Sheila Jansen grew up [...] her mid-twenties she m[...] London, where she spent ten years before going to America. There she read English and French and now teaches English in California, where she lives with her husband, a professor of wild-land sciences.

Also by Sheila Jansen

Mary Maddison

Della Dolan

Sheila Jansen

HEADLINE

First published in 1993
by HEADLINE BOOK PUBLISHING LTD

First published in paperback in 1994
by HEADLINE BOOK PUBLISHING LTD

10 9 8 7 6 5 4 3 2 1

ISBN 0 7472 4241 0

Typeset by
Letterpart Limited, Reigate, Surrey

Printed and bound in Great Britain by
HarperCollins Manufacturing, Glasgow

HEADLINE BOOK PUBLISHING LTD
A member of the Hodder Headline PLC Group
Headline House
79 Great Titchfield Street
London W1P 7FN

**To my husband, Henricus,
and my sister, Shirley**

Chapter One

'Della! How many times do I have to tell you? You'll get chilblains on your backside.'

Grinning, Della ignored her mother's warning. She lifted her skirt higher, backed closer to the fire, and sighed with pleasure. 'Oh, it was so lovely not to have to get up for school, I turned over and had another snooze.'

Mary poured two cups of tea. 'Well, you might as well enjoy it while you can. Once you start work you'll wish you *were* back at school.'

'Never!' Della skipped to the table and joined Mary. 'The snow's thick enough for sledging. I thought I'd take Johnny out.'

'That would be nice, luv.' Mary's green eyes clouded, and the tiny lines on her brow deepened as she frowned. 'Anne could do with a break. She looked peaky at New Year, and I don't like the way her legs are swelling. I don't think this one's going to be as easy as Johnny. *And* I have a feeling there's something fishy going on with her and Dan.'

Della looked down at the tablecloth. 'Aw, don't be daft, Mam. She loves him, and she's excited about the new baby. You just worry too much about everybody. She looks healthy enough to me.'

Pushing an auburn curl off her brow, Mary shook her head. 'I know she puts on a good act, but I'm sure there's something wrong. I wish Dan spent less time at

1

the pub and more with her and Johnny. Has she ever said anything to you? I know I'd be the last person she'd want to worry if anything was wrong.'

Della shot her a wary glance. When suspicious, Mary probed like a surgeon with a scalpel. Della was no match for her and knew Anne would never forgive her if she let anything slip. 'Look, Mam, it's a pity you don't like Dan, but Anne loves him and that's all that matters. Whenever you have nothing to worry about you start looking for something. Next you'll be picking on me.' To end the conversation, she helped herself to corn-flakes.

Mary sighed and looked at her daughter with her usual pride. Soon it would be time to worry about this one. Always a pretty child, at fourteen Della was becoming a beauty. Even the heavy wool skirt and jumper couldn't hide the swelling breasts and tiny waist. And the black mane of hair falling over her shoulders dramatised the white skin and dark brown, almond-shaped eyes. Everything about her was Walter – the fine straight nose, the sensuous mouth. Mary hoped her daughter's good looks wouldn't get her into trouble as her own had done and, stifling a sigh, smiled and patted Della's hand. 'Well, at least I don't have to worry about you just yet – but not for much longer.'

'Aw, come off it, Mam. That won't be for ages. Like some more tea?'

'Yes, I'll have another cup and relax a bit. Getting that lot off to work wears me out.' Mary stretched her slim legs and rested her feet on the neighbouring chair, lowering them with a groan as a heavy knock rattled the back door. 'No peace for the wicked. Would you get that, luv?'

Della darted to the door and admitted Mrs Bowman, their next-door neighbour.

The old woman employed her customary wheedling

tone when asking favours. 'Eey, hinny, I know I'm a pain in the neck, but do you think your mam could lend me a cup of sugar? I was just startin' to make a batch of scones and I've run out.'

'Yes, come in, Winnie,' Mary shouted from the kitchen. 'We're just finishing breakfast. Would you like a cup of tea?'

'Aye, I wouldn't say no, hinny. You know me. I can never say no to a cuppa. I'm like me old man with booze.' She waddled to the kitchen and eased her short, squat body on to one of the wooden dining chairs, her mammoth hips bulging over the sides.

Mary's green eyes were polite, though not exactly welcoming, and her gentle mouth was set firmly. She had learned to be on her guard with Mrs Bowman. 'Did you have a good New Year?' she enquired.

'Aye, hinny – quiet like. Eey, I can't believe how the time goes. 1934! And it just seems like yesterday I brought in last New Year with you lot.' She raised her hooded lids and fixed her watery blue eyes on Mary. 'I heard you all havin' a good time, though,' she finished slyly.

Mary understood the implication. 'We just had a small *family* gathering this year, Winnie.' Despite herself, she smiled as she remembered how her neighbour had to be lifted off the lavatory and carried home the previous year. Winnie Bowman was well known for her acid tongue and prying eyes, but Mary now knew how to deal with her.

Della returned from the scullery with the teapot. 'I've just made some fresh,' she announced, pouring Mrs Bowman a cup.

'Eey, well, you shouldn't have done it special for me.' The old woman eyed the table and screwed up her nose in distaste. 'Never could get away with cornflakes.'

'I'll get you some fresh bread then, Mrs Bowman.'

Della returned to the scullery for a new loaf.

'Eey, well, that's kind of you, hinny.' Winnie Bowman knocked back the contents of her cup and emitted a grunt of satisfaction. 'Eey, that's a good cuppa! I could do with another one.' She helped herself. 'So, when are you goin' to start workin' for your livin', lass, an' get yoursel' off your mam and dad's hands, eh?' Her ferret nose twitched in disapproval. 'When I was your age I'd been workin' for three years, scrubbin' offices in the mornin's an' houses in the afternoons.'

'Those days are over, Winnie.' Mary poured herself more tea before Winnie Bowman could finish the pot.

Trying not to smile, Della cut a slice of bread and set it before Mrs Bowman, who now examined the butter dish closely. 'This butter or margarine?'

'It's margarine, Winnie. We can only afford butter on Sundays,' Mary said drily.

'Aye, all right. I'll have that with some marmalade. I can't get marge down on its own.' Mrs Bowman adjusted one of the metal curlers covering her grey head as she turned to Della, who had resumed her own place at the table. 'So, why aren't you out lookin' for a job, then?'

'I *am* looking, Mrs Bowman, and I've had an interview at Binns. I even said a prayer last night that I get it.'

Mary laughed. 'Well, if God heard you, I hope he recognised your voice after all this time.'

'Don't laugh, Mam. It's a serious matter. I swear, if I don't hear by the end of the week I'll eat worms and die.' Della swallowed a mouthful of cornflakes and addressed their visitor: 'Oh, it would be smashing to sell glamorous clothes and get a discount. I could buy smart things for Mam as well.'

A faint smile touched Mary's lips. Approaching thirty-four, she was still beautiful, having kept her trim

4

figure and burnished auburn hair, though her piquant face had a tired air. Her smile widened. 'Do you think your dad would even notice?'

'He noticed when you borrowed my white blouse at Christmas.'

'Only because it gaped about my bust. But never mind about me. I just want you to find a job you enjoy.'

'Eey, a job you enjoy! Them's hard to come by, hinny.' Mrs Bowman shook her head gloomily. 'School days are the happiest. And as soon as you start to earn a bit to help your mam and dad, you'll up and get married and dump them in the dust bin – just like my lot. They came over for Christmas dinner and paid for the pork. First penny I've had out of them since last Christmas – and their father out of work for five months.' She spread more marmalade on her bread. 'That's gratitude for you!'

'But, *we* won't do that, Mrs B,' Della insisted. 'The boys have been working for ages and they're still at home and helping out.'

'Aye, but not for long, hinny. I saw them two lasses comin' in here at New Year – the same ones your Michael and Billie had last year. Goin' steady now, eh? Those lads won't be long for the choppin' block. An' I saw your David walkin' down Northumberland Street holdin' hands with that Langham lass. He'll be next. Mark my words.'

Smiling despite herself, Mary put down her teacup. 'And what about Wally, Winnie? Can you tell us anything about *him* we don't know?'

The sarcasm was lost on Mrs Bowman, who continued querulously. 'Aye, Wally won't be long neither. I wouldn't give him more than a year before he starts bringin' lasses home. Then that'll be the end of him an' all.'

'Aw, going out with girls doesn't mean they want to get married,' Della protested.

'Oh, aye? That's what you think, hinny.' Mrs Bowman spoke with her mouth full. 'I've seen it all before. Just look at my lot . . . an' Jennie down the road. Lost three sons in two years, poor soul. They say you don't lose a son but you gain a daughter. That's a laugh! I never see hide nor hair of any of mine.'

Mary put down her empty cup and broke in wistfully: 'I must admit that when they were little and we were very hard up, I used to look forward to the time when they'd grow up and earn some money. But it does seem to happen so fast.'

'Aye, and then the ungrateful little beggars just diddle off and leave you to rot . . . never a thank you for all you done for them,' Mrs Bowman whined.

Not allowing the old woman time to start on her well-known monologue about her ungrateful family, Della cut in quickly: 'Mam's talking rubbish. It'll be donkey's years before we're all gone. *I* haven't even got a boyfriend.'

'Indeed not, madam,' Mary said firmly. 'You're still too young for that, and no need to jump into it. You could get on well at Binns – maybe even become a buyer and have a proper career before you settle down.'

'But *you* were young when you married Dad, Mam, and you don't regret it, do you?'

'Of course not, silly. What a stupid question!' Mary dismissed Della with a warning glance. 'More tea, Winnie?'

'Nah, luv. I'd better be gettin' back. I put the oven on before I found out I had no sugar. It'll be eatin' up me gas. Ta for the tea.' She rose heavily and laboured to the scullery.

'Your sugar! I'll get it.' Della followed her.

'And while you're at it, hinny, do you think you could spare a few raisins an' all? I'm a bit short.'

'They're in the pantry,' Mary shouted through the

door, smiling to herself. 'And how are you off for flour?' she added under her breath. Mrs Bowman, amongst her other quirks, was a notorious scrounger. Mary grimaced at Della when she returned. 'I wonder she has time to make scones; she's always so busy nosing into other people's business.'

'Why did you glare at me like that when I asked you about Dad, Mam? I didn't say anything wrong, did I?'

Mary reassured her with a pat on the hand. 'No, you didn't, pet. But you know I don't like to talk about anything too personal in front of Mrs Bowman. The question alone is quite enough to start her twisted mind ticking and her tongue tittle-tattling to the neighbours. I can just hear her now.' She assumed a disgruntled expression and mimicked Mrs Bowman's peevish tone: ' "Well, the bairn wouldn't be worried about her mam being sorry she married her dad if there was nowt to be sorry about, now would she? If you ask me, there's a lot goes on in that house they keep under the mat. Of course, Mary being such a snob and all, she wouldn't want her dirty washing aired in public." ' As Mary finished, she nodded knowingly, after the manner of Mrs Bowman.

Della laughed. 'You should have been an actress, Mam. Anyway, nobody would believe the old goat.' She looked closely at Mary. 'But, seriously, there never *was* a time when you regretted marrying Dad, was there, Mam?'

'Of course not, you dumb-bell! Though at first I did wish I'd had more freedom before bringing up a family, and I'd like you to have what I missed. I hope you're a lot more mature and ready for responsibilities than I was.' Mary's brow furrowed and, for a moment, she looked far away. 'I made a lot of silly mistakes I could have avoided if I'd known a little more about life.'

Della looked puzzled. 'I don't see any mistakes you

made. I mean, marrying Dad and bringing up a happy family, I don't see anything wrong with that.'

'Of course not, you silly girl. That was the first *right* thing I did. Being poor didn't stop us from being happy, thank God!' Mary looked far away for a moment. 'No, I made the mistakes before I married your dad. And I want to make sure you don't fall into the same trap.' She wagged her finger in warning. 'I want you to have fun and enjoy being single before you marry your Prince Charming.'

'I wouldn't exactly call Dad a Prince Charming,' Della chuckled.

Mary's bell-like laugh tinkled as she poured Della another cup of tea. 'No, me neither! But you know your dad. He never was a man of many words.'

'But I wouldn't change him, Mam . . . except I wish he didn't work so hard and come home so tired. Once I start work, couldn't we talk him into looking for a lighter job? We'll all be earning then.'

Mary shook her head. 'You know he's too proud to rely on his family in his old age, even if he could find another job during this Depression. And anyway, he wants to put away as much as he can for his retirement.'

'But, Mam, you've only got a few pounds in the money tin.' Della looked dismayed. 'That's not going to help much when you're old. You know we'll all help you out. We're not like Mrs Bowman's lot.'

Mary smiled at her daughter's serious expression. 'I almost let the cat out of the bag, didn't I? Your dad wanted it kept a secret till we needed it, but if it'll stop you worrying – he opened a savings account when Anne started work, and he's been putting more in every week since the boys started. And for heaven's sake, don't let on I've told you,' she warned as she saw Della's eyes widen.

8

'Crikey! You mean we've got a bank account? How posh! How much?'

Mary's laugh rang again. 'Don't be silly, Della. You don't think your father would actually tell me, do you? I only discovered it by accident because I found the book in his pocket when I was washing his overalls.'

Della almost choked with mirth. 'Oh! Was he mad, Mam? Crikey, I wish I'd been there.'

'No, he wasn't mad. He just said he'd wanted to keep it a surprise, but he admitted he was glad I knew when he saw how relieved I was.'

'And you still don't know how much?'

'I've no idea, and it doesn't matter. If I know your dad, it'll be enough,' Mary assured her. 'And it isn't a bank account; it's a Post Office savings account.'

'Oh, well! That's almost as good. Gosh, he's a dark horse, isn't he?'

'You can say that again.' Mary stood up and stretched. 'And now I'd better clear these things away and do my errands. The larder looks like Mother Hubbard's cupboard.'

'I'll come and help you.'

'No, dear.' Mary shook her head. 'I'd rather you went to Anne's and took Johnny off her hands for a while. I made a sponge cake for her yesterday.'

Ten minutes later Della arrived at Anne's council flat in Highdene Street. She balanced the cake on one hand and turned the knob. It was locked. Anne never locked her door. She banged on the knocker. No answer. She thumped again. This time she heard footsteps followed by Anne's muffled voice through the door: 'Who is it?'

'It's me, you idiot! Why've you got the stupid door locked?'

'Oh, Della!' Anne sounded dismayed. 'I just wasn't feeling well and didn't want to be disturbed.'

'I'm not disturbing you, you numbskull!' Della cried in exasperation. 'I've come to give you a hand. Open the door, for goodness' sake! It's freezing out here.'

The downstairs flat door opened slowly and Anne stood in the dim hall. She turned down the passage to the kitchen, where she sat at the table and put her face in her hands.

'Goodness, Anne, you're all in the dark!' Della cried in astonishment. She put the cake on the table and opened the heavy green curtains. 'Are you all right?' She looked anxiously at her half-sister, whose face was still covered by her hands.

Anne said nothing and Della, now frightened, gently lowered the hands. She saw what she had dreaded. 'Oh, no, Anne! He's beaten you again!' She looked aghast at the blanched face. The lips, purple and swollen, had a deep cut in the centre encrusted with dried blood, and one eye was half closed and black. Anne's pretty, delicate features were almost unrecognisable, and her fine blonde hair, usually smoothed back and curving in sleek waves to her neck, hung in a matted mess.

'Oh, Della, I wish you hadn't seen me like this. Please don't tell Mam, will you?' Anne's voice was distorted to a hiss through the disfigured lips.

'Well, I won't this time, but I can't promise to keep this a secret much longer,' Della said firmly. 'She's bound to find out sooner or later . . . and she suspects something now anyway. Good Lord, Anne! He's half killed you this time. What in heaven's name happened?' Angrily, she threw off her outdoor clothes and filled a bowl with cold water from the scullery tap. Anne didn't answer, and Della knew her sister would have to take her own time. 'I'm just going to bathe your face to get the swelling down,' she began but, suddenly remembering the reason for her visit, asked fearfully: 'Where's Johnny?'

'He's all right . . . making a snowman in the garden.'

'Dan didn't touch him?'

'No, oh no, thank God! He's never touched him. I'd leave him in a flash for that. It's only me he goes for when he's had a skinful.'

As Della dabbed at the swollen eye, Anne's tears mingled with the water droplets on her face.

'That's right, luv, have a good cry. And then I'll make you a nice cup of tea and you can tell me what happened.'

'Oh, the same as the last time and the time before,' Anne began wearily. 'He just came home drunk and in a bad mood, complained that his meal wasn't hot and then went for me. But he's not a bad man. He's just depressed again. When the mood's on him he's like a man possessed. He never seems to learn, Della! When he's down he gets drunk to feel better, but when the effects wear off he feels even worse.' She winced as Della dabbed at the eye and went on in Dan's defence: 'And he's fed up selling shoes for a living, and not very many at that. With his brains he should be doing something better.'

'Well, Dad should be doing something better than welding, but he doesn't complain about it and beat Mam.' Della's voice was angry. 'It's time Dan grew up and thought about his responsibilities. He doesn't know how lucky he is compared to some. Look how he came into this flat when his mother died, when we were on the waiting list for years. And he doesn't have to get his hands dirty and sweat all day in a factory like Dad.'

Anne had to agree. 'I know, luv, but he doesn't see it that way. There's more to it than just his black moods; he wants to get on in the world. He hates his job. Oh, if only he didn't get drunk.' Her voice broke again. 'He's all right when he's sober.'

'Hates his job, my foot! He should be thankful he's

11

got a job at all – any job. Stop being so soft on him, Anne. You've got to stand up to him. If you act like a doormat, you can expect people to wipe their feet on you.' Della hoped to stir up what was left of Anne's spirited nature, which had ebbed since her marriage to Dan. 'Dad has a few drinks at weekends, but he doesn't come home and hit Mam. Being drunk's no excuse. Though it would be nice if Dan could cut it down a bit. And he's a beast to hit you when you're having a baby.'

Anne winced as Della bathed the cut lip. She pushed her hand away. 'Sometimes it's hard to believe you're ten years younger than I am – you're so much more sensible and practical. But I love him, Della. I can't help it. I like trying to please him.'

Della kissed the damp forehead and relented. 'I know you do, luv.' She handed her a fresh towel. 'Come on now, pat your face dry while I make the tea. Mam sent a sponge cake.'

Glancing through the scullery window as she filled the kettle, Della assured herself that Johnny was happily occupied with his snowman. She carried the tray into the kitchen which, like their own and most other kitchens, served as living room and dining room during the week, the sitting-room fire being lit only on Sundays.

Anne, now looking more composed, said in a firmer voice: 'I know you're right, Della, but what can I do to stop him? I just couldn't bear to leave him.'

'Well, first of all we should tell Dad,' Della said, pouring milk into the cups. 'But not Mam – at least not yet. She'll just worry too much. Dad'll give Dan a piece of his mind, and a piece of his fist as well if he starts on you again. And the boys! They'd massacre him if they knew what he was doing to you.'

Anne's hand flew to her mouth. 'Oh, God, Della! Don't let the boys know. They'd half kill him.'

12

'Maybe that's just what he needs to bring him to his senses,' Della said more sharply than she had intended. Penitent, she added gently, 'It's just that if he knew the boys were looking out for you, he'd be too scared about his own skin to touch you again.' She poured the tea and handed Anne a cup.

Anne sipped awkwardly through her swollen lips and waved away the slice of cake Della offered. Despite her handicap, her voice was adamant. 'No, you mustn't tell the boys.' She put down her cup and looked thoughtful for a moment. 'But maybe if you told Dad on the quiet, he could come over tonight and just talk to Dan – just talk, mind you. If you could get Dad to promise not to start any rough stuff, it might be worth a try. And please!' She grasped Della's hand and gave her a pleading look. 'Make him swear not to tell Mam and the boys?'

Della squeezed her hand in reassurance. 'I promise, luv. If I know Dad, he'll want to sort it out himself anyway.'

Chapter Two

Walking home in the afternoon, Della devised a plan to get her father on his own. She'd make an excuse to meet him at the tram stop. It would be impossible to talk to him with everyone home from work.

When she reached the house, Mary was making pastry for bacon and egg pies. She looked up anxiously. 'Hello, luv. You were a long time. How's Anne?'

'Fine,' Della lied, her back to her mother as she hung her wet coat on the scullery door. 'She sent her love.' She sat before the fire warming her hands, her back still to Mary. 'Do you mind if I pop out again around five, Mam? I promised to help Rose cut out that dress for the party. She can't make the pattern fit.'

Mary whisked the eggs briskly. 'Why not go now and be back in time for dinner?'

'Because she won't be home,' Della countered. 'She's got her interview at Binns this afternoon.' That part was true. Thank goodness she hadn't had to think up something on the spur of the moment. Eager to keep busy in the meantime, she joined Mary and began the washing up. 'I'll do these and then finish the ironing before I go out.'

At five-fifteen Della pulled on her still wet outdoor clothes.

'You'll catch your death of cold, girl,' Mary scolded.

'Why didn't you dry them in front of the fire? Wear *my* coat, it's dry.'

'Stop worrying, Mam. I'll be soaked again in two minutes anyway, it's sleeting now.' She escaped quickly and closed the door with relief.

The tram was at least fifteen minutes late, and the longer Della waited, the more nervous she became about her father's reaction to the news. She stamped her feet to keep warm.

'Why hello, lass. What are you doing here?' Walter looked at her in surprise when he finally alighted.

Della drew in a deep breath. 'I have to talk to you, Dad, and this is the only way I could get you alone.'

Her father's face was covered in grime, but the cloth cap pulled over his forehead concealed his mop of black hair without a single strand of grey; his long, sensitive face was still good-looking for all his forty-five years and life of hard work, and his mouth still full and sensuous. When Walter was dressed in his Sunday suit, women's eyes turned in his direction.

He looked at her shrewdly. 'What's all the secrecy, then?'

'It's Anne, Dad,' she blurted out. 'Dan's beaten her and she wants you to give him a talking-to. She made me promise I wouldn't tell anyone but you; she's worried about Mam knowing and afraid the boys'll have a go at him if they find out.'

Though they walked briskly, Walter stopped dead. 'That bugger! Beating our Anne! I'll knock the living daylights out of him,' he hissed through clenched teeth, punching his left palm with his right fist.

'Dad . . . please!' Della timidly put a restraining hand on his arm. 'Anne begged me to make you promise you wouldn't touch him. She says he gets depressed, and when he's like that drink makes him violent. Please just give him a good talking-to. He

16

knows he'll have to listen to you, of all people.'

'How long has this been going on?' Walter's voice now sounded like gravel as he trudged again through the slush. Della was afraid of that voice.

'He's done it three times since Johnny was born – that I know of. She may be covering up for him, but I know it's been at least that often because I popped in to the flat and saw the bruises on her face. She says he only does it when he's drunk and doesn't know what he's doing.'

Walter's lips tightened. 'I'll let him know what he's doing all right. I'll fettle his hash once and for all.'

'What are you going to do, Dad? Promise you won't hit him . . . please?'

'I'm not making any promises, lass. You know me when my temper's up. But if that's what Anne wants, I'll do my best. And her havin' a bairn an' all! The swine!' He shook his head in disbelief.

'Can you go round tonight, Dad?'

'Aye, I'll make up some excuse to your mam.'

At the house in Brigham Gardens, Della's stomach lurched with relief as Walter greeted Mary in his usual voice.

Mary took one of the pies from the oven. 'You're late and the boys aren't home yet. Is it the tram lines?'

'Aye, they have to clear them every few yards,' Walter muttered. 'It'd be quicker to walk.'

Mary looked at Della before setting the pie on the table. 'Did you manage to get Rose's dress cut out?'

'Well, we got a good start but we didn't have time to finish it,' Della lied. She would go to see Rose tomorrow on her way back from Anne's. That way Mam wouldn't need to know she hadn't been today.

Walter had removed his overalls in the scullery and washed his grimy hands and face. Sitting at the table, he said casually. 'I'll have mine now, lass, in peace and quiet before the lads get back. I promised Ernie I'd see him at the pub.'

Mary's eyebrows arched in surprise. 'The pub? On a Tuesday! What's got into you?'

'Ernie just said he felt like a game of darts and I wouldn't mind one meself, and a pint,' he added, avoiding her eyes.

The meal over, Walter scraped back his chair. 'Well, I'm off now. Nice pie!' Within seconds, the back door slammed.

Mary was disappointed he was going out. Though he rarely talked much, she enjoyed his companionable presence in the evenings. As she settled by the fire waiting for the boys to arrive, she smiled affectionately, remembering her wedding day. Walter's pleasantly lilting Geordie voice hadn't changed, although she had spent her life trying to teach the children to speak 'correctly', as she called it, in order to stand a better chance of getting 'clean' jobs.

Anne and Della had naturally emulated her, despite ridicule from the rougher girls at school for talking lah-di-dah. But, regardless of her efforts, the boys had modelled themselves on their father, too embarrassed to sound different from their friends. Still, they had mostly managed to get the sort of jobs she had always wanted for them – quite an achievement considering that over a fifth of the working population was unemployed.

Yes, she thought gratefully, they were all turning out as well as she'd hoped: Michael, a rent collector for the council; Billie, training as an insurance agent; Wally, not as bright as the others but with an overdose of charm, apprenticed to a barber; and David – at the moment a bit of a mixture – labouring at Walter's factory because, as he said, 'Where there's muck there's

18

money.' But he was studying book-keeping at night school.

Della interrupted Mary's thoughts. 'I think I'll start on these dishes before the boys come in, Mam.' She'd have to keep busy till Dad got back. Although Walter was strong for his lean build, Dan was a burly man, and younger. What if Dan got rough with him?

Mary raised her eyebrows. 'My! You *are* fidgety tonight! Why not wait and do them all together? You'll use twice the hot water, and—'

She stopped as David burst through the door, his six-foot frame soaked from the top of his head to the toes of his working boots. His childhood blond hair had turned a mid-brown, with red lights like his mother's. Nevertheless, his face was a model of the father he had never known. He had Joe's square jaw, rugged features and determined expression. To Mary's distress, he had also inherited Joe's bad moods, although these were becoming less frequent as he got older.

'Rotten weather!' He shed his overcoat and overalls and washed at the sink. 'Can I have my dinner now? I'm going to be late for night school.'

Della volunteered, 'I'll get it.'

'Ta, pet,' he said as she handed him his plate.

Mary waved her hands in protest. 'David, those friends of yours at work are having a bad influence on you. Can't you say "thank you" like everybody else?' But she looked fondly at her firstborn and thanked God for the hundredth time that she had not married his father. She had heard from her friend Doreen in London that Joe had gone into the flower shop two years previously and bought flowers for the young girl hanging on his arm. Still playing around at his age! God, she'd been a poor judge of character in those days, she thought. But David brought her back to the present.

'Everybody else around here says "ta" except us,' he

grinned. 'Don't worry, Mam! By the time I'm a book-keeper I'll be talking like a toff.'

Billie and Wally arrived together, blond hair hanging in wet ringlets. Walter's first family had all retained the youthful blond of their hair and had their mother's pale blue eyes and fine features. Mary sighed; she often wished Annie could see how well her family had turned out.

'I'll see to them, Mam.' Della bustled to the scullery.

'My goodness! You're like a cat on hot bricks tonight.'

'You need a break, Mam, and I'm bored. I need something to do. I think I'll bring my sewing down later.'

'Bloody awful night,' Billie grunted, unbuttoning his overcoat.

'Careful,' David laughed. 'I just got told off for saying "ta". Mam's on one of her pure language campaigns.'

Sniffing exaggeratedly, Wally joined him at the table. 'Nice smell. What's to eat?'

Della set two plates before them. 'Find out.'

'I saw our Michael on the way home, Mam.' Wally pronged a piece of pie. 'He told me to tell you he won't be home till late. He's gone to Ellen's.'

'Oh, really now! That's the second night this week he's gone there for dinner,' Mary remarked.

'Ellen calls it "tea", Mam, like everybody else,' Wally corrected her. 'You're the only one around here who calls it "dinner".'

'I've called it dinner all my life and dinner it is in this house,' Mary said emphatically.

David held his empty plate towards her with a grin. 'I'll have Michael's tea then – I mean dinner.'

'No, you will not. You'll have your pudding. I'll save Michael's. Perhaps he'd like it when he gets home.'

Wally shook his head. 'Nah, he'll be stuffed when he

gets home, Mam. Ellen's mam's a fantastic cook.'

'Are you trying to tell me he likes her cooking better than mine?'

'I wouldn't say that.' Wally grinned his impish fifteen-year-old grin. 'But he prefers Ellen's company to our Della's. Girlfriends are more exciting than sisters. Our Michael's in love.'

'That's not funny,' David cut in. 'Bloody sad, I'd call it.'

'*You* can talk, our David. What about Barbara Langham?' He jabbed his finger at David's face. 'Look, you see! He's gone beetroot just because I said her name.'

David snorted and stalked to the scullery. 'I'm late for class. I'm not putting up with any more of this rubbish.'

'What about your rice pudding?' Mary asked.

'I'll have it when I get back, if I'm desperate,' he snapped, before slamming the back door.

Sitting opposite Mary, Della pretended to listen to her brothers' banter, though her eyes were fixed on the fire and her mind fixed on her sister and her father.

Walter knocked on Anne's door and waited impatiently. He tried the handle. It was locked. He knocked again, louder. Eventually the door opened a crack and Anne's voice whispered, 'Who is it?'

'It's me, lass. What's this I hear about that bugger hitting you?' He pushed the door open further and stepped heavily inside. He stopped when he saw her swollen face in the lighted hallway. 'I'll get him for this,' he rasped.

'Please, Dad.' Anne pressed her hands against Walter's chest. 'He's said he's sorry and he won't do it again. Please don't make any trouble.'

Walter ground his teeth. 'He's the one making the trouble. Where is he?'

'In the kitchen having his tea. Everything's all right

now, Dad, honestly. Please don't get mad.'

Pushing his way past her, Walter flung open the kitchen door. Dan's sandy head was bent over his plate as he forked mashed potato and peas into his mouth. He looked up, startled on seeing Walter, his loose lower lip hanging in surprise.

Walter placed his face an inch from Dan's, whose florid complexion turned pallid as his father-in-law grabbed him by his tie. Dan's shifty grey eyes grew round and alarmed.

'You dirty, filthy coward!' Walter yanked the tie tighter. 'How dare you hit our Anne! God knows how long this has been going on, but I'll tell you this, you bastard: now that I've got something to say about it, you've done it for the last time.'

Dan squirmed under the pressure on his neck and tried to loosen Walter's grip, to no avail. 'I told her I was sorry,' he whined, before attempting to assert himself. 'And just what the hell do you think you're doin', walkin' into my house without a by-your-leave?'

Walter let go of the tie. 'I can walk into my own daughter's house whenever I like. Now just remember that, because if you so much as lay a finger on our Anne again we'll *all* be walking in here – her brothers and all. And if that doesn't fettle your hash, the next time we'll invite the coppers as well.'

'I just lost my temper,' Dan snivelled. 'I've told her it won't happen again.' His colour had returned, but his craggy face was rigid with suppressed anger. 'You've got no bloody right interfering in our business.'

'What you do to my bairn *is* my business. And you remember that.' Walter turned to Anne, who stood white and still in the doorway. 'It's all right, lass. I won't knock his block off this time. But this is the only warning I'm giving him. If he starts on you again, he's as good as dead.'

'Oh, he won't, Dad. Everything's all right now. He's promised.' Anne swallowed hard in relief that at least they hadn't used their fists.

'Aye, promises, promises! You'd better bloody well keep *this* one,' Walter flung over his shoulder at Dan as he turned to leave.

No sooner had the front door closed than Dan jumped up, grabbed Anne by the shoulders, and shook her violently. 'What do you mean by snivelling to your blasted father? What goes on in our house is our business and nobody else's. Do you hear me?'

'I didn't tell him, Dan,' Anne sobbed. 'Della came over today and saw me. I had to let her in.'

'Well, next time I belt you I'll put it where nobody can see it,' he said grimly, before marching into the scullery.

Anne waited for the door to slam and sank into the chair by the fire. The tears she'd managed to hold back so far suddenly released like a dam. Dear God! Had he not meant his promise? Would he do it again?

In order to make his evening out look realistic, Walter stopped for a couple of pints on the way home. When he returned, Della rushed to greet him. 'Hello, Dad. How was the game? Did you win?' she asked obliquely.

'Aye, lass, I won. I fettled his hash,' he assured her.

Chapter Three

The following morning Della got up early. She couldn't wait to see how Anne was and to find out about Walter's visit. Michael, always the last to leave for work, sat at the table while Mary carried a steaming bowl from the scullery and set it before Della. 'To what do we owe the pleasure of your company this morning?'

'Aye, what's the matter? Couldn't you sleep?' Michael gave her a wide grin as he emptied three spoons of sugar into his tea.

Della ignored her brother's remark. 'Oh, good! Porridge! I'm starving. I told Rose I'd go over and finish off the dress this morning.' It was only half a lie; she'd be seeing Rose after Anne.

'How did her interview go yesterday?' Mary took her place again at the table. 'You didn't mention it.'

'All right,' Della stalled, 'but she doesn't know if she's got the job yet.'

Michael drained his teacup. 'I'd better get a move on. Where are my sandwiches, Mam?'

'Where they always are – in the larder,' Mary said patiently. She always made the men's sandwiches the evening before and wrapped them in greaseproof paper to keep them fresh.

Breakfast over, Della helped her mother with the washing up before hastily donning her outdoor clothes. 'I shan't be long,' she said, her hand on the doorknob.

'I thought maybe I'd pop over to Anne's today.' Mary hung the wet tea towel on the rail beside the sink. 'I've finished Johnny's gloves and hat, and he could use them this weather. The slush has turned icy; it's still cold enough for more snow. If you want to come with me I'll wait till you get back.'

Della's hand gripped the doorknob tightly as she searched wildly for an excuse. 'Anne said she was going out today, Mam. She won't be back till tea time.'

'Really? Where's she going this weather?' Mary, head bent, wiped down the draining board, and Della was glad she didn't have to look her in the face as she mumbled the lie.

'She's going to see Muriel in Gateshead.' Mercifully Anne's friend's name had popped into her head.

'Well, then, I'll go over to see Auntie Jane instead. I'll wait for you if you'd like to come.'

'No, I want to do some sewing, Mam. Give Auntie Jane my love.' Della closed the door behind her and sighed with relief. She'd got out of that tight spot. But what about tomorrow? Mam would surely go to Anne's tomorrow instead.

Anne's door was unlocked. 'It's me, luv,' Della shouted as she pulled off her Wellingtons in the hall.

Anne looked up from her ironing on the kitchen table. 'Oh, Della! You scared me. Sometimes your voice sounds so like Mam's.'

'No, I stalled her. But I'll tell you about that later.' She hugged her sister, then pushed her away to examine her face. The swelling was less obvious, but the discolouration round her eye and the cut on her lip were still all too evident. 'How are you feeling?' She threw her outdoor clothes on the sofa.

Anne had arranged the kitchen the same as the one at home, squeezing into the tiny room a dining table, sideboard, sofa, and two armchairs by the fire. Della dropped into one of the chairs and looked searchingly at her sister. 'Dad said he'd won last night . . . whatever that means. He couldn't say any more in front of Mam. What happened?'

Anne put the iron back on the trivet and wearily sat opposite Della. 'Dad told Dan off and said if he ever touched me again he'd set the boys on him, and then the coppers. But he'd already promised not to.' Unconsciously, she fingered her cut lip.

Della remained unconvinced. 'But you said he promised that after the last time, *and* the time before. How can you know he means it this time?'

'I'm sure he means it, Della. I swear it!' Avoiding Della's gaze, Anne picked up the poker and stirred the failing fire.

'Well, he'd jolly well better mean it.' Della's words came out as if sieved through her teeth. 'Now that Dad knows, he'll be keeping an eye out for you. And guess what? Mam was coming round today. I had to do some quick thinking to put her off – I told her you were going to Muriel's. But I bet she comes tomorrow. She's worried about you. I swear she suspects something. And I don't need to tell you she's never been very keen on Dan.'

Anne's hands flew to her face. 'Oh, God! How can I explain *this* if she comes tomorrow?'

'Well, you could camouflage it a bit with make-up,' Della suggested half-heartedly, 'but that's not going to fool her. You'll still have some explaining to do. Why not say you slipped on the ice on your way back from Muriel's and banged your head on the kerb or something?'

'That's a good idea! I didn't know you were such a good liar.'

'Neither did I!' Della managed a giggle, but Anne looked hesitant now.

'Do you think she'll believe it?'

'Your guess is as good as mine. You know Mam as well as I do.'

'Yes, unfortunately.' Anne grimaced as much as her sore lips would allow. 'And we both know she's no fool.'

Della, until now preoccupied with Anne's predicament, suddenly noticed Johnny's absence. 'Where's Johnny?' she asked.

'He's with Cath, next door. She's been very good to me, Della. She heard the shouting through the wall but thought it was just a row, so she kept her nose out of it. But she popped in after you left yesterday and nearly had a fit when she saw me. So now my family *and* my neighbours know.' Anne groaned. 'I feel so ashamed.'

'*He's* the one who should feel ashamed, you daft thing!' Della's anger flared at her sister's meekness. 'And anyway, not *all* your family and not *all* your neighbours know, and nobody else needs to know if Dan keeps his word. But, honestly, Anne,' she went on more softly, 'I know he's your husband and I don't know anything about that sort of love, but I just don't understand how you can love a man who beats you.'

'You'll know what it's like to love a man one day, Della,' Anne said enigmatically and changed the subject. 'Have you heard anything from Binns?'

'Not yet. I'm hoping there'll be something in the post today. I just popped in on my way to see Rose. I'm helping her to cut out a dress. Is there anything I can do before I go?'

Anne shook her head. 'No thanks, luv. Cath got me what I needed this morning. I couldn't go out looking like this. You be off now. I'm fine, honestly.'

Frowning, Della walked quickly to Rose's house. Anne seemed in very low spirits, despite Dan's having promised not to do it again.

28

Rose greeted her with a pleased expression on her pretty, round face. 'Hello, pet! Oh I *am* glad to see you. Come on in. I've got something to tell you.' Her emerald eyes sparkled as she hugged Della.

The modern semi-detached house was expensively furnished. Although her father was only a railway signalman, they somehow managed to rent a private house on Grange Road, near the Lonnen. When Della had told Mary where her new friend lived, she had remarked suspiciously that she didn't know there was money in the railways. Nor did she approve of the freedom Rose's parents afforded her. She had been allowed to go out with boys and wear make-up since she was thirteen and, in Mary's opinion, Rose's extensive wardrobe was much too flashy for a girl her age.

Della and Rose had attended the same school but had been in different classes until the final year, when Rose had suddenly decided to work and had been promoted to Form IVA. Since then they had become inseparable. Della admitted that Rose was high-spirited and a little wild, but she was also a warm and caring friend.

'Gosh! You do look smart,' Della complimented her as they walked down the hall. Rose's formerly long red hair had been cut short and permed in fashionable Marcel waves, ending in frothy curls on her neck. The style made her look older than her fourteen years, the effect enhanced by a liberal layer of powder over her freckled nose and a vivid red 'cupid's bow' painted on her lips. She wore a tight-fitting green dress and high heels that clicked on the green linoleum as she led Della into the kitchen.

'Mam let me have my hair done for the interview and she says I can keep it like this,' Rose announced proudly as she relieved Della of her coat and hat.

Della sat in an armchair by the fire and Rose joined her. Money seemed no object in this house, unlike most homes locally, yet the sitting-room fire was lit only on Sundays.

'Well, don't keep me in suspense, Rose. How did it go?' Della asked eagerly.

'Well, it was the manager who interviewed me – a man, Della, when I was expecting some crabby old crow. I couldn't believe my luck. So I just fluttered my eyelashes, smiled and agreed with everything he said. I'm sure I've got the job and – wait till you hear the best bit – it's in cosmetics! He said they needed pretty girls to show off their products and he took me through the department. All the girls are young and stunning, so I won't have any frosty old fuddy-duddy telling me what to do.'

'But how are you so sure you've got it? I'm still waiting to hear.'

Rose waved her red-tipped hands confidently. 'Oh, he said he'd write and let me know. But I know already, Della; I just know he liked me. It's a pity you were interviewed by a woman,' she added sagely, 'and it's a pity your mam won't let you use make-up and do something with your hair. It would make you look older and more sophisticated.'

'Mam says there's time enough for that when I'm sixteen.' Della spoke airily, pretending not to care.

'Sixteen! That's two years away! My mam was married at sixteen. When was yours married?'

'I'm not sure.' Della pondered a while. 'I never thought to ask. But David is Mam's son from before she married Dad, and he's seventeen, and Dad's *my* father. I know they got married some time after his first wife died having Wally. Wally and the others are Dad's first family, you see.'

Rose's jaw dropped in surprise. 'Gosh! You never told

me you were such a mixed-up family.'

'We're not mixed up!' Della's voice rose in indignation. 'We're just like one big family. If I never told you, it's because I never think about it. They're all just my brothers and sisters.'

Rose looked puzzled. 'If your dad's not David's father, then your mam must have been married twice. That means she was even younger than *my* mam the first time.'

'I don't know. I expect so,' Della said vaguely. 'Things were different in those days anyway. She doesn't like to talk about David's father, but she says she grew up too quickly and she wants me to enjoy being young and having no responsibilities before I settle down.'

'Well, in that case, why doesn't she let you do your hair and wear make-up? You'd have a lot more fun if you didn't look like a schoolgirl still.'

Unable to counter the argument, Della changed the subject. 'How's the dress coming on? I came to give you a hand.'

'Oh, that's wonderful, Della! Thanks a mill! It's not coming on at all. I can't get the pattern to fit on the material. I'll get it now and we can spread it out on the floor.' Rose jumped up and two minutes later returned with a bundle of glittering green taffeta topped by an untidy mix-up of creased paper patterns.

'Where's your mam?' Della asked, as they placed the material on the floor and juggled the pattern to fit.

'Gone to Granny's,' Rose muttered through a mouthful of pins. 'Do you think you could help me finish this by Saturday in time for the party?' She paused, removing the pins as an idea dawned. 'Hey, Della! Why don't I get you an invitation? I never thought of it.'

'Don't be silly! I don't know your cousin.' Della

continued to smooth out the creases in the bodice pattern.

'That doesn't matter, you nitwit. I'll tell her you're my best friend, and you helped me with the dress. She's all right. She'll let you come. She's sixteen and knows *loads* of boys. It'll be a smashing party.'

'I'd have to ask Mam first.' Della looked doubtful. 'And anyway, I've got nothing to wear.' She felt it wiser to dismiss the idea.

'Don't be a dope! I can lend you one of my dresses. You loved the blue one I wore at Christmas.'

'Oh, thanks, Rose, but I don't think so.'

'You mean your mam won't let you! Aw, come on,' she coaxed. 'We'll walk over to Eileen's when we've finished cutting this out and I'll ask her if you can come. She's writing invitation cards, so if you get an official invitation your mam can't say no.'

Mary scanned the white, gold-edged invitation card, then glanced at Della. 'But you don't even know Rose's cousin.'

'I met her today, Mam. She's nice! You'd like her. And you wouldn't believe the house she lives in. It's a semi-detached like Rose's, but it's huge and it overlooks the Lonnen, and her dad's got a car, a shiny blue Austin. He works at the railways like Rose's dad, but he works in the office. Rose says he's a manager or something.' Della stopped for breath and waited expectantly.

'Indeed! Another one getting rich working for the railways!' Mary looked sceptical. 'The family must have money from some other means. And I hope this girl's not as flighty as Rose,' she added with a disapproving twitch of her nose.

Della jumped to her friend's defence. 'Mam, Rose isn't flighty – she's just fun. You said you wanted me to

32

enjoy myself before I settle down . . . please, please! It's my first invitation to a grown-up party.'

'All right,' Mary consented half-heartedly. 'But you'd better be home no later than ten, do you hear?'

Della hugged her. 'Oh, thanks, Mam.' Ten o'clock was awfully early but better than nothing, which she had expected.

'Now we'd better think what you're going to wear.' Mary rubbed the bridge of her nose with her forefinger and frowned.

'Rose said I can borrow her blue dress, the one she wore here at New Year,' Della ventured timidly.

'That dress! That's not for you, Della. It's much too low in the neck and too tight in the bodice. Rose's mother ought to know better than to let her parade herself like that.'

Della's face fell. 'But, Mam, it wouldn't be so tight on me.'

'No!' Mary was adamant. 'We'll go to town this afternoon and get you some material and a new pattern. You'll have plenty of time to make a dress before Saturday. I don't want you going to your first party in borrowed plumes anyway.'

'Oh, thanks, Mam.' Della's face brightened.

But, in Binns, her face fell again as her mother decided on a simple pattern with a high, square neckline, puffed sleeves and gathers across the bodice. 'This one's just right. It'll do for a party and it's simple enough to shorten for a day dress later on.'

Della moaned. 'Aw, Mam, it's so plain.'

'No, it's not plain; it's simple. And simple is good taste,' Mary insisted.

Knowing there was no point in arguing, Della bit on her lip. 'Oh, all right, if I have to have it. But can I choose the material?' Maybe if she got some shiny material it would look more eveningish, she thought.

'All right,' Mary smiled. 'That's a bargain!'

Della's eyes roved over the bales of material on the shelves and alighted on a peach satin. 'Ooh, that's lovely, Mam!'

'Indeed it is, but remember it's got to do as a day dress later on.'

Reluctantly, Della settled for a mid-blue crepe that would do double duty, after which they bought a box of embroidered handkerchiefs as a present for Eileen.

On the tram home, she wondered if Mary would notice if she cut the neckline a little lower than the pattern and decided to do so – just an inch. Excited at the prospect of the party, she had for the moment forgotten her worries about Anne.

But the following day, while washing up after breakfast, Mary dropped the bombshell Della had been expecting. 'I'm going over to Anne's today. Do you want to come?'

Della stopped in the act of drying a plate. 'Er, no, Mam. I want to get on with the dress.' Silently, she debated whether it might be better if she went. No! She'd probably give herself away . . . better let Anne handle it on her own.

Mary shouted a greeting as she opened Anne's door.

Anne, awaiting the visit with dread, called out, 'In the kitchen, Mam.'

'How are you—?' Mary stopped dead when she saw Anne's face. Although she had obviously disguised her eye with powder and smeared lipstick on her lips, the face was unmistakably bruised, and the lipstick only accentuated the congealed blood encrusting the healing cut. 'My God! What have you done to yourself?' Mary threw her bag and parcels on to the sofa and examined Anne's face more closely.

'Don't panic, Mam. I just fell down on the ice.' Anne

34

silently thanked Della for her creativity.

'Fell? On your face?' Mary asked shrewdly.

'I . . . I hit my face on the side of the kerb.'

Mary looked anxiously at Anne's growing belly. 'Did you hurt yourself anywhere else?'

'No, thank goodness! I only hurt my face. Stop worrying, Mam. Nice to see you. I'll put the kettle on.' But Anne knew her attempt to change the subject would be futile.

'Where did you fall?' Mary pursued relentlessly.

'On my way home from Muriel's yesterday.' Anne gratefully recited Della's lie and retreated to the scullery to fill the kettle.

'You only did it yesterday, and it's turning green already!' Mary followed her, probing suspiciously. 'You're not lying to me, are you? You haven't had a fight with Dan?'

'Don't be ridiculous, Mam.' Anne concentrated on filling the kettle. 'Dan would never touch me. We shout a bit sometimes, but that's all. I've got make-up and powder over it; that's probably why it looks funny.' She shrugged off Mary's suggestion that she was lying and placed the kettle on the gas stove, striking a match with shaking hands. 'Johnny's outside playing. I'll get him in now before I make tea.' She opened the door and called Johnny in, hoping he would take Mary's mind off her suspicions.

'Granny, Granny!' he whooped, running in from the back garden and throwing himself into Mary's arms.

'Well, look what a big boy you're getting!' Picking up the four-year-old with difficulty, Mary beamed with pleasure. 'Let's see if this hat and these gloves fit. I swear you've grown since last week.'

Anne carried the cups to the kitchen, heaving a silent sigh of relief that Mary was occupied with Johnny – for the moment at least. But, as it turned out, not for long.

'How's Dan?' Mary asked when the three were seated at the table.

'Fine!' Anne kept her eyes down as she buttered Johnny's bread.

When Mary returned at three o'clock, Della sat by the fire tacking the seams of the new dress. She looked up fearfully. 'You've been a long time,' she said as casually as she could. 'How's Anne?'

'Did you know she had hurt her face?' Mary looked at her almost accusingly.

'No! What's happened? Is she all right?' The concern in Della's voice was genuine, but even Rose would have been proud of the innocent look she feigned.

'Well, she says she is.' Mary threw her coat and hat on the sofa. 'She said she slipped on the ice yesterday. But I've dealt with enough cuts and bruises in my time to know when a wound's fresh or not. And a black eye doesn't turn green overnight.'

Della groaned inwardly. Anne was right! Mam was nobody's fool. 'She was fine when I saw her the day before,' she lied.

'Well, I don't believe that cock-and-bull story about falling on her face. I think Dan's been at her.' Her expression grim, Mary sat by the fire.

'Aw, Mam!' Della protested, horrified that she had guessed the truth so easily.

'Don't "Aw, Mam" me!' Mary looked at Della closely. 'I know what I'm talking about. I've suspected for a long time that something's going on with those two. Of course Anne's too loyal to tell on him, but she gets a guarded look on her face whenever you mention his name. I even asked her outright if he'd touched her and she said he'd never laid a hand on her. But she couldn't look at me when she said it.'

'*Mam*, you're imagining things. I know you're not

awfully fond of Dan, but Anne loves him and they're all right.' Della consoled herself that they *could* be all right if Dan kept his promise.

'Not fond of him! That's an understatement if he's up to what I think he is.' Mary poked the fire furiously. 'And if he is, I'll find out. You can't keep that sort of thing hidden for ever.'

That evening, Mary told Walter about Anne's face and her own suspicions, but he simply replied, 'Well, if Anne says she fell and hurt herself, then that's what she did. She wouldn't lie to you.'

Chapter Four

Saturday arrived and the dress was finished, pressed and hanging in the airing cupboard. Mary and Rose had each given Della some dancing lessons, though she swore she wouldn't set foot on the dance floor. She had just washed her hair and was brushing it dry before the fire when Walter came in with the post.

'There's a letter for you, Della.'

'Oh, Dad, let me see.' She almost snatched the envelope from his hand, tore it open, and devoured the letter. 'It's Binns! They want me to start a week on Monday.'

Mary rushed in from the scullery, wiping her hands on her pinafore. 'Well, congratulations, dear!'

'And I get ten and six a week to start!'

'Aye . . . time you earned your keep.' Walter lit another Woodbine from the one he was about to stub out.

Wally poked out his head from behind the *Daily Herald*. 'Hey, Dad! Maybe you can afford to buy Players now instead of those stinky Woodbines.'

'That's enough of your lip, lad,' Walter grunted.

David, sitting quietly at the table doing his homework, closed his book with a thud and yawned. 'Have you finished with the sports page, Wally? I'm bored.'

'Aye, you can have it all.' Wally threw the paper at his brother. 'Are you coming to the match this afternoon, then? Michael and Billie are.'

'What do you think, you daft thing?' David smoothed out the paper. 'I couldn't miss seeing our lads flay those Scots buggers.'

Della was relieved her brothers were going out. There was never much peace when the boys were in the kitchen on a Saturday afternoon, and it was too cold to go up to her room. Now she'd be able to savour the anticipation of the party quietly.

At five o'clock, she took her bath, extravagantly sprinkling a few Sylvan soap flakes into the water to soften it. She soaked for almost an hour, then carefully put on the dress, turning this way and that before the full-length mirror in her parents' room. She screwed up her face. The dress was all right but not very grown-up looking, despite the illicitly lowered neckline. And the lisle stockings and sensible lace-up shoes were embarrassing. Only the toes of the shoes showed beneath the hem, but a thought suddenly struck her, and tentatively she took a step towards the mirror. She wanted to cry. Why hadn't she thought of that before and made the dress longer? When she walked, the shoes and an inch of lisle stockings peeked out from under the skirt.

She pouted as she went down to the kitchen. 'Aw, Mam, I look like a schoolgirl – especially with these shoes and stockings.'

'There's nothing wrong with them, and the dress looks very nice, very suitable.' Mary surveyed Della more closely. 'That neckline is lower than I thought, though. And, anyway, you know you're too young for high heels and silk stockings, so don't start asking for them.'

'I'll bet everybody else is wearing them,' Della said huffily.

'And everybody else there is older than you.'

'Rose isn't,' Della insisted.

'And you know what I think about Rose and the way her mother lets her carry on. Just be grateful I'm letting you go to the party at all. And any more whingeing and I've half a mind not to,' she said sharply.

'Oh, Mam! You wouldn't?' Della's face crumpled as if she were about to cry.

Mary relented. 'Don't be silly, luv. Go and splash your face at the sink and pinch those cheeks to get some colour into them. You'll be the prettiest girl there in any case.'

'Aye, if I was a lad I'd chase you.' Walter added his piece. 'And it looks like a nice dress to me.'

Della hugged him. 'Oh, thanks, Dad.' She was nervous and needed reassurance. It was strange. Mam was usually the one who gave her that. Why was she being so difficult about this party?

'Your dad'll come for you at ten. Have a nice time, dear,' Mary said more gently now.

Della's face looked as if it were about to crumple again. 'Oh, Mam, please don't make Dad come. I can walk back. I'm walking there! I'll be a laughing stock if Dad comes to get me.'

'Yes, but you'll have Rose with you going, and you know I don't like you being out on your own late at night.'

Though Della couldn't see the difference between walking there in the dark at six or walking home in the dark at ten, she knew better than to argue.

Rose opened the door and posed in the shiny green taffeta dress they had both worked on. Della felt even dowdier than before. 'Gosh, you look like a film star, Rose! And I love your shoes.' She looked enviously at the black patent leather high-heeled pumps and silk-clad instep peeking out from Rose's long skirt.

'Thanks, luv. I'll just get my coat.' Rose disappeared

41

into the hallway and returned wearing her black astra-khan coat and hat, a Christmas present from her parents. 'Ta ta, Mam, Dad!' she yelled as she shut the door.

Della pulled her navy blue velour coat more tightly about her. It was her only coat and had been bought for school the previous year. Oh, it must be wonderful to have money! She sighed inwardly as they made their way to the Lonnen, the tap-tap of Rose's high heels and the rustle of her taffeta dress resounding in the quiet street.

'Your Dan came round today to see our Tommy,' Rose said. 'He's so handsome, I get the shivers whenever I see him. Gosh, your Anne's lucky.'

Della's ears pricked up. She knew Dan and Rose's elder brother had gone to school together, but she didn't know they were still friends. 'What did he come for? I didn't know they saw each other any more.'

'They don't much now, but they met in town and Dan said he was looking for a new job, so our Tommy said he might be able to help him get work on the railways.'

'But Tommy's only a clerk there. How can he get him a job?'

'Don't forget the railway's a sort of family business for us,' Rose reminded her. 'My Uncle Albert's got a lot of pull. He got Dad and Tommy their jobs, and Tommy said they were looking for a new clerk they could trust.'

Trust? Della pondered. Mam always said she wouldn't trust Dan as far as she could throw him. 'Well, it would be nice for Anne if he got a better job,' she said, hoping it might improve his temper.

The house on the Lonnen was ablaze with lights, and Della was impressed at the half dozen cars parked outside. Eileen answered their knock. She looked rav-ishing in turquoise satin. Only two narrow straps held up the tight-fitting bodice, and the daring neckline

42

showed off a gold pendant with a matching turquoise stone. Her hair, the same red as her cousin's, was also cut fashionably short and permed. Della felt more drab than ever.

Eileen ushered them to an upstairs bedroom. 'Leave your coats in here and do your make-up in the bathroom. Come down when you're ready,' she flung over her shoulder as she floated off.

Della took off her coat and laid it on the pink satin eiderdown, her eyes taking in the matching curtains and pink and green Indian rug. Now she felt shy and overwhelmed as well as dowdy.

Rose laughed. 'Come on! Don't stand there gawping. If you don't shut your mouth you might catch a fly in it. Let's go and tidy up in the bathroom.'

Della placed the box of handkerchiefs on the pillow for Eileen to find later and followed Rose. Standing before the bathroom mirror, she slowly ran her comb through her shining hair. She still looked like a gawky schoolgirl, she thought miserably; she might as well have put a bow in her hair.

'Come on, cheer up!' Rose pulled down her mouth in imitation of Della's expression. 'You look as if you've lost a pound and found a penny. I'm going to put some colour on that miserable mug.' From her black satin evening bag she took out a lipstick, a powder compact and a tiny jar of rouge.

'No, I daren't. Mam would have a fit.' Della backed away.

'Your mam isn't going to see it, you ninny, so stop worrying. You can take it off before you go home.' Rose tipped up Della's chin and applied a bright red lipstick, paler red rouge on her cheeks, and a final dusting of powder over her face. 'I wish I had black eyelashes like you,' she said enviously. 'You don't need mascara, but a little bit of Vaseline wouldn't hurt.' She took a tin from her bag and ran her fingers across the surface, smearing the grease upwards on Della's lashes. She stood back to admire her handiwork. 'Wow, what a difference! I'm a bloody idiot. Now I've got real competition.'

Della gazed at her reflection, half in delight and half in doubt. She turned to Rose. 'It doesn't look like me.'

'Of course it does – like you only better,' Rose assured her, dabbing more rouge on her own cheeks and expertly renewing her lipstick. 'Now let's see what the talent's like.' Grabbing Della's arm, she almost dragged her down the stairs and into the large front room.

The gramophone was playing *I'm Just Wild About Harry*, but Della noted with relief that the area cleared for dancing was still deserted. The party was just getting under way and most people hovered around the dining table and sideboard. The table was loaded with savoury snacks, sandwiches and cakes, in the centre a huge birthday cake with sixteen candles waiting to be lit.

The sideboard, however, seemed to be even more popular. On it stood a bowl of punch, bottles of beer, sherry, and a bottle of clear liquid that looked like gin.

'Well, there you are!' Eileen joined them. 'I thought you'd died up there.' She ladled punch into two glasses and handed one to each with a wink. 'Secret recipe. I can recommend it.'

Della was glad to have something to do and sipped her punch, glueing herself to Rose's side. 'What's in this?' she whispered. 'It tastes like cough medicine.'

'Tastes like rum to me.' Rose took another sip. 'And cider, and something else. It's anybody's guess. And who cares! Drink up!'

Della gingerly attempted the drink again. 'It burns when it gets down,' she croaked.

'That's the booze – warms your cockles.' Rose giggled and surveyed the guests. Her attention was taken by some new arrivals. 'Hey, look who's just come in. It's Eileen's new neighbour, Jim Parker. I'm going to get her to introduce me. He's dreamy!' But she hesitated when she saw Della's stricken face. 'Oh, you'll be all right on your own, won't you? Nobody's going to talk to us while we're stuck together like Siamese twins. This is a party! You've got to circulate. We can talk to each other any old time.' She eyed Jim Parker as she spoke.

'I'll be fine, don't worry,' Della said without conviction.

'Look! I promise I'll come back and see how you're doing.' Rose's eyes still weighed up Jim Parker. 'But I bet as soon as you're on your own, somebody's going to chat you up. Wish me luck.'

Della nodded. She remained by the sideboard for a few moments before deciding she'd be less conspicuous in the crowd round the table. She helped herself to a ham sandwich. As the room filled up with more guests, she gravitated towards an empty armchair by the window, slumped down in it, and balanced her plate and glass in her lap. She checked that her shoes weren't showing. They were! *And* the stockings! She pulled the skirt down over her toes. She must remember to sit down more carefully.

'Are you a friend of Eileen's? I haven't seen you here before.' The voice came from high above her, and Della looked up to see a tall, slender boy looking down at her.

She quickly swallowed the last of her sandwich. 'Well, I'm really Rose's friend – Eileen's cousin.'

'May I join you?' He nodded towards the chair arm. 'Seating's getting a little scarce.' He perched on the arm and smiled again.

Now that she could get a better look at him, Della saw that he had brown curly hair, wide-set, humorous brown eyes and, despite his determined jaw line, a long, almost delicate face. She liked what she saw.

45

He indicated her almost empty glass. 'Can I get you some more punch?'

'Yes, please,' she said recklessly. Her head felt funny from the first glass; she'd better just pretend to sip this one, she thought, as he returned with two glasses.

He resumed his position on the chair arm. 'I'm Jonathan.'

'I'm Della.' She hoped her voice didn't give away her nervousness.

'It's a pretty name.'

'Thank you. I was christened Elizabeth after my grandmother and Della after my great-grandmother, but my father liked Della better, so it stuck.'

'It was my great-grandmother's name, too. It must have been the fashion then. Do you live in Newcastle?'

'Yes, the West End. And you?'

'No, I'm from Carlisle, but I usually come into town at weekends. I don't really get on with my parents, so I like to get away whenever I can.' He shifted a little in embarrassment that he'd confided in this girl so quickly. 'I . . . I stay with my friend; he moved next-door here recently. But I'll be living in town permanently next year when I go to university.'

His friend must be the one Rose likes, Della deduced, and if he were going to university next year he must be at least seventeen. 'My mother used to live in Carlisle,' she said, suddenly realising there'd been a gap in the conversation while she'd weighed him up.

'Whereabouts?'

'Oh, I don't know. That was centuries ago. She was only ten when she left. Her uncle married the maid and she threw my mother and grandmother out of the family house.' She was glad to let him know that her mother had once had a maid, even though their circumstances now were humble.

46

Jonathan raised his eyebrows. 'Threw them out! What for?'

'Well, according to my mother, because the ex-maid wanted to run the house without my grandmother having any say in matters. And, of course, because of the money.'

'Sounds like a Gothic novel.' He smiled down at her again.

'I suppose it does.' She resolved to look up 'Gothic' when she got home.

They chatted easily. Della was amazed at how comfortable she felt talking to him. And he only asked her to dance the slow dances; she was grateful for that. The evening flew and, with a shock, she caught sight of the clock on the mantelpiece. Twenty-five to ten! She'd have to leave soon and say goodbye to Eileen and Rose before washing her face. How could she manage that? She mustn't let Jonathan see her without her make-up. She allowed herself another ten minutes before saying in a forced casual tone: 'If you'll excuse me, I've got to go now, and I must say goodbye to Eileen and Rose first.'

'You're going already? But it's hardly started.' He looked dismayed.

Della lowered her eyes. 'My father's coming to pick me up.' She hoped Jonathan would at least think she was being driven home.

'Well, er, may I see you again?' He coloured a little.

Della coloured also, from pleasure and embarrassment. Now she'd have to tell the humiliating truth. 'I'd have to ask my parents first,' she confessed, feeling extremely foolish.

Jonathan shot her a surprised glance, then smiled. 'You seem to have old-fashioned parents. I suppose we'd better make it formal.' Taking out a pocket address book, he tore off a page and wrote on it before handing it to her. 'Why don't you ask them and write and let me know if you could see me next weekend? We could go for a walk on Sunday afternoon, and I could come to pick you up so they can give me the once-over. Surely they can't object to that . . . unless they object to *me*, of course.' He laughed nervously, again colouring slightly.

Della clutched the paper and stood up. 'All right. But I have to go now. Goodnight.' She moved with assumed casualness, taking care not to take big steps and show her shoes, yet making her exit as fast as she decently could. She saw Rose on the dance floor, draped around the boy from next-door, and whispered in her ear that she was leaving.

'Ta ta then, luv. Hope you had a nice time,' Rose said over her partner's shoulder, her voice a little slurred.

After thanking Eileen, Della flew upstairs. She scrubbed her face with soap and water, but still there were traces of the lipstick and rouge, and the water simply beaded on the greased lashes. She must make the water hotter and use more soap. Two scrubs later, she patted her sore face dry and peered at it through bloodshot eyes. It was impossible to wash her eyelashes without getting soap in her eyes. Only then did she notice the jar of cold cream on the window sill. Oh, well – too late now. She must be outside waiting when Dad arrived.

Making her way carefully down the stairs without lifting her skirt, her coat collar pulled up as far as possible over her face, she managed to avoid encounters. Walter was opening the gate as she gratefully closed the door behind her.

Mary put down her knitting when they arrived. 'Did you have a nice time, dear?'

'Yes, Mam, thanks.' Della nodded and tried to skulk through the kitchen to the hall. 'I think I'll go straight up to bed. Goodnight.'

'What's all the hurry? I've got your cocoa ready and I'm dying to hear about the party. Come and have it while it's hot.' Mary picked up a steaming mug from the hearth.

Della, knowing it would be better to behave normally and hoping the cool air had toned down her face by now, returned and sat by the fire. 'It was very nice, Mam.' She cradled the mug. 'There was lots of food and a fruit punch.' Now for it! She might as well get it over with. 'And I . . . I met a very nice boy. He asked me to go for a walk next Sunday. May I, Mam? Dad?' She hoped vainly that she might stand a better chance if she brought Walter into the decision but knew that he would go along with whatever Mary said.

Walter half-glanced up from his library book. 'What are you asking *me* for? You know your mam's word's the law on those things.' His gaze returned to the book.

'All right, let's hear more.' Mary's tone was encouraging. 'Who is this boy and how old is he?'

'He's a friend of Eileen's,' Della began excitedly. 'He lives in Carlisle but stays with his friend, Eileen's next-door neighbour, at weekends. And he's very well spoken and well educated. He's going to King's College next year.' She realised too late that mentioning university had been a mistake.

Mary frowned. 'If he's going to university next year, that means he must be at least seventeen. I think that's just a bit too old for you, Della.'

'But Mam!' she persevered. 'He could be a real lout and be my own age. But he's a perfect gentleman. He gave me his address so I could ask your permission first and then write to him. And he said that to make it extra proper, he'd come and pick me up so you could meet him.'

'Well . . . he certainly sounds determined.' Mary wavered. 'How much do you like him?'

'Oh, a lot, Mam. I told you.' Della held her breath waiting for permission, but none came.

'What's his name, then, and whereabouts in Carlisle does he live?'

'His name's Jonathan and he gave me his address.' She pulled the paper from her handbag. 'Here it is. See for yourself.'

Mary took the proffered sheet and, glancing at it, turned white. 'Della!' she shrieked, a look of disbelief on her face. 'You absolutely cannot see this boy!'

At her tone, Walter again looked up from his book. 'Why all the hysterics? Can't a man read in peace?'

'This is the boy who's asked Della out.' Mary's hand shook as she handed him the paper.

As Walter read, he let out a low whistle. 'Do you know who this is, lass? It's your own cousin.'

Della looked puzzled. 'My cousin? Don't be daft, Dad! Let me see!' Her mouth gaped as she grabbed the paper from him and read. 'Maddison!' She looked incredulously at Mary. 'Oh, no, Mam! I didn't know his surname. How awful! Is it the same address?' By now she felt close to tears.

'Yes, it's my old house,' Mary replied stonily. 'And he, no doubt, is my Uncle Joseph's youngest, born shortly after David.'

'But wait a minute, Mam,' Della implored. 'He can't be *my* cousin. If he's your Uncle Joseph's son, he's *your* cousin. That means that to me he's only a great cousin, or half cousin, or second cousin once removed or whatever they call it. And he told me he doesn't get on with his parents, so you might like him, Mam. Please, please, just meet him once and you'll see.'

Mary's expression remained rigid. 'I don't want to hear any more about this boy. Do you understand? Write and tell him you can't see him, not next week nor any time.'

Chapter Five

The following afternoon Della trudged dejectedly to Rose's house to tell her the awful news. She greeted Rose glumly and waited until they were seated by the fire in the sitting room before relating her story.

'I don't believe it!' Rose looked incredulous. 'I wondered why you had such a long face. Of all the lads in that room, you had to go after your own cousin.'

'I didn't go after him,' Della corrected her. 'He came after *me*. But I really liked him, Rose . . . and besides, he's *not* my cousin.'

'Well, whatever he is, your mam won't let you see him, so what's the difference? You poor thing. What rotten luck! And I had such a fantastic time with Jim.' She sighed and feigned a swoon. 'He's dreamy, Della. And he's taking me to the pictures tomorrow night. He walked me home, and all he did was give me a goodnight peck on the cheek. I thought he'd try to neck the first time, but in a way I'm glad he didn't. Waiting sort of builds up the excitement.'

'That's nice. I'm glad one of us was lucky,' Della said graciously. She lay back listlessly in the chair and wondered what a goodnight kiss on the cheek from Jonathan would have been like. Then she remembered the new job. 'Oh, Rose, I can't believe I forgot to tell you in all the excitement last night. I do have *some* good news, I suppose. I got the job at Binns.'

'Ooh, that's fab, Della. I still haven't heard, but I can't think about anything but Jim at the moment anyway.' Rose swooned again, then giggled.

'I'm glad one of us is happy. I'd better go home now and write that letter.' Della rose reluctantly.

'What if I see him, then? I mean, if I see more of Jim, and Jonathan stays with him, I might. Shall I tell him you're writing to him?'

'Don't you dare, Rose Johnson!' Della flared. 'Not a word about me! Do you hear?'

Rose pulled a face. 'All right, keep your wool on. See you during the week, then. Come over any time during the day, but I'm keeping every night free in case Jim asks me out again.'

'Don't worry, I won't butt in on your love affair.' Della saw herself out.

When she arrived home, Mary and Walter were reading the Sunday papers in the sitting-room. 'Did you have a nice time at Rose's?' Mary asked in an obvious effort to break the ice. Della had been very strained at breakfast, and it wasn't like her to sulk.

'All right.' Della shrugged and retreated to the kitchen to write her letter in private. She decided she wouldn't give her address so Jonathan couldn't write back. Thank goodness the boys were out again today; she needed to think hard to write this. And thank goodness also it was Sunday and the sitting-room fire was on. She wanted to be alone in her misery.

As Della left, Mary turned anxiously to Walter. 'She's taking it very hard, Walter. It's not like her to be moody.'

He grunted from behind his newspaper. 'Aw, she'll get over it. It's the first lad who's asked her out, that's all. Stop worrying about her. If you're going to worry your head about anything, I'd be more concerned about what's going on in Germany with that damned Hitler and his Nazis. Now that he's gained strength in the Reichstag, there'll be no stopping him. It's a pity they didn't succeed in burning down the place, and him with it.'

'Walter! For God's sake stop meeting trouble half-way. We've got enough *real* problems without worrying about what else may happen.'

He tutted and lit a cigarette. 'It does no good to bury your head, woman. We've got to face facts and be prepared for the worst. God knows where it'll end if that maniac gets in. They're already stepping up their rearmament, and what for if they're not planning to start another war? It sounds as if it's coming anyway, but if Hitler gets in I'd say it's a dead cert. And we're not going to be ready for it this time any more than the last. "The war to end all wars." That's a bloody laugh!' He spat the last words. 'Barely fifteen years since the end of that slaughter and those bloody Jerries are getting ready to have another go.'

'Walter, please!' Mary waved her hands in despair. 'I couldn't live through another war, especially with the boys . . .' She shuddered.

On Tuesday, as Jonathan sat down to breakfast, his father handed him an envelope. 'Letter for you,' he said.

'Thanks.' Jonathan slit open the envelope with his knife, noting with pleasure the Newcastle postmark. It might be from Della. It was. He read eagerly:

Dear Jonathan,

I feel very embarrassed writing this, but I have to tell you that I am not allowed to see you again. It would be unfair not to tell you the reason, so here it is. Remember that story I told you about my mother and grandmother being turned out of their home? Well, strange as it sounds, it seems it was your parents who were responsible. Your father is my mother's uncle, and the rest you know.

I don't think it's fair that things that happened to our parents years ago should still affect us, but it seems they do.

Della

After reading the contents twice, his expression incredulous, Jonathan laid the letter on his plate and looked at his father with disgust. 'You never told me you had a sister and a niece you threw out of the house.' His voice shook despite his efforts to control himself.

Joseph Maddison's pale, thin face twitched, then flushed. 'Don't you use that tone of voice to me, lad,' he spat. 'And what the devil are you talking about?'

'This! Read for yourself.' Jonathan pushed the letter towards his father.

Joseph snatched it, his bushy black brows drawing together as he read. He then glared at his son with steely brown eyes, his thin lips curling beneath his narrow black moustache. 'That was a long time ago and there was good reason for it.'

'I know the reason,' Jonathan retorted, seething with suppressed anger. 'And *I* don't think it was a good one.'

'What's going on here?' His mother entered. Her thick make-up and rouged cheeks accentuated her round, flaccid face, and her heavy corsets impeded her movements as she lowered her plump body on to her chair.

Not wishing to confront his mother as well, Jonathan simply handed her the letter.

She bent her immaculately coiffured head, the chestnut brown he remembered from his childhood now tinted black to conceal the grey. She read slowly, arching her high pencilled eyebrows even higher. 'And what's this girl got to do with you, Jonathan?' She coolly placed the letter on the table and poured herself a cup of tea. As she looked down, her heavy eyelids veiled the displeasure in her piercing brown eyes.

'I met her at a party and wanted to see her again. And I will! I won't let old family feuds stop me,' he added daringly.

For a moment Roseanne's composure faltered. She put down the cup she had raised to her lips, which had been sensuous in her youth but now sagged and curled downward. 'You'll have nothing to do with this girl! Her mother was a no good tart – two children before she was married. Oh, yes, she married the second father all right, but not till after the daughter was born.'

'How do you know what her mother's like? You haven't seen her since the day you threw her out as a little girl,' Jonathan threw back at her, marvelling at his own daring.

'I read the Births and Marriages,' Roseanne snorted, 'and she wrote us begging letters when she got into trouble the first time. Mark my words, that girl will be a trollop just like her mother. Like mother, like daughter, and like her grandmother before that! Thank your lucky stars she'll have nothing to do with you.' She waved her white, scarlet-tipped hands in dismissal.

But Jonathan was not to be overruled on this subject, unlike so many before. 'We'll see,' he said, anger loosening his tongue further. 'And Della's not a trollop!' He looked closely at his mother's expressionless face and shook his head in puzzlement. 'Why on earth did you have to keep it secret that you used to be a maid here, Mother? There's no disgrace in the fact that you bettered yourself. And what other skeletons are there in our family cupboard? Don't you think we're all old enough now to know the truth?'

'That's enough!' Joseph cut in, his face now blotchy with anger. 'As long as you live in this house you'll hold your tongue. Don't you dare speak to your mother like that, especially when you know she's not well. Now apologise to her!'

Jonathan suddenly lost heart. Yes, he thought, if I don't apologise she'll have another fainting fit, or another so-called heart attack. 'I'm sorry, Mother,' he grunted, scraping back his chair. There was no point in prolonging this.

He made his way dejectedly to his room. Why couldn't he be like his brothers – acquiescent, dutiful, and loyal? Well, loyalty should be earned! Ever since he'd been old enough to think for himself he'd questioned his parents' values and resented the iron discipline they used to keep their sons under their thumbs. And, of course, he resented his mother's simulated ill health. This she used as a weapon to get her own way, even with his father. Yet in all the years she'd been having her convenient bouts of illness, the doctors had diagnosed nothing wrong with her physically. He reached his room and sat on the bed with his head in his hands, lost in thought and miserable.

His brother's voice interrupted him. 'Yoiks! I heard all that.' Charles plunked down on the bed beside him and ran his hands through his fair hair. 'Thought I'd better stay out of it. Take my advice and keep your nose clean if you want to stay all right with the old man – and the old lady.' He pulled down his mouth in an exaggerated grimace, his long face, a model of his father's, lengthening even further. Yet he had a rugged look about him, and a freshness that the wildest imagination couldn't associate with Joseph, even in his youth.

'I don't care about staying all right with either of them,' Jonathan said grimly. 'As soon as I'm old enough, I'm going to get out of here. If I were your age I'd go today.'

'Yes, twenty-one and got the key of the door! But

that's not enough my boy. Some day I'll have more, if I play my cards right,' Charles said in a satisfied tone. 'And so could you. You don't know when you're well off.'

'I don't care about their lousy money. I just want to finish university and get away from them.'

'Glad to hear it, then – all the more for James and me.'

'You're welcome to it,' Jonathan said fervently. 'It's all right for you and James. You don't seem to mind kowtowing to them, but I'm just not made like that.'

Charles smiled. 'Oh, really! How *are* you made, then?'

'I don't know.' Jonathan punched the pillow in frustration. 'But I do know I'll never find out till I get away from here.'

Anne was putting Johnny to bed when Dan arrived home on Thursday evening. He was late again. 'Hello, luv,' she shouted from the bedroom. 'I'll be out in a minute to get your tea. It's keeping hot in the oven.' Johnny was whining and it took longer than usual to get him settled. When she finally entered the kitchen, Dan was sitting at the table.

He glowered at her. 'Some bloody welcome I get! I work my flaming arse off all day for you and the bairn. The least you can do is be here when I get home and have my meal ready. That blasted kid means more to you than I do.'

From across the table where she stood, Anne could smell the beer on his breath. She was afraid. 'He's yours as well, Dan, and I have to look after our son.' She kept her voice deliberately light and went to the scullery.

'And what about looking after your husband for a change? That bairn takes up all your time. You've spoiled him rotten. Whinge, whinge, whinge! He knows that's all he's got to do to get his own way.'

Anne carefully placed Dan's plate on the table. She knew she must placate him before he got any worse. 'I'm sorry, Dan, but he was crying. Here's your dinner. It's liver and onions.'

'That's the second time we've had bloody liver and onions this week. Can't you think of anything else, woman?' He threw his plate and the contents to the floor.

Anne, shaking now, ignored the mess and, with an effort, kept her voice steady. 'I know, Dan, but it's cheap and tasty, and it was all the housekeeping I had left today.' She must try harder to defend herself in future. In these moods, it irritated him to see her nervous. But he got more irritated anyway.

'Money! That's all you women go on about. If you had to go out and earn it yourself, you'd bloody soon learn how to make do on less!' His voice was almost a scream, and he thumped his fist wildly on the table. At the noise, Johnny began whimpering once more. 'And there's that bloody brat of yours, whingeing again. Go on, run to him like you always do.'

Anne knew she mustn't go to Johnny. She must keep Dan calm. 'Shall I make you a cheese sandwich, then?'

'I don't want anything.' He jumped up from the table and slumped into an armchair.

Yes, she thought, because you've got a belly full of beer. But she knew better than to say it and, leaving Johnny crying, went for a cloth to clean up the mess. Dear God! It was only a week since the last time. Surely Dan wouldn't touch her again? But as she knelt, cloth in hand, he towered over her and undid his belt.

'That's more like it,' he snarled, 'get on your hands and knees and say you're sorry.'

'What for, Dan?' She forced herself to speak and straightened up on her knees. But, in an instant, he had pulled her jumper over her head, her arms imprisoned and her back bare above her thin cotton vest. She was helpless against the wild thrashing of the leather, scorching her flesh again and again. Clenching her teeth, she tried not to shout for fear of distressing Johnny even more, but her moans grew louder. And then the thrashing stopped. Whimpering, she painfully eased the jumper down over her head and dragged herself up by the table.

Dan had thrown himself back on the sofa, his hands covering his face. 'I'm sorry, lass,' he snivelled. 'I don't know what gets into me.'

'I do. It's the beer,' Anne sobbed. 'It's only when you've had a bellyful you take it out on me.'

'Aye, maybe! But I can't stop the beer. It's the only pleasure I get when I'm depressed. I've had a rotten day at work,' he whined like a child.

'You'll have to stop if you want to keep me and Johnny.' Still standing by the table, Anne rocked back and forth in pain and anguish.

'Aye, well, I'm seeing Tommy on Saturday to see if that job's going to come off. Maybe things'll get better if it does. I promise I won't hit you again, Anne. Please don't leave me, please!'

'I've heard your promises before, Dan.' Anne's voice was dead and her shoulders hunched with pain and despair. She trudged to the bedroom to comfort Johnny.

By Friday Della had regained some of her good humour, but the thought of Jonathan was never far from her mind. It was boring just staying at home and helping Mam with the housework. She would go to see Anne today. Maybe they'd take Johnny for a walk on the Lonnen.

The door was open and she found her sister in the kitchen, a pile of mending on her lap. Anne looked up, startled. 'Oh, Della, I . . . . I wasn't expecting you.' Her face was pale, but the bruising had disappeared and the cut had healed.

'It's mild out so I thought we'd take Johnny for a walk. I'm bored and fed up,' Della said truculently.

'Well, I can see why you're bored with no school and no work yet, but why are you fed up?' Anne kept her eyes down on her mending.

Della sat down and poured out her tale while Anne listened, at last looking up in amazement. 'Good Lord! How strange he had to be a Maddison! Oh, you poor lamb. Did you like him very much?'

'Yes, heaps, and I don't see why I shouldn't be allowed to see him. All that family business was centuries ago.'

'But you've got to remember that it was pretty awful for Mam. I can understand her not wanting you to have anything to do with that family.'

'But he's not like them, Anne. He's nice! He's—'

The back door opened and Johnny hurled himself at Della. 'Auntie Della!' He climbed on her knee and fixed his round brown eyes on her expectantly. 'What you got for me?'

Della tousled the fair head. 'Johnny, you mustn't expect a present every time I come. I thought your mam and I would take you for a walk.' She turned to Anne. 'Do you feel like a walk?'

'Not really, luv, but you go ahead and take Johnny.' Anne kept her head down. 'I'll make a cup of tea and a sandwich when you get back.'

'Are you all right?' For the first time, Della looked suspiciously at Anne's bent head.

'I'm fine, luv . . . just a bit tired today.' She forced a smile. 'You two go off now and get some fresh air.'

When they returned, Anne still sat in the chair, the pile of mending in her lap. 'Oh my! You're back early,' she said guiltily. 'And I haven't got tea ready yet. I'll just put the kettle on.' She placed her hands on the chair-arms and, wincing, eased herself up.

'Anne! What's wrong?' Fearfully, Della took her by the shoulders.

Anne winced again, then her face crumpled. 'Oh, I didn't want you to know, Della. Please don't tell Dad – or anyone – please. It'll be better when he gets that new job.'

'Oh, God! No! Not again! What's he done to you?' Della's hands dropped from Anne's shoulders.

Slowly, Anne sat down again, weeping freely now. 'He took his belt to me across my back,' she stammered between sobs, all pretence gone. 'He said last time that in future he'd put it where no one would see it.'

Della sank to her knees and held the pathetic figure gently. 'Oh, no, Anne!' She forced back her own tears. 'You said he'd promised.'

Anne sniffled. 'He did. But after Dad came round he got mad at me again.'

'Why's Mammy crying?' Johnny tugged at Della's coat.

'She's just got a pain in her tummy. It'll go away in a few minutes. Why don't you go out and play and she'll be better when you come in?'

'I don't want to go out to play.'

'Do as I say, Johnny!' Della ordered, still holding Anne's sobbing figure. The back door finally slammed. 'It's all right, Anne.' She stroked the silky blonde head. 'Now tell me what happened.'

Haltingly, Anne related the previous evening's events. When she'd finished she looked up. 'I . . . I can't believe he's jealous of his own child. I don't know what's going to happen when another one comes.'

'Why don't you leave him and come home?' Della urged. 'You and Johnny and the new baby could have my room. I'd be fine in the sitting-room.'

'No!' Anne shook her head. 'I've just got to pray he gets over this period. I'm hoping the new job will make a difference if he gets it. If he's got a job he enjoys, he won't need to get drunk to drown his sorrows, and he won't need my attention so much. I've got to give him another chance, Della . . . he was so pathetic last night . . . afterwards.'

Della sighed in resignation and took Anne's hand. 'It seems there's no way to talk sense into you. But at least I'm going to tell Dad he's done it again.'

Anne's wide blue eyes grew even wider. 'Oh, please don't tell him this time. He threatened to bring the boys with him if it happened again.'

'But that's just what Dan needs! He needs to know you've got people to look out for you,' Della said firmly. 'Now let's get that jumper off. I want to see what he's done to you.'

With difficulty, Anne raised her arms while Della gently lifted her wool jumper. 'Good God!' Della winced when she saw the red weals on Anne's back, the skin broken in several places. 'I'd better put some Germolene on those cuts, and then I'll put a cloth over so your jumper doesn't rub.'

Later, walking home, Della pondered what to do. She would have to tell Dad and let him decide. This didn't take him long. When he arrived that evening, she greeted him in the scullery and whispered the news to him.

'That's done it!' he shouted fit to burst his lungs. 'I told him what I'd do and I'm damn' well going to do it. It's bloody well time he had a good hiding.'

'What's all the shouting about?' Mary rushed in from the kitchen.

'There's no point in keeping it quiet any longer, lass.

Dan's been at our Anne again. I'm going over there with the lads tonight.'

Mary's hands flew to her face. 'Oh! I knew it! I knew it! What's he done to her?'

'He used his belt on her back, Mam, but she's all right,' Della tried to placate her.

Mary looked stupefied. 'How long have you been keeping me in the dark about this?'

'I only found out last week.' Walter tried to keep Della out of the conspiracy. But it didn't work.

Mary drew in a deep breath. 'So she didn't fall and hurt her face and you both knew?'

Walter put a hand on her shoulder. 'We just didn't want to worry you, lass. But now he's been at it again, it's time you knew and time we put a stop to it. I'm going over with the lads tonight to give him something he won't forget in a hurry.'

'Dear God! Why doesn't she leave the swine and come home?'

Della shook her head hopelessly. 'She won't, Mam. I've tried.'

With an effort, Mary pulled herself together. 'Well, I suppose I'd better finish making the dinner if you're all going over there. The boys'll be home any minute.'

The boys' reaction was predictable.

David exploded. 'I'll blast the bugger to smithereens.'

'No, you won't, *I* will.' Michael thrust out his jaw pugnaciously.

'Not before *I've* punched his face in,' Billie added, slamming his right fist into his left palm.

Walter ended their discussion. 'That's enough of that! We're just going over to frighten him – no punching up. Let's hope it'll be enough. Dan's a coward at bottom. He'll think twice when he see's he's got the whole family after him.'

★ ★ ★

Dan was sprawled on the settee when they all marched in without knocking. He sat up with a start, his jaw dropping.

The group advanced and, although Walter was a good two inches shorter and a stone lighter, he grabbed Dan by his shirt and pulled him to his feet. Dan's eyes popped and his face turned grey. 'I told you I'd get the lads to you next time,' Walter bellowed, 'and I'm a man of my word.'

'Yes, you bloody coward!' David pushed his father out of the way and, towering over Dan, twisted his ears till he winced. 'This is just a little taste of what you'll get if it happens again.' He twisted further.

'That's right, only it'll be a lot worse next time,' Michael joined in, forcing Dan's right arm behind his back. 'How would you like your arm broken?'

Billie lunged forward and waved his fist close to Dan's eye. 'And what about a black eye from me, the same as you gave to our Anne?'

'All right! That's enough, lads!' Walter shouted.

Wally pushed Billie out of the way. 'Oh, no! Not till I've had *my* turn, Dad.'

Walter restrained him. 'Nah, not now! We'll let you have first go at him if there's a next time. And that'll be the real thing!' He gave Dan a shove that sent him crashing back on to the sofa.

Anne, standing rigid in the doorway, her clenched fist to her mouth, tried to pacify Walter. 'Oh, Dad, there won't be a next time. He's promised!'

Walter turned to her. 'Aye, and we all know what his promises are worth. But he'd better mean it this time.' He looked closely at Anne's white face. 'How are you feeling, lass?'

'I'm all right, Dad, honest.'

'Well, that's not what our Della says. I'm telling you,

if he touches you again he's going to end up in the hospital.'

'Or the mortuary.' David poked Dan in the chest.

Pale and shaken, Dan said quietly, 'You needn't worry. It won't happen again.'

Chapter Six

On Monday Della got up early, washed in the cold bathroom, slipped on her new black wool dress, and fastened the white detachable collar with difficulty. She grimaced as she pulled on the lisle stockings and flat shoes, knowing that the other girls would be wearing high heels and silk stockings. Despite the businesslike dress, she still felt like a schoolgirl.

'Well, you do look nice, dear,' Mary remarked, when Della appeared in the kitchen. 'I'll get your porridge.'

'I'm not hungry, Mam. I'll just have a cup of tea.'

'You'd better get something down you,' Mary insisted, disappearing into the scullery and returning with a steaming bowl. 'It's going to be a long morning.'

'Are you nervous, Della?' Billie asked. 'I know I was on my first day, but you get over it.'

'I wish the first *week* were over,' Della groaned. She forced a spoonful of porridge down.

Wally grinned and tried, in his way, to comfort her: 'Aw, it's nowt to be nervous about. You'll probably only be sweeping floors and running messages. That's all I did for the first few months.'

To Della's dismay Wally's comment turned out to be not far from the truth. Miss Bane, head sales lady of the department, a slim, well-preserved woman in her forties with peroxided hair and heavy make-up, introduced

Della to the other girls, all looking as elegant as she had dreaded.

'And this is Nora.' She came to the last in line, a slight girl of about Della's age. Nora's light brown hair hung naturally to her shoulders the same as Della's, and her open, pretty face was devoid of make-up. Della also noted with relief that she wore flat shoes and thick stockings.

'How do you do?' she said shyly.

Nora's hazel eyes smiled sympathetically. 'Hello.'

'Nora's been with us a year now and she's moving up to the floor. You'll be taking over her job, but she'll work with you and show you the ropes for the first few days.' Miss Bane waved her hand in dismissal.

Taking Della's arm, Nora led her to the back of the department and down some stairs. 'The Bane of our lives,' she muttered when they were out of hearing, rolling her eyes upwards. 'Here, just hang your things up there.' She indicated an empty hook.

Della looked at her curiously. 'Why are you going upstairs? Don't you like the dress department?'

'Upstairs?' Nora sounded puzzled.

'Miss Bane said you were moving up to the next floor or something.'

'Oh, no, I'm moving "up to the floor", to start as a sales lady,' Nora laughed. 'You will as well, one of these days.'

Della looked dismayed. 'But you've been here a year. Does it take that long to train?'

'Training! That's a laugh!' Nora pulled a face. 'I spend most of my time in the back room ironing the dresses, making the tea, washing the dishes, dusting the racks, packing dresses for delivery, and running messages. I'm only allowed on the floor to stand and watch what the other girls do when I've got nothing else to do, and that doesn't happen much. I had to clean up my tongue as well and talk nice like the other girls. They told me that at the interview.' She puckered her lips and imitated Miss Bane: 'Yes, modom, that one's just perfect on you. All it needs is letting out here and a little more room here and the buttons moving over there.' She spluttered with laughter. 'When what modom really needs is a new pair of corsets and the next two sizes up.'

Della's spirits sank even further. 'You mean I won't be selling dresses for a year?'

'Maybe it won't take so long for you. You don't have to learn to talk posh the way I had to,' Nora replied, adding mischievously in broad Geordie, 'But when I gerr oota this dump, I please mesel' the way I tark.'

Della smiled. 'You sound like two different people.'

'Aye, that's what me dad says. He thinks I'm gettin' airs an' graces, but me mam wants me to get on in the world,' Nora continued in her Geordie voice.

'Mine too,' Della said. But she was still thinking – twelve more months!

'Come on, we'd better get back before the old faggot comes looking for us.' Nora resumed her shop floor voice and led Della back up the stairs to a small room at the rear of the department. 'This is new stock to be ironed.' She indicated three racks of dresses. 'And this is where you make the tea,' she added, pointing to a grubby sink, a gas ring and a wooden bench littered with chipped mugs. 'You'd better start the ironing. I've got to deliver a dress, and those new ones have to be ready for the floor tomorrow morning.'

At least they've got an electric iron and an ironing board, Della thought gratefully. At home they still used flat irons and spread a sheet on the corner of the kitchen table. She plugged in the iron experimentally and was working diligently on a silk dress when Miss Bane came in.

'Miss Jones and I have our tea at ten,' she said,

somehow turning the statement into an order. 'And the others come in at ten past.'

Della nodded meekly. 'Yes, Miss Bane. I'll have it ready.' But, since Miss Bane's entry, she'd forgotten the iron in her hand.

Miss Bane sniffed, as a strong singeing smell filled the air. 'Look what you're doing, girl!'

Too late, Della lifted the iron to reveal a triangular brown patch on the grey silk. 'Oh, I . . . I'm sorry, Miss Bane,' she stammered.

'And so you should be! Didn't your mother teach you how to iron?' Miss Bane's voice hissed through her teeth as she bore down on Della and pulled out the plug. 'You're supposed to check the temperature regularly and switch it off when it's too hot for fine materials.'

'I'm sorry, Miss Bane. It's the first time I've used an electric iron,' Della confessed.

'You're just lucky it's at the bottom of the hem,' Miss Bane grunted, examining the damage. 'The alterations girl can take it up and we can sell it as a shorter fitting – otherwise it would have had to come out of your wages. You must be more careful in future,' she added in a voice rising with impatience.

'Yes, I will, Miss Bane,' Della said miserably.

'And you'd better start the tea now.' She slammed the door as she left.

'Don't let the old faggot get you down, luv.' Nora attempted to console Della when she returned after the staff tea break. 'Come on! We can have a cup now.' As she poured the tepid, stewed brew into two cups, Della looked on with distaste.

'Ugh, I hate cold tea,' she grumbled, 'and I hate that old bitch already.'

'She's got a soft spot in her sometimes, though.' Nora tried again to reassure her. 'She sent me home once when I had the curse and couldn't stand up straight for the pain. And she bought a lovely baby present for one of the girls she had to fire for getting into trouble.'

'That's a joke!' Della remained unconvinced. 'Firing someone and buying them a present!'

'Well, she had to,' Nora insisted. 'The shop wouldn't stand for a single girl on the floor with a belly on her. Mind you, I'm not saying I like the old bag, but I can't help feeling sorry for her. She had a fiancé who jilted her when she was nineteen, so the story goes, and she hasn't had a man since. All she's got to go home to is a grouchy old mother she looks after. The rumour is that she locks herself in her room and gets drunk most nights. Her job is all she's got, and she takes her responsibilities too seriously,' she added kindly. 'When she gets on at me I just remind myself that I'm glad I'm not in her shoes.'

'Thanks for the pep talk.' Della smiled, putting down her cup untouched. 'I'd better get back to the ironing.'

When she arrived home she was exhausted, but Mary greeted her at the door, eager to hear her news. 'How was it, luv?'

'Well, all I can say is that Wally wasn't exaggerating this morning. The only thing I haven't done today is sweep floors, but no doubt that will come tomorrow.' Wearily, Della hung up her coat before flopping into the nearest armchair.

Looking crestfallen, Mary sat opposite her. 'What happened, sweetheart?' After hearing Della's tale, she did her best to soothe her: 'I'm sure Nora was right, dear. *You* won't have to wait a year, and it'll be easier tomorrow. Why don't you put your feet up while I see to the food?'

In the evenings, Della was too tired to go out after work and waited until Saturday to see Rose.

As usual, her friend greeted her warmly. 'Oh, Della, I've been dying to see you. How was it? Come on in.'

Della followed her to the kitchen. 'Well, the "training", if you can call it that, isn't exactly what I had expected, and the last girl had to wait a year to get on to the sales floor. But it was nice to get my wage packet yesterday,' she added, feeling slightly more hopeful about the job now. 'Mam's giving me three and six pocket money out of it. Let's go to the matinee this afternoon? Charlie Chaplin's on at the Embassy in *Hard Times*.' But before Rose could answer she went on: 'Oh, I forgot to ask. Have you heard from Binns?'

'Yes, I heard this week and I start on Monday, but I'm so excited about Jim I've hardly thought about it,' Rose said ecstatically. 'Let's go to the pictures then, and I'll tell you my news on the way.'

A few furtive rays of sunlight peered through the clouds as they made their way to the Embassy and Rose embarked on her news. 'He's absolutely gorgeous, Della. I'm in love! We went to see Mae West in *Angels with Dirty Faces* and he held my hand at first, but when it got to the dirty bits he gripped my knee.'

'Rose!' Della cried, shocked. 'You mean you let him?'

'Only my knee. What's wrong with that? But I admit it made me feel so funny I couldn't concentrate on the film. I can't tell you what it felt like, Della. I mean, I know boys have kissed me before, but I've never felt anything so . . . so exciting.'

'Don't be a meany! Tell me what it was like,' Della begged.

'Well, it's not easy to put into words, but I'll try. I got the tingles all over, especially *you-know-where*, and I wanted him to leave his hand on my knee for ever, but then the lights went on. He walked me home with his arm round me.' She paused to enjoy Della's astounded expression. 'And I couldn't wait for him to kiss me properly on the mouth. I asked him in because I thought Mam and Dad would be in bed, but just my rotten luck they were up. So I'll have to wait till tonight to continue the story. He's taking me to the Oxford.'

'The Oxford!' Della repeated, impressed. That was the biggest dance hall in town.

'He only asked me out once last week and all I got was a peck on the cheek again, but he's stepping it up now. I think he likes me.' Suddenly Rose stopped, looking guilty. 'Oh, crikey, I forgot to tell you and it's your own fault for making me talk about myself. Jonathan stayed with Jim at the weekend and he gave him this for you.' She pulled an envelope from her bag. 'He found out from Eileen that I was your friend.' Della took the envelope and stared at it. 'Go on, open it, you dope,' she urged.

Without a word, Della opened the letter and slowly read:

Dear Della,

You can't know how sorry I was to receive your letter and hear the unfortunate news. To think that I made that flippant remark about it sounding like a Gothic novel when you told me the story at the party – if only I'd known!

I had a row with my parents about it, but rows can't change history. I wish I were older and had the means to make amends now for what my parents did . . . but I will one day. In the meantime I can only ask you not to judge me by my family.

I understand why your parents won't let you see me again, but that doesn't stop me feeling very sorry for myself.

Yours,
Jonathan

Della folded the letter and stood mute. Impatiently,

Rose prompted her, 'Well, come on you ninny. Don't just stand there dumbstruck. What does he say?'

Della handed over the letter without a word. Rose read it eagerly. 'Well, it seems as though he really had a pash on you. Oh, and you on him and all, luv. What a filthy rotten shame! Can't you see him without letting on to your parents? Why should they rule your life anyway? I know I wouldn't let my mam and dad get in my way,' she added fiercely as she handed back the letter.

Della found her voice and continued walking towards the Embassy. 'You don't understand, Rose. Your parents are different and you have a different relationship with them. If I tried to see Jonathan on the sly, it would be bound to come out sooner or later. And nothing could ever come of it anyway,' she added hopelessly.

When Della returned, Mrs Moyihan was seated in the sitting-room, the fire lit specially for the occasion. 'Oh, Mrs M!' She bent to hug her. 'I didn't know you were coming today or I wouldn't have gone out. It's ages since we saw you.' Della loved her mother's old neighbour and friend as much as Mary did. The white hair was scraped back into a neat bun, and the large, bony frame that Della remembered so well from her childhood was more stooped than ever. But the clear brown eyes in the gaunt face still smiled, and the wide mouth still turned up at the corners.

'Wey, hinny, I didn't know I was comin' mesel' till I got up this mornin',' she bellowed. 'I just decided to leave that bugger to fend for hissel' and get on the train and come to see you lot while me legs can still carry me.'

'Oh, is your arthritis bad?' Della looked anxiously at the misshapen feet in their surgical shoes, and the deformed knuckles on the swollen hands.

'Aye, hinny, not gettin' any better, but while I can still hobble an' hold me stick, nowt's goin' to keep me a prisoner in me own house.' But, never one to dwell on herself for long, Mrs Moynihan changed the subject. 'I hear you're a workin' lass now then?'

'Yes.' Della pulled a face. 'It's not much fun yet, but it should get better when I'm allowed to sell.'

'Why aye, hinny, that's the spirit! Always look on the bright side.'

Mary interrupted, handing Mrs Moynihan a glass of rum which she had uncharacteristically taken to since her arthritis had worsened. 'Eey, thanks, pet, and cheers,' she said, taking a large draught. 'Puts hairs on your chest, this stuff.'

'I'm trying to get Mrs Moynihan to come here for a while for a rest,' Mary said, sitting on the sofa. 'That brother of hers still expects her to wait on him hand and foot. She could do with a break, at least while the weather's so bad, and she could sleep in Anne's bed in your room.'

Della quickly agreed, though had it been anyone else, she would not have relished the thought of her precious privacy being invaded. 'Of course, Mrs M,' she said. 'Why don't you?'

'There might come a day, luv, when I have to load mesel' off on me friends and relations, but it hasn't come yet.' Mrs Moynihan chuckled. 'You know me. I'll probably die on me feet makin' dinner, or on me knees scrubbin' the floor, an' when I'm pushin' up the daisies, I'll be the one doin' the weedin'.' She looked up as Michael arrived.

'Well, look who's here,' he said, bending to kiss Mrs Moynihan's cheek.

'Eey, lad, what a proper young man you're gettin'.'

'Yes, going on twenty-two and courting,' Mary said wistfully. 'He'll be the first to be whisked from under my nose.' She turned to Michael. 'Why aren't you at the match with the others?'

He flushed. 'I didn't go, Mam. I took Ellen to town to buy a ring. We're engaged.' His colour deepened.

'Well, congratulations!' Mary's eyes misted as she hugged him warmly.

Della jumped up and did the same. 'You dark horse,' she accused. 'Why didn't you tell us? When's the big day?'

'I wanted it to be a surprise.' Michael looked at his shoes, embarrassed by the attention. 'And it won't be till June next year. We might have the ring paid off by then, if we're lucky.'

Mrs Moynihan nodded at Mary. 'Aye, hinny, there goes the first one! After that they go like ninepins. I should know!'

'Oh, no, Mrs M,' Della cut in anxiously. 'The rest of us aren't going yet, and *I'll* be here for years and years.'

Nine years old when Anne had married Dan, Della had thought only of her new bridesmaid's dress and the excitement of the day, not realising until later how much she missed her sister. Now she had a real fear of the family breaking up and life changing.

Chapter Seven

By March Della and Nora had become good friends. They often went out after work, although only to the coffee rooms as Nora received only one and sixpence pocket money from her parents out of her wages. There were seven younger ones still at school and, though Della understood that money was short, she couldn't understand why Nora's father, who had been out of work for almost a year, did nothing about looking for a job. He spent most his time at the pub when it was open, and when not, sleeping off the effects of the beer.

Over coffee one Friday evening, Della dared to voice her thoughts. 'Look, Nora,' she ventured, 'you're free to tell me it's none of my business, but I think it's a rotten shame that your parents keep you so short of money when you work for it. I earn less than you and I get more back from my mam.'

'Della, you know your mam's got all the lads working as well,' Nora said defensively. 'I'm the only one working in our family, and I feel guilty about getting one and six. The kids go to the rectory on Saturday mornings for a free sticky bun – their weekly treat – and that's where they get their clothes from and all. Charity!' She bit hard on her lip. 'Dad's dole barely covers the rent and his booze, and the allowances for the bairns and Mam come to about one and ninepence each. That doesn't nearly cover the food, and every week there's something extra. Mam had to buy a new frying pan on tick at Farnon's this week. She gets everything she can there because she can't buy with cash, but then her payments mount up. We just get more and more in debt . . . and I can't see any hope of Dad ever finding work the way things are.'

'I know, Nora, and I suppose that's what I mean.' Della's tone was sympathetic, but she wanted to make her point. 'Does your dad ever *try* to find work? I don't get that impression from what you say.'

Nora rubbed at a stain on the white tablecloth. 'He did when he was first laid off, but for months now he hasn't bothered; he just picks up his dole every week and goes straight to the pub . . . I think he's got disheartened,' she added protectively. 'He lies to them at the dole and says he's been looking, or he wouldn't get anything. He's picked up more than he contributed when he was in work, and now he's on one of those special extensions.' She stared forlornly into her coffee. 'But it can't go on for ever. Mam says it'll be the parish soon if he doesn't get off his backside and find work. But any rate,' she looked up and added more cheerfully, 'our Maureen'll be finished school this summer, so if she can find a job, things'll be easier.'

'Well, I think that if your dad can still have his booze, you can have a better treat than a cup of coffee now and then. I'm taking you to the pictures next week whether you like it or not.'

'You know I can't take your money.' Nora shook her head in protest.

Della opened her mouth to silence her, but it remained open, her eyes fixed on the door, as Rose entered followed by Jim and Jonathan. She was about to lower her gaze and pretend she hadn't seen them when Jonathan's glance alighted on her. He spoke to Rose and

Jim, and the three approached the table.

'Hello, you two.' Rose greeted them as though it was nothing unusual.

Jim, who had met Della several times, greeted her warmly. His handsome, craggy face creased into a wide grin. Everything about him contrasted with Jonathan's dark, lean good looks – his pale blue eyes, his fair hair, his muscular build. Jonathan's deep brown eyes fixed on Della. 'Hello. Nice to see you,' he said without embarrassment. Struck dumb, she managed a nod and a smile.

'Mind if we join you?' Rose said, smiling wickedly.

Della found her voice. 'No, of course not.' Rose and Nora knew each other from work, but she had to introduce the boys. 'Oh, er,' she said, with assumed nonchalance, 'Nora, this is Jim . . . and Jonathan,' she added, hesitating noticeably.

The two greeted Nora and sat down, Jonathan taking a chair from the next table. Della had time to compose herself. But she hoped Jonathan didn't notice she wasn't wearing make-up.

'We're going to the second house at the Odeon. Want to come?' Rose invited.

Della shook her head. 'No, thanks. I said I'd be home early.'

'Me too.' Nora knew they would be going in the best seats in the back stalls or circle at ninepence or a shilling.

'Is there nothing we can do to persuade you?' Jonathan addressed both of them yet somehow kept his eyes on Della. 'It's Friday evening . . . and Laurel and Hardy are on,' he enticed further.

'No, but thanks anyway. I've got to be home by eight in any case. I'm expecting a friend,' Della lied, hoping Jonathan would think it was a boyfriend. She stood up, wishing she wasn't wearing the black work dress. Now they would have to walk to the coatstand and, worse still, wait at the cash desk to pay; he would see her shoes and stockings.

Nora cast Della a knowing glance and gulped the last of her coffee. 'It was nice meeting you,' she said, pushing back her chair.

The boys rose politely as the girls grabbed their bags. Jonathan then cleared his throat and said as if to both of them, 'Is there no chance you might change your mind, if not this evening then some other? *My* treat, of course.'

'That's very kind of you—' Nora began, but Della interrupted her.

'Thank you for the offer. We'll keep it in mind.'

Rose grinned mischievously. 'Well, I'll see you tomorrow at lunch-time then. You don't know what you're missing.'

'The cow . . . I'll kill her tomorrow,' Della muttered to Nora as they reached the cash desk.

'You'd better shut up and keep smiling,' Nora warned, 'Jonathan's looking at you still.'

They smiled and waved at the exit. But, when safely outside, Nora whistled. 'Phweeeooo! So that's Jonathan! I knew by the look on your face even before you said his name. He's dishy, and so's Rose's boyfriend.'

Della gripped her arm as they walked. 'Oh, I've got the collywobbles again, just like last time. And I'd hoped that after almost three months I was beginning to forget about him. Trust Rose to go to the coffee rooms. She knows that's where we always go.'

'Now you can't blame her for that, luv. Everybody goes there, and you didn't tell her we were going tonight, did you?'

'No,' Della admitted before bursting out, 'Oh, Nora! I've often imagined seeing him again, but I didn't dream I'd feel sick and get the shakes like this.'

'Well, luv, many a girl wouldn't have taken any notice of their parents anyhow. If you really want to see him that much, why don't you? They don't need to know.' It was out of character for Nora to encourage such deceit.

'Go against my parents' wishes!' Della's voice was horrified. 'You know I could never do that, Nora. I'm just not made that way.'

They parted on Grainger Street and went to their separate tram stops. Della's mind raced. Dare she go out with Jonathan – just as a friend? If Nora and the others went, it wouldn't be as if she and Jonathan were courting. Mulling over the prospect, she felt heady at the thought, but decided no. She'd always respected her parents' wishes and this was so important to them, especially to her mother; she simply couldn't deceive them.

At home, Mary and Walter sat chatting with Michael and Ellen. Now that they were saving up to get married, the couple spent most of their evenings at each other's homes and, though Della liked Ellen, she felt annoyed tonight that she would have to make conversation when she wanted to creep up to bed and think about Jonathan.

Mary's voice interrupted her thoughts. 'Hello, dear. You're home early. Are you all right?'

'Yes, Mam,' Della said irritably. 'You're always asking if I'm all right. Can't I come home early if I want to?'

Mary pulled a face. 'Oh, sorry I spoke. It's just that you look a bit pasty as well.'

'Well, I don't *feel* pasty, so stop worrying,' Della assured her in a lighter tone. It wasn't right to take it out on her mother because she was upset.

Ellen's hazel eyes smiled at Della, breaking the tension. 'My mam's always getting on at me for looking peaky as well. I suppose it's just part of being a mam. I'm sure I'll be just the same when *I'm* one.' Her round face dimpled as she smiled lovingly at Michael.

He ruffled her brown curls. 'Crikey, that day's a long

way off, I hope. We can't even afford to get married yet.'

'Aye, and a good thing too,' Walter growled. 'This is no time to bring bairns into the world, not with another war likely to start any minute.'

'Walter, get off your soap box,' Mary admonished. 'You're always prophesying doom. This is a happy occasion.'

'Aye, maybe, but you can't ignore the facts. That maniac's in total control now. He's a bloody dictator with four years of unrestricted power – him and his blasted stormtroopers!' Walter's face was dark, his voice angry. 'And now Japan's left the League of Nations, it's going to give Hitler the same idea. Mark my words, we're in for another world war.'

'Come off it, Dad.' Michael tried to dispel his father's gloom. 'I read the papers as well and it's not as bad as you say. Hitler'll have his hands full keeping his own house in order, and as for Japan – a tiny country like that isn't going to be a major threat to the world.'

'Michael's talking sense, Dad,' Della said, seeing her mother's worried face. But inwardly she respected her father's political opinions more than Michael's. To end the discussion, she asked. 'Who's for a cup of cocoa? I'm going to have one.'

'Aye! Change the subject, as usual,' Walter muttered.

Later, in bed, Della tossed uneasily, her confused dreams switching back and forth from Jonathan to soldiers on a battlefield.

Returning home from the cinema, Jim helped Rose off the bus and the three walked towards Dene Road. Jim's arm was round Rose's waist and Jonathan's hands in his overcoat pockets, his shoulders hunched forlornly.

'Cheer up, man!' Jim urged Jonathan, producing

from his inside pocket a small bottle of whisky. 'What you need's a drink.'

Jonathan shook his head. 'No, thanks.'

'I'll have some,' Rose said eagerly. 'I thought we'd finished it in the pictures.'

'*You* almost finished it, you mean.' Jim handed her the bottle. 'You can drink a man under the table.'

Rose tipped the bottle and drained it. 'Under the table! That's not a bad idea. We've never tried it under the table.' She tittered as she handed back the empty bottle.

Jim replaced it in his pocket and turned to Jonathan. 'Why don't you come with us to the Oxford tomorrow and meet another one? They're all the same with a bag over their heads.'

Jonathan shot him a glance in the dim gaslight and said nothing.

Rose tittered again and then hiccuped. 'Jim Parker, are you saying you wouldn't recognise me if you saw me with a bag over my head?'

'Well, maybe some parts I would.' Jim's face broke into a pleased grin. They had passed Rose's house and approached Jim's. 'You go on in,' he said to Jonathan as he steered Rose across the road to the Lonnen. 'Tell them I'm at Rose's.'

Jonathan punched his friend playfully on the shoulder. 'One of these days I'm going to let you do your own lying, Jim.'

'Don't worry!' Jim's grin flashed again. 'One of these days I'll pay you back.'

He and Rose picked their way across the damp, unkempt grass towards their usual clearing in the bushes, about ten yards from the main road and secluded from passers-by. It had taken them only a few weeks after their first meeting to graduate from a goodnight kiss and cuddle outside Rose's house to their private spot where, with youthful curiosity and desire, they had experimented with love, exploring each other's bodies as far as they dared. Jim took off his overcoat and laid it on the grass, shivering in the dank night air as he sat and pulled Rose down beside him. But his shivering stopped as he kissed her, slipping his hands underneath her coat and feeling the warm flesh under her jumper. Rose trembled with delight, and soon the two were lost in their now familiar game of love, experiencing anew the forbidden delights.

Rose moaned as Jim's hand slipped under her skirt and slid up her thighs. She tugged at his clothing and uncovered him as much as she could lest anyone pass by, caressing him with her recently gained expertise. Jim groaned with pleasure. After a while, he rolled his body over hers and Rose gasped under his full weight. This was the first time he had gone that far. She felt his hand pushing her cami-knickers aside, and then – oh! That wasn't his hand! Wild with excitement at the feel of his body in that forbidden place, she was unable to stop him as, out of control, he began to press himself into her. But then she tensed.

'Relax,' he said hoarsely.

She tried to – she wanted him too much to stop now. Her head was spinning, and she was aware only of the wild pulsations in her loins – until he thrust further. No, that hurt! 'Jim! Jim!' she cried. 'Don't move any more!' But he *was* moving, unable to stop himself, and his cries of passion equalled her cries of pain as his body shuddered violently and he fell on top of her, perspiring profusely despite the cold.

'Jim! You didn't stop!' Rose accused. She felt only a raw, burning sensation now. All the wonder of the moment had suddenly vanished. Was this *it*? All those marvellous feelings led up to this? It couldn't be! She started to cry.

Jim still gasped for breath. 'How the hell did you expect me to stop after you'd let me go that far?' he protested, flinging himself on to his back.

'I . . . I didn't mean you to stop altogether,' Rose whimpered. 'But you went so fast and it hurt so much.'

Jim sighed. 'I know . . . I'm sorry. But what did you expect? I got carried away. Did it hurt much?'

'A whole lot,' Rose replied dejectedly. 'So that's what it's like! I never want to do it again, Jim Parker, never! Do you hear?'

He rolled towards her again and put a comforting arm round her shoulders. 'It only hurts the first time, honestly.'

'I don't care!' Rose was adamant. 'Even if it didn't hurt, I don't see what people see in it – there was nothing to it. It was all over in a flash. I liked it better before. And anyway, I don't want to risk getting into trouble so you can just forget it ever happened.' Feeling cheated, she sat up and rearranged her clothes.

'Aw, Rose,' he grumbled, replacing his own dishevelled clothing. 'I swear you'll like it better next time. Don't be upset, please. I know you wanted it as much as I did.'

'Well, I wouldn't have wanted it if I'd known what it was like, so there!' she pouted, standing and dusting off her coat.

They walked silently to her door and, when he tried to kiss her goodnight, she averted her face. 'Come on, Rose,' he pleaded. 'You're not going to sulk about it, are you?'

'I'm not sulking! I'm just upset and disappointed.'

He tipped up her chin. 'I promise you won't be disappointed next time. George's parents are away and he's having a bit of a do after the dance tomorrow night. We could have a whole bedroom to ourselves.'

'I don't care. I'll come to the dance, but nothing else.'

Rose turned her back and let herself in.

But, lying in bed, she pondered over the event. It *had* to be better after the first time or why would women go on doing it? And now she'd lost her virginity, there was no point in pretending she was saving it till she got married. She would give it one more try, but she'd make sure Jim got some of those things. There'd be no harm in it so long as they took precautions. It was lucky she had just finished her period and it was her safe time. She'd read enough books to know that.

She couldn't tell Della and Nora she'd gone all the way, though. They'd be shocked. This would be the first secret she'd kept from them. Up to now she had delighted in regaling them with every detail of her sexual exploits with Jim, feeling sophisticated and worldly as they eagerly sucked up the information. Oh, well – she justified her behaviour – she was in love with Jim. It wasn't as if she would do it with just anybody.

The following morning Della couldn't wait for lunchtime to find out from Rose what Jonathan had said about meeting her. At one o'clock, after the senior staff's lunch hour, she took her lunch to the staff room. There was a small counter where the staff could buy food and drinks, though most brought their own food to save money. She bought a cup of tea and had just seated herself when she saw Rose carrying her tray from the counter. Della bit heavily into the cheese sandwich she'd brought, feeling ashamed of the twinge of envy she felt at her friend's affluence.

'Hello, pet,' Rose said gaily as she sat down. She wondered if she looked any different after last night. She'd regained her spirits and was looking forward to being alone with Jim again at the party, curious to know what it might be like when it didn't hurt. 'Bit of a mess bumping into you last night.' She looked closely at her friend. 'How did you feel?'

'How do you think? Rotten! I just hope you didn't know I was at the coffee rooms when you took him there.'

'Course I didn't, luv. Honest!' Rose embarked on her fish and chips.

It smelled appetising and, eyeing the plate hungrily, Della took a ferocious bite of her sandwich. She was tired of sandwiches every day. 'Did . . . did he ask about me after I'd gone?' she asked hopefully.

Rose pulled a face. 'He talked about nothing bloody else if you ask me. The only time he shut up was when we were watching the picture.'

'What did he say?'

'Oh, he just went on about how upset he was that your parents wouldn't let you see him, and then he asked if you had a boyfriend and I told him you hadn't.'

'Rose! How could you? Why did you tell him that?'

Rose, poised in the act of inserting a chip into her mouth, looked up in amazement. 'Well, because that's bloody well the truth! You didn't tell me you wanted me to lie to him.'

'I'm sorry, Rose.' Humbled, Della lowered her head. 'It was only to save my pride a bit that I hoped you might have told him I had a boyfriend.'

'Well, he hasn't got a girlfriend neither, so I don't know what you're worrying about.' Rose shrugged. 'Ever since that flaming party he hardly ever comes to town, and when he does he just hangs around Jim or both of us – like a bloody third thumb. I like him, Della, but sometimes Jim seems to prefer seeing him to me. You know what they're all like about going out with the lads. He says Jonathan's staying at home more weekends to study, but when he starts King's next autumn he'll be in town all the time, and that means I'll hardly ever see

Jim.' She put down her knife and fork and looked earnestly at Della. 'Why don't you make a foursome with us? It'd be much better that way . . . and your mam and dad don't need to know,' she added archly.

'That's what Nora said. But you know I couldn't deceive them, Rose.'

'Well, think about it. Strikes me it would make life a lot easier for both of us.' Rose pushed her unfinished meal away and stood up. 'I have to go now. Mabel's promised to do my face with some new cosmetics we've just got in. I want to try them out for tonight. Jim's taking me to a party after the dance. Come over on Monday after work and we can have some sherry and a chat. Mam and Dad are going out. See you then, luv.'

Della nodded.

The front door was open when Rose and Jim arrived at his friend's house in Elswick. They could hear the gramophone playing. After hanging their coats on the overburdened hallstand, they made their way down the dimly lit hall to the darkened sitting-room, from which came strains of unidentifiable music. 'Smooch music' Jim called it, because you couldn't dance to it. From the light of the fire they could see couples lying on the sofa or the floor, the music punctuated by the occasional giggle or grunt.

Jim took Rose's hand. 'This is kids' stuff,' he whispered. 'John said we could use his bedroom, second on the right. He bagged his parents' room for himself.'

As they passed the first room, they noticed a pair of high-heeled shoes outside. The second door was closed but there were no shoes denoting occupation. Jim opened the door and fumbled for the switch. Light shed on a small room with only a single bed, a wardrobe and a chest of drawers. But they were both excited at the luxury of a warm room and a bed, whatever its size.

'Put your shoes outside the door and close it,' Jim ordered impatiently. Rose did so and within minutes they had removed their clothes and were enjoying the sight of each other fully naked for the first time. Rose gasped with pleasure and anticipation as Jim pulled her roughly down on the bed and began kissing her all over. She was eager now to try the ultimate experience once more; it had to be better than last time. And it was. Though still feeling a little tender from her first experience, Rose also felt the promise of new delights. She moaned, partly with pleasure, partly with pain, until the pleasure overwhelmed the pain, as Jim, managing to control himself longer this time, finally reached what seemed to be the core of her being. So that was lovemaking, she mused dreamily, as afterwards they lay in each other's arms.

'Didn't I tell you it would be better next time?' Jim panted beside her.

'I'll say! Does it get any better than that?'

Jim tried to sound worldly, and spouted as if from first-hand experience the information he had gleaned from his friends and from books: 'It's sort of different every time,' he informed her importantly, 'and some women feel it and some don't. You're a natural though, Rose. I'll bet it gets better every time for us.'

She grinned. 'Well, let's have another try and find out, then.'

'Just give me another five minutes,' he boasted.

On Friday evening Della and Nora again went for a coffee after work. They sat at their usual table.

'Crikey, it's good to get off me pins and get me shoes off,' Nora groaned, furtively slipping off her shoes under the table.

'I think I'll do the same,' Della said. 'I've been standing the whole day ironing the summer stock.'

Nora yawned. 'I'm beginning to think I was better off where you are than being on the floor. Standing around doing nothing and trying to look busy is worse than ironing. I swear there was no more than a dozen customers today, and do you think I got any? Not bloody likely! Old Bane and her gang copped the lot.'

They ordered two coffees and sat zombie-like, waiting for the reviving drink, until Nora gripped Della's knee under the table. 'It's him again,' she hissed, indicating the door with her head.

'Oh, Lord, no.' Della kept her eyes on the tablecloth. 'Don't look and he might not see us.'

'Are you kidding? That's what he's come for, you dope. I bet he comes straight over.'

True to Nora's prediction, Jonathan approached their table. 'Hello,' he said shyly. 'I see this must be your regular Friday night meeting place.'

'Not really,' Della contradicted him. 'I mean, we go to other places as well.' She didn't want him thinking he could meet them any Friday he pleased.

'May I join you?' he asked.

'Of course,' she said, coldly but politely.

Jonathan took the chair next to hers as the waitress brought two coffees. 'Another coffee, please,' he said before turning to the girls. 'I've just got into town and the train was freezing. I thought a hot drink would be nice before I go on to Jim's.'

Nora, trying to become invisible, picked up her cup and buried her nose and eyes in it, while Della, realising her friend's ploy, nudged her knee to no avail.

Jonathan looked at Della. 'You missed a good picture last week. I wished you'd come.'

His coffee arrived, allowing her a moment to think of an intelligent reply. But all that came out was, 'I told you I couldn't.'

'Yes, but you did say perhaps some other time. How about this evening?'

She felt cornered and looked pleadingly at Nora for help. But her friend still busily examined the contents of her coffee cup. Della decided it was better to stop skirting the issue. 'You know I can't.'

But Jonathan persisted. 'Do you really think your parents would object to us just being friends? Say, going to the pictures occasionally. That's all I'm suggesting.'

'Yes, I do, Jonathan. They've forbidden me to see you. Isn't that enough?'

He looked uncomfortable and shifted in his chair. 'You're right, I suppose. I just hoped we could get round it that way. It's not really fair that I'm being judged by my parents, you know. As I told you that first night, I don't see eye to eye with them. What they did was inexcusable, and I wish I could do something to put it right.'

'I told them you didn't agree with your parents, Jonathan, but it didn't make any difference,' Della said with a note of finality. She glanced at Nora, now tactfully studying the menu. 'We'd better be going or we'll be late.' She kicked her on the shin, to her chagrin being reminded they had taken off their shoes.

Nora nodded, and both girls surreptitiously stuffed their feet back into their footwear. This task was easier for Nora who had worn slip-ons since she'd been working on the floor. At last successful, she stood up and summoned the waitress for the bill. But when it arrived Jonathan intercepted it and, placing it under his saucer, said graciously, 'Please, allow me.'

'Well, thank you very much,' Nora said, feeling like a lady.

Della, both shoes on but laces undone, was also on her feet. 'Thank you,' she said serenely, and proceeded carefully to the exit behind Nora.

'Della,' he called after her. 'Your laces are loose.'

'Oh!' She feigned surprise and bent to fasten them with her back to him so he wouldn't see her pink face.

Outside, Nora said, 'Well, he's determined to see you one way or the other.'

'We can't go there on a Friday again.' Della's voice shook. 'I suppose I should be flattered that I'm being followed, but it just upsets me to see him when I can't see him, if you know what I mean.'

'I know, luv, but I wish such a handsome, well-mannered lad would chase me like that. That'll be the day,' Nora said wistfully.

'I'm sorry our coffee was cut so short. I'd like to go home now. Do you mind?'

'Course not, luv. I'm knackered anyhow. See you tomorrow, then. And don't spend the whole night pining.'

But Della slept little and lightly, her sleep punctuated yet again by dreams of Jonathan, though this time there was no battlefield. She had forgotten her father's prophecy about war.

Chapter Eight

Anne was preparing the evening meal when Dan came home carrying a large box. 'What have you got?' she asked.

'What you got?' Johnny echoed, jumping with glee.

'Wait and see,' he gasped as he set the heavy object on the table. 'I need a knife.' Anne handed him the bread knife, and he slashed and cursed until the contents were unveiled.

'A wireless!' She drew in her breath. 'Oh, Dan, can we afford it? It's such a big one!'

Dan looked very pleased with himself. 'It's not just any wireless, lass. It's a Philips – the best there is. And of course we can afford it, now that I'm not selling bloody shoes for a living.' Reverently, he bowed to the set. 'Here's to the London North Eastern Railways.'

Johnny jumped with glee, shouting, 'A wireless, a wireless, no bloody shoes!'

But Anne bit her lip nervously. 'It's just that you got that eiderdown last month. We must be going into more debt. It frightens me, Dan.'

'No need to worry your head,' he boomed confidently. 'Haven't I always done all right by you?' He heaved the wireless on to the sideboard. 'And it's short wave an' all.'

'It must have cost a fortune!' Anne stroked the shiny mahogany case nervously.

'Aye, enough! But we deserve the best. And it's not before time.' Dan twiddled the knobs. 'There we are,' he said with satisfaction as the strains of *When You and I Were Young, Maggie* wailed out of the set. He grabbed Anne's swollen frame and attempted to glide her around the kitchen. 'Eey, listen to that song, then. We're going to live life while we're young, lass, before we're too flaming old to enjoy it.'

Anne giggled as he pushed her to and fro, Johnny hanging on to her skirt in delight. Finally, exhausted, she pushed him away. 'Oh, Dan, get off it! I'm out of breath. You'll bring the bairn on at this rate.'

'Well, I wish it would get a move on. It's time I had me wife back instead of this great, lumpy sack of potatoes. Much longer without me husband's rights and I'll be forced to go elsewhere.'

Anne's face fell. 'Oh, Dan, you would never do that, would you?' Suddenly, she felt as if cold water had been poured over her.

'Now if I was going to do it, I'd have done it before now, wouldn't I? And instead of buying all these presents for you, I'd be buying them for her, wouldn't I?' He continued to dance Johnny around the room.

'I know, I'm just being silly.' Anne smiled with relief. 'It's just that I've been feeling a bit off all day. I think my time's getting near.'

Dan grunted as he hoisted Johnny on to his shoulders. 'Wey, if anything starts the night you'll have to knock on the wall for Cathy. I've arranged to see the lads from work.'

'Cathy and Dick have gone to her mother's,' Anne informed him, dismayed that he was going out again.

'Well, then, get Della to come over,' Dan said casually, dropping Johnny to the floor and twiddling the knobs again. The wireless emitted a high-pitched screech, which Johnny attempted to imitate.

'How can I? I can't walk that far and back, and I'd have to take him. Johnny, stop that noise!' Anne put her hands over her ears, her nerves now feeling raw. Johnny pouted and was about to cry. 'Come and help Mammy get tea ready,' she coaxed. 'You can carry the plates in.'

'I suppose you want me to go and get Della before I go to the pub, then?' Dan said slightly sulkily, and then in a more cheerful tone, 'All right! I'll go. Keep your wool on.'

'Thanks,' Anne said, relieved. She thanked God silently that Dan had been so much better since the new job.

Mary's hand flew to her face when she answered the knock on the back door; Dan rarely paid them a visit and never without Anne. 'What's wrong? Is it Anne?' she cried.

'Don't panic! She's fine!' he pacified her. 'She's just feeling a bit off and wondered if Della would go and sit with her in case anything starts. I have to go out,' he added, knowing this statement would meet with disapproval but showing no sign of discomfiture.

'I see,' Mary said stiffly. 'Well, I'll go too. If anything happens Della couldn't cope on her own.' As she spoke she scrambled for her coat among the clutter of garments on the scullery door, and Della, who had heard the conversation from the kitchen, quickly joined her.

'What time will you be home, Dan?' Della asked, knowing that his outings often ran into the small hours. 'I have to be up for work tomorrow.'

'Not too late,' he said evasively. 'Ta ra then. See you later.'

'*Not too late*,' Mary muttered into her coat collar as he disappeared down the path. 'What sort of an answer is that? Don't worry, luv. If it gets late, you can go home.'

★ ★ ★

When they arrived, Anne lay on the sofa, the dirty dishes still on the table. 'Don't worry! I'm just tired, Mam,' she said, as she saw Mary's anxious face. 'It was a hard job getting Johnny into bed. He had a tantrum.'

'I hope that one doesn't take after his father,' Mary said sharply, throwing her coat on to a chair.

'I'll see to the dishes, Mam. You sit down.' Della added her coat to her mother's and rolled up her sleeves.

'It's nice to see you, anyway, luv.' Mary sat in an armchair, looking closely at Anne. 'Still another week to go! Do you think it's going to be early?'

'I don't know. But I feel very tired and my back's aching a lot.'

Suddenly Mary's gaze caught the wireless. 'A wireless! Good God! How can he afford to buy a wireless with a new baby coming? And you haven't paid off the furniture yet!'

'It's all right, Mam. Dan says we can afford it.' Anne hoped this would be enough to appease her mother, but it wasn't.

'How much is he making at this job, then?' Mary asked suspiciously.

'I don't know, Mam, and I don't care. He's giving me an extra three and six a week for the housekeeping and he's happy at his job. That's all I know.' Then, to get off the subject of Dan, she suggested: 'Let's have a game of snap? I feel much better now. I'll put the wireless on as well.' She attempted to rise but moaned and eased herself down again.

Mary's eyes grew large. 'Good God! Is it starting?'

'I don't know, Mam,' Anne gasped. 'It's my back.'

'You'd better lie on the bed.' Mary tried to help her up but, halfway, Anne sat down heavily again. Della looked on with a paper white face.

'Della, help me,' Mary ordered, and together they managed to get Anne on to the bed.

'It doesn't feel like before, Mam,' Anne whimpered. 'I'm frightened.'

'Don't worry, luv. Della felt different from David as well,' Mary comforted her. 'Now let's get you undressed. Get me a bowl of cold water and a flannel, Della, to keep her cool, and then we'll start timing the pains.' As she spoke she glanced at the alarm clock on the bedside table.

Della felt herself trembling. 'Shall I go for the midwife?'

'No, there'll be no need for a while,' Mary replied nervously.

But half an hour later, as soaked in perspiration as Anne, she called into the kitchen where Della sat biting her fingernails and trying not to hear Anne's agonised cries: 'You'd better go, Della. Now!'

The midwife rode her bicycle and arrived before Della had returned. She set her black bag on the bedside table and took over from Mary, who whispered urgently, 'I know it's early but something doesn't seem right. I thought I'd better get you.'

The huge woman nodded and almost thrust her out of the way. She began poking Anne's belly. 'It's all right, hinny! Let's have a look at you.'

But it wasn't all right. Another wave of pain washed over Anne, taking control of her tortured body. She screamed, raising her head, and the woman pushed her back. She held her down and repeated, 'It's all right, hinny. Nowt to scream like that about . . . just take deep breaths now.' She turned to Mary. 'You go and have yourself a cup o' tea, hinny. I'd rather be on me own than have worried mothers to deal with an' all. It looks like a long job, but she'll be all right. I'll shout if I need you.'

Reluctantly, Mary returned to the kitchen where

Della, her eyes luminous in her ashen face, nursed a whimpering Johnny. 'The noise woke him up,' she explained. 'Is everything all right Mam?'

'Nurse says so, but it's going to take a while. We'll just have to have that cup of tea and be patient. Nurse doesn't want me in there – a right bossy one, that.'

After an eternity of listening to Anne's pitiful cries, she jumped up. 'I can't stand this much longer. I'll make some more tea.'

'I'll help.' Shaking, Della followed her mother into the scullery, both glad to be further out of earshot of Anne's agony.

Back in the kitchen, Mary looked at the clock on the mantelpiece. 'Good Lord! Twelve o'clock and that bastard's not back yet. You'd better go home when you've finished your tea. You've got to get up for work tomorrow.'

'Oh, please let me stay, Mam,' Della begged. 'I couldn't possibly sleep anyway.'

'All right.' Mary gave in with a weary sigh. 'Dear God, there's Johnny off again. This is much too upsetting for him. Why don't you take him in to Cathy? Their kitchen light's on, so they're back now.'

As Della returned from next-door, footsteps sounded down the hall. It was Walter.

'What's wrong?' he bellowed as he pushed open the kitchen door. 'I went to bed, but I woke up after a bit and you still weren't there, so I came straight over.'

'Anne's having a bad time,' Mary told him in a trembling voice. 'The midwife's with her.'

'Is it going to be all right?' He sat beside her on the sofa and took her hand.

'I don't know, Walter. I'm worried.' Tears began to flow.

'There now, bawling isn't going to make it any better,' he said with gruff concern, taking out his handkerchief and thrusting it in her hand. 'Is it the bairn or Anne?'

'It's a bad labour the nurse said. That's all.' Mary dabbed at her eyes with the handkerchief.

'Well, that's all it is, then. What are you getting so upset about? And where's that bloody husband of hers?' Walter had only just noticed Dan's absence.

'He hasn't come back yet,' Della said quietly, praying that Walter wouldn't cause trouble with Dan.

'That bugger!' Walter yelled. 'Can't even be here when his wife needs him!'

Della tried to soothe him. 'I've made some tea, Dad.' She rose to get another cup from the scullery – anything to take his mind off Dan. 'And then you go home and get some sleep. Mam and I can manage.'

'No, you're going with him,' Mary said firmly. 'You both have to go to work tomorrow.'

'All right, Mam,' Della grumbled, pouring the cooling tea into a cup for Walter.

Mary stood up. 'I'll take that one in to the midwife. Pour your dad—' But her hand flew to her mouth and she dashed to the bedroom as Anne gave a single ear-piercing scream.

Anne cried hysterically while the sweating midwife wrapped a white bundle. 'I'm sorry, luv. There was nowt I could do,' she informed Mary. 'The cord was round its neck.'

'Oh God, no!' Mary knelt and stroked Anne's wet face. 'Will she be all right?'

'Aye, but she's going to need a good, long rest after what she's been through.'

'Oh, Mam,' Anne wailed as Mary cradled her. 'It was a little girl as well. I want to see her.'

'Better not,' the midwife said firmly as she disappeared into the bathroom with the bundle.

Mary tried to calm Anne, though not believing a word she said: 'It was God's will, luv. And there'll be more.' As she spoke, she looked up at the returning midwife for confirmation, but the woman shrugged and shook her head in a soundless reply.

'Oh, if only we'd got you to the hospital, maybe this wouldn't have happened.' Mary tried not to weep in front of Anne, but heedless tears trickled down her cheeks.

'No, luv,' the midwife assured her. 'It'd been dead for a while. There's nowt any doctor could have done either. Don't fret yoursel'.'

Two hours later, Walter, Mary and Della still sat in the kitchen, while exhaustion had mercifully allowed Anne a fitful sleep. Walter and Della had steadfastly ignored Mary's plea for them to leave, and the three sat in silence, the first rush of grief having played itself out. Della froze as heavy footsteps sounded in the hall.

'Quarter past two.' Walter sucked in his breath. 'Where does that bugger think he's been?'

Dan, startled by the light from under the kitchen door, pulled himself together before opening it. 'Did something happen, then?' he asked coolly.

'You're dead right something happened,' Walter spat. 'Your wife almost died and the bairn's dead. Where were you when Anne needed you?' As he spoke he clenched his fists as though for action, but Mary put a restraining hand on his arm.

'You and Della go home now, Walter,' she said calmly. 'I'll sleep on the sofa and Dan can sleep in Johnny's room.'

He slumped in a chair and ran his hands through his hair. Then he turned to Walter and whimpered, 'Look, I know you don't think so, but I do love her, you know.'

'Aye, I'll believe that when you start showing it,' Walter retorted, flinging on his coat and stalking out.

Chapter Nine

One fine August day four months later, Walter came home from work, hung his cap on the door, and slumped into his chair without washing.

'Walter, are you all right?' Mary cried in alarm. In their fourteen years of marriage he had never sat at the table dirty.

'I'm not ill if that's what you mean,' he muttered, drumming his fingers on the table as he often did when agitated. 'I've got me cards.'

'You've *what*!' Her mouth open in horror, Mary dried her hands on her pinafore and sat opposite him.

'Aye, lass, what I said,' he replied dully.

'But, Walter, you've been with them since you were thirteen. Why you?' Mary's face had drained of colour and the hands on her lap trembled.

'Don't worry, it wasn't only me; they've laid off twenty, and some have been there longer. There'll be more to come and all,' he added grimly.

'Dear God, Walter! How are we going to manage?'

'Just like all the rest, I suppose. At least we've got a bit put by. That's more than most have.'

'But that was for our old age, Walter. What's going to happen to us then if we use it now?' As she spoke, Mary twisted the corner of her pinafore into a knot.

'There's nowt for it, lass. There's not much point in trying of a Saturday, but I'll have a scout around in the morning anyway. I might get some leads. I'll start looking seriously Monday morning first thing . . . aye, and every day after that,' he added, rising and going to the sink. 'But I'm not banking on anything turning up, mind you. We're in a world slump. It's not only us, if that makes it any better,' he said, soaping his hands and face. 'I suppose I'm lucky I've had work for so long. I've been expecting me cards since the Wall Street Crash – aye, and before that. If those bloody speculators hadn't withdrawn their funds from Europe, we wouldn't be in this mess.' His voice sounded muffled behind a towel. 'Aye, that started the drop in exports and in home consumption. We can't bloody well afford to make the goods any more, so who needs ships to transport them? And as long as Macdonald sits twiddling his thumbs in Parliament, nothing's going to change.' He went to the kitchen and slumped back into his chair. 'How about some dinner then?' he said wearily. 'A man's still got to eat.'

'Don't you want to wait for the others?' Mary asked in surprise.

'No, I'll just have mine now and then I'll go out for a pint. It's still Friday night, isn't it?'

Remembering how he used to drink heavily before they were married, Mary's mouth set in a grim line as she served him a plate of rabbit stew. She prayed silently that he wouldn't turn back to drink – so many men took to drink when they were unemployed. No, she told herself, she was being stupid. Walter always went out for a drink on a Friday. She mustn't get this thing out of proportion. 'I wish I could be like those people who just sigh and say "It's God's will",' she said drily, putting the pan back on the gas stove and joining Walter. 'If there *is* a God up there, why would he want to heap such misery on people?'

'Aye, God comes in handy as a scapegoat for some,'

Walter said almost with a sneer. 'I suppose they're the lucky ones – they've always got somebody to take the blame. In *my* book, it's man that does all the dirty deeds every time, not God.'

Della, always last home, was surprised to see Walter at the kitchen door, already changed to go out, and everyone else seated gloomily round the table. 'What's up? Why's everyone looking so dreary on Friday night? And where's Dad going?'

'Your dad's been laid off.' Mary's voice was without emotion as she placed Della's stew on the table.

'Oh, no! For good?'

'It's always for good until and unless you can find another job, you ninny,' David said scornfully. 'And I'll be next on the list.'

'I'm off then,' Walter muttered, slamming the back door.

'Where's he off to?' Billie asked with his mouth full of stew.

'Don't talk with your mouth full, Billie,' Mary admonished. 'And, not that it's any concern of yours, he's gone to the pub.'

'Bit early, isn't it?' Wally remarked tactlessly.

Michael glared at him. 'So what then? And that's where I'm going.' He scraped back his chair noisily.

'Aren't you seeing Ellen tonight?' Mary asked.

'No, and if she comes round, tell her I've gone to keep Dad company. Everybody sitting around here looking morbid isn't going to make him feel any better.'

The door slammed again and Della toyed with her stew. 'It could be worse, Mam.' She tried to sound encouraging. 'At least *we're* all working.'

'Aye, and we'll all tip up a bit more. We won't starve.' Billie picked up on Della's tone.

Mary nodded. 'Yes, I suppose you'll have to. But I

can't take any more from Michael when he's saving up to get married.'

'If you ask me he's barmy to take on responsibilities now,' David snorted. 'There's no knowing how long any of us might last.'

Wally shot him a warning glance. 'Cheerful Charlie, as usual! I don't know about anybody else but I'm going to the youth club. There's a social on. Life must go on, you know.'

'Why don't you all go?' Mary suggested. 'Have a good time and relax a bit, then maybe Della and I can have some peace and quiet.'

Della smiled weakly as her brothers left. 'Thank the Lord for the youth club. I didn't want to say anything in front of the boys, Mam, but what about the money in the post office?'

'I'm sure your dad'll tell you all about that now to ease your minds. Yes, thank God! That'll help to eke things out a bit. But we'll have to go very carefully with it. I know your dad'll want to keep as much as he can for his dream of a comfortable retirement.'

'I can make do with less pocket money. Nora only gets one-and-six, plus her tram fares, and she doesn't complain.'

'No, Nora wouldn't. We'll see how things go, luv.'

Della frowned. 'Oh, Mam, I've just remembered. I said I'd see Rose tonight, and I don't want to leave you on your own. I'll just pop over for a few minutes. I don't want her to wait in for me specially.'

'No, you go out and enjoy yourself. I'll be happy to get on quietly with the dishes and then do some knitting.' Mary spoke wearily, and Della was worried about her as she made her way to Rose's house.

'I can't stay long, Rose,' she said, sitting at the table. 'I want to go back and keep Mam company.'

'Well, aren't you the dutiful daughter?' Rose scoffed. 'Mam and Dad are at the boozer so I got the sherry out.' She poured two glasses and sat beside Della with a quizzical look. 'Why on earth do you want to stay with your mam on a Friday night, then?'

'Dad's been laid off,' Della told her miserably.

'Crikey! That's lousy, luv. How are you going to manage?'

'I don't know – but we will. Mam's been through hard times before and she's always managed.'

Rose sipped her drink thoughtfully. 'Well, you know, it's funny, but Dad came home all upset about *his* job tonight and all.'

'Why? Are they laying people off the railways as well?' Della looked incredulous. It just didn't seem possible for Rose and her family ever to be short of money.

'No, something funny's happened.' Rose's tone was unusually serious. 'One of the goods vans was signalled to the wrong track and an inspector, who just happened to be off his own beat, saw it. But that's not all – there was a lorry parked beside it and two men had broken into the van and were unloading the cases on to the lorry. They scarpered like scared rabbits when they saw the inspector.'

'You mean, they were stealing the cases? How exciting! But what's that got to do with your dad?'

Rose didn't look at all excited. 'Well, it was one of the vans on his lines that was misrouted. It was a mistake, but the security officers interviewed him today. They're trying to find out how it happened. It could be serious if they charge him with negligence. They interviewed our Tommy and your Dan as well to see if it could have been a clerical error.'

Della, who had been listening sympathetically, suddenly felt cold. Please God, she thought, don't let it be

Dan who made the mistake. Don't let it be Dan who loses his job. 'When will they know?' she asked in a whisper.

Rose shrugged. 'I don't know. Dad said they're all going to be questioned again tomorrow. He was nervous about it, though, and so was our Tommy.'

Della thought quickly. Dan would probably be at the pub if he was upset. If she left now she could call in to see Anne on her way home. No doubt she would need cheering up as well. She put down her glass. 'I'd better go now. Thanks for the sherry.'

'Oh, well, here's your hat! What's your hurry!' Rose said in an injured tone.

'I'm sorry, Rose, but I told you I couldn't stay. See you tomorrow.'

Anne was in the kitchen nursing a sleeping Johnny. 'Oh, hello, luv. Nice to see you.' She got up slowly under Johnny's weight. 'I've just got him off. I'll put him to bed and make a cup of tea.'

'I'll put the kettle on,' Della said, trying to sound cheerful. But she had scanned Anne's face and seen that it was even paler than usual. 'Are you all right, luv?' she asked when Anne returned. 'I heard the news about the trouble at work. How's Dan?'

'How did you find out?' Anne asked in astonishment.

'Rose told me. How's he taking it?'

'How do you think? He's very upset. I'm just praying he doesn't get drunk tonight.' She sat nervously on the sofa.

'So am I. That's why I came.' Della joined her and took her hand. 'Why don't you and Johnny come home and stay the night, just in case?' she pleaded.

'Oh, no!' Anne shook her head adamantly. 'I can't do that and worry Mam.'

'She'd worry more if Dan beat you again,' Della countered.

'Oh, he's been so good lately, I'm sure he won't.' Anne managed a reassuring smile. 'Stop worrying your head about nothing.'

But Della remained unconvinced. 'Well, if you won't come home, promise me you'll knock on the wall for Cathy if he gets nasty? I'll tell her to keep her ears open on my way out.'

'All right. I promise.'

After a cup of tea, Della called on Cathy before hurrying home. She hadn't told Anne about Dad. That could wait until the worry about Dan was over. And she wouldn't tell Mam about Dan. That could wait until they knew for sure. What a day!

Walter returned at noon the following day and slouched in an armchair.

'Any luck?' Mary asked, knowing the answer from his weary face.

'No, lass,' he muttered, untying his bootlaces. 'I tried Vickers and Laird's and then a few smaller places. There were more men outside the gates than inside. But I'll be back again on Monday,' he went on doggedly. 'Any chance of a cup of tea?'

'I've got some leek soup ready,' Mary coaxed.

'No, I'll just have a cup of tea now. I'm not hungry.'

On Saturday evening, Della couldn't wait to go back to see Anne. She rushed home, barely touched her dinner, and announced casually: 'I promised I'd go to Rose's again tonight, Mam, as I couldn't stay long last night. Do you mind if I pop off now? I'll do the dishes when I get back.'

Mary looked surprised. 'Won't Rose be seeing Jim? It's Saturday.'

'Eh, no, Mam. He's away for the weekend.' As usual, Della had anticipated her mother's reaction and prepared her answer.

'Well, off you go then, and don't worry about the dishes.' Mary rose wearily. Walter had been quiet and dejected all day and had now gone to the pub. It wasn't unusual for him to go out for a quick pint on a Saturday evening, but his mood worried her. Perhaps she should have gone with him, she thought, though she hadn't been in a pub since they were married.

'Are you all right, Mam? You look . . . preoccupied.'

Mary shooed her towards the door as if with a broom. 'Of course I'm all right. Out you go!'

As she walked down Anne's hallway, Della heard male voices in the kitchen. She stood still. Should she leave and come back later? No, she decided, Anne was her sister and she had every right to visit her. She marched on, but as she passed the sitting-room door, Anne's voice hailed her. 'I'm in here, luv. What are you doing back so soon?'

'I came to see how you are, you ninny.' Della was relieved that Anne seemed all right. She and Johnny were doing a jigsaw puzzle on the floor. 'Hello, monkey face,' she greeted Johnny.

'What you got, Auntie Della?'

'Nothing,' she said firmly.

Anne patted his head. 'Auntie Della has come to talk to me. Why don't you go into the garden and play with your new football? If you go this minute, we'll both have a game with you later.'

Johnny stuck out his lower lip. 'I don't want to play in the garden.'

'Yes, you do,' Della insisted, grasping his hands and pulling him to his feet.

Anne stood up quickly. 'I'll take him. They're talking

business in the kitchen. That's why I came in here.'

'Who? I heard voices. What happened at work?'

'It's all right, luv. I'll tell you when I get him outside.' Anne grimaced as she dragged a reluctant Johnny from the room.

Della sat down and looked around. Something was different. What was it? Good Lord! A new carpet! She noticed for the first time the plush green and beige patterned rug. Where on earth was the money coming from? 'You've got a new carpet!' she cried in a mixture of surprise and dismay when Anne returned.

From Della's tone, Anne sensed the unspoken question and lowered her eyes in embarrassment. 'Yes, Dan brought it home last week. He got it cheap from a man he knows.'

Della thought it best not to say any more about the matter. It was none of her business anyway. 'What's happening at Dan's work?' she asked eagerly.

'Oh, thank God, Della!' Anne's face was jubilant as she flung herself into an armchair. 'It all turned out all right. The inspectors couldn't find anything wrong with the paperwork, and Tommy's dad said he could have made a mistake with the signal. Sometimes these things happen. Anyway, with Tommy's uncle speaking up for his brother and saying what a good, reliable man he was, they just gave him a warning to be more careful in future. Isn't it wonderful?'

'And was Dan all right when he came home last night?' Della asked tentatively. With Anne looking so cheerful, surely nothing could have happened?

'Yes, he came home early and sober. Said he didn't want to have a hangover when he faced the inspectors,' Anne replied happily.

Della hated to dampen her sister's joy by delivering the news about Dad, and Anne would be coming home for tea tomorrow anyway. It would be better to say nothing till then. At least Anne would be honestly surprised and Mam wouldn't get suspicious about how she knew. Nobody need know about Dan's trouble at work and Della's secret visits to Anne.

Chapter Ten

By early April 1935 Walter had been out of work for eight months, and Della had been working at Binns for well over a year with no mention of promotion. Today she had plucked up her courage to ask Miss Bane and waited for an opportunity but, so far, had seen her only at first tea break when the others were present. She confided her nervousness to Nora during their break. 'I'm scared stiff, Nora, but I've got to mention it. It's been a year and three months now, and Mam could really do with the extra money with Dad still on the dole.'

'Well, I only got an extra three bob on the floor, luv, but I suppose every little helps. How *is* your dad anyway?'

Della shook her head sadly. 'Well, he's still getting odd jobs when he can. He had two days as a day-labourer last week and one carting meat at a meat wholesaler. He's better when he gets work, no matter what it is. When he doesn't work he goes to the pub in the afternoons. He says he can't stand hanging around the house all day. And Mam gets upset when he does that.'

Nora nodded sagely. 'I know all about that.'

'Yes, I know you do, luv. But things have got to pick up soon,' Della went on hopefully. 'I always feel optimistic in the spring, though not that you'd know it's spring from the weather. But Dad's dug up the back garden and planted veggies. That'll help to keep him busy and save some money as well. I wish you had a garden for your dad to do,' she added wistfully.

Nora smiled. 'I suppose he could always hack up the back yard, but I don't think the people upstairs would appreciate it.'

Rose interrupted them, poking her head through the door as much as she dared in the vicinity of Miss Bane. 'Come to the staff room at dinner time. I've got something to tell you,' she hissed. Her head disappeared.

At five minutes to one, as Della combed her hair at the mirror over the sink, Miss Bane stormed in.

'What do you think this is – a restroom?' she bellowed.

'I'm sorry, Miss Bane. I . . . I was just going to lunch. I've finished parcelling those dresses.' That morning Miss Bane had complained about her tea being cold when it wasn't, and Della had an idea that this might be one of her off days.

'Well, you'll just have to wait,' Miss Bane said acidly. 'Go downstairs and get me a bottle of Aspro.'

'Yes, Miss Bane.' Meekly, Della accepted the three pennies the woman thrust in her hand and disappeared. So that's why Baney's in a rotten mood, she thought. She's got a hangover! That was that for today. She'd better postpone her request until a more propitious time.

On her way out to the stairs, she passed Nora and hissed sideways through her teeth. 'Go to the staff room and get two cups of tea. Rose's there. I'll pay you back for the tea – treat's on me.'

Nora nodded. In the staff room, she bought the tea and joined Rose. 'Della's coming. She had to go a message.'

112

Rose grunted a greeting, fingering an Elastoplast on her cheek.

'What's wrong with your face?' Nora enquired. But before Rose could answer, Della appeared and asked the same question.

'I've got a pluke,' Rose pouted. 'And I'm seeing Jim tonight.' She fingered her other cheek. 'And I can feel another one coming up. Just my luck!'

Della inspected the fledgling red blotch and wanted to commiserate but burst helplessly into laughter. 'Oh, I'm sorry I'm laughing, Rose, honestly! It's just that you look as if someone's biffed you one with that Elastoplast stuck on your face. Don't you think you'd look better without it, and the spot would heal quicker?'

'I can't let it show,' Rose said miserably. 'It's got a yellow head and it's oozing.'

'Ugh!' Nora nudged Della under the table to stop laughing.

Della endeavoured to sober her expression. 'Well, I'm sure you didn't want us to come here to talk about your spots.'

Rose's face brightened. 'No. Guess what? I'm having a party on Saturday night. Mam and Dad are going to a wedding at Otterburn, and they won't be back till Sunday. Uncle Willie's driving them and he says he'll be too blotto to drive home. I just hope these spots have gone by then.'

'Your parents are letting you have a party?' Della's voice rang with excitement.

'Not exactly. I didn't bother to ask them. They'll never know anyway.'

'Oh, Rose, you *are* terrible,' Della scolded. 'You should have asked first. They let you have just about whatever you want anyway.'

She grinned. 'I thought it would be more exciting to have a secret party. You're both coming, aren't you?'

Nora contemplated her wardrobe – one brown wool dress and one skirt and jumper, apart from her black work dress. She sighed. 'I'd love to, honestly, Rose, but I haven't got anything to wear.'

'Aw, that's nothing, you nitwit. I've got plenty that would fit you,' Rose insisted. 'Mam and Dad are leaving at twelve o'clock, so why don't you both come over at half-past and help me get the food and drinks, and we can try on dresses? You can have one too, Della. You need something more glam than that blue thing you wore to Eileen's party.'

'I'll have to ask Mam and Dad,' she said cautiously. But Mary had been more lenient since Della's fifteenth birthday. She was almost sure she would say yes. Already she was feeling a little excited at the prospect. And then a thought struck her. 'You're not asking Jonathan, are you?'

'No, you ninny! He's not coming to town this week-end anyway,' Rose assured her.

'Who *are* you inviting then?' Della pressed further.

'Oh, just some of my friends and some of Jim's.' She winked. 'And he knows some nice boys from the rugby club.'

Della glanced at Nora, who had been unusually quiet since Rose had mentioned the party. 'Your parents will let you go, won't they, Nora?' she asked gently.

'Aw, they'll say yes so long as I don't have to mind the kids that night, but I feel funny about borrowing a dress. Won't your friends recognise it?' She turned to Rose doubtfully.

'Not if you pick something I haven't worn for a while. So that's settled, then,' Rose said with an air of finality. 'If I don't see you before, I'll see you at half-past twelve at our house. Now I'd better go and brave that queue. I'm starving.'

★　★　★

That evening Della waited to broach the subject to Mary until the boys had gone out; that is, all except David who was studying at the kitchen table. 'Mam, Rose is having a party on Saturday. May I go? Nora's going,' she added, knowing that Mary approved of quiet, sensible Nora.

Mary looked doubtful. 'And how's she going to get home?'

'Gosh, I hadn't thought of that! Can she stay here, Mam? We could come back together, so Dad won't have to pick me up.'

'It's not Rose's birthday. What's the party for?' Mary's voice was light but she still hadn't given an answer.

'Nothing in particular . . . just a party.'

'Della wants to go to a party at Rose's.' Mary addressed Walter, who was invisible behind a newspaper as always.

'Oh, aye? Well, what about it?' he asked without looking up.

'She wants to know if she can go, that's what.'

'Well, I don't see why not, if you think it's all right.'

Mary let out a deep breath, wishing Walter didn't think it was solely her job to supervise the girls. But, she thought thankfully, when they're in trouble, he's the first to protect them. 'All right,' she said to Della, 'providing you're back by half-past ten. And Nora can stay.'

'Oh, Mam, thank you!' Della flung her arms about Mary. She didn't complain about the curfew; it was half an hour longer than she'd been allowed at Eileen's party.

'What's all this about a party?' David asked. 'Can I come? I'm not doing anything on Saturday night.'

Della turned on him. 'No, you can't, our David. You've never taken me to a party with you.' That would be all she'd need to dampen her fun, she thought. The boys were as protective towards her as her parents.

'All right, all right! Keep your wool on,' he grunted.
'I only asked.'

Nora knocked on the back door at twenty minutes past
twelve on Saturday. Della, dressed in a skirt and
sweater, quickly ran to the scullery and picked up her
coat and the carrier bag containing her long blue dress –
a blind for Mary. 'That's Nora!' she said excitedly.
'We're off now to do the food and things. I promise we'll
be back by half-past ten.'

'See that you are,' Mary shouted from the kitchen.
'Have a good time, luv. And you'd better iron that dress
again at Rose's. It's going to be creased to death by the
time you get there.'

'Yes, Mam.' Della guiltily dashed back to kiss Mary
before opening the door. But, she consoled herself,
there was no harm in borrowing one of Rose's dresses.

On the way, she and Nora talked about the party and
Della felt a surge of excitement. 'You know, Nora, all
along I've had a funny feeling that something wonderful
is going to happen tonight, though I'm not sure to which
one of us – maybe it's both,' she added hopefully.

Rose answered their knock irritably. 'Well, I'm glad
to see you've finally got here. I thought you'd changed
your flippin' minds. Come on in.'

'We're only five minutes late,' Della objected, peeved
by Rose's manner. 'What's got into you then?' But once
in the kitchen, she saw her friend's face in the daylight
for the first time. Immediately, she understood and
tactfully said nothing. Rose's skin had broken out in
further angry red blotches, disfiguring her entire face.

'Look at these stinking spots,' Rose wailed. 'I wish I
hadn't invited everybody now. Jim's going to find
somebody else tonight, I just know it.' She flopped
down in a chair and her face puckered.

Nora came to the rescue. 'Don't cry, Rose, you daft thing. Do you want red eyes as well? You can put make-up over the spots. And I read a book once about a middle-aged woman who invited a young man to dinner and, so he wouldn't see her wrinkles, only used candles to light the room. Why don't we get plenty of candles so you don't have to put the light on? It's romantic as well,' she encouraged further.

Rose considered for a moment. 'That's not a bad idea. You're a gem, Nora!' She peered into the mirror above the fireplace and examined her spots for the umpteenth time that morning. 'Come on, then, we'd better get on with it now. Let's do the shopping first, then you can both try on some dresses, and then we'll put the food and booze out – and the candles.'

They staggered home under the weight of their heavy shopping bags, dropping them gratefully on the kitchen floor.

'All right, we'll do the food later. Let's try on some dresses first,' Rose said bossily.

Upstairs in her pretty blue bedroom, she opened the shining mahogany wardrobe and ran her fingers along her amazing array of dresses.

Nora's mouth gaped. 'Gosh, Rose! Where did you get all those super dresses?'

'Mam bought most of them for me and some were hers,' she answered nonchalantly. 'She goes to a lot of dances with my dad and she doesn't like to be seen in the same one more than a couple of times, so she passes them on to me. And I used to sew a bit but I don't have much time for it now.' She pulled out a shimmering blue taffeta and considered it. 'Nora, I could see you in this, and I haven't worn it for ages. Try it on.'

Nora gazed at the creation with wide eyes. She'd only ever seen dresses like this on the racks at the shop. 'Oh,

117

Rose, I couldn't wear that. It's so expensive! What if I spilled something on it or something?' She fingered the shiny material reverently.

'Don't be an idiot!' Rose dismissed Nora's concern impatiently. 'It can go to the cleaners. And I told you, I haven't worn it for ages anyway. I've gone off it.'

Nora demurely undid the buttons of her best brown wool frock which, as she was painfully aware, looked even cheaper and shabbier than usual in these opulent surroundings.

Della helped her pull the blue taffeta over her head. 'Oh, Nora! The colour is wonderful on you.'

Rose being plumper than the others, the dress was predictably a little loose, especially in the bosom. But, as always, Rose was full of bright ideas. 'Now all it needs is a sash around the waist,' she announced, producing a grey satin sash from behind the wardrobe door. 'Here, try that.' Then she searched in her chest of drawers. 'And these.' Grinning, she waved a pair of white cotton socks.

'Rose!' Nora spluttered. 'I couldn't possibly wear those with a dress like this.'

'You're not going to *wear* them, you daft thing! You're going to stick them up your brassiere – *under* your tits, mind you, so they don't show.'

'Oh Rose! I couldn't!' Nora creased with laughter, and Della joined in.

'If you don't do as I say, you can't wear the dress,' Rose threatened. 'Without a bosom to put in it, it looks like an empty sack of spuds. But remember to take the socks out before you let any lads put their hands down there.'

'Rose, you're the giddy limit.' Nora laughed, but obediently stuffed the folded socks into the bottom half of her brassiere. The effect was stunning. Her hitherto almost childlike figure now looked voluptuous, her bosom curving upwards above the low, boat-shaped neckline, and her tiny waist shown off by the wide grey sash.

Della gazed at her in awe. 'Gosh, Nora! You look ravishing – like Mae West.'

Uncertainly, she studied her reflection in the wardrobe mirror. 'I feel like Cinderella – without the glass slippers, though.' She pulled a face as she poked out a foot, clad in a black leather work shoe.

'Never fear, Rose is here!' She searched through the shoe drawer at the bottom of the wardrobe and came up with a pair of silver high-heeled pumps. 'I'll be wearing my black satins, so you can have these.'

'But they're too big,' Nora protested. 'I only take a four.'

'Then we'll just stuff your feet the same as your tits.' Rose went to the dressing table and returned with two wads of cotton wool. These she packed into the shoe toes. 'Now try them.'

Nora tentatively tucked her feet into the shoes and walked to the window, wobbling only a little. 'What do you think, Della?' she asked, obviously needing reassurance.

'I think you look lovely, Nora,' she said truthfully.

Rose nodded in satisfaction and ran her hand along the rail again. 'Now it's your turn, Della. How about this one?'

'Oh, Rose . . . really?'

She held out a soft, clinging cream silk with a skirt neat around the hips and fluting out into a delicate swirl at the hem. The neckline, as with most of Rose's dresses, was daringly low, and the bodice held up with only two ribbon-like shoulder straps.

'Go on.' Rose pushed the dress under Della's nose. 'I haven't worn it for at least two years and I've grown a bit since then,' she boasted, pushing out her large bosom and wiggling her round hips. 'I bet it fits you.'

In a trice Della was out of her skirt and jumper and into the soft silk. It felt heavenly.

'Oh, it looks gorgeous on you!' Nora cried. And indeed it did, clinging to and accentuating every line of her body.

'Maybe I shouldn't give you that one.' Rose considered, fingering her chin. 'You look too sexy in it – too much competition for me.' But she laughed as Della hastily began to take off the dress. 'You daft bugger! I was only kidding. But, I'm warning you, you'd better not flaunt yourself in front of my lad.' She hunted amongst the shoes again, triumphantly pulling out a pair of cream satin pumps. 'They go with the dress, but they'll need padding.'

The shoes suitably stuffed, Della stepped into them and walked gingerly to the mirror. 'Oh, Rose, thank you!' She continued to stare open-mouthed at her reflection.

Rose sighed with satisfaction. 'Well, now that you're both tarted up, you'd better get them glad rags off and we'll make the sandwiches. I'm keeping my dress a secret till unveiling time.'

By six o'clock the sitting room looked festive: the table groaned under an assortment of sandwiches and cakes; glasses gleamed on the sideboard, accompanied by punch made to Eileen's 'secret' recipe; the remaining rum, sherry and lemonade stood by two dozen bottles of brown ale; and candles stuck on saucers glowed strategically around the room.

Rose surveyed the sideboard and screwed up her nose. 'We're going to need some more beer. The lads'll polish that off in no time. I'll go, and while I'm out you two can light the fire in here. We'll need some more coal on the kitchen fire and all. And one of you'd better have first bath. We'll have to make them quick if you want me to do your faces; they'll be here at seven.' With that she made for the front door.

Nora was bathed by the time Rose returned with the bottles. 'Here!' Rose thrust the heavy bag at Della. 'I'm going to have my bath.'

By five minutes to seven all were dressed and, with the help of Rose's artistry, made up. Rose's dress turned out to be a clinging black crêpe, showing off her plentiful curves and white skin. It had the deepest neckline Della and Nora had ever seen, revealing at least an inch and a half of cleavage.

Rose studied herself in the mirror. 'Yes, a little more perhaps,' she mused aloud, grabbing a pair of socks from the drawer and stuffing her already bulging bosom. 'This'll keep their eyes off my spots,' she giggled, pulling the dress even lower. The blemishes she had painstakingly covered with a thick layer of tinted foundation before liberally adding powder.

The doorbell rang. Della was glad she had Nora to talk to as no doubt Rose would be drooling over Jim most of the evening. She and Nora had spent enough time in Rose's company when Jim was around to know that she almost forgot their existence.

'Let's get some food and punch and sit on the sofa,' Della suggested, remembering her tactics for becoming inconspicuous at Eileen's party. She sighed, wishing that Jonathan would be coming – and that he wasn't who he was. Nora was nervous, but Della felt slightly more self-confident than she had at Eileen's party, especially since Mary and Rose had given her more dancing lessons. She tried to reassure Nora. 'Don't worry, luv, the night I met Jonathan I could hardly dance a step.' A piercing sadness went through her as she uttered his name, and she smiled, hiding the longing she felt. 'Just say you've got a bad foot and, if they really like you, they'll sit out with you.'

By eight o'clock most of the guests had arrived. Both girls had been asked to dance, and Della had braved a two-step and a foxtrot without mishap. Nora had claimed a bad foot, but several boys had opted to sit out and chat with her. Nevertheless, neither had seen anyone they'd taken a fancy to.

'Maybe I was wrong about something exciting happening tonight,' Della whispered as she rejoined Nora after dancing. 'How was the one who chatted you up?'

'He had spots,' Nora giggled. 'And may lightning strike you if you tell Rose I saw them in this light. What was yours like?'

'*My* age – and awkward with it.' Della pulled a face. 'Oh, Nora, I wish I'd never met Jonathan. Everybody I dance with I compare with him.'

'There's one coming now that looks smashing and doesn't look your age neither,' Nora warned. 'I saw him looking at you earlier.'

A tall, blond boy approached them. He smiled shyly, showing perfect white teeth, his fresh, rugged face looking out of place above his formal pinstriped suit and white shirt. He nodded to Della. 'May I have this dance?' Her heart fluttered as she smiled acceptance and took his proffered arm.

They didn't really dance, but rather swayed to the music as he talked. 'What's your name?' he inquired, holding her so close she was aware of the smell of his shaving soap – Gillette, she thought, smiling secretly, the same as Dad and the boys used.

'Della,' she answered a little breathlessly. 'What's yours?'

'Jeremy, but most of my friends call me Jerry. They don't think Jeremy suits me.' His voice was soft and cultured; it didn't seem to go with his rugged features.

'I agree,' she said shyly.

They chatted amiably, and Della was sorry when the

dance ended. She found Nora also making her way back to the sofa and said in surprise: 'I'm glad to see you decided to dance at last.'

'It was only old spotty again.' Nora made an unlady-like face. 'I decided I might as well use him for practice. But that's his lot for tonight. To tell you the truth, I just didn't have the heart to say no to him again. But I will if he comes back,' she said with determination. 'I've got to be harder or I'll get stuck with him all night. Yours looks dishy. How was he?'

'As nice as he looked. I hope he asks me again. He's from Jesmond and he plays rugby and he's sixteen and when he finishes at the Royal Grammar he's going to go into his father's factory. Just imagine! His father has his own factory.'

'It sounds like you've struck gold,' Nora said without a trace of envy. 'No, don't sit down.' She caught Della's arm as she was about to return to the sofa. 'Let's stand up now. It looks more inviting. I just wish these shoes crippled me a bit less.'

The two picked up their half empty punch glasses from the side table and struck a nonchalant pose. 'Is Handsome one of Jim's friends?' Nora was pleased that the evening was going well for one of them.

'No, he's a friend of Eileen's – but he's not her boyfriend. She's with someone else.'

The gramophone wailed again, and this time it was a quickstep. Putting one hand behind her back, Della crossed her fingers, whispering to Nora to do the same.

'If I'm crossing my fingers for anything, it's that Spotty doesn't pester me again,' Nora muttered, managing to keep a smile on her face. 'If lover-boy comes back, ask him if he's got a friend for me?'

Jerry did come back, and this time they danced the quickstep, which allowed little conversation. But when the record stopped, he asked shyly: 'Would you mind if

I joined you and your friend?'

Della cheered inwardly while replying lightly, 'No, of course not.'

Nora came back with a long face but smiled when Della introduced Jerry. 'Well, if you'll excuse me now, I've got to go and get some sandwiches from the kitchen.' She hissed sideways to Della, 'I've got to escape from Spotty. He just doesn't give up.'

Aware of the secret message but unable to hear it, Jerry looked embarrassed. 'I hope I didn't scare your friend away?'

'No, not you,' Della laughed. 'Someone's been pestering her all evening and she's too polite to say no.'

'You're . . . you're not just being polite to me, are you?' he asked earnestly, shifting a little from one foot to the other. 'Please tell me if you want me to leave?'

'But I don't.' Della was amazed at her boldness. By saying that, she'd actually admitted she liked him.

For the rest of the evening she thought she was in heaven, nevertheless keeping a wary eye on the clock. If they were to be home by ten-thirty, they would have to be upstairs by ten in order to change and remove their make-up. She had already concocted a partial excuse that would explain their spending so long upstairs and, at two minutes to ten, explained to a baffled Jerry: 'Nora and I have to go upstairs now. It's just that we came over early to help with the party and had a nap and got dressed and everything in Rose's mam and dad's room, so we have to make the bed and clear up before we leave.' She flushed as the lie tumbled out.

He looked disappointed. 'But why do you have to leave at all?'

Oh, well, now for it, Della thought. She had no choice but to be honest about this one. 'Well, you know what mothers are like about their daughters, and I've got a particularly old-fashioned one.' She laughed to lighten the admission. 'She still hasn't realised I'm a working woman . . . and I have to be home by half-past ten.' Her voice trailed off as she finished, her poised act crumbling.

'Gosh, that's a shame! But . . . but may I take you and your friend home?'

For the second time in her life, the thought flashed through Della's mind: His parents are rich. What will he think when he sees our lowly council house? Oh, well, she tried to convince herself, if that put him off then he wasn't worth bothering with anyhow. She smiled and said. 'Thank you. I'd better find Nora now. We'll see you in the hall.' If he was a snob, better to find out now than later.

Having learned from her first experience the art of removing make-up when leaving parties, Della cleaned both their faces with Rose's cold cream and they slipped on their own clothes.

'Let's go down and find Rose first,' she said, buttoning her coat.

Nora frowned. 'The last I saw of them, Jim was holding her up on the dance floor. I don't think she can stand by herself.'

'Don't worry about her. Rose can take better care of herself tiddled than we can sober.'

They found Rose lounging in an armchair, a glazed look in her eyes and a glass of punch in her hand. 'Are you all right?' Nora asked anxiously.

She hiccuped loudly. 'Course I'm all right, luv. Jim's just gone to the lavvy. I think he's worse than me.'

'We're going now,' Della said unnecessarily.

Rose giggled. 'Well, I didn't think you'd put your coats on to go to bed. Now see that you come back in the morning to help me clean this mess up.'

'Of course we will, Rose.' Della took Nora's hand and edged out into the hallway. Jerry was waiting, wearing an expensive Harris tweed overcoat. Della managed to greet him with her head lowered so he wouldn't see her clean face.

Out in the cold air, Jerry walked in the middle and tucked each girl's arm in his. Della hoped he wouldn't notice in the dim lamplight that she was now wearing a dark blue dress under her coat and that Nora's legs were sticking out from under hers.

'I feel honoured to be escorting two lovely ladies home,' he said, seeming not to notice anything unusual about their attire.

'Well, I did get an offer to take me home,' Nora assured him, 'but it was from Spotty.' She burst out laughing.

'Oh, Nora, it's not like you to laugh at someone's afflictions,' Della remonstrated, giggling with her nevertheless.

Nora lowered her voice. 'Well, normally I wouldn't. But, honestly, he was as thick as two planks. I did everything but tell him to go to blazes and he still followed me around like a lap dog. And it's not fair! After every time I refused him, I had to refuse some nice-looking boys. I wish we didn't have to sit out the whole dance afterwards.'

'I always thought girls had the best of the deal,' Jerry said. 'All they've got to do is wait until someone asks them; they don't have to summon up the courage and risk being turned down.'

'But they don't have the freedom of choice men have,' Nora pointed out. 'Look how I've had my whole evening ruined by one persistent idiot.'

'I never saw it that way before,' he said thoughtfully.

Della couldn't resist asking, 'Did you have to pluck up your courage to ask me? And did you think I'd refuse?'

He laughed. 'Yes to both questions. I watched you

dance with three other blokes before I got up the nerve.'

As they neared the house Della tried to slow their steps, but all too soon they arrived at the front gate. 'We're here,' she said a trifle self-consciously.

Jerry shifted his feet and mumbled awkwardly, 'Well, I'm glad I got you home safely.'

Nora knew he would be embarrassed to ask Della out in front of her and saved the situation. 'I'm going in. Thank you, Jerry.' Tactfully, she tiptoed down the path to the back door.

'Well, er . . .' He cleared his throat, both hands now in his pockets and his eyes on the pavement. 'I'd like to see you again,' he said, once more shifting his feet.

'That would be nice.' Della thought with relief that he obviously wasn't a snob or he wouldn't have asked her once he'd seen where she lived.

His voice was suddenly eager. 'How about Wednesday, then? I could pick you up from work and we could go to the pictures in town.'

Della jumped in with both feet. 'That would be fine . . . just after six then, main entrance.' She would bother about getting her mother's consent later and, if the worst came to the worst, she'd just have to meet him to say no. 'Goodnight, then. Thank you for walking us home.'

'Goodnight, Della. See you Wednesday.'

She almost ran down the path, to find Nora huddled outside the back door. 'I was trying to be quiet so as not to let anybody know you were still at the gate,' she hissed. 'And now you come barging down here like a baby elephant.'

'He asked me out on Wednesday,' Della squealed, heedless of Nora's caution. 'I said yes, but now I'll have to ask Mam.'

Mary put down her knitting and listened with interest to

the tale of the evening, only raising her eyebrows a little when Della reached the part about Jerry asking her out.

'I don't see why not,' she said finally, 'if it's only the pictures. But if he asks you out again, he must come and pick you up so we can meet him. And ten-thirty, remember,' she added, wagging a warning finger.

'Oh, thanks, Mam!' Della planted a kiss on Mary's forehead.

She couldn't sleep for excitement, at last turning over and shaking the other bed to wake Nora. 'Nora, I can't keep it to myself any longer – I'm in love.'

'Aw, Della, whadja have to wake me up for?' Nora muttered uncomprehendingly, turning her back and breathing heavily again in seconds.

Chapter Eleven

After a hurried breakfast, Della and Nora made their way to Rose's house to help clean up. They thumped on the knocker several times before Rose emerged, hair dishevelled, mascara spread all over her still blotchy cheeks, clutching a blue satin dressing gown around her shivering body. 'Bloody hell! You're early!' She groaned and shaded her eyes from the daylight.

'It's nearly nine o'clock, Rose.' Della grinned. 'You look like something the cat's dragged in. If only Jim could see you now.'

'That's not bloody funny,' she said tetchily. 'Well, now you're here, I suppose you'd better come in.'

Nora politely stifled her laughter and they followed Rose to the kitchen, now arrayed with empty bottles, glasses, curled up sandwiches, and, worst of all, pervaded by a sickly smell of fermenting punch and stale beer.

'Phew!' Nora twitched her nose in disgust. 'Looks like a bomb hit it and stinks like a brewery.'

'I hate to think what the sitting-room's like,' Della moaned. 'But let's start in here.'

Rose sat down heavily in an armchair and delivered her instructions. 'There's enough coal in the scuttle. Would you put the fire on and the kettle? I'd kill my granny for a cup of tea.' She clicked her tongue in distaste. 'My mouth tastes like the bottom of a parrot's cage.'

'Aye, an' your face looks a bit like the parrot's bottom, an' all,' Nora tittered, lapsing into Geordie as she often did when attempting humour.

'Get off it, Nora! You're not funny.' Rose's teeth chattered as she spoke. She huddled in the chair, pushed a tangled lock of hair from her face, then paused for several moments before announcing hesitantly: 'I . . . I've got something to tell you – Jim's upstairs.'

Nora, poker poised, stopped attacking the fireplace, while Della, kettle in hand, rushed back from the scullery open-mouthed. They stared at Rose in horror, as if she had said she had indeed killed her grandmother.

'Don't look so stricken,' she said hotly. 'It'll happen to you one day. I didn't tell you before because I knew you'd be shocked, and I didn't want to lose your friendship.' She curled into a tighter ball and folded her arms, a defiant look on her face but a pleading note in her voice. 'I know your mother already thinks I'm a tart, Della. The first time it happened I'd had a bit to drink and I was shocked at myself, but once you've gone all the way you grow to need it, you know.'

Della found her voice and managed to stammer: 'Oh, Rose, it's none of our business, and . . . and of course it doesn't affect our friendship.'

Nora, still standing awestruck by the empty grate, confirmed Della's statement. 'Of course not, Rose. It makes no difference to us.'

'The only thing is, we'd hate anything to happen to you, Rose,' Della said uneasily. 'I hope you're being careful.'

'Do you think I'm stupid, you daft thing?' Rose half grinned, more relaxed now that her friends were taking the news all right. 'We use French letters,' she informed them importantly.

Della and Nora showed even more interest now.

'What's it like, Rose?' Nora replaced the poker and knelt expectantly at her feet.

Della joined her, setting the kettle beside her. 'And how long have you been doing it?'

'Hey, wait a minute!' Rose flapped her hands to shoo them away. 'One question at a time, and I'll tell you after you get that bloody fire on and make some tea.'

The eager slaves jumped up. A few minutes later, the fire smoking promisingly and a cup of tea in Rose's hand, she embarked on her tale of forbidden delights, while Della and Nora curled up at her feet again. Rose felt like a queen giving audience. 'Well, it's absolutely heavenly, honestly. I used to think necking and petting was fab till we went the whole hog, but there's no comparison. Mind you,' she paused dramatically, 'I'll warn you, the first time isn't marvellous. It hurts something awful, so don't be disappointed. I wondered why everybody made such a big fuss about it. But after that, it just got better and better. I didn't actually come till the second time, but Jim says I'm a natural, because it takes some women a long time and some never do. We manage to come together almost every time now,' she announced proudly, adding with a giggle, 'except when we've had too much to drink like last night. We both conked out in the middle of it.'

'You come . . . together?' Della repeated, astonished.

'What's it like, Rose – coming, I mean?' Nora asked eagerly. Then, smelling the heavy smoke from the fireplace, she jumped up, took a newspaper from the pile on the hearth and stretched it across the opening as a damper.

'I'm going to keep my trap shut till that fire's blazing and I've got another cup of tea in my hand,' Rose said imperiously. Thoroughly enjoying being the centre of attention, she drained her cup and exaggeratedly sealed her lips.

Her eager lackeys spun into action and, the fire spluttering and her teacup refilled, Rose was ready to continue. Her audience sat expectantly at her feet once more.

'Well, actually,' she began thoughtfully, 'I had come before, when we were petting. I didn't tell you that bit earlier in case you were shocked, but it's sort of different when you go all the way – a fuller experience, if you know what I mean?' She tittered, forgetting her hangover now that she had such avid listeners.

Della tut-tutted impatiently. 'How could we possibly know what you mean, you nut? Describe it then.'

'Do you mean, describe it "out" or describe it "in"?' Rose teased.

'Both, you ninny,' Nora urged.

'Well, it's hard to describe a feeling.' Rose drew her brows together in exaggerated thought. 'But you get smashing tingling sensations all over, and especially down below, and they rise and get bigger and bigger and you can't stop until – poof! You sort of explode. Sometimes it's a long explosion and sometimes it's short, but it's always incredible. I suppose the best thing I can liken it to is a sort of sneeze all over your body, but much nicer, of course.'

'Is that what it's like "in" or "out"?' Della asked, impatient for more detail.

'Well, let's say that's "out", and "in" is just like "out" except that when you're actually . . . joined . . . oh, you know what I mean, you feel the sensations more *inside* as well. And it's extra nice that you're both feeling it together.' She moaned ecstatically. 'Ooh, and it's wonderful when you're naked and can feel each other's whole bodies.'

Nora groaned and sat back on her knees. 'Oh, you're making me want to try it.'

'I wouldn't if I was you, luv.' Rose shook her head sagely. 'You've got to be in love with the boy, or at least I'm told it's a lot nicer that way. I wouldn't know because I've only done it with Jim and, as we all know, I'm head over heels with him.'

'I never dreamed when you met him at that party you'd still be seeing him more than a year and three months later,' Della said, unable to control a twinge of envy as she thought of her doomed meeting with Jonathan that same night.

'Aye, well, your mam might say I'm a tart, but she could never say I'm fickle, could she?'

'Mam doesn't say you're a tart, Rose,' Della said defensively. 'She thinks you're a little bit fast, that's all.'

'Stop arguing, you two, and get on with the story,' Nora interjected. 'Where do you do it when your parents are here?'

'Sometimes his house when his parents are away; sometimes in the bushes on the Lonnen in the moonlight.' Rose sighed romantically, then grinned. 'And, when it's very cold or raining, the park shelter, or absolutely anywhere if we're stuck and desperate – even a shop doorway once.'

'Rose, you didn't!' Nora looked horror-stricken.

'Well, obviously it's not so much fun as in a bed, but once you get carried away, it doesn't matter where you are, and it sort of adds a bit of spice that you might get caught.' Rose looked at them mischievously, expecting a shocked reaction, but they both turned their gaze towards the door.

The floorboards creaked loudly as Jim lumbered in, wearing his shoes, Rose's father's dressing gown, and a very foolish expression. 'Oops! Er, excuse me,' he stammered, backing out.

'No, come on in and have a cup of tea,' Rose beckoned. 'They knew you were here anyway.'

He returned and greeted them sheepishly, a dull red colour creeping up his neck. 'Hello, Della, Nora.' He sat on the sofa, self-consciously pulling his dressing gown over his legs.

'How about a cup of tea for Jim then and another one for me?' Rose demanded rather than asked. She took her superior position for granted now.

Della jumped up. 'I'll do it.' She was glad of something to do, not knowing quite what to say in front of Jim.

'And I'll get on with the sitting room,' Nora offered, also eager to get out of the situation.

'Well, while you girls are at it, do you mind if Jim and I take our tea back to bed?' Rose yawned loudly. 'We're both feeling a bit fragile this morning, and we've got some catching up to do . . . on sleep.' The pause was deliberate and Jim's colour rose further.

'No, of course not.' Della poured more tea, relieved that they were leaving.

'Ta ta, then,' Rose grinned, rising and taking the cups. 'Come on, Jim. Let's sleep it off while the slaves are at it.' She winked over her shoulder as she followed him.

Nora carried through a pile of dirty dishes and set them on the table. '*Well!* What do you think of that?'

Della grimaced. 'I think we'd better hurry and clean up and get out of here. I feel uncomfortable.'

'Me too. She's got a bloody nerve, going back to bed to have it off with him while we clean up the mess!'

'Oh, that's Rose,' Della said resignedly. 'She'd probably have gone back to bed whether he'd been here or not. You can't help but like her though,' she added loyally, 'she's so honest about herself, and kind, and she did give us a great time last night and lent us her clothes.

Come on, let's get on with it. We've got nothing else to do anyway.' She marched into the scullery to attack the dishes. 'I wash, you dry.'

As they put away the first load, a car drew up noisily outside and voices carried up the path. They looked at each other in horror.

'It couldn't be her mam and dad already,' Della whispered fervently. 'Oh, Nora, it couldn't.'

But a few seconds later the front door creaked. Della sprang into action. 'Nora, quick, whip upstairs and say you've been to the lavatory. You've got to warn Rose.' She pushed her towards the hall. 'I'll just have to confess about the party, but you get Rose down here. She'll have to talk herself out of her own mess.'

Mrs Johnson's nostrils twitched as she stepped into the hall. 'Smells like a pub in here.'

'Aye, what the devil's been going on?' Mr Johnson's gruff voice sounded even gruffer than usual.

'Oh, er, hello, Mr and Mrs Johnson,' Della stammered as they came into the kitchen. But mercifully she was saved an explanation as Rose, looking even more dishevelled than earlier, miraculously appeared in the doorway.

'Hello, Mam, Dad. Sorry about the mess,' she said blithely. 'We'll have it cleared up in no time. We just decided on the spur of the minute to have a party last night. We didn't expect you back so early.'

'Aye, I can see that,' Mrs Johnson remarked sourly. She jerked her head toward the heaps of dirty dishes on the kitchen table. 'Got all my best china out an' all.'

'What do you mean by carrying on like this behind our backs, our Rose?' Mr Johnson bellowed, still looking about him in bewilderment.

'But, Dad, you know I don't have to go behind your backs. If you'd been here I'd have asked you, but I only thought of it yesterday,' she wheedled skilfully.

Mrs Johnson stooped to scrutinise a dark stain on the carpet. 'Aye, maybe so. But I still want to know what's been going on here? It looks like you've had a wild old time. And you'd better get that stain out, whatever it is.'

'I will, Mam, and it wasn't wild, honestly. We just had music and dancing. But there was a lot of people, that's why there's so much mess. I know next time to keep it smaller,' Rose finished lightly, trying to mollify her mother.

Reluctantly, Della admired her aplomb. But what, she wondered, could have happened to Jim . . . and Nora? Hurriedly, she dried the dishes she had just washed, mouthing silently: Please God let Jim have got out.

Rose continued her penitent daughter act in the kitchen, while Della listened in wonder.

'Let me take your coats and I'll make you a cup of tea,' she cajoled. 'Honestly, we'll have this place cleaned up in a wink. Or, better still, why don't you go out for a walk till we've finished? It's a nice day.'

'I'm not going nowhere,' her father shouted, taking off his tweed overcoat and throwing it on the sofa. 'And neither is your mam. We expected to come home to a bit of peace and quiet, and that's what we intend to get.' His bushy black moustache quivered with the force of his voice, and his thin lips set in a tight line.

Bemused, Mrs Johnson sat on the sofa, still wearing her elegant black coat and fox fur. The feathered hat poised on her red-tinted curls appeared like a blackbird ready to take off in flight. She looked exactly like an older version of Rose, and equally as ravaged after her previous day's celebration.

Rose, standing by the fire, turned to the scullery. 'Well, if you're staying in, I'll make you some tea then,' she said calmly, as if the matter were settled. But, as she joined Della, she rolled her eyes in despair.

'I don't know what the world's coming to.' Mr Johnson shook his head and sat slowly at the table without removing his Homburg. 'You can't bloody turn your back for a minute in your own house.' He turned to his wife accusingly. 'Look what you've done to your precious daughter – you've spoiled her rotten.' His moustache twitched again as he unconsciously screwed up his bulbous nose, which was even pinker than usual after his wedding binge.

'Oh, *my* daughter is she, when she does something you don't like!' Mrs Johnson rallied. 'I don't want to hear no more about the matter. I'm going to have a cup of tea and then go up for a lie down. I shouldn't have had that champagne yesterday; I should've stuck to gin. Champagne always upsets me stomach, and our Willie driving home at that speed hasn't helped.' She burped loudly. 'Why don't you have a lie down an' all? The mess'll be gone by the time we get up.'

'No, I think I'll go out for a hair of the dog and let those lasses get on with it,' Mr Johnson muttered. 'I don't feel up to a row this mornin' anyway. But, mind you, our Rose'll have to answer for it if she's been at my booze.'

She popped her head round the door. 'No, I haven't, honestly, Dad,' she insisted, for once truthfully. 'I bought the booze.' She'd known better than to raid her father's precious drinks cupboard.

Within half an hour, Mrs Johnson was safely tucked up in bed and Mr Johnson at the pub. Rose's laugh tinkled. 'I've never seen Jim move so fast.'

'Rose, how can you laugh about it?' Della asked, shocked. 'And what happened to him?'

Nora provided the answer. 'While you were all yapping in the kitchen he sneaked downstairs like greased lightning and bolted out the front door. He was still doing up his trousers under his coat. I made the bed.' Visibly drained by the experience, she ran a shaky hand over her forehead.

Della turned on Rose. 'You mean you were in your parents' bed? Oh, Rose, one of these days you're going to go too far.'

'Aye, I nearly did this time, didn't I?' she agreed. Then she clapped her hand to her mouth, her eyes popping. 'Good God! Nora, did you find any of those things in the bed?'

'What things?' She raised her eyebrows questioningly. 'I found your knickers under the pillow and threw them into your bedroom with your other clothes which were all so neatly hung up on the floor.'

Rose whimpered and sat on the nearest chair. 'Thanks, Nora, but I meant French letters. Jim had a packet in the bed.'

Nora let out a long breath. 'Well, I wouldn't know what they look like, but I made the bed pretty thoroughly considering I was pushed for time and panicked out of my mind. Jim must have taken them,' she finished hopefully.

'Just pray he did.' Rose sounded very subdued and stood up shakily. 'I'll have to be more careful in future. I'd better keep out of their way till they simmer down. I'll go back to your house with you and we can have a post mortem on the party. I want to hear all about that fella that took you both home, but not right now. My head's splitting!' She groaned and put her hand to her forehead in a theatrical gesture. 'Would you mind if I had a little lie down on the sofa while you finish cleaning up?'

Chapter Twelve

Monday morning provided Della with her first chance to talk to Miss Bane since the day of the hangover. The one in question arrived early and alone for tea break, displaying what passed for a genial expression.

Della drew a deep breath and dived in. 'Miss Bane, I was wondering when I'm going to be promoted to the floor? I've been here for a year and three months now.'

Miss Bane's pencilled eyebrows rose almost to her peroxided hairline. 'There's not going to be any promotion that I can see, Della. The management isn't employing any new staff at the moment. They have to cut back. So unless one of the floor girls leaves, and I can't see that happening at the moment, you'll just have to stay where you are.' She terminated her announcement by taking a large bite of her mid-morning slice of rich cake and opening a back copy of *Woman's Own*.

Della's spirits plummeted, but she wasn't going to let the matter rest there. 'Does that mean I shan't even be getting a rise?' she dared to ask.

The eyebrows shot up again. 'Rise! There won't be any more rises until business picks up. If you don't like your job and your wage, you can always leave and make way for someone who'd be glad of both. And there are plenty who would,' she snapped, ending the discussion by picking up her magazine again.

The others arrived, and Della was left dumbstruck

and miserable. She'd patiently waited her time – more than her time – and now no promotion, and not even the rise she'd been banking on to help out at home.

At late tea break, Nora listened sympathetically to Della's news. 'Eey, it's rotten luck, luv, but what can you do? At least you've got a job, and that's something to be grateful for these days. You'll just have to be patient a bit longer.'

A knock on the door interrupted them and Monica, one of Rose's workmates, poked her blonde head into the room. 'Rose says to meet her in the staff room,' she whispered. 'She couldn't get away for break.'

Della wearily picked up the dirty cups. 'Well, I wonder what's happened now? I hope her parents didn't find that packet.'

At four minutes past one they arrived at the staff room and stood in the queue for tea. Already seated, Rose waved them over.

'What's up, Rose?' Della asked. 'Is everything all right with your mam and dad?'

She grinned. 'Right as rain! By the time I got back yesterday they'd forgotten all about it. And Jim remembered to grab the packet.'

'Phweew!' Nora pulled out her sandwiches from her bag. 'My mam and dad would have hanged, drawn and quartered me.'

Della noticed that Rose was also eating a sandwich. 'What's the matter? Have you joined the working class? I've never seen you bring a sandwich before,' she remarked a little sullenly, still brooding over her bad news.

'I spent all my pocket money on the party, and I didn't want to ask them for more money on a Monday or they'd have wanted to know where it had all gone.' Rose paused, noticing Della's long face. 'And why've you got a face on you today? I thought you were in love. Don't tell me you've gone off him already.'

Nora cast her a warning glance. 'She's had bad news about the job, Rose. Old Baney told her no promotion and no rise, unless somebody leaves, and there's a fat chance of that.'

'Oh, I'm sorry, pet,' Rose said feelingly. 'Look, I've got something for you. Maybe it'll cheer you up.' She fished under the table and produced two large carrier bags, giving one to each. 'One for you and one for you.'

They peeked into their bags. On top of Della's was the cream silk dress she'd worn at the party and on top of Nora's the blue taffeta. Underneath both was an assortment of garments, too many to pull out and examine in the staff room.

'Oh, Rose, we can't take these,' Nora gasped. 'All your beautiful clothes!'

'Yes, it's very kind of you, Rose, but we can't possibly accept them,' Della agreed reluctantly, fingering the familiar softness of the cream silk.

'Don't be daft, the both of you! They're all too tight for me anyway, since I put on my extra inches in the right places.' Rose proudly puffed out her chest. 'And if you don't take them my mam'll end up giving them to the girl down the street, and I can't stand her. I'd rather give them to the rag and bone man. I . . . I just wanted to thank you for being such good friends this weekend and to say I'm sorry for taking advantage of you.' She bit her lower lip and hung her head in mock penitence.

Della was touched. 'Rose, you ninny, you would have covered for us just the same. There's no need for this.'

'Eey, you should know me better than that, luv,' she spluttered. 'Never bank on me covering for you if it means washing dishes and doing housework. But, honestly,' she went on more seriously, 'please take them. I swear I'll never wear them again. You can have a proper look at them in your tea break; there might be some things you want to swap.'

'To tell the truth, Rose, I'm not sure that Mam would let me accept them,' Della confessed. 'You know how proud she is. Remember, she wouldn't even let me borrow a dress from you for Eileen's party.'

Rose sniffed. 'Well, she can't afford to be so proud now your dad's out of work. And it's not charity – it's a present.'

'The only trouble I'll have with *my* mam is keeping her greedy hands off,' Nora laughed, now persuaded by Rose's arguments.

Della relented happily. 'You win, as usual, Rose. Do you mind if we rush back now and have a look at them?'

'No, luv. I have to go early anyway. I need some heavier make-up for these spots. I want to try out some samples.'

'They look better than they did at the weekend,' Nora remarked, screwing up her eyes to scrutinise Rose's face.

'Only because I've got three layers of grease paint on them,' she pouted. 'Let's go then.'

In the stock room, Della and Nora eagerly examined the contents of their bags. 'Crikey,' Nora breathed, over-awed by the pile of silk blouses, wool skirts and sweaters and, at the bottom, several expensive-looking summer dresses. 'Hey, look!' She picked up a white silk blouse. 'This one's still got the price tag on it. The little fibber! They aren't all old things that are too small for her.'

'I told you she's kind,' Della said, examining her similar goods with delight. 'It would be ungracious of us not to accept them.'

Nora grinned. 'Now that's a good argument to use on your mam.'

'You're right! And, oh, Nora, they've come just in

time. I'll have something decent to wear to go out with Jerry.'

'I think Rose probably had that in mind. As you say, sometimes there's more to her than meets the eye.'

'Yes, I know there is. She's like a split personality – one minute she's completely self-centred and the next she's thoughtful and generous.'

At home that evening, Mrs Moynihan was ensconced in an armchair by the fire and the boys and Walter seated at the table, impatiently waiting for Della to arrive.

'About time, an' all,' Billie grumbled when she finally appeared. 'We're starving. I don't know why we all have to wait for you every night.'

Della ignored him and hugged Mrs Moynihan. She had forgotten their old friend was coming that day.

'Hello, Mrs M. How are you?'

'Eey, can't complain, luv. Still waitin' for the spring to come so I can get these old bones movin'. Your mam and me's had a good old natter the day, an' I heard what you been up to.' She grinned, showing a wide gap where her front teeth used to be.

'Oh, Mrs M, what happened to your teeth?' Della asked in dismay.

'Eey, I had a little fall, hinny, when I was carryin' the coal scuttle. But it's nowt! So long as I can still chew the cud, I'm not complainin'.'

'Della,' Mary interrupted, 'can you help me with these plates – and mind, they're hot! I'm giving Mrs M a tray on her lap.'

'Ooh, lovely! Shepherd's pie!' Della cried.

'Well, stop standing there sniffing it,' David grumbled. 'If you don't get it on the table I'm going to be late for night class.'

'Sorry, sir. It's the maid's night off.' Della set his plate down with an unnecessary thud.

143

'Eey, now, you bairns, you should be glad you've got meat on the table at all, never mind moanin' about the service,' Mrs Moynihan pointed out, picking up her knife and fork awkwardly with her misshapen hands.

Billie winked at her. 'Don't believe all you see, Mrs M. This is only because *you're* here. We usually get tripe and onions on a Monday.'

'Aye, and you lot should be glad o' that an' all, with your dad out o' work,' Mrs Moynihan retorted, painfully raising her fork to her mouth.

Della gave Walter a sidelong glance. 'Any luck today, Dad?' But she knew the answer from his face and decided to postpone the bad news about her promotion.

'No, not today.' He shook his head, the thick black hair now beginning to show a few strands of grey. 'I worked in the garden all day to keep out of the way of these two old crows.'

As Mary and Della washed up, Mary noticed the bag Della had stashed under the scullery bench. 'What's this then?'

'It's some clothes Rose gave me,' Della said offhandedly. 'She gave Nora some as well. They're too small for Rose, and she said if we didn't take them she'd give them to the rag man.' She finished on this note, knowing that Mary could never countenance such wastefulness.

Mary scrutinised the cream silk on top. 'They look like expensive rags to me.'

'Is it all right to keep them?' Della held her breath.

'I don't see why not,' Mary answered abstractedly. 'God knows you could do with some more clothes.' Then she lowered her voice and said what was really on her mind. 'I'm worried about Mrs M, Della. She's not getting any better. I've got to go to see her more often.'

'Aye, aye! I heard me name mentioned,' Mrs Moynihan bellowed from the kitchen. 'Nothin' wrong

144

with me ears yet, you know. Stop talkin' about a poor bugger behind her back, you two. And don't you worry, Mary, I'm not goin' to kick the bucket just yet. I'll let you know in good time when I decide to.' She paused, prising herself up from the chair with difficulty. 'Eey, well, thanks for a lovely dinner, luv. I'd better get me lazy carcass to the station or I'll miss that train.'

'I'll take you, Mrs M.' Walter pushed away his empty plate. 'I need to work that shepherd's pie off anyway.'

At closing time on Wednesday, trembling with excitement, Della swiftly changed from her uniform dress into the blue wool sweater and beige tweed skirt she had brought with her, thanking Rose silently. She cursed that she hadn't seen her at lunchtime; she'd intended to borrow a lipstick and some rouge. Well, he'll just have to see me as I am, she thought nervously. She left by the back staff exit and walked to the front of the building. Jerry was waiting. The last few straggling shoppers and shopgirls made their way to tram stops, and a couple of fur-coated women stepped into taxis.

Shivering, Della pulled her old navy blue velour coat more tightly about her, wishing the weather were warmer so she could have worn her beige serge jacket. She greeted him shyly. 'Hello.'

'Hello,' he returned, removing his hands from his overcoat pockets. He looked every bit as nervous as she felt.

'Sorry I'm late.'

'That's all right.' Hesitantly, he took her arm and guided her off the pavement and across the road. 'I'm just glad you're here. I thought perhaps your mother wouldn't let you come.'

'Oh, she always lets me come. It's just a formality really that I have to ask,' Della lied convincingly, determined not to let him know he was the first boy she'd been out with.

'I . . . I expect you're hungry?' he stammered, steering her towards Blackett Street. 'We've got time for something to eat first.'

As her stomach was rumbling, Della decided not to demur. 'Thank you, that would be nice. But I'm not very hungry.' She lied again, wondering how much pocket money his father gave him. 'Perhaps a snack, though.'

They reached the YMCA building and entered Carricks Cafe downstairs. Inside, Jerry helped her off with her coat and hung it on the rack with his own. Underneath he wore casual flannels and a sports jacket. They looked much more fitting on his huge frame than the tailored suit he wore to the party, Della thought.

He found a quiet table in a corner and pulled out her chair. She felt like a queen and wondered whether to thank him or simply to accept his manly attentions as her right. She decided to thank him – better too polite than rude.

He handed her the menu with a nervous cough. 'What would you like?'

'Just a snack, I think.' She scanned the menu, trying to look unobtrusively at the right-hand column. 'I think I'll have Welsh rarebit,' she finally said, satisfied that she had found something more than a sandwich, which would have been too obvious, yet less than an entrée.

'Umhh.' Jerry laid down his menu. 'Are you sure you won't change your mind and have something more substantial?'

'I'm sure. I had a late lunch.'

'And what would you like to drink?'

'Some coffee later, please.'

'All right then.' He addressed the waiting waitress.

'We'll have one Welsh rarebit and one roast beef, please, and coffee later.'

Della mentally kicked herself. Well, that was lesson number one! If he could afford roast beef, she needn't worry about his pocket in future.

'That blue suits you,' Jerry remarked, less self-conscious now that the formalities of ordering were over. 'And so did that dress you wore at the party.'

'Thank you.' Della was angry with herself for feeling so tongue-tied. He must think all she could say was 'Thank you'.

'Charlie Chaplin's on at the Odeon and there's a Laurel and Hardy first,' he went on. 'Do you like comedies?'

'Yes, I love them.'

He glanced at his watch. 'We'll be in time for the second house at eight. What time do you have to be home?'

At the innocent question, dismay engulfed Della like a wave of cold water. 'Ten-thirty,' she said miserably.

'Well, we can probably still do it,' he said, though he looked doubtful. 'It should be over by ten or shortly after, and if we get on a tram straight away—'

'Don't worry,' she interrupted, lying recklessly. 'It won't matter if I'm a few minutes late.' She looked down as the waitress set her plate before her and lied again. 'This looks delicious.' She embarked on her single slice of toast and cheese and tried not to look at Jerry's steaming mound of roast beef, Yorkshire pudding, peas and mashed potatoes.

They left the cinema at five minutes past ten and raced to the tram stop just as one was leaving. Jerry pushed her on and jumped on after her.

'Oh, you can't come all that way, Jerry. It's too far! Please get off at the next stop.'

'Of course I'm taking you home,' he insisted. 'I want to anyway.'

At her gate, he looked at his watch, screwing up his eyes to see in the lamplight. 'Almost twenty to eleven. Will you get into trouble?'

Della hid her misgivings. 'No, don't worry. I had a lovely evening, Jerry. Thank you.'

'So did I, Della. When am I going to see you again?'

Mentally saying, tomorrow, the next night and the night after that, she cautiously suggested, 'I'm free on Saturday.'

'Would you like to go to the rugby club dance then?' he said with a mixture of relief and pleasure in his voice. 'I'll meet you outside at seven.'

'Yes, all right,' she agreed, feeling even greater misgivings. Would Mam let her go to a rugby club dance? The rugger crowd were notoriously wild. Her thoughts were interrupted as she felt Jerry's lips softly and briefly touch her own. Was this what Rose had meant? Her head felt as if it were floating above her body. 'I must go,' she gasped. As she darted down the path, she touched her lips in wonder. How could a simple kiss make her feel so giddy?

Mary was waiting by the fire in her dressing gown, a stern look on her face.

'Sorry I'm late, Mam.' Della tried to sound composed. 'But it's impossible to do it any quicker from the second house pictures in town, and I don't get out of work in time for the first house.'

Mary's expression softened. 'All right, but only when you go to the pictures, mind you. Did you have a nice time?'

'Oh, wonderful, Mam!' Della's face glowed as she bent to kiss Mary's cheek. 'And he's asked me to go to the rugger club dance on Saturday. I can go, can't I, Mam?'

Mary pondered for a moment. 'Well, so long as this boy's escorting you and you'll stay with him all evening, and so long as he has you home by ten-thirty. But it's time we met him. Bring him in for cocoa after the dance.'

Della flinched. How unromantic! Cocoa! And how dreadfully embarrassing to have him formally approved by her parents. But *anything* was worth it to see Jerry again.

Chapter Thirteen

One warm, sunny Sunday in August 1936 Jerry took Della to Durham for a day's punting and a picnic. They had been going out together for almost eighteen months and Mary, who liked the quiet religious boy Della had fallen in love with, had no hesitation in giving her permission for the outing.

They walked hand in hand along the river bank, Jerry carrying the basket of sandwiches Mary had prepared, a bottle of lemonade wrapped in a teatowel at the bottom. Della took off her shoes. The grass yielded soft and springy beneath her feet, while the flimsy white cotton voile of her dress fluttered against her body in the breeze.

The university students, in their straw boaters, cream flannels and dark blue blazers, enjoyed their last days of freedom before the autumn term. The whole world was having fun today, Della thought delightedly, gripping Jerry's hand more tightly.

He smiled down at her. 'Happy sweetheart?'

'Mmm.' She nuzzled her head into his arm. 'This is much nicer than Sunday walks on the Lonnen.'

'You may not think so if I douse you in the river. I told you I'm a novice punter.'

'I trust you implicitly,' she said confidently. Nevertheless, a few minutes later, she felt a little apprehensive as the boatman helped her step into the shallow, bobbing craft.

Jerry took control and, after a few awkward and wobbly manoeuvres, they soon glided smoothly by the weeping willows. Della lay back and trailed her hand in the water, the liquid notes of a song thrush on the bank echoing her joy.

'Don't move! I want a snap of you just like that.' Jerry braced his long legs to keep his balance and poised the pole precariously across the punt. He lifted the Brownie box camera strung round his neck and focused it with difficulty in the swaying craft.

'If one of us is going to fall in, it'll be you,' Della teased.

'Never,' he said, turning slightly to get the sun directly behind him. The camera clicked, the punt wobbled, and Jerry grasped frantically at an overhanging willow. 'Grab the pole,' he yelled, as the punt tipped sideways and the pole slid into the water.

Della grabbed the end just as it was about to disappear over the side for ever. 'I can't pull it up,' she cried in dismay.

'Don't move! Just hold on. Don't let go!' Regaining his balance, Jerry bent his knees slowly until he could grab the tip of the pole. 'Eureka!' Hand over hand, he heaved it up until he was master of it once more. 'No more snaps on the boat,' he grinned. 'But it was worth it.'

Della giggled. 'What if it doesn't come out after all that?'

'Then we'll just have to do it again,' he said, still breathless from the rescue effort. 'I think we need that picnic now.' Laboriously, he guided the punt towards the bank. 'Hold on to those branches and keep her still,' he shouted, jumping out and hauling the stern up on to the mud.

Della, now on dry land, laughed hysterically. 'I don't think Mam would have agreed to this if she'd known you were bent on drowning me.'

'Well, I haven't managed it yet,' he laughed, 'but I'll have another try on the way home.' He set the basket on the grass and flung himself down beside it.

Happy that they had managed to find a secluded spot with no other boats moored nearby, Della spread the tea towel as a table cloth and laid out the food: tinned salmon sandwiches with cucumber, two hardboiled eggs, two tomatoes and two apples. A pang went through her as she realised that her mother had not eaten her egg at breakfast in order to leave two for the picnic.

After the meal, lying back on the grass with Jerry's arm round her, Della thought the day couldn't be more wonderful.

'There's something I've got to tell you,' Jerry said softly. He propped himself on one elbow and gazed intently into her eyes, which were flecked with gold from the dappled sunlight. 'I want to marry you and take care of you for the rest of your life.'

After Della had found her voice, she gasped, 'Marry me! But, Jerry, you know I'm only sixteen . . . and you're only seventeen. My parents would have a fit.' She sat up and stared at him with round eyes.

'I know all that,' he said, sitting up also. 'And we wouldn't have to tell them just yet. But will you marry me when you're old enough? You'll be seventeen in December and we could get officially engaged then and be married when you're eighteen. That's old enough. In the meantime, though, we could be secretly, unofficially engaged. It's just a promise between us. Please say yes.'

'Oh, Jerry, yes, yes, of course, yes!' Della almost shouted. 'How could you think I'd say no? You know I love you.'

'Yes, I know,' he whispered, brushing her ear with

his lips. 'I just wanted it settled for the future. I want to love you and look after you and spoil you for ever.'

She smiled. 'You're always saying you want to look after me. I don't need looking after; I just want to spend the rest of my life with you.'

He bent and kissed her gently on the mouth, and she wound her arms about his neck, pulling him closer. She stirred, feeling the familiar pleasure of his kiss wash over her like a warm tide. Then he released her mouth and kissed her softly on her eyelids and forehead. She sought his mouth again, her entire body tingling with pleasure until, breathless, he pulled away and fell back on the grass. He closed his eyes. 'Oh, Della, I love you so much.'

'And I love *you* so much.' She lay down beside him and kissed him.

He returned her kiss lightly. 'Temptress!' he teased, pressing her head into his chest and stroking her hair.

Della sighed. She respected his religious beliefs and knew she shouldn't encourage him and make it harder for him, but she longed for his touch. That's all she wanted; she wouldn't tempt him into doing anything they would both regret. Yet it was wonderful also to have a man who held love so sacred, even though it was difficult for him at times. But now they were to be married in less than eighteen months! She longed for their wedding night, when they would discover the joy of total physical love.

'Jerry,' she began tentatively, 'I've been thinking a lot lately about going back to church. You've been a good influence on me.' She smiled and traced his chin. 'And, now that we're getting married, I'm definitely going to start next Sunday. It would be confusing for our children to have a good Catholic father and a lapsed mother.'

'Oh, Della, that's wonderful!' He jerked up excitedly and propped himself back on his elbow. 'But I hope I didn't influence you too much. I never tried—'

'Of course you didn't.' She stopped him, pressing her finger to his lips. 'If you had, I'd have resisted. You should know me well enough by now.'

'I want three little girls just like you.' He kissed the tip of her nose.

'Why no boys like you?'

'Girls are much nicer.'

'Jerry,' she said, thoughtful now, 'of course I want Anne to be my maid of honour and Rose and Nora to be bridesmaids, but I'd like to have your sister as well. I know how fond of her you are. Will she have taken her vows by then?'

'She takes them next June.' Absently, he plucked a blade of grass and twisted it between his fingers. 'But she'll still be able to come to the wedding.'

'I'm a bit nervous about meeting her,' Della confessed. 'I've never known a nun personally, only the ones at church and at school, and they always seem so . . . so formidable.'

Jerry guffawed. 'Veronica, formidable! You've never known anyone so shy and withdrawn. She'll be more nervous than you. In fact, you'll meet her next June. We'll be officially engaged when she takes her vows, so you can attend the ceremony like one of the family.' As he spoke he tickled her nose with a dandelion. 'How does Mrs Jerry Davidson sound to you?'

'Della Davidson,' she enunciated slowly. 'It's all right, but I think Della Dolan sounds better.' Suddenly, she clapped her hand to her mouth. 'Oh, dear! Davidson and Dolan! I never thought of it before. They both start with "D".' She shrieked with laughter. 'You know what our jolly next-door neighbour always says: "Change the name and not the letter, change for worse and not for better". Both her daughters did it and she swears their marriages will come to a bad end. I've no doubt she'll warn me off you when she hears the news.'

'Ah, the delightful Mrs Bowman! I admire your mother for being so patient with her. You're lucky you've got two such wonderful parents, Della.'

'Yes, I know. But Dad's been a bit grumpy since he's been out of work. It's awful to see him so miserable when all he wants is an honest job.'

'I can see why he's never got a good word for the Conservatives,' Jerry sighed. 'I've learned better than to mention Baldwin's name in your house.'

Della smiled wanly. 'Yes, Mam's forbidden anyone to mention politics at the table any more because he gets so mad it gives him indigestion. He wants to go on the Jarrow working men's march to London in October, but they've already got two hundred volunteers, and Mam's begging him not to go anyway. She's convinced there'll be trouble.'

'No, it's a peaceful march, though I don't know that carrying a petition to the House of Commons is going to create any work for the area,' Jerry said doubtfully. 'But at least it'll advertise the situation up here. Sometimes I feel guilty that I have a good job on no merit other than that it's my father's company.'

'Darling, you mustn't feel guilty,' Della scolded. 'Your father's company creates jobs for people.'

'Not so many as it used to. He's had to cut back, too. Companies don't need cardboard boxes to pack goods they can't afford to manufacture any more. Most of the business that's left is packaging for food and other essentials – like booze.' He paused, grimacing. 'But Father's still doing all right. He was born with the luck of the devil.'

Della looked surprised. 'You say that as if you didn't like him, Jerry. Your parents are nice . . . even if they

156

are rich,' she finished with a grin.

'Oh, my mother's all right, but the old man can be a bastard at times,' Jerry said in a low voice.

'You've never said that before. I thought you got on with both of them?'

A pained expression crossed his face. 'I do . . . I have to for Mother's sake. But now that I'm working with the old man all day and living in the same house, I get a bit too much of him. I never told you before because I don't like to talk about it, but you'll find out when we're married anyway.' He took a deep breath before continuing, 'They don't get on, I'm afraid. They just put up a front. He treats Mother badly at times. That's one of the reasons she goes out with her bridge crowd so much.'

'But he's always been nice to me. I don't understand what's wrong with him.' Della's voice revealed her surprise. 'I know I've only met them occasionally for Sunday tea, but I usually get feelings about people.'

'You'd know well enough if he were your father,' Jerry muttered grimly, and then smiled. 'But that's enough of this talk. It's better to dwell on people's good points than their faults.'

'Oh, I wish I could be as good as you, Jerry. You never say a bad word about anyone. I try not to be critical of people, but it's not always easy for me,' she admitted.

'Nor me,' he murmured feelingly.

'Rose does bad things at times,' Della went on, seeming not to have noticed the emotion in his voice, 'but I never criticise her because she's nice with all her badness, if you know what I mean?' She hesitated, a thought striking her. 'Oh, Rose and Nora! Would it be all right if I told them about our engagement? I'd swear them to secrecy. I just couldn't keep a secret like that from my two best friends.'

Jerry smiled at her serious tone. 'I imagine Rose will

explode with the effort of keeping it in, but if you want to tell them, that's all right. It wouldn't make it official – not like telling family.'

'Mrs Jerry Davidson,' Della breathed, savouring the sound again.

'To love and to cherish, from this day forward,' he murmured, kissing her again.

She embraced him and the familiar thrill of his lips and his body against hers surged through her once more as they lay back on the grass. As they clung together, their passion mounted. Through the thin cotton dress, Jerry's big hands caressed her shoulders, her back. And then, panting, he pulled away and flung himself face down on the cool grass.

They lay composing themselves until Jerry sat up slowly.

'We'd better start moving. It'll take at least an hour to get back to the boat-house, barring accidents.' He grinned down at her. 'And your mam'll tan my hide if I don't get you home on time.'

Della sighed. Back to reality, and the shop the next morning! But work wasn't so bad now that she'd finally been promoted to sales. And today had been the most wonderful day of her life.

Although bursting to tell her news to Rose and Nora, Della decided to wait until lunch time to announce it to them together. On her way in to work, she dropped a note off at the cosmetics department to say she had some news.

'Well, what's all this about?' Rose set down her tray of sausage and chips and sat beside Della.

'Oh, nothing important,' she said offhandedly. 'It can wait till Nora gets here. She was still busy with a customer when I left.'

'Here she comes,' Rose said as Nora arrived, a cup of

tea in one hand and a bag of sandwiches in the other.

'What's the meeting in aid of?' she asked as she sat down.

Della felt she would explode if she kept it in a moment longer and burst out: 'Jerry and I are engaged.'

Four round eyes stared at her in amazement.

'Engaged!' Rose clapped her hand to her mouth as she choked on a large piece of sausage.

Nora's eyes grew even larger. 'Already! I can't believe it!'

'It's a secret,' Della warned sternly. 'You're the only ones who know, and you mustn't tell a soul. We can't announce it till after my birthday, and then we'll be married the following year on my eighteenth.'

'Oooh, Della,' Nora breathed. 'That's wonderful!'

'Well, what happened? How did he ask you? Did he get down on one knee? Tell us *all*!' Rose stabbed the air impatiently with her fork.

Flushed with pleasure and pride, Della related the previous day's incidents.

' . . . to love and to cherish, from this day forward.' She sighed as she repeated Jerry's words.

'Don't tell me that even after he asked you to marry him, all you did was kiss and cuddle?' Rose asked incredulously. 'You mean, he didn't even put his hands anywhere?'

'Rose, your problem is that you judge everyone by yourself,' Nora rebuked her. 'I think it's very romantic that Jerry treats Della with respect. There aren't many fellas like that left nowadays.'

'Well, I admit I wouldn't have minded if he had,' Della confessed, 'but I was glad afterwards that he didn't. I always am. Only eighteen more months now till we're married, and I want to save everything till then anyway.'

'It doesn't sound long if you say it fast,' Rose said

drily, resuming her interest in the now cold sausage. 'Better you than me, luv.'

Della ignored Rose's remark. 'Oh, and I almost forgot. You'll both be my bridesmaids, won't you?'

Rose swallowed her sausage and giggled. 'I suppose unofficially you might call me more like a maid-of-honour. But I can still pass for a bridesmaid.'

'Crikey, Della,' Nora said, 'you know I'd love to. I'm so happy for you. I wish someone nice like Jerry would cross my path. All I ever get is gropers.'

'You'll meet the right one soon, luv.' Della worried about Nora, who had never been out with the same boy more than two or three times, although boys liked her and asked her out. 'It's wonderful that you're so particular, Nora,' she said encouragingly. 'Rose and I were just lucky that we met the right ones so soon.'

'Aye, one of these days some lad'll come and knock you on the head and you won't know what's hit you.' Rose pushed away the cold greasy chips with a look of distaste. 'And when it does happen, I hope you're not going to waste good time by staying a vestal virgin like our Della.'

Nora chewed thoughtfully on her sandwich before asserting, 'Oh, yes, I am. It's . . . it's not a criticism of you, Rose, but everybody's different, you know. I want to be swept off my feet, then swept up the aisle, and then swept into bed, in that order – if ever I'm that lucky.'

'Don't worry, your luck's got to change,' Della reassured her. 'Jerry always says the Lord heaps troubles in this world on those he loves, so they can skip purgatory and go straight to heaven in the next.'

'Well, he must bloody well love me more than he does Nora,' Rose said vehemently. 'First He gave me pink eyelashes and freckles and, as if that's not enough, now He's given me plukes and scars.'

160

Nora moaned. 'Rose, stop going on about your scars. Nobody but you can see them anyhow. They're microscopic. And, anyway, you wouldn't get scars if you didn't pick the blasted things.'

'Microscopic! You wouldn't say that if you saw them before I put my face on in the mornings. It takes me half an hour to fill up the craters with make-up.'

Della stood up. 'I'd rather look at wedding dresses than talk about spots. Anybody want to come with me? We've got twenty minutes left to survey the bridal department.'

'A bit early to be buying a wedding dress, isn't it? One of *us* might need one before you,' Rose said haughtily.

'I'm only going to look, you idiot. I just want to get some ideas.' Knowing that Rose longed for Jim to ask her to marry him, Della understood that she must feel envious.

'I'm coming.' Hastily, Nora drained the last of her cold tea.

Rose jumped up. 'Me too!'

As the trio made their exit, Rose marched ceremoniously behind Della, holding up an imaginary train and noisily singing to the tune of Mendelssohn's wedding march:

> 'Here comes the bride
> Fifty inches wide
> She couldn't get in the taxi
> She had to walk behind.'

Della turned pink under the staff's amused stares.

Chapter Fourteen

Della's seventeenth birthday on 15 December fell on a Thursday. As it was early closing day, Jerry was to meet her outside the shop when they would go home to break the happy news to Mary and Walter and, later, the boys. After that they would call on Anne and Dan before visiting Jerry's parents. Della trembled with excitement as they reached home. She hailed Walter who was working in the garden. 'Dad, come on in. We've got some good news.'

'Can't it wait? I've got to get these potatoes in before they freeze. I've left it too late already,' he retorted impatiently, his foot poised on the spade.

'No, Dad. Please come in,' Della begged. 'You'll be glad when you do.'

'Will I now?' he muttered, scraping his boots clean on the edge of the spade. 'The world's coming to something when a man's bossed around by his own daughter. But seeing it's your birthday, I'll let you off.'

Mary sat by the fire peeling turnips, her feet in a bowl of water. 'Well, you caught me at it,' she laughed. 'I was just soaking my corns. Why aren't you at work, Jerry?'

'I took off early for Della's birthday,' he croaked, nervous now that the moment had arrived.

After hanging their coats, they sat stiffly on the sofa.

'What's all the fuss about?' Walter stood impatiently in the kitchen doorway, drying his hands.

163

Jerry, feeling more nervous than he had expected, cleared his throat and came straight out with it: 'I'd like your permission for Della and me to get engaged, sir.'

Walter sat down suddenly on the nearest dining chair, and Mary dropped the turnip she was peeling, unaware that it fell with a splash into her foot basin.

'Well!' Walter exhaled heavily and ran his fingers through his hair. 'It's quite something for a lad to ask permission these days, but you know there's no need for me to tell you she's a bit young, and so are you, lad.'

'I know that, sir. But we're going to wait to get married until she's eighteen, and I'll be nineteen by then. We love each other,' he finished simply.

Uncomfortable with his responsibility, Walter looked to Mary for help. 'I think it's up to her mam to make that sort of decision.'

'Well,' Mary said in a choked voice, 'you *are* both young, but you've certainly known each other long enough to know what you're doing. I suppose eighteen isn't really too young. Anne was only nineteen.'

'Oh, Mam!' Della jumped up and hugged her, then Walter.

'Aye, well, if her mam says so, I suppose that's it,' Walter said to Jerry.

'Thank you, sir.' In his relief that the ordeal was over, Jerry's shoulders dropped at least two inches.

Della beamed. 'We knew you'd say yes, so we bought the ring last week.'

'But we made sure we could return it if you refused,' Jerry put in tactfully as he took a red velvet box from his pocket.

'You can put it on my finger formally now.' Della sat beside him and looked at him with her heart in her eyes. He slipped the ring on her finger and she skipped across the room to show Mary.

'Oooh!' She gasped at the size of the brilliant solitaire

diamond. 'Jerry, are you sure you can afford this?'

'Not really.' His mouth turned up at the corners in a wry smile. 'But I've been saving up. I wanted the best for Della.'

'Aye, it's a beauty.' Walter nodded approval as Della held her prize before him. 'Must've cost a bonny penny, but I suppose you know what you're doing.'

'I'm sure he does, Walter,' Mary said. 'And now I'm going to put the kettle on and make a cup of tea to celebrate. I expect you two would like something to eat.' She dried her feet on the towel spread on the floor and rescued the turnip from the bowl. Averting her head to hide her brimming eyes, she waited until she was safely in the scullery before letting the tears of sorrow and joy flow – sorrow that she would soon be losing her daughter, but joy that Della had chosen such a fine boy, and that she would never know the hardship of bringing up a family in poverty. First Anne, then not six months ago Michael, and now Della, she thought wistfully, remembering how she used to look forward to the time when they would all be grown up. Ah, well, she consoled herself, at least Wally and Billie and David still needed her.

A few minutes later she returned, dry-eyed, 'We've already eaten, but we'll have a cup of tea with you.' She set a jar of chutney, a home made loaf, and a hunk of Cheddar cheese on the table. 'I'm afraid that's the best we can do today, but we'll have a real engagement party on Saturday, and you can invite all your friends.'

Embarrassed, Jerry looked at his shoes. He was unwilling to impose any further hardships on Della's parents. 'That's not really necessary, Mrs Dolan, but if Della would like a party, I'd be happy to pay for it,' he suggested, trying to sound tactful.

Walter shook his head. 'No, lad, she's our daughter and we've always done the best we can for her. She'll be your responsibility for long enough.'

'I'd really just like the family and Nora and Rose, and of course Jim. Can't we just have a family dinner on Sunday?' Della said diplomatically, not wanting her father to have to deplete his post office account any further.

'All right, if that's what you want then,' Walter said.

Thinking the same as Della, Mary was happy to agree, even though Walter had just found his first full-time job. 'Well, now that's settled, sit down and eat before the tea gets cold,' she ordered briskly. 'And it's time for *our* good news. Your dad's got a full-time job.'

'Oh, Dad, that's marvellous! Where? What?' Della was overjoyed. The day was turning out even happier than she had expected.

'Aye, I start at Vickers-Armstrongs on Monday, back at me old trade,' Walter announced matter-of-factly.

Della looked puzzled. 'Well, what's the matter? You don't sound very pleased.'

'Aye, I'm pleased to have work, I don't deny that. But I wish it wasn't building warships. Vickers have had new life since May last year with government rearmament orders. I'll be working on *The Sheffield*, a new aircraft carrier, and they say there'll be more orders for battleships after that.' His expression was solemn as he went on, 'It's a sad state of affairs when it takes the threat of a war to boost the economy. I'd rather build merchant ships.'

'I know what you mean, Mr Dolan,' Jerry said. 'Our business is stepping up steadily as well, but the increase is mainly in munitions boxes. I wish it were for food and civilian goods.'

'Oh, you two!' Mary admonished. 'Better work than no work, and it's only for precautions. Just knowing that we can retaliate will make the Germans think twice. That's the whole idea.'

Walter raised his eyebrows at Jerry. 'Women!' he said in despair. 'They're like bloody ostriches, always burying their heads in the sand.'

'And I'd rather keep it there,' Mary retorted, 'until and unless there's a war. What's the point of getting into a stew about it when it hasn't happened? And isn't going to happen,' she added firmly, determined not to let the prospect of war spoil the present. 'Will you do as you're told and come and eat?'

As they took their places at the table, Della groaned. Mrs Bowman's stout figure had just marched past the window.

'Come in, Winnie,' Mary shouted reluctantly in answer to her knock.

In an instant Winnie Bowman waddled in, waving the early edition of the *Evening Chronicle*. 'Have you seen this?' she screeched. 'He's goin' to abdicate. They say here it's going to be officially announced tonight.'

'As if the country hasn't got enough problems,' Walter muttered, 'and more important ones than who happens to be sitting on the throne. Baldwin should be spending the taxpayers' money on improving the economy, not settling the Royal Family's rows.'

'Eey, I didn't mean to interrupt your teas,' Mrs Bowman said, eyeing the table. 'I didn't know you were eatin'.'

Mary forced a smile. 'That's all right, Winnie. Della and Jerry are eating. We're just having a cup of tea with them. Would you like a cup?'

'Ta, hen, I wouldn't say no.' She pulled out the chair next to Della's. 'Eey, that looks a nice bit o' cheese,' she hinted, her sly eyes sliding over the table again.

'Yes, it's Della's and Jerry's lunch,' Mary said tartly. She had a hard enough job feeding the family these days without subsidising Mrs Bowman's housekeeping.

Della kicked Jerry's foot under the table and grimaced, carefully hiding her left hand in her lap.

'Well, what do you all think o' the news, then?' Mrs Bowman went on, unperturbed by Mary's snub.

'I think it's very romantic,' Della sighed. 'He must love her very much to give up the throne for her.'

Mrs Bowman snorted. 'I don't know how any man could love a hussy like that. Twice divorced already, and I'll bet it won't be long before he gets the boot an' all. Ta, luv,' she said as Mary handed her a cup of tea. 'Would you pass the sugar, hinny?' She addressed Della who forgetfully passed the bowl with her left hand. 'God's truth!' the old woman exclaimed. 'What's that you've got on your finger?'

'Jerry and I are engaged,' Della told her reluctantly. She had wanted this to be strictly a family day, but nosy Mrs Bowman would have found out soon enough anyway.

'Engaged? At your age? I hope you know what you're doin'.'

'Yes, we know, Mrs Bowman,' Jerry said quietly.

'Eey, let's have a look then, hinny.' She turned to Della, her hawk's eyes raking in every detail of the shimmering stone and broad gold band. 'Eey, by God! That must have cost a mint.' Her eyes bored through Jerry. 'How much did it set you back then?'

'Enough,' Jerry retorted sharply.

Annoyed now, she turned to Della. 'Well, I hope it doesn't prey on your conscience, havin' that much money on your finger when some folks hasn't got enough to keep body and soul together.'

'And how's your new wireless working?' Mary asked cuttingly. But the implication passed over Mrs Bowman's head.

'Oh, aye, all right,' she answered, puzzled by the sudden turn of the conversation.

'It's getting on for two o'clock. There might be

something about the king on the news,' Walter suggested hopefully to Mrs Bowman.

'Aye, you're right. I'd better get back then. Ta for the tea. Oh, and congratulations you two,' she flung over her shoulder as she bustled out.

Mary and Della burst out laughing and Jerry joined in. But Walter wasn't amused. 'I'll never know why you put up with that old bitch,' he said angrily.

Mary stifled her laughter. 'Only because I'm so sorry for her. She's lonely and unhappy. Nobody else lets her past their doors any more.'

'You're too good to live, woman,' Walter said, shaking his head.

Della stood up. 'I'll help clear up, Mam.'

'No, this is your birthday and your engagement day. You're not lifting a finger,' Mary said adamantly, standing up. 'Off with you both. Walter'll put the sitting-room fire on, won't you, Walter? And you can have some quiet time together till the boys get home.'

Another figure passed the kitchen window, but this time Della cried out in delight. 'Oh, wonderful! Here's Anne! What perfect timing!' But she turned pale as, sobbing, Anne rushed into the kitchen and flung herself into Mary's arms.

'Oh, Mam,' she wailed. 'Dan's being held at the police station. They're going to put him in prison.'

'Dear God!' Mary gripped Anne's shaking shoulders.

'No, oh, no!' Della cried, running to them. The three clung together, too shocked to speak.

But Walter jumped up, his face red with anger. 'God in heaven! What's that swine been up to now?'

'Calm down, Walter,' Mary said firmly as she began undoing Anne's coat. 'Let's get your coat off, luv, and you sit by the fire and calm yourself down, then you can tell us all about it. Della, get her a cup of tea.'

Anne slumped in an armchair and, between sobs,

stammered her story: 'He . . . he's been stealing goods from the railways. The police have got Rose's father and brother as well, and they were on their way to pick up the uncle. He's been running a racket for years.' She covered her face with her hands, wailing, 'Oh, why did they have to get Dan into it?'

'All right, luv,' Mary soothed, sitting on the chair arm and stroking Anne's fair head. 'Take your time now. Here, Della's got you a nice cup of tea. Dad'll put a tot of brandy in it.'

Walter, who stood clenching and unclenching his fists, obediently went to the sideboard and poured some brandy into Anne's cup, while Della shakily joined Jerry on the sofa. He put his big arm around her shoulders comfortingly.

Anne sipped the spiced tea and, haltingly, began again: 'It was the same guard as last time who spotted that van on the wrong tracks, remember? Well, he saw another one on the same siding with a lorry parked near with the back open. He guessed someone must be in the goods van unloading it and didn't want to scare them away like last time, so he went to the office and called the police.' She groaned in despair, her teacup rattling in the saucer in her trembling hands. 'The police were suspicious because of the last time, and this time they found out that some of the books had been altered. It was Dan and Tommy and Rose's dad who did all the dirty work, but the uncle was the organiser. That's why he only got people he knew to work for him. They took them straight to the police station and got a confession from them.'

Walter thumped his fist on the table. 'By God! I should have killed that bugger when I had the chance.'

'Shut up, Walter,' Mary snapped. 'Can't you see she's upset enough? Go on, luv.'

Anne sniffed and continued: 'It was Dan's and Tommy's job to doctor the paperwork so that missing items didn't show on the records, and Rose's dad changed the signals to divert the vans to an unused siding. Then at night the three of them loaded the contents on to a lorry and took it to a warehouse on the quayside. That was the end of their job. The warehouse owner paid them and got rid of the goods. Sometimes, though, if there was something they wanted, they took goods instead of money. Oh, Mam,' she sobbed, 'that's how Dan got our wireless and gramophone and all the other things. I was so blind! I should have suspected something.'

'Don't blame yourself, luv.' Mary stifled a sigh. 'You weren't to know.'

'I'd like to get my hands on that bugger,' Walter snarled, sitting astride his chair now, white knuckles gripping the wooden back. 'As if he hasn't given you enough trouble! You've got to leave him after this, Anne.'

'Walter,' Mary said sharply, 'Anne has to make her own decisions. How long do you think they'll get, pet?'

'I don't know, Mam. I've been at the police station all morning, but they were still questioning them when I left. They told me to go back later this afternoon. Cath's picking up Johnny from school and I'm going back to the police at four.'

Jerry, silent up to now, feeling that he should not intrude in the family's problems, said gently: 'Della and I'll go with you, Anne.'

'It's nice of you to offer, lad,' Walter cut in, 'but her mam and I'll go.'

'And you're not going back to that empty flat tonight,' Mary said emphatically. 'Perhaps Della and Jerry could go round and pick up Johnny from Cath and any things you need for tonight. We can talk better about what we're going to do when we have more news.'

Della stood up. 'Of course, Mam, we'll go.' As she

spoke, she twisted the ring on her finger and thought of the planned visit to Jerry's parents to make the announcement. That would have to wait now. Poor Anne, she thought miserably, her own happiness crushed for the moment.

The following morning Della again dropped off a note at the cosmetics department for Rose to be sure to meet her and Nora in the staff room. At one o'clock, the two waited anxiously. Rose finally appeared, looking pale under her make-up and carrying a cup of tea and a bag of sandwiches.

'Oh, Rose, we're so sorry,' Della commiserated.

'How are you feeling, luv?' Nora pulled out a chair, and Rose sank into it silently.

'Have you heard any more news?' Della asked.

Rose swallowed hard before answering. 'Mam stopped at the counter this morning after she'd been to the police station. They're all out on bail for the moment. Auntie Agnes put up the money. The stupid buggers!' she cried in fury. 'They might have known they couldn't get away with it for ever.'

'I can't believe how they managed to get away with it this long,' Nora said. 'I just don't understand how they could cover up the entire contents of goods vans going missing.'

'Oh, they were clever at it all right,' Rose said grimly. 'Tommy and Dan didn't book in the receipts and claimed they had never received the goods. And, of course, with Uncle Willie backing them up, the police believed them and investigated the losses from the London end to Doncaster. But when they came up with nothing, they began to get suspicious again here.' She paused, shakily lifting her cup to her lips.

'Have you any idea how long they'll get?' Della asked.

'No, it's too soon to tell yet. They'll have to go to

court first. But Mam was moaning last night that she's
sure it won't be months.'

'Did your mam know about it?' Della asked awkwardly, remembering Mary's suspicions about the family's money.

'No, only Auntie Agnes was in on it. That was part of
the method. Women blether, Uncle Willie always said.
They'd have been a bloody sight luckier if one of them
had blethered though. They'd have got less time than
they're going to get now.'

Puzzled, Nora shook her head. 'I don't understand
how their wives didn't wonder where all the money and
things came from.'

'Oh, don't worry, Uncle Willie had that covered,'
Rose said angrily. 'That's where Auntie Agnes came in.
He told us years ago she'd inherited some money from a
distant relative and he'd invested it wisely. We all
thought what a kind uncle he was, taking care of his own
family the way he did.' Tears trickled down her cheeks,
and Della patted her hand comfortingly.

'Don't cry, luv . . . your mascara's going to run,' she
added with the suggestion of a smile, knowing that Rose
would pull herself together at the thought of damaging
her make-up.

Rose sniffed and wiped her tears away with the back
of her hand. As she did so, she noticed the ring on
Della's finger. 'Good grief! Your engagement ring! Let
me see.' She grabbed Della's hand and scrutinised the
diamond, her mouth falling open. 'Crikey Moses! I've
never seen such a big one.' Then she looked penitent.
'Oh, Della, I'm sorry. With all this trouble going on I
forgot you were going to make it formal yesterday, and I
forgot to buy you a birthday present.'

'Don't worry about that,' Della reassured her. 'Everything sort of fell flat after Anne arrived anyway. And it
was so wonderful just minutes before. Dad had his own

announcement as well. He's got a full-time job.'

'Oh, that's nice, Della,' Nora put in feelingly. 'He'll be a different man now. I know my dad is since he got his job at Laird's.'

'It couldn't have been better timing,' Della said. 'We'll have two more mouths to feed now that Anne and Johnny are living with us. She'd have had to go on the Parish if she hadn't come home. But anyway, at least Mam and Dad agreed to our engagement, and we don't have to keep it a secret any more. In twelve months I'll be Mrs Jerry Davidson . . . and surely by then this trouble will be over and they'll be out of prison?'

Chapter Fifteen

By June 1937 Dan had served six months of his two-year sentence, and Anne and Johnny were living with the family, sharing Della's small bedroom.

It was Thursday, early closing day, and Rose had arranged for the three girls and Anne to go to South Shields to a popular fortune teller. Anne met them outside the shop. The day being warm and sunny, perfect for a trip to the coast, they had changed from their uniforms into light floral print cotton frocks – no need even for cardigans today. They walked to the station, Anne and Della a little apprehensive but Nora and Rose eager.

Rose comforted Della in her fashion. 'Don't worry, you daft thing. They don't tell you anything bad, or if they do, they say it's only going to be a minor set-back or something like that.'

'It's not only that,' Della confessed. 'Now that I'm going to church again, I shouldn't be doing this sort of thing.'

Nora tried to reassure her. 'Aw, Della, it can't be more than a venial sin. And you can go to confession on Saturday.'

Anne linked her sister's arm as they walked. 'You already know what your future's going to be, anyway. You're going to marry Jerry and live happily ever after. I wish I could be so certain about what's going to happen to me.'

'Nobody can know exactly.' Nora's voice came from the rear, where she walked arm in arm with Rose. 'Della knows she's going to marry Jerry, but she can't know how many children she's going to have, or what sexes they'll be.'

'All I want to know is if and when Jim's going to pop the question,' Rose said crossly. 'Della started after me and now she's miles ahead.'

Anne smiled at Rose's impatience. 'You've got to remember that Jim's still at university; he couldn't keep a wife yet. It's different with Jerry. He's got a good job with his father.'

'Well, Jim could at least ask me to get engaged. That would only cost him a ring, wouldn't it?'

'That reminds me, Della,' Nora said. 'You'd better hide your ring. You don't want to give this woman any tips.'

Della obediently removed her ring and put it in her handbag. 'Shouldn't you take off your wedding ring, Anne?'

She shook her head. 'No, I don't care if she knows I'm married. All I'd like to know is if Dan'll get out early, if he'll find a job, and if we'll have any more children. I'm longing for more babies. I don't want Johnny to be an only child.'

Della took her hand and squeezed it. 'It's got to be all right soon, luv. You've had your lifetime's share of rotten luck already.'

The train was at the platform as they reached the station. Hurriedly, they bought their tickets and piled into the nearest empty carriage.

'I wish we could have brought Johnny,' Anne sighed as they slowly pulled out into the sunshine. 'He loves the seaside, and the sea air would have done him good.'

'He wouldn't like standing in a queue to hear an old

woman babble on about grown-ups' things,' Della assured her. 'And anyway, Mam's taking him to the park.'

'Ugh!' Rose wrinkled her freckled nose. 'Is it really worth having kids, Anne? It strikes me they're just a nuisance and a lot of work, and I can't stand snotty noses – never mind nappies and all that.'

Anne smiled nostalgically. 'You love them from the moment they're born . . . even before. They're worth all the work they cause and more. I'm glad now I didn't manage to get pregnant again before Dan went to prison, but I want to try as soon as he gets out.' Her pale blue eyes clouded as she added reluctantly, 'That is, providing he finds a job and we have our own home.'

Rose shook her head gloomily. 'Don't bank on him getting a job. Mam says that with a prison record they're going to have trouble finding work, even if the job situation's better by then. And that's another good reason I want to get married,' she went on, taking her compact from her bag and powdering her nose. 'I'm sick of living at home with no money and our Tommy's wife and kids living in. Mam's selling the last of the sitting-room furniture this week, so now I'll have nowhere to escape to.' She clicked shut the compact and dropped it in her bag, her face full of self-pity. 'It's bad enough having to share Mam's bedroom when she's well, but since she's been depressed, she spends most of her time in bed. The house is always so crowded now, I can't stand it.'

Nora gave her a sympathetic look. 'I know what you mean. My life's always been like that. But you've got to look on the bright side – you had an easy time for so long, and you still live in a nice house and have your nice clothes.'

'But there's hardly anything left in the house,' Rose

protested. 'At the rate the furniture's going to the sale rooms, we'll soon be eating off the floor. And, anyway, if my mam has her way, we won't even have the house much longer. She's gone on the council housing list.' Unconsciously Rose curled her lip in distaste at the thought of lowering her social status in such a way. 'The money she gets from the Parish barely covers the rent, and my wages and Margaret's Parish money don't even cover the food. If we didn't have the lodger, we'd be in an even bigger mess. And it's not funny.' She thrust out her lower lip in a childish fashion.

'Well, it's never been funny for us,' Nora insisted. 'Since my dad got the job at the shipyard, I get half a crown a week pocket money, but that's still not half as much as you get. You shouldn't grumble, Rose.'

Refusing to be cheered by the pep talk, she glowered out of the window. However, by the time the train pulled in at South Shields, she had regained her good humour.

Madam Ruby's establishment turned out to be a rickety wooden hut near the beach, a covered lean-to down one side as shelter for the waiting customers in bad weather.

There were a dozen people ahead of them in the queue. Della groaned. 'Why don't we go for a walk on the beach instead? We'll be here all day.'

But Rose was determined. 'I wish you'd shut up, Della, and stop moaning. Mam says she only spends a few minutes with each one, so it won't be all that long. Who wants an ice-cream cornet while we're waiting?'

By two-thirty they had consumed their penny cornets and by three-thirty were at the head of the queue.

Nora cleared her throat nervously. 'You go first, Rose. I'm getting cold feet.'

'Scaredy-cat,' Rose said, nevertheless feeling her stomach churn as she entered the booth.

Five minutes later she emerged, looking slightly pale. 'What did she say?' Della asked nervously.

'I'll . . . I'll tell you later, when we get out of here. You go now.' Rose pushed Della towards the door. 'And remember, don't answer any questions. Let her do the talking.'

Filled with apprehension, Della entered the dingy booth. Through the gloom, she saw a wizened old woman with a dirty red scarf knotted round her head. She sat at a small round table covered with a grey chenille cloth, in the centre a crystal ball.

'Take a seat, hinny.' The woman indicated the wooden chair opposite her. 'Have you been here before?'

Della hesitated a second, remembering Rose's advice. Of course she must answer the woman. 'No,' she whispered.

'Don't be nervous, pet. Just give me your hands.' Madam Ruby's gnarled fingers picked up Della's proffered white hands and turned them over to examine the palms. Della swallowed hard, trying not to recoil at the sight of the black finger nails tracing her palm.

The woman then clasped Della's slim hands firmly and closed her eyes. 'That's good! Now I've got your vibrations.' After rubbing her palms together, she cupped her hands around the crystal ball and peered into it intently. She let out a long breath. 'Now I'm getting it. I see a tall man in your life and a wedding ring. No . . . no, hinny, I see two rings. One has some decoration on it, but I can't make out what it is. Ah, and now I see a J . . . no, two Js.' She looked at Della strangely. 'Would that be right, lass?'

Della forgot her vow of silence and happily supplied the information: 'Yes, his name's Jeremy John.' She felt excited now. There must be something to this after all.

Madam Ruby again peered into the ball and furrowed

her brow. 'And now I see two Ds.' She eyed Della again.

'His surname's Davidson. That has two Ds. Could that be it?'

After a pause the old woman nodded. 'Aye, it could be. I see some sort of interruption in your married life, and it's not a good time, but it gets over,' she added quickly, 'and you'll be happy again.'

'Could that be a war?' Della looked dismayed. 'My dad's convinced there's going to be a war soon.'

'Aye, that's a right possibility, hinny. But you don't need me to tell you that. Everybody's talkin' about it these days.'

'But . . . but if I'm going to be happy again, that means he'll come back all right, doesn't it – if there is a war I mean?'

'Well, I don't see you alone for long, hinny.' Madam Ruby still peered into the crystal ball. 'An' I see you livin' in a big house with bairns, two girls and a boy.'

Della smiled. So Jerry would almost get his wish for three daughters. 'And if I'm not going to be alone for long, that must mean that if it *is* a war it won't last long,' she ventured hopefully.

Madam Ruby clicked her tongue before answering. 'Aye, that part's a bit fuzzy, hinny. If I could tell exactly when a war's goin' to start an' end, I wouldn't be doin' this for a livin' – I'd be workin' for the government.' She cackled and returned her gaze to the ball. 'I can tell about people better.'

'Do you see anything else?'

'I see you wearin' black, hinny, but not for long.'

'I wear a black dress for work, but I shan't be working after I'm married.'

Madam Ruby's eyes left the ball and bored through Della. 'I don't see nothin' more,' she muttered, waving her hands in dismissal. 'That'll be ninepence, hinny.'

'Thank you.' Della dived into her purse and thrust the money into the woman's hand. She was sad that there might be a short war, but everything else was wonderful news.

Rose was the first to greet her. 'Button your lip. We don't want to hear a word till we're out of here,' she said bossily.

Anne looked anxious and took Della's hand. 'Just tell us, was it good news?'

'Wonderful, except for one little bit, but everything's all right in the end. Who's going next?'

'I will.' Nora squared her shoulders and marched into the booth.

After Anne's turn, they escaped as fast as they could and found an empty spot on the beach, crowded though it was with deck chairs and children playing.

'All right, girls, now for it,' Rose announced when they were seated on the warm sand. 'We'll take it in the order we went in, so I'll go first.' She drew in a deep breath and paused for dramatic effect. 'Well, would you believe it? She said I'm going to marry a tall, dark, handsome man and I've already met him. It can only be Jim, although I wouldn't exactly call him dark.'

'I'd call him fairish.' Nora frowned. 'Do you think it could be somebody else?'

Rose gave her a withering look. 'No, you numbskull! I've already met him, so it's got to be Jim. He's the only man in my life. They can't get everything exactly right, you know. Sometimes things get confused. My dad's dark, and she said that someone in my life was either going away or had already gone, so she must have mixed him up with Jim. Oh, and she said she saw a uniform – that must be my dad in clink. Anyway,' she continued, 'she saw a long journey across the sea . . . and Jim *has* vaguely thought about emigrating to America when he's got his degree. Oh, wouldn't that be marvellous!' She raised her eyes to heaven, an ecstatic expression on her face.

Nora hugged her knees and sighed. 'Gosh, it would be dreamy. We could come to visit you.'

'Don't be daft! Where would you get the money from?' Rose burst Nora's bubble. 'Unless she's told you you're going to marry a rich man . . . has she?'

'I'm not saying anything till it's my turn,' Nora said. 'My lips are sealed. Go on, then, what else?'

'Well, I'm going to have either three or four children. I could do without that. But she said I'm going to be happy,' Rose finished in a satisfied tone.

'Is that all?' Anne asked, surprised. 'You were in a long time for that little bit.'

'Oh, well, she waffled on a bit about other things that don't make much sense. It seems I've got a talent I haven't discovered yet, but I'm going to use it eventually.' Rose winked at the group mischievously before going on, 'There's only one talent I've got that I know of, and you all know I've already used that. So, that's me over and done with! Come on, you're next, Della.'

Della, who had been lying on her back listening quietly, eyes closed against the hot sun, rose to her knees. Absently, she picked up a handful of sand and let the warm, white grains run through her fingers as she related her story.

'She told you all that!' Rose said huffily when Della had finished. 'She even saw two Js and two Ds? She didn't tell *me* any initials.'

Anne shook her head uneasily. 'I don't like the bit about the war.'

'Oh, Anne, she wasn't at all sure about that part,' Della insisted. 'I mean, the separation could just be a business trip or something. Don't take any notice of Dad's proclamations. He's been saying that for years and nothing's happened.' She turned to Nora. 'Come on, it's your turn.'

'Well, she saw a wedding ring. And I haven't met him yet, but I will soon. Of course, he's tall, dark and handsome, and not rich but well off. She says I shan't have any worries over money. Isn't that marvellous?'

'I wish she'd said that to me,' Rose said sourly.

'Oh, shut up, Rose,' Anne butted in. 'You know you'll be all right for money if you're going to marry Jim. Let Nora finish.'

'Well,' she continued, 'let's see. She said there'll also be another man in my life, but I'm going to marry the rich one. She saw a P and an H. She seemed a bit confused about that. And I'm going to have two children. That's good news. I don't want a mob like my mam has. And she said I've had a hard life, but it's going to get easier. And that's all. Doesn't it sound wonderful?'

'Yes, Nora, but you know we shouldn't take any of this too seriously,' Anne cautioned. 'I know they *seem* to hit some things on the head, but that could be coincidence, and most of what they say is very vague.'

'Oh, come on, Anne.' Della was anxious to hear if her sister had any good news to look forward to. 'Stop being such a spoilsport. What did she tell you?'

Anne wriggled into a cross-legged position, keeping her eyes down. 'She told me I'd had a lot of troubles and that I was separated from someone I love. I can't deny that. But she said she saw two men in my life – that's a laugh!'

'But it could have been Dick she saw. You went out with him for a year before you met Dan,' Della reminded her.

'I suppose . . .' Anne went on almost reluctantly. 'She told me as well that I've got a talent I haven't used yet, and I'm going to make money out of it. That must be her stock saying for the day.'

'Did she tell you *when* Dan was coming out?' Rose asked.

Anne shook her head. 'No, she didn't say when. But she said she saw me happy again though I must be patient. She saw a child as well, but I don't know if she meant Johnny or another one. She couldn't say if it was a boy or a girl. And she saw me living in a big house and said I'd have no worries about money.' She looked at them unsurely. 'So, you see, she told us a lot of the same things. I think it's a lot of tommy rot.'

'But you can't deny that some of it sounds right, and she got the right letters for Jerry,' Della said.

Rose nodded. 'Well, *I* think there's definitely something in it. Let's stop arguing about whether it's phoney or not. I've got an idea how to prove it. In twenty years from now . . . let's see . . . that'll be 10 June 1957, wherever we are, we'll all meet on this spot at three o'clock and compare our life stories with what she told us.'

'That's a pact,' Nora agreed. 'By that time Madam Ruby will be pushing up the daisies, but at least we'll know whether she was right or not.'

Chapter Sixteen

In December that year Della would be eighteen and, despite Mary's pleas for them to have a spring wedding, the couple were determined to be married on her birthday.

The weeks beforehand were a frenzy of excitement and preparation. During the final days, Anne, the best seamstress in the family, still frantically worked on Della's dress, copying from a model in a magazine. Not having made a garment without a pattern before, it was an ordeal, made more difficult by the slippery white satin she was using.

Mary decorated the three-tiered cake, and Della sewed her trousseau and shopped with Jerry to furnish the two-bedroomed flat they had rented in Jesmond. It was quite a find, for most houses in that area were large, expensive family homes. Jerry was determined they wouldn't share his parents' house, and Della was overjoyed to have their own home so soon, thanks to Jerry's parents' foresight. In order to save on death duties, they had decided to give their children some of their inheritance when they came of age or got married. This also enabled Jerry to present Della with one hundred and fifty pounds to buy her trousseau and to help with the wedding expenses.

'Don't be late back,' Anne called, as Della flung on her coat on her way to visit Jerry's family. 'It'll be ready for the final fitting tonight.'

'I'm only going for lunch. We'll be back for tea.' Della blew Anne a kiss and darted out.

She took one of the new trolley buses into town. The system had started two years earlier but was now extensive enough to travel to Jerry's house in Jesmond with only one change in town. Today they were to have a quiet celebration lunch with Jerry's parents. His sister had gone to Kenya while still a novice, deciding she could do more good at the mission school abroad than in England, and had taken her final vows there. Della was disappointed that Veronica couldn't attend the wedding, but nothing else could mar their perfect day.

Jerry was at the bus stop on Jesmond Road. The waiting passengers looked approvingly at the slim girl in the simple grey tweed coat, her fresh face adorned by no more than a touch of lipstick. As she alighted, a gust of wind tugged playfully at her glossy black hair, and her eyes shone with happiness.

'Hello, darling,' she said, pleasantly surprised to see Jerry. 'You didn't have to meet me. I should know my way by now.'

His blue eyes greeted her with pride and pleasure as he tucked her arm in his. 'I want to talk to you before we see my parents.' He seemed excited. 'I've got some good news, Della. Dad's office manager is retiring and one of the clerks is emigrating to Australia, so there'll be two jobs going by the beginning of the year. There's not enough work for two men really, so Dad's combining them. It would be a wonderful opportunity for your dad. He's got brains and deserves a chance to use them. Welding's going to make an old man out of him before his time.'

Della gave a little skip of delight. 'Oh, Jerry, that would be marvellous!' Then, more subdued, she shook her head. 'But I can't imagine him accepting it, can you?

I mean, he'll think it's just a handout because he's my father. You know how proud he is.'

'It's nothing of the sort,' Jerry said adamantly. 'Look, I know your dad. He's one of the brightest men I know, and a hard worker. His mind's wasted doing manual work, and there are plenty to fill his place. You know my father's not the sort to give charity. He'll get the better bargain in your dad and, from the few times he's met him, I know he likes him – and that's saying something. My father's not any easy man to please.'

'Well, you'll have to put it to Dad like that.' Della was still doubtful, though her hopes were rising.

'I've worked it all out with my father,' Jerry went on. 'He wants your dad to come for an interview tomorrow. I shan't even be there, and there's no reason why he should know there aren't any other applicants.'

Della gripped Jerry's arm tightly in her excitement. 'I can hardly believe it – a white-collar job. Mam'll be thrilled!' She paused, looking up at Jerry earnestly. 'It's so incredible that so many wonderful things are happening all at once! Just think, Jerry, if we hadn't both gone to Rose's party that night, we'd never have met, and this fairy-tale would never have happened.'

Jerry looked down at her seriously. 'No, it was meant, Della. It would have happened anyway. Don't you know that by now?'

She smiled. 'Yes, it was all arranged in heaven, I suppose.'

As they turned into Fern Avenue, Della stopped abruptly, but only for a second. Jonathan approached them, a pretty, blonde girl on his arm. Della felt her face flush. Oh, well, she thought, gripping Jerry's arm proudly, she had done just as well as Jonathan Maddison.

He looked almost as startled as she felt. 'Hello, Della.'

'Hello, Jonathan.' He seemed leaner, she thought, but as handsome as ever, his brown hair ruffled by the wind and his King's College scarf slung casually round his neck.

'Gosh, it's been ages,' he went on, obviously determined that this should be more than a passing meeting. 'Let me introduce you. This is Vera Jackson – Della Dolan.'

Vera Jackson's china doll pink and white face was framed by a grey fox fur hat. Her cornflower eyes scanned Della from top to toe, and Della could have sworn her turned-up nose twitched. A polite 'How do you do?' issued from her scarlet lips, while she held out a tiny hand encased in expensive calfskin.

Della wished she weren't wearing wool gloves and longed to take them off to show her ring. Instead, she returned the handshake and said proudly, 'This is my fiancé, Jerry Davidson.' She watched Jonathan summing up Jerry.

'Jim told me. Congratulations!' He shook Jerry's hand.

'Thanks.' Jerry returned the handshake.

'We've got to go,' Della urged. 'Nice to see you, Jonathan, and nice to meet you, Vera.' The girl's eyes had now left Della and gazed up adoringly at Jonathan.

'I gather that's the distant cousin who's a friend of Jim's – good-looking chap,' Jerry remarked as they moved on.

Della gripped his hand tightly. 'Yes, but he's no handsomer than you – in fact, you're even handsomer.'

Pleased with the compliment, Jerry grinned as he opened the gate to the house.

Mr and Mrs Davidson awaited them in the elegant sitting-room.

'Nice to see you, Della. Lunch is almost ready,' Mrs Davidson greeted them in her rich, refined tones. 'Jerry, why don't you pour us all a sherry while I put the finishing touches to the gravy?' She stood up and smoothed down her smart black wool dress. The fair, greying hair was pulled back softly into a sophisticated coil low on her neck, and the once beautiful face, with high cheekbones and a perfectly straight nose, was ageing gracefully. The grey-blue eyes, however, had a sad, haunted expression. Except for the eyes, Jerry had his mother's looks.

Mr Davidson grunted a greeting. His portly stomach bulged over the trousers of his expensive suit, and his steely grey eyes rested on Della as Jerry took her coat, revealing her simple beige jumper and tweed skirt. As always, and she didn't know why, Della felt slightly awkward when Mr Davidson looked at her.

'Jerry's just been telling me about the job, Mr Davidson. It's very nice of you.' She sat on the blue velvet sofa.

'Balderdash!' he retorted gruffly. 'I need a good worker and I know one when I see one.'

Mrs Davidson returned, followed by Jerry balancing four glasses of sherry on a silver tray. She took a glass and sat in the armchair by the fire. 'Here's to the happy couple.'

'Time enough for toasts next week,' the father growled as he grabbed a glass and threw back the contents. 'I'll have another, Jerry.'

For a second, he hesitated before refilling the glass. But Della noticed the hesitation. She was used to Mr Davidson's drinking habits, and again thanked God silently that Jerry didn't take after him.

Mrs Davidson ignored her husband. 'How's the flat coming on?'

'The three-piece suite and the dining table and chairs arrived this week, but we're still waiting for the bed and the rest of the stuff. And I still have to make the curtains.' Della sighed. 'I think I'll have to leave that till after the wedding.'

Jerry sat beside her and took her hand. 'That's all right. We can always make do with sheets at the windows. You'll have all the time in the world to make curtains afterwards. If anything, I'm worried in case you get bored just looking after a little flat and cooking meals for me.'

Della squeezed his hand affectionately. 'It sounds a lot more exciting to me than what I've been doing for the past four years.'

'You'll probably find you'll need some outside interests as well, though,' Mrs Davidson cautioned. 'Even this big house doesn't keep me busy enough. I'd die of boredom without my bridge.'

'But you've got help, Mother,' Jerry pointed out. 'And, anyway,' he added shyly, 'Della will be kept busy before long looking after a family, we hope.'

Mr Davidson gave them a sour look. 'I wouldn't be in too much of a hurry with that. Families only bring more troubles. Being married's hard enough to get used to at first.'

'Don't be such a Jonah, William,' Mrs Davidson said sharply.

Jerry gripped Della's hand, and Mrs Davidson stood up abruptly. 'Lunch will be getting cold. Let's go and eat now.'

After lunch, Della and Jerry went to the flat to make a list of the remaining items they needed. Della was so excited she dismissed Mr Davidson's disagreeable mood over lunch. He was usually polite enough, though cold and distant, but today he had seemed in a particularly bad frame of mind. Once again, she marvelled at Jerry's warm nature, despite having been brought up by such cool, formal parents. But Mrs Davidson was more relaxed when her husband wasn't around, Della reasoned; she must have been a good mother to Jerry and his sister when they were younger.

After walking hand in hand around the small flat, they once more took stock of the wedding presents they had already received. These were piled on the dining table ready to be shown off at the reception. Della giggled again at the statue from Rose – a slender woman poised on one foot, her remaining limbs floating behind her in an anatomically impossible position, and her diaphanous dress not even attempting to hide her womanly charms.

Jerry chuckled with her. 'If I hadn't read the card, I'd still know that came from Rose.'

'We'd better hide it in the bedroom when our folks come. I'd love to go through all the presents again, but we have to make a list of what we still need. We should get at least one set of sheets to start,' she said shyly, 'even if we do get more for presents.'

'Practical as usual.' Jerry took her in his arms and kissed her.

Della returned his kiss eagerly and they clung together until Jerry pulled away, leaving her with her usual feeling of aching longing. She buried her head in his chest. 'Oh, Jerry, only one more week to wait.'

'To love and to cherish, from this day forward,' he whispered, stroking her hair.

'You're such a romantic!' Reluctantly, Della pulled herself away. 'Come on! We'd better get on with the list or we'll be late for tea.'

They took the trolley bus back to Brigham Gardens and, as usual, Della was struck by the contrast between the warm, happy atmosphere in her home and the aura of forced politeness in Jerry's. And it wasn't even polite today, she thought, sad for Jerry. But she was determined to give him in their own home the same loving surroundings she had always known.

Although it was Sunday, the whole family was crowded into the kitchen. Anne had taken over the sitting room as her workshop, the floor littered with bits and pieces of material and patterns cut from newspapers.

'You can't go in the sitting room, Jerry,' Mary warned him as Della hung up his coat. 'You mustn't see the dress.'

'Believe me, you wouldn't want to go in,' David shouted from the kitchen. 'It's like Paddy's Market in there.'

'Hello, Jerry,' Wally greeted him. 'Have you got the heeby- jeebies yet?'

Billie grinned, showing his slightly crooked teeth. 'There's still time to call it off, you know.'

Jerry smiled and sat at the table, leaving the only available space on the sofa for Mary and Della. He loved to be in this crowded room with this noisy family. 'It's too late. I'm as good as dead already,' he joked. 'And we'd have to send all the wedding presents back.'

'I wish you'd stop trying to put the lad off,' David said. 'We might not get shot of our Della.'

Billie assumed a serious expression. 'Aye, that's right. We're all looking forward to that. I don't see why Dad should have the pleasure of giving her away. I've always wanted to. There were times when I'd have happily given her free to the rag and bone man.'

'I can hear you in there.' Della carried in the dishes from the scullery. She was happy to have all her loved ones around her, and Michael and Ellen would be visiting that evening. 'Come on everybody . . . Anne, you too,' she shouted through to the sitting room. 'Tea's ready, and when you're all seated, Jerry's got an important message from his father for Dad.'

Chapter Seventeen

Saturday morning proved cold but dry, a few weak rays of sunshine managing to find occasional holes through the clouds. At ten minutes to one, Anne, Rose and Nora waited at St Bede's church, shivering in their long peach satin dresses and cream skull-caps. Feeling silly in his white silk sailor suit, Johnny sat glumly on the cold stone steps.

'God knows why she insisted on getting married on her birthday,' Rose complained through chattering teeth. 'I'm freezing to death. I don't know why she wouldn't have a sensible June wedding, and then she'd have two celebrations and two lots of presents.'

'I don't think Della cares about that, Rose,' Anne said.

Nora stamped her feet to keep her circulation going. 'Trust you to think of presents, Rose. If Jerry had asked *me* to marry him, *I* couldn't have waited till June either.' She hugged herself and rubbed her arms. 'Thank God your mam made us those woolly vests and knickers, but we should have worn wool socks as well. My feet are dropping off.'

'It'll be warmer in the church,' Anne reassured her.

Johnny yelled as the shiny black car drew up. 'There's Auntie Della!'

Anne took his hand firmly. 'All right, Johnny. Now you be quiet and come with us. We're going to put

193

Auntie Della's train right, and you're going to walk behind me and do just what you did at practice.'

The crowd already gathered to see the spectacle oohed and aahed at the sight of the bride in her shimmering white satin. Anne had excelled herself. The dress's bodice was decorated with white rosettes of the same material, continuing in a cascade down the long full skirt, and the white veil covering Della's face and floating behind her was topped by a garland of pink hot-house roses to match her bouquet.

'Are you nervous, luv?' Nora whispered, as they all fussed around her.

'A bit,' Della confessed. 'I'm afraid I'm going to muff my lines.'

The church clock struck one and, on Walter's arm, Della made her way slowly up the steps. Rose and Nora followed, each holding an end of the train with one hand and their cream rosebud bouquets in the other. Anne followed the trainbearers, Johnny walked obediently at the rear.

Della forgot her nervousness when she reached Jerry at the altar and glanced sideways at his solemn face. She had a strong desire to whisper 'Cheer up', but thought better of it.

The service went without a hitch, though Della felt her eyes brimming as they each repeated Jerry's favourite lines: 'To love and to cherish, from this day forward.'

Mary, in the front pew with the boys and Ellen, frequently dabbed her eyes with the lavender handkerchief Della had bought her to match her costume. Though embarrassed, David put a comforting arm about her waist.

The ceremony over, everybody stood patiently in the cold while the photographers fussed with the bride's dress and rearranged the two families into various groups. Everyone was pleased when the cars eventually left for the reception at the Denton Hotel and, after the official congratulations, all sipped cold champagne, yet felt warmer.

After the meal of fresh salmon, sautéed potatoes and garden peas, followed by sherry trifle, it was time to cut the cake and make the toasts and speeches.

Rose giggled as Walter, having imbibed too much champagne, garbled on about not losing a daughter but gaining a son. She kicked Nora's foot under the table. 'I bet those two have fun tonight. I hope Jerry knows what to do. Just think – both virgins. Oooh, how I'd love to be a fly on the wall.'

'Rose, don't be disgusting,' Nora chided. 'I think it's very romantic. And I hope my husband's a virgin, if and when I get married. You're just jealous because you can never have a *real* wedding night, and you know it.'

Unperturbed, Rose grinned. 'No thanks! No more first times for me. I want my wedding night to be perfect, and only practice makes perfect.'

'Keep your voice down, Rose. People are looking at you.'

She pulled a face. 'Oh, stop nagging. I wish they'd cut out these bloody speeches. I want to dance.'

Ten minutes later, the guests trickled to the function room, where tables and chairs were arranged around a small dance floor. The pianist broke into a waltz, and Della and Jerry shyly led the dancing, Della holding her train gracefully over her arm and Jerry looking very debonair in his grey tailcoat. Mary sat next to Mrs Moynihan and held her hand.

The old woman beamed, displaying her broken front teeth. 'Eey, Mary, I've never been to such a posh weddin'. You must be very proud. Don't they make a lovely couple?' She wiped her eyes with a white handkerchief. 'I'm that happy for her – a lovely husband and

no worries about money. They've got a grand life ahead
of them.'

'Yes, I'm very grateful,' Mary said softly. 'But even
though I know it's selfish, I wish she'd waited at least
another year – she's so young.'

Mrs Moynihan snorted. 'By God! You're a fine one
to talk! By the time you were her age you already had
David. She's getting off to a lot better start than you
did, hinny . . . though things worked out for you in
the end. Thank God you did marry Walter and not
that Joe fella, though I had me doubts about both o'
them at the time.'

As if hearing his name, Walter appeared. 'Would one
of you ladies like to dance?' he asked with a tipsy grin.

'Why aye, man, I'd love to trip the light fantastic,'
Mrs Moynihan chortled. 'But them days is over. You'll
just have to make do with your wife.'

Walter bowed to Mary, who coyly allowed him to
float her on to the dance floor.

Della felt almost sorry when the girls smuggled her into
the dressing room to change into her going away outfit.

'Come on,' Anne said. 'It's after six o'clock. You can't
stay here all night.'

As they pulled the heavy wedding gown over Della's
head, Rose giggled. 'You'd better get those woolly
knickers and vest off. You'll kill the groom's ardour on
the first night.'

Della delved into her suitcase. 'Don't worry, Rose.
I've made good use of Jerry's trousseau money. What do
you think of these?' She flourished a pair of white satin
cami-knickers.

'Whoah!' Nora fingered the flimsy garment. 'Once he
gets an eyeful of you in those, I bet they don't stay on for
long.'

Anne spluttered with laughter. 'Nora! That sounds

more like one of Rose's bright remarks. I hope she's not beginning to affect you.'

'Stop larking about and let the poor girl get into her knickers,' Rose interrupted. 'She's getting goose pimples.'

Finally, dressed in her new grey costume over a red silk blouse, a tiny matching feathered red hat perched on her black hair, Della surveyed herself uncertainly in the mirror. 'I've never worn a fancy hat before. I feel too dolled up.'

'This is one day in your life when you ought to be dolled up,' Rose assured her. 'And here, don't forget your coat.' She folded the new grey wool coat neatly over Della's arm. 'Don't wear it unless you're freezing to death. You look super in that costume.'

'My luggage!' Della cried, suddenly noticing its absence.

Anne soothed her. 'Calm down. It's already in the car. Go out there and say your goodbyes.'

'Wait a minute!' Rose handed Della her bouquet. 'And don't forget, you've got to throw it to me.'

Della looked at her sternly. 'Don't be selfish, Rose. I'll close my eyes and give everyone a chance.'

Outside, the guests waited to cheer them off. Mary and Walter stood by the car and Jerry's parents at the doorway. Della hugged Mrs Davidson and, though feeling slightly awkward, did the same to Mr Davidson.

'Have a wonderful time, dears,' Mrs Davidson said, blinking away her tears.

'Bye, Mother.' Jerry kissed her cheek before shaking his father's hand stiffly. 'Bye, Father.'

'Good luck to you both.' As he spoke, Mr Davidson swayed heavily on his feet.

At the car, Della flung her arms round Mary. 'Bye, Mam, and thank you for all your hard work. It was a wonderful day. And thank you, too, Dad.'

His eyes glistening, Walter returned Della's hug before pushing her away. 'Get off with you, lass. Only a few hours married and you're keeping your man waiting already.'

Jerry kissed Mary and shook Walter's hand more warmly than he had his own father's. He was about to help Della into the waiting car when the crowd, dousing them with confetti, shouted, 'Bouquet!'

Della threw the bouquet into the air with closed eyes, opening them just in time to see Nora catching it.

Inside the ribbon-draped limousine, a large placard on the bumper saying 'Just Married', they sat back with a joint sigh of relief.

'Thank goodness it's all over.' Jerry put his arm round Della's shoulders.

Her face clouded. 'Didn't you enjoy it?'

'Of course I did, darling.' He grimaced, loosening his tie with his free hand and dusting confetti off his shoulders. 'But it's a relief to be out of the limelight and alone with you. I feel as though my face is about to crack from all that smiling.'

Della snuggled into him. 'I know what you mean, but it was a wonderful wedding. I'll never forget our wedding day, Jerry.'

'It's not over yet.' He looked at his watch. 'I've got dinner booked at seven-thirty; that'll give us time to check in and have a quiet celebration drink first.'

At the hotel, the driver helped them out before getting their luggage from the boot. Della had never felt so grand. As they had chosen an afternoon wedding, they would spend the first night at the Station Hotel before taking a train to Edinburgh the following morning. There they would spend three days, returning in time to settle into the flat before Jerry went back to work.

Della smothered a giggle as a slightly pink Jerry

signed the register 'Mr and Mrs J. Davidson'. Everyone in the lobby had seen the wedding car, and amused eyes watched them as Della dusted some tell-tale confetti off Jerry's shoulder.

When the porter took them to their room, Della gasped with delight. Jerry had booked one of the best rooms with its own bathroom. She flung her arms about his neck as the porter closed the door. 'Oh, Jerry, it's beautiful! But you shouldn't have spent so much money.'

'We only get married once and we only have one honeymoon,' he murmured, nuzzling her hair and accidentally knocking off the little red hat. 'That's better,' he grinned. 'It didn't look like you with that little bit of frippery on your head.'

'I . . . I suppose we should unpack first.' Shyly, Della laid her handbag and coat on the large blue velvet-covered bed.

Jerry threw his coat down beside hers. 'No, let's have that celebration drink and dinner first. I hardly had anything at the reception. I didn't get much of a chance, and anyway I'd lost my appetite.'

'Me too! I was too excited.'

When they were seated in the lounge, the waiter brought the dinner menus and Jerry ordered two sherries.

He glanced down the list. 'And no looking on the right side of the menu tonight, Mrs Davidson! I know you and your little tricks.'

'I already know what I'm going to have.' Della set down the menu after a brief glance. 'The shrimp salad to start, then the sole almondine, followed by profiteroles and coffee. Is that expensive enough?'

'Good choice! I think I'll have the same, and we'll have a bottle of Chablis. How does that sound, Mrs Davidson?'

Della took his hand under the table and gazed into his eyes. 'Wonderful!'

Blushing, Jerry looked away. 'Della, you'd better not look at me like that. We've got to try to behave like a married couple. I've had enough amused stares for one day, and—'

The waiter interrupted him, a knowing smile on his face. 'Your table is ready, sir.'

'Er, thank you.' Jerry dropped Della's hand as if it burned him and stood up.

Heads turned to follow them as the waiter led them to their table. 'I warned you,' Jerry muttered when they were seated.

Della laughed. 'Have you thought that people might be looking at us simply because we make a handsome couple?'

'Modesty!' he exclaimed, raising his eyebrows.

By nine-thirty, sipping brandy with their coffee, Della was beginning to feel sleepy from the wine.

'Like another brandy, sweetheart?' Jerry drained his glass and stubbed out his umpteenth cigarette.

'No, thank you. I can't manage this. I had too much wine.'

'Then I'll finish it.' Jerry drained the glass, coughing as the fiery liquid seared his throat.

Della looked at him in surprise. 'Jerry, I've never seen you drink like this. It's plain to see you're an amateur.'

'Well, it's not every day a man gets married. We're supposed to be celebrating, aren't we?'

'Yes, darling, and it was a wonderful celebration.' Again, Della sought his hand under the table.

But he lit another cigarette, took a couple of puffs, picked up his coffee cup and noticed it was empty. Then, looking rather sheepish, he asked: 'Do you mind if I have another cup of coffee, sweetheart?'

'Of course not.' She smiled, though impatient to be alone with him. 'Tell you what, then. I want to have a long hot soak. I'll have it while you finish your coffee. I need to unpack anyway.'

Jerry looked relieved. 'All right, darling. I'll see you in a few minutes.'

When Della emerged from the bathroom in her cream satin nightdress and matching dressing gown, Jerry lounged in an armchair, stubbing out another cigarette in the overflowing ashtray.

'Oh, I didn't hear you come in.' Della flushed as he gazed at her in her nightwear.

'I . . . I didn't want to disturb you,' he croaked. 'You look beautiful, Della.'

'This was part of your trousseau present.' She smiled shyly and bent to kiss the top of his head. 'I unpacked for you. Your pyjamas are on the dresser.' She waited for him to pull her down into his arms, but instead he jumped up.

'Thanks, darling. I'll have a quick bath now.'

She smiled. He was nervous, she knew, and so was she. As he disappeared into the bathroom, she slipped between the fine sheets. It seemed an age before Jerry returned, looking embarrassed in his grey striped pyjamas. He switched off the bedside lamp before sliding into bed beside her.

Della tingled with excitement as he slipped his arm underneath her shoulders and kissed her cheek. 'Oh, darling, it's so wonderful to be like this with you,' she murmured, turning toward him. He kissed her gently on the lips, and her whole body throbbed. Returning his kiss, she drew him closer, feeling every contour of his body through the soft cotton pyjamas.

He ran his free hand over her bare shoulders, down her side to her waist, then, slowly, over her hips.

Della was in paradise. She clung to him fiercely, pressing her body against his. As she moved, her nightgown strap slipped over her shoulder and she wriggled to free the remaining strap. Jerry kissed her neck tenderly, her throat, and then stroked her shoulder, her breasts. He seemed to flinch as he felt the bare flesh of her bosom and the now hard nipples. Her own body jerked in excitement. Oh, God! So this is what heaven's like, she thought, as she slipped her hands under his pyjama jacket and caressed his muscular back. She longed to feel his hard chest against her. Slowly, she undid his pyjama buttons, while he buried his head in her neck once more and groaned. Then, almost encircling her tiny waist with his large hands, his lips travelled down her throat and between her throbbing breasts. Della pressed his head hard against her, moaning with pleasure. Her body cried out to him, clung to him. Almost involuntarily, her hands travelled down to his bare waist and over his pyjama-clad thighs. He groaned again, and then his whole being stiffened. Their bodies separated as if a cleaver had been thrust between them.

'Darling, what's wrong?' she asked fearfully.

With an anguished cry, Jerry buried his head in the pillow and sobbed like a child. 'No . . . no . . . I can't hurt you, Della . . . I just can't.'

Della's voice was shrill with distress. 'But, darling, you're not hurting me! I love you and I want you. What are you talking about?' She leaned over him and stroked his head anxiously. His tear-stained face turned towards her and she clasped him to her, rocking him like a baby. 'Tell me, my darling. Tell me what's wrong.' Suddenly she felt very frightened and alone.

'You know I've always wanted you. And I . . . I thought it would be all right when we were married in the eyes of God,' Jerry whimpered, then drew a laboured breath. 'But I still can't hurt you, Della. I love you too much.' He buried his head in her shoulder, overtaken by another fit of sobbing.

Still rocking him, she implored, 'Jerry, Jerry, why on earth do you think you're hurting me?'

'I . . . I'm not like him,' he moaned into her shoulder, his whole body shuddering. 'I'm not a beast.'

'Like who, Jerry?' Della's voice shook uncontrollably. 'Of course you're not a beast . . . you're talking nonsense.' Her own tears flowed freely now and her body trembled with fear. 'Tell me, darling,' she pleaded. 'I need to know what's wrong. Like who, Jerry?' She clutched him tightly to her and stroked the back of his head as a mother would.

Jerry's voice was cracked and hoarse as he began: 'My father . . . he'd pulled my sister's nightdress up . . . around her neck . . . and his hand was over her mouth to stop her screams. But I'd heard the first one, and . . . and I went to her bedroom door to see what was wrong. He was kneeling over her. Oh . . . I never wanted you to know this, Della.' He whimpered again and buried his head in her neck.

'Oh, my poor darling,' she moaned, stroking his head.

He went on, mechanically now, as if in a trance, 'I saw her eyes . . . wide open . . . screaming silently. Have you ever seen a little girl's eyes scream, Della?' He paused, as if gathering strength to go on. 'It was horrible. He was like an animal . . . and I saw blood. His . . . his . . . trousers were down, but he still had his socks and shoes on. I don't know why I remember that so vividly.' His voice choked as he relived the scene, and his large frame trembled before he broke down and wept again.

Della's stomach lurched and she swallowed hard to quell the wave of nausea that washed over her at Jerry's words. She finally stammered, 'Your . . . your father did that – to your sister?'

'Yes,' he whispered, regaining his voice slowly. 'Veronica was twelve years old.'

'But where was your mother?' Della asked in horror.

'She was at a bridge party . . . She's never forgiven herself for not being there. When she came home she saw me at the bedroom door. My father had finished by then and . . . and was buttoning his trousers.' His voice broke as he went on, 'Veronica was lying rigid in the soiled bed. Her eyes were still wide open and screaming.'

'Oh, my poor darling! And you were only ten years old.' Della felt ten years old herself at this moment – ignorant, at a loss to deal with this blow, and very frightened. Ashamed, she also realised that she felt hurt – hurt that Jerry didn't want to touch her. How could she be so selfish when he was suffering so much?

Jerry went on almost as if she weren't there: 'I still dream about it often. Life changed then. Mother sent Veronica away to a convent school, and when she came home for the holidays she was different.' He paused and swallowed hard. 'She used to be a happy, playful little monkey – always bossing me around and playing the big sister. But after that she became quiet and withdrawn, and my mother never left her side; she never played bridge during school holidays after that.'

'Oh, my poor darling! How terrible for you!'

'Yes, it was terrible for me. I can't even imagine what it was like for Veronica . . . and for my mother. Oh, she hushed it all up, of course, to keep up appearances. But they've slept in separate rooms ever since . . .' His voice trailed away, empty and drained.

Della finally understood Jerry's strained, distant family life, so unlike her own. Her heart ached with sorrow for what he had missed. 'Oh, my darling, how awful! Is that why Veronica became a nun?'

'Nobody ever says so, but I . . . I know that's what changed her. She even used to go rigid when I hugged her after that. I'm sure she couldn't stand the idea of a man touching her again . . . or maybe it was especially me,' he finished bitterly. 'I *am* my father's son.'

'Darling, you mustn't think you're like your father.' Della's voice was almost sharp. 'You couldn't be more different. And I'm your wife and I love you and I *want* you to make love to me. It's very different between a man and wife who love each other.' She wanted to hold him tightly, to melt into him, to show him how much she loved and wanted him, but she was afraid.

Jerry gulped in a deep breath. 'I know, and that's what I thought till tonight . . . but I couldn't. I was holding you and wanting you desperately . . . and . . . and yet I had a vision of my father forcing himself into Veronica. And I saw her eyes again, and her bleeding little body.' He shuddered violently. 'I just couldn't do that to you, Della.'

He laid his head back on the pillow, his breathing steadier, and Della fell back, struggling to clear her mind. She must help Jerry to forget his nightmare, but how? She felt drained and lost and strangely discarded. But it was only because he loved her, she reasoned. He really did want her. She squeezed his hand. 'It'll be all right, my darling. Just remember how much I love you and want you. It doesn't matter about tonight. We're going to be together "from this day forward", remember?' she said with forced lightness. 'I'm glad you've told me what's wrong. Now that you've talked about it, it'll be all right . . . I know it will.'

Jerry gripped her hand and closed his eyes wearily. Della listened to his breathing grow heavier, until he finally fell into an uneasy sleep.

Her bewildered mind was suffused with anguish and

pity for Jerry. She must help him with love and assurance; she must seem normal and cheerful tomorrow. But she felt sorry for herself too. She knew Jerry loved her, so why did she feel rejected – even unclean? She bit hard on her lip. No. It was Jerry's father who was unclean! Jerry's love for her would overcome his nightmare.

Emotionally and physically exhausted, she closed her wet eyes. But sleep eluded her.

Chapter Eighteen

Feeling as exhausted and miserable as she had the night before, Della woke at six-thirty from a short and fitful sleep. The events of the previous night flooded back as she glanced at Jerry, now sleeping deeply. Part of her wanted to take him in her arms and hold him close, but another part of her told her it would be better if she were up when he awoke.

Slipping silently out of bed, she took a long, hot bath and, in view of Jerry's fear of hurting her, decided to take Rose's pre-nuptial advice. She inserted first one finger into the unfamiliar place, then two, and then, biting hard on her lip and tensing against the discomfort, forced a third finger into the tight opening. A searing pain shot through her, and the water between her thighs turned pink. Gritting her teeth, she made a slow circular motion with her fingers to stretch the opening further. One final thrust assured her the job was done, and she lay back gasping with relief. Now there would be no blood stains to remind Jerry of that night. Her gaze returned to the pink water. But was it only his fear of hurting her? Did he find her unclean? Was lovemaking unclean? No! It was perfectly natural. And Jerry loved her and wanted her. She must stop these silly thoughts.

Afterwards, she slipped silently into a fresh white blouse and her going-away costume. With nothing left to do, she sat in the chair by the curtained window, waiting for Jerry to wake up.

At eight o'clock he opened his eyes. She ran to him and sat on the bed, kissing his cheek. 'Good morning, darling,' she said as cheerfully as she could. 'How are you feeling?'

'Um, er, all right, sweetheart.' Jerry took her hand. 'Oh, God, I'm so sorry for what I put you through last night. What a wedding night for you!'

Della kept her voice light. 'Darling, don't be silly. We'll have plenty more wedding nights. I'm going to help you to forget your fear.'

'If anyone can, it's you.' He lifted her hands to his lips. 'I wish I deserved you.'

'And I wish I deserved you.' She forced a smile and stood up. 'But I do think I deserve breakfast. I've been up since half-past six listening to you snoring. Get your lazy bones out of bed or we'll miss the train. Come on!' She pulled back the blankets, but wished she hadn't. His pyjama jacket, still open from the night before, revealed his bare chest, and she wanted to tear off his clothes and hurl herself into his arms. 'I'll open the curtains,' she muttered, turning away.

After breakfast, they caught the nine-thirty train to Edinburgh with five minutes to spare. Della's eyes widened as Jerry ushered her into a first-class carriage. 'Jerry, you're being extravagant again,' she chided.

'Nothing's too good for you, my sweet,' he said, helping her up the steps.

Della had never been to Edinburgh, nor indeed anywhere further than neighbouring Darlington, so the train journey was exciting to her. Jerry chuckled at her delight. She thought how wonderful it was to see him laughing and gripped his hand. Last night seemed a million years away.

★ ★ ★

After checking in at a small but elegant hotel behind Princes Street, they walked hand in hand to the castle. 'Oh, I've never seen anything so beautiful!' She looked awestruck by the imposing fortress on the hill.

'Yes, Edinburgh's one of my favourite places, and I'm going to show you a lot of others, Della.' Jerry put his arm possessively round her waist. 'We're going to go somewhere different every year. Where would you like to go for the summer holidays?'

'You mean, we're going away again?'

'Of course, darling. I'll still get my annual two weeks' holiday in July. Would you like to go to London?'

'Oh, I'd love to, Jerry. I just can't believe all these wonderful things are happening to me.' Again, she pushed away the memory of the previous night.

'Don't lie,' he teased. 'I know you married me for my money.'

'You know I'd scrub floors every day just to be with you – but I'm glad I don't have to. And I'm glad I don't have to go to the shop every day. I have to admit it's nice not to be poor any more.'

A drop of water alighted on Jerry's face. 'It's raining, wouldn't you know?' he grinned, putting up his umbrella and drawing Della under it. 'Let's go back to the hotel and have a drink before dinner.'

'Who cares about the rain! But dinner sounds lovely, and I'd like to change first.'

This time the bathroom was next-door on the landing and Della, still too shy and uncertain to undress in front of Jerry, changed while he slipped out for some ciga-rettes.

'Della, you look marvellous,' he said when he returned, taking in her soft, clinging beige dress.

She threw a red cardigan over her shoulders and they went down to the hotel lounge where they enjoyed a sherry before dinner – simple roast beef this time, followed by cheese and biscuits.

'Coffee and two brandies, please,' Jerry ordered as the waiter took their plates.

Della's heart sank. 'Just coffee for me.' She knew he must still be nervous to order brandy again. But, happily, after only one glass and two more cigarettes, he said, smiling. 'Shall we go up now?'

'Yes.' Relieved, she stood up. He was obviously feeling better tonight.

Upstairs, she took her nightwear to the bathroom and bathed quickly, again inserting her fingers to check for any remaining blood. She felt a little tender, but the water remained clear. She had done a good job. After drying herself, she smeared Vaseline around the tender area. That would make it still easier for Jerry. She thanked Rose silently for the advice, although at the time she had laughed, declaring that she wanted her husband to do his own deflowering duty. Shivering in the cold corridor, she returned in her satin nightdress and negligee of the night before. Her heart thumped. Was it going to be all right tonight?

Jerry, already in his pyjamas and dressing gown, sat on the big brass bed smoking. His eyes took her in from head to toe, her white skin slightly flushed from the hot bath, her negligee flowing back as she walked.

'Bathroom's free.' She was pleased at the way he had looked at her.

'Er, yes.' He stubbed out his cigarette. 'I shan't be a mo'.'

Della slipped between the crisp sheets and felt the warmth of the heavy silk eiderdown. Please God, she prayed, let it be all right tonight.

Jerry returned and, switching off the bedside lamp, eased himself into bed. The springs groaned under his weight. He half turned toward her, sliding his arm under her shoulders and drawing her to him. She let herself be held, stroking his shoulder softly. She must let him take his own time tonight.

After a few moments of waiting that seemed like an eternity, she felt his lips on hers, then on her closed eyelids. Her body began to throb again. 'I love you so, Jerry,' she breathed.

'And I love you,' he whispered into her hair, kissing her ear.

They held each other and kissed softly and tenderly, until finally she felt the pressure of his lips increase and his hands pull down her nightdress straps, seeking her breasts again. Oh, it *was* going to be all right! Relief washed over her body like a warm wave. Excited now by his caresses, she returned his kisses passionately. She undid his pyjama buttons, her hands urgently exploring his chest, his back. 'Darling,' she whispered to encourage him, 'you can't possibly hurt me tonight. I prepared myself for you this morning. I'm ready for you now.'

Jerry leaned on one elbow and looked down at her in the lamplight shining through the curtains. 'You didn't have to do that, Della,' he said huskily. Then he turned back the bedclothes and inched down her nightdress over her waist, her thighs, her feet. 'Oh, God, you're beautiful,' he muttered.

Della shivered with delight. 'That's not fair, darling.' She fumbled at his pyjama cord. As she slowly removed the garment, his body tensed, but only for a second. Her eyes raked in every detail of his maleness. Gently, he pulled her up and laid her beside him again, gazing at her white form in the dim light and stroking her softly. She moved closer, running her fingers down his side, his thighs, thrilling at his nakedness. His body shuddered and he bent over her, kissing her hard on the mouth. Her arms wound round his back, pulling him down until she could feel the length of his body over hers. She gasped slightly at his weight, and instantly he pulled himself off her and buried his face in the pillow.

'Dear God, I can't,' he groaned.

She sat up and bent over him. 'Oh, darling, darling, it's all right! I want you desperately. You're not hurting me!' She tried to stem her tears of disappointment and shame. Had she been too eager? Had she frightened him?

'It's no good, Della.' He moaned and hit his forehead against the pillow. 'I can't . . . I can't . . . I can't!'

Della couldn't bear to hear the pain in his voice; her own pain was unimportant now. 'My darling, it doesn't matter,' she soothed, pulling the bedclothes over his shivering body. She lay beside him, careful not to touch him. 'Do you want to talk some more?'

'There's nothing more to say,' he said bitterly. 'It's the same as last night. I want you terribly, but when it comes to it, I just can't go on.'

'It'll be all right, sweetheart. We'll take it very slowly. It really doesn't matter. Close your eyes and get some sleep now.'

He turned towards her and they lay naked in each other's arms, he eventually dropping off to sleep, she alert and distressed. Again, why did she feel abandoned and unclean? Jerry wanted her. He had just said so. He would never lie. She must stop this ridiculous notion and try to help him all she could. But how?

Chapter Nineteen

Two days after the honeymoon, Della felt even worse. Since the second night, Jerry had not even tried to make love to her, simply kissing her tenderly before they slept in each other's arms. Not wishing to upset him further, she tried not to show her pain, deciding she must be patient until he overcame his fear. The subject had not been mentioned again, and she knew she must wait Jerry's time. Although he seemed a little withdrawn at times, he was as affectionate as usual, and she forced herself to settle for this affection until his fear had more time to heal.

They were kept busy putting the flat in order, making curtains, painting and pottering. By Friday the new carpets were down, the mahogany furniture shone like glass, the cream and green painted kitchen sparkled, and the main bedroom looked elegant with the addition of a new wardrobe and tallboy.

Della paused in the act of dusting the sitting room. 'It would be nice to have Mam and Dad to dinner tomorrow, darling. I'd like them to be our first guests. Would you mind?' she asked tentatively, wondering if Jerry would want her to include his parents but not wishing to see his father until she could find forgiveness in her heart.

'That would be nice, sweetheart.' Jerry climbed down the ladder, where he'd been hanging the pink velvet curtains Della had chosen to repeat the roses on the chintz suite.

She decided to ask in case he felt hurt. 'Would you like to invite your folks as well?'

'No, sweetheart. I'm seeing Mother this afternoon anyway; I've got to go over to pick up some more of my things. And I'll be seeing Father at work on Monday.'

'Then I'll pop over home.' Della grinned, correcting herself. 'I mean I'll pop over to Mam and Dad's and ask them to come tomorrow.'

'Why not ask Anne as well? She needs to get out of the house more.'

Della straightened from stirring the fire and stood on tiptoe to kiss his cheek. 'You're a sweetheart. I wanted to ask Anne, but you know she'll have to bring Johnny.'

Jerry grinned wryly. 'That's all right. We can tie the little monster to the bed in the spare room and lock the door.'

Della frowned; she was worried about Johnny. Although now eight, he was still unruly and, despite Anne's efforts to control him, his tantrums always beat her down in the end.

'Maybe we can slip some booze into his lemonade and knock him out for the evening,' she said wishfully.

On Saturday evening Mary, Walter and Anne arrived with Johnny in tow. Della and Jerry fluttered around their guests, taking their coats, showing them the improvements to the flat, and finally relaxing in the sitting-room for a glass of sherry.

Mary raised her glass, though with a slightly worried expression. She thought Della looked pale and seemed nervous and preoccupied, just as she'd been when she'd called at the house the previous day. She didn't have the glow of a blooming bride.

Walter toasted the pair jovially. 'Here's good health to both of you.'

'May the rest of your lives be as wonderful as your wedding day,' Anne said. 'I've never seen such a beautiful wedding. Johnny, lift your lemonade to toast Auntie Della and Uncle Jerry.'

Johnny did as he was told, slopping lemonade over the sofa.

The evening went pleasantly, and Mary told herself she'd been silly to have thought Della seemed off-colour. She had experimented with her new Mrs Beeton's cookery book and served mulligatawny soup, steak and kidney pie, and caramel custard for dessert.

Della looked at her family seated round the table in the tiny dining room and felt thankful for her good fortune. One of these days she and Jerry would be sitting there with their own family. A sharp pain shot through her at the thought. Would it ever happen? Maybe she should encourage him a little tonight.

Their guests departed, Jerry put his arms about her and kissed her. 'You were a marvellous cook and hostess, darling. I didn't know I'd married such talent. Even Johnny kept reasonably quiet and ate his dinner.'

'You know, when I saw him sitting there being semi-angelic and enjoying his food, I thought how rewarding it must be to bring up a family. I never thought Johnny would give me that idea,' she laughed, holding Jerry close.

He nuzzled her hair. 'Shall we wash up now or leave it till the morning?'

'I'll do it tomorrow. Let's go to bed. I've spent enough time in the kitchen tonight.'

After her bath, she found Jerry already propped up in bed reading the newspaper. He put it down when she entered. 'That was a quick bath.' His eyes approved her as she approached him wearing a demure, long-sleeved white cotton nightdress. 'You look like an angel in that nighty.'

'Do you prefer me all covered up?' she teased. She switched off the lamp before climbing into bed and snuggled cautiously into him. Please God, let it be tonight, she prayed silently.

He put his arms about her and drew her closer, kissing her mouth, nose, eyes. Although her body ached for him, she simply lay still and pliable in his arms, feeling his lips travel over her face. But then, in a surge of love and desire her hands travelled beneath his pyjama jacket, gripping his muscular back so tightly that her nails dug into his flesh. He winced, and she felt his body stiffen before he gently drew away. Dear God! She had meant to be patient and she had got carried away – had even hurt him. Shame filled her. 'Darling, did I scratch you?'

'No . . . no, of course not. Goodnight, sweetheart.'

Della lay awake all night in an agony of guilt and misery.

On Monday she went to Binns to invite Rose and Nora to lunch on Thursday, early closing day. She had only been able to whisper the invitations while pretending to look at merchandise and was looking forward to catching up on her friends' news.

By one o'clock on Thursday the table was set simply with a white damask cloth and the plain white kitchen crockery. Della had toyed with the idea of using the best Doulton china for fun but had decided it might seem as if she were flaunting her rise in status.

When the doorbell rang, a simple beef and vegetable casserole was keeping warm in the oven, and a loaf of home made bread waiting enticingly on the table.

'Eey, it's nice to have you back, luv.' Nora flung her arms round Della.

'It's nice to *be* back.' Della started a smile but froze as she saw Rose's face. 'What's wrong, Rose? Are you all right?'

Rose gave her a perfunctory hug. 'Not really, but it's still nice to see you.'

'Well, come on in. And let me take your coats. Tell me what's wrong?' As Della hung their coats on the hall rack, Nora shot her a warning glance behind Rose's back. Oh, dear, she thought, as she led them to the dining-room. It must be serious. 'What's wrong then?' she enquired again as Rose slumped into the first available chair, putting her elbows on the table and her head in her hands.

'That bugger's two-timing me,' she sobbed.

'Not Jim!'

'Yes, Jim.' Nora put her arms protectively round Rose's shoulders. 'She's suspected something since the wedding, but she saw him out with her last night. She was from Jerry's side, a second-cousin or something.'

Della drew in a breath. 'Ellie!' She had seen Jim dancing with her at the wedding, but she wouldn't have thought Ellie would be his type. She was pretty enough, but quiet and withdrawn and a devout Catholic. Jim certainly wouldn't get his way with her. She couldn't be more different from Rose. 'Oh, Rose, I'm so sorry!' Della sat next to her, the casserole in the oven forgotten.

'Just wait till I see him tonight!' Rose burst out angrily. 'The rotten sod! I've only seen him three times since the wedding, and he told me it was because he had to study to retake one of his finals before Christmas or he'd flunk. He doesn't know I saw him last night. There he was, as large as life, walking down Pilgrim Street with that . . . that bitch!'

'Oh, you poor thing,' Della commiserated.

Nora sniffed suspiciously. 'I smell something burning.'

'Oh, no!' Della ran to the kitchen. 'I think it's still edible,' she said dismally, as she returned with the casserole and placed it on the table-mat. 'It's just a bit burnt on the bottom. But it's too hot to eat. I'll get us a glass of sherry first . . . or would you like something stronger, Rose – a brandy?'

'Yes, please.' She straightened her shoulders and sniffed loudly. 'I'm not going to cry any more; it always gives me a stuffy nose and a headache.'

'Good!' Nora sat down. 'If he really is two-timing you, he's not worth crying over anyway.'

'What do you mean *if*? I saw him with her!' Rose accepted the brandy from Della and finished it in one gulp.

'Well, I mean,' Nora continued encouragingly, 'he could have been studying on the other nights he couldn't see you, and maybe this was just a chance meeting, or at the worst, maybe a one time thing. Men aren't angels, you know. Couldn't you forgive him if it was just a passing fancy and he still loves you?'

'He'll have to get down on his knees and bloody well beg me to first.'

'Oh, come on, Rose.' Della joined them at the table again. 'Nora's right! Give Jim a chance to explain himself. I'm sure he loves you, and I can't see him having much in common with Ellie.'

Rose's curiosity got the better of her. 'What's she like? Apart from being a man-stealer, I mean.'

Della looked thoughtful for a moment. 'Well, I've only met her once. But I'd say that's just exactly what she's not. She's quiet and very religious and rather dull, in fact. I can't see her keeping Jim's interest for long, if at all – not after you, Rose. Why don't you stop thinking the worst until you have it out with him tonight? And, in the meantime, we can eat this lovely casserole.' She smiled ruefully as she served the dried-up meat and vegetables.

Suddenly Rose looked at Della as if noticing her for the first time. 'Eey, I'm sorry, luv. Until last night I was excited about seeing you and hearing all your honeymoon news, and I haven't even asked you how it was.'

'Oh, yes, Della, I'm dying to hear.' Nora almost drooled with anticipation.

Toying with the food on her plate, Della answered hesitantly: 'Well, as you know, the first night we stayed at the Station Hotel, and then we went to Edinburgh, and—'

'Hey, who's interested in where you went?' Rose slapped the table in impatience. 'We want to know what you *did*. How was it in bed?'

Della fixed her eyes on her plate. 'Wonderful, of course. What do you think?'

'Wonderful!' Rose shrieked. 'Is that all you're going to say? We want to know all the gory details, don't we Nora?'

'Speak for yourself, Rose,' she said tartly. 'Not everybody likes to discuss their sex life the way you do . . . and besides, marriage is different – it's private, between husband and wife.'

Rose made a face. 'Aw, codswallop! Sex is sex, whether you're married or not, and if it's too disgusting to talk about, then it should be too disgusting to do.'

'Of course it's not disgusting,' Della broke in, eager to end this conversation. Her stomach felt as though it had screwed itself into a ball. 'It's the most wonderful thing in life to love a man and make love with him.' She lowered her eyes, thinking of the long nights she had lain awake in anguish and longing while Jerry tossed in troubled sleep.

'There you go again. "Wonderful",' Rose mimicked.

'That doesn't tell us anything. Did it hurt the first time? Did you both know what to do?' She giggled and winked at Nora. 'Could he get it up? Could he get it in? Tell us all.'

The knot in Della's stomach tightened. She must end this conversation. 'Rose, you're incorrigible! The answer is yes to all those questions. Does that satisfy you?'

'Not bloody much,' Rose grumbled, 'but I suppose that's all we're going to get out of you.'

'That's right.' Della needed to escape for a few moments. 'Now I'm going to make some coffee and get the cheese. You haven't tried my home made bread yet. Sorry about the casserole. I'll do better next time.'

She returned with the coffee and cheese and deliberately turned the conversation to Nora. 'Rose and I've been gabbling on about ourselves, Nora. What about you? What's happening, if anything?'

Nora's face glowed. 'Oh, I had a lovely time at the wedding, Della. And guess what – I met someone nice, really nice.'

'Who?' Della asked in surprise.

'That friend of Jerry's from the rugger club.'

'Which one?'

'Phil, the shortish, stocky one with the nice face. He's an apprentice engineer at Parsons.'

'Oh, he *is* nice, Nora!' Della was thrilled that Nora had finally found someone she liked.

'Well,' Nora went on, her voice high with excitement, 'after you left he asked me to dance again, and then he asked if I'd go out for a drink with him the next night.' She paused, reliving the experience. 'Oh, it was fab! We just talked and talked, and then he insisted on taking me home and, would you believe it, at the front door he just took both my hands and asked when he could see me again. He didn't even try to grab me.'

'Gosh, he took you all the way to Jarrow! He sounds like a gentleman, Nora.' Della was impressed.

'Oh, he is! I've been out with him twice since, and all he's done so far is kiss me goodnight. He's taking me to the Christmas rugger club dance on Saturday night and I'm so excited I can hardly wait. I've fallen for him.'

'About time as well,' Rose snorted. 'You're the only virgin left now. It's time you did something about it. If you don't use it, it dries up and withers – and *you* with it. You know, like poor old Miss Bane.'

Della ignored Rose's remark. 'Jerry will be thrilled you've hit it off with his friend, Nora. Why don't you stay in our spare room when you go out with him? It's a long way for him to take you home to Jarrow every time, and after a late dance he'd have to walk back or hitch a lift.'

'That would be marvellous, Della. Thanks a mill. But I'm glad he's taken me home so far. At least he's seen what a dump I live in and it hasn't put him off.'

Della smiled. 'He wouldn't be one of Jerry's friends if things like that bothered him.'

'You know, it didn't occur to me at first,' Nora said thoughtfully. 'But remember, that fortune teller said there'd be two men in my life and I'm going to marry the rich one. And she saw a P and an H, but she didn't know which was which. Well, Phil starts with a P *and* an H, and he won't be too badly off when he's qualified. Do you think he could be the one she meant?'

'It's possible,' Della agreed.

Rose shook her head. 'No! She said he was going to be tall, dark and handsome. That doesn't exactly fit Phil.'

'He's five feet nine, and I'm only five four,' Nora insisted, 'so he's tall by comparison.'

'And he's nice-looking, though not handsome like a film star,' Della added. 'I mean, he's got a pleasant, open face.'

'Well, time will tell,' Rose said. 'I suppose you could do a lot worse, Nora. You sort of go well together.' She cut another slice of bread. 'Nice bread, Della – better than the stew or whatever it was. You're turning into quite a little housewife. Next thing you know, you'll have a bun in the oven and start getting all motherly.'

'Some day.' Della put down her coffee cup. 'If you've finished now, why don't I show you around the flat and then we can go in the sitting room? I banked up the fire.'

'Eey, it's smashing, Della,' Rose said after the tour. She stifled an envious sigh as she curled up in one of the chintz armchairs in the sitting-room. 'I'm glad you've done so well for yourself. I wish I had Jim hooked the way you have Jerry.'

Della managed a grin as she sank into the sofa. ' "Hooked" doesn't sound very nice. You make it seem like landing a fish.'

'Well, just pray for me tonight that my fish isn't the one that got away,' Rose said bitterly. 'And after all the time I've invested in him . . .'

'How are your dad and Tommy?' Della asked in an effort to take Rose's mind off Jim.

'Oh, all right. Mam goes to see them every week, but it just makes me depressed. How's Dan?'

'Thin and quiet, Anne says. She always goes upstairs and has a good cry after she's seen him. But it can't be much longer. A year's already over, and they'll get time off for good behaviour.'

'Well, I hope I'm married and out of the house by then,' Rose said vehemently. 'It's bad enough living with Tommy's wife and the kids, but with those two back as well, it'll be pandemonium.'

Della smiled ruefully. 'It's funny, I'm so used to living in a noisy, crowded house that this place seems too quiet when Jerry's at work. It's wonderful to have you both to talk to today. Why don't we do it every

Thursday, and I can try out a new recipe on you each time?'

'Suits me,' Nora agreed.

'Aye, me too. We miss you at work, luv,' Rose said with feeling. 'But I'd better get home now. I've got to have a bath and change and meet Jim back in town at six. Say a prayer for the sod if he's been up that bitch's skirt. And I've bought his rotten Christmas present as well!'

Nora wagged her finger in warning. 'Don't meet trouble half way, my mam always says. Give the poor lad a chance to explain himself. He might have just met her accidentally, and he might be telling the truth about having to study.'

'Aye, maybe.' Feeling somewhat more comforted than when she had arrived, Rose stood up to leave.

Dressed in her new cream cashmere sweater and pencil-line black skirt, Rose grabbed her mother's best black wool coat from the hallstand. She intended to look stunning tonight so Jim would know what he was missing. She glanced at her reflection in the hall mirror and reached out for her mother's fox fur, which lay temptingly over the banister. Slinging it round her neck, she gazed at her reflection once more. That was better! But the fur was dressy; now she needed a hat. Daringly, she picked up her mother's latest creation – a grey felt, with a trilby-like brim and a large green feather curving over the crown. That was it! She would slay Jim tonight.

Her stomach jumped at the sound of the door knocker. She took a deep breath before opening the door wide. She wanted Jim to see her in her finery in the hall light. They were going to the pictures and wouldn't be able to talk. She'd better start lacing into him now. She couldn't sit through the picture without knowing the truth. 'Hello, Jim,' she greeted him sullenly.

'Hello, luv.'

Had she imagined it by the brief light of the hall or did his face look strained? On the street, he took her hand as usual, but was it a little self-consciously? Rose's mind raced. When should she start? But Jim saved her the decision. 'My parents are out tonight. I thought we'd go home instead of to the pictures.'

'All right,' Rose replied coolly. They could talk privately there and, if everything was all right, could make love by the fire. But she wasn't going to think about that until she knew for sure. 'I saw you the other night,' she found herself saying, unable to wait till they reached the house. 'You were with that girl from the wedding.'

Jim's pace slackened and his grip on her hand loosened. He stuffed his hand in his pocket. 'I . . . I was going to tell you, Rose,' he muttered uncomfortably.

'So I was right, then!' She stopped dead and faced him in the street light. 'Jim Parker! Do you mean to tell me you've been cheating on me?'

Nonplussed, Jim scratched his head. 'Well, no . . . I mean . . . I only took her out a couple of times. We didn't do anything.'

'No! I'll bet you didn't – not with that snot-nosed little madam! No lad's going to get up her knickers till she's dragged him to the altar.'

'Rose, look, I didn't even try.'

'No, you wouldn't! Not at first anyway!' She was near to tears, but anger overcame her misery as she flung a furious torrent of words at him: 'I suppose you think you can have your cake and eat it, Jim Parker? Well, you can't! We're finished! And don't come crawling back to me when you get bored with Minnie Mouse!' She turned and ran home, leaving him standing stupefied.

That'll teach him to play around with me, she thought, hot, angry tears scalding her cheeks as she ran.

But once in her bedroom, having flung off her clothes in a frenzy, she sat on the bed, feeling numb. He would come back to her! Surely he couldn't throw her over for that colourless little nothing? She loved him, and he'd said he loved her. She mopped her eyes and dressed again, then sat on the bed waiting for his knock. He'd come back once he'd had time to think things over.

After a while, shivering, she lay down and pulled the eiderdown over her. The grandfather clock in the sitting room chimed every hour on the hour until she counted three o'clock. Tears flowed again.

Chapter Twenty

One sunny July Monday in 1939, Della went to town to shop for Jerry's birthday. After much thought, she decided on a gold tie pin and matching cuff links, revelling in the luxury of having money to spend on him. She felt much happier today. After all her months of agony and loneliness, waiting patiently for Jerry to overcome his fear, it seemed that something was finally happening. The past two nights he had kissed her urgently and held her so close all night that she could barely breathe. She had become accustomed to his kissing her goodnight and turning over abruptly to feign sleep, while she lay, aching with love and longing and plagued by self-doubt. But he was beginning to want her as a real wife. Her patience was going to work in the end.

As arranged, at one o'clock she met the girls in Binns' staff room. She smiled as she carried over her tray of egg salad and tea.

Rose hailed her. 'Well, you look pleased with yourself.'

'So do you, Rose. What's up?'

'Only another man.' Nora yawned, already bored with Rose's frequently changing romances since Jim had jilted her.

'Another one!' Della reproached Rose. 'When are you going to stop playing the field and settle for someone nice?'

'Well, I might just settle for this one,' Rose replied smugly. 'I realise now I've been flitting around like a batty butterfly looking for a replacement for Jim, when what I need is somebody completely different . . . and this one fits the bill exactly.'

'How's he different?' Nora asked without interest.

'For one thing, he's older. And for another, he's rich – I mean *very* rich.'

'How old and how rich then?' Della asked, but at that moment discovered a slug on her lettuce. She pushed her plate aside in disgust. 'Ugh, how revolting!'

Rose jumped on her. 'What do you mean, revolting? I said he's older, not *old*. And what's revolting about being rich?'

'There's a slug on my lettuce, you idiot!' Della laughed. 'I didn't mean your boyfriend.'

'Well, just chuck it off the plate and eat the rest,' Rose said, mollified. 'You pay extra for slugs here.'

Della grimaced and pushed away her plate. 'I've lost my appetite.'

'Come on, Rose,' Nora coaxed, her interest aroused. 'We're waiting with bated breath. We'll be late for work if you don't get on with it.'

'All right then! He's tall, dark and handsome . . . and forty. Very distinguished.'

'Forty!' Nora interrupted in amazement, while Della's jaw dropped.

'*Yes, forty*.' Rose stressed her words mutinously. 'And what of it? He's sophisticated, charming, a fabulous lover – everything a girl could want, even if he didn't have money. But, of course, it makes it even more exciting that he does.'

'He's a fabulous lover!' Della repeated Rose's words in dismay. 'You mean you've been to bed with him already?' Even for Rose, who had been sleeping around in a desperate attempt to find a substitute for

Jim, to go all the way so early in the relationship was unusual.

Rose grinned impishly. 'The second night, not the first I'll have you know. I met him at the tea dance at the Old Assembly Rooms on Saturday, and he took me for a meal afterwards and then to the dog races at Gosforth Stadium. It was exciting. I'd never seen a dog race before, and he lost twenty pounds and didn't bat an eyelid. The first night he took me home in a taxi and we necked a bit on the way. We couldn't do much with the taxi driver looking through the rear view mirror anyway. And then he asked me out again last night and took me to dinner at the Station Hotel. He stays there when he's in town. He's got a house in Durham.' Rose paused for breath and Della jumped in.

'You mean you stayed the whole night with him at the hotel?' Della's eyes widened, then clouded as she tried not to think of her miserable night at the Station Hotel with Jerry.

'Well, not exactly the whole night.' Rose supplied the information happily. 'I had to get up at six and go home to change for work. He put me in a taxi and paid the driver. Oh, it was dreamy to be bought an expensive dinner and made love to by an experienced man. And then to be put in a taxi! I felt like a princess.'

'More like a tart, if you ask me,' Nora said, giving her a disapproving look.

'Aw, don't be so old-fashioned,' Rose defended herself, though subdued somewhat by Nora's tone.

'I just hope you were careful.' Della looked at her with concern. 'I'm getting worried about you, Rose. I mean, it was one thing when you were in love with Jim, but now all these others you don't love . . . and what if you got into trouble?'

'Rubbish! Not me. But let me finish. Bill's got

properties in Newcastle and Durham. That's why he lives there and comes here on business. He owns a lot of big houses, and last year started converting some of them into flats. He says the days of big houses are numbered; people can't afford them any more, but there's always a market for small flats. He's a good businessman with an eye to the future. And now – wait for the best part – he's offered to let me have one of his flats in Gosforth, and he'll stay with me when he comes to town.'

'But how could you ever afford a flat?' Nora asked innocently.

Della shook her head in dismay. 'I think I know. It's rent free, isn't it?'

'Of course it is, you daft thing,' Rose admitted freely. 'You know I couldn't afford to pay rent. He's giving it to me because he likes me.' But she hesitated as she saw Della's and Nora's horrified expressions. 'Oh, don't look so bloody disapproving, both of you. It's no different from letting a man pay for your dinner or your seat at the pictures. And it's just the same as that for him; he's got money to burn. Can't you see how wonderful it is? I'll get away from that house before Tommy and my dad get out, and I'll have my own posh flat. And, if all goes well, I might even end up Mrs William Fraser. Remember that fortune teller woman said I was going to mary a tall, dark handsome man, and she saw a journey across the sea? Well, this one's certainly got the money to travel.'

'But she said you'd already met him,' Della pointed out.

Not to be put off, Rose dismissed the idea with a wave of her hand. 'Aw, they can't be right on everything. She might have got confused with Jim.'

'But if this man's so eligible, why isn't he married already?' Nora asked sensibly.

'You're a right dampener, you are!' Rose snapped at her. 'He says he just never found the right girl to settle down with. But, you never know, it could be little me.'

'But he's old enough to be your father,' Della countered.

'So what!' Rose gave her a defiant look. 'He's got a lot more to offer than a young lad. You know how the song goes: "I'd rather be an old man's darling than a young man's slave". Well, I learned that lesson from Jim. No more pining away over young lads who don't know how to treat a girl.' She paused before adding mournfully, 'I can still hardly believe he jilted me for that skinny little Ellie bitch. And after all those years I was faithful to him!' She took a deep breath and wagged her head as if to shake Jim out of her thoughts. 'Well, I've decided I'm going to be in control of my own life from now on. No more teenage passions! Older men are more appreciative – and more faithful.'

Della lowered her eyes and rubbed an imaginary stain off the wooden table with her fingers. 'Well, Rose, if you're sure it's what you want, and if you're sure it'll make you happy, we'll be happy for you, won't we, Nora?' She looked warningly at her to agree.

Nora nodded and forced a smile. 'Of course, luv. We're just worried about you, that's all. And it's all so sudden. It's none of our business to disapprove of what you do.'

Rose looked satisfied. 'Thanks, kids. I know we disagree about a lot of things, but I forgive you for being so pure.' She giggled loudly. 'I don't know why you're still my best friends, despite your goody-goody ways. And speaking of goody-goody, how's Phil, Nora?'

'Wonderful as ever.' Nora's face brightened at the mention of Phil's name. 'But he's not so goody-goody as you think, you know. He gets carried away like any lad, and I have to keep him in check, but he always stops when I say so.' She looked closely at Rose, an idea brewing. 'We're going to another rugger club dance on Saturday. Would you like to come?' It would be nice, she thought, if Rose could meet someone else to take her mind off this older man.

Not catching on to Nora's subterfuge, Rose waved her hand in refusal. 'No thanks, luv. Bill's coming this weekend. He's taking me to see the flat and we're going shopping for furniture. I'll have you both over as soon as I move in. Gosh, it's so exciting, I can hardly wait. I'm going to lead a completely new life.'

'Aye, it might be a completely new life for all of us, Rose. Have you thought of that?' Nora said seriously. 'I hope the house has a proper Anderson shelter – if not, you might be better off staying with your mam. *We've* only got a Morrison shelter.'

Rose looked slightly alarmed. 'What's a Morrison shelter?'

'The kitchen table, you daft thing,' Nora snapped. 'And all of us have to get under it. We haven't got a garden to put an Anderson shelter in.'

'Oh.' Rose paled. 'It's a big house; it's bound to have a garden.'

'I wish Jerry and I had a garden,' Della said nervously. 'Mam and Dad had their shelter delivered in February. Dad and the boys dug it in. It looks scary – a bit like a bunker in a battlefield – but if anything does happen, God forbid, they're prepared.

'Aw, nothing's going to happen,' Rose said flippantly. 'It would have happened by now if it was.'

But Nora looked serious. 'I wouldn't bank on it not happening. I joined the Air Raid Precautions last night.'

'What for?' Della asked in dismay. Although she had followed Mary's insistent advice that she stock up with tinned goods and sugar, she wouldn't allow herself to believe a war would really come. 'All these precautions are just to *prevent* a war, Nora, to show those Germans that we're prepared and armed enough to knock their blocks off. Now that Germany knows we're ready for them, they're less likely to try to take us on.'

Nora nodded. 'That's right, luv. And that's why, whether it happens or not, we've got to be ready for them. I'm going to my first lecture tonight and, after the course, I have to sit an exam. At least I'll learn something useful, even if I don't have to put it into practice.'

'Aw, come off it, Nora, you're so bloody patriotic,' Rose scoffed. 'This country hasn't exactly given you an easy time so far, why should you care so much about it? And anyway, if anything has to be done, let the men do it. It's not a woman's job.'

'That's the whole point, you dimwit!' Nora returned, exasperated. 'All the young, healthy men will be away fighting. That's why women will have to do it.'

Rose's face lit up with relief. 'Hey, I never thought of that! That's another good reason for having an older man – he won't be going away to fight like the young ones. I'll be living it up with Bill while Jerry and Phil are doing their bit for their country,' she said thoughtlessly.

'Rose, sometimes you can be an absolute cow,' Della shot at her. 'I've had enough of this morbid conversation and, anyway, you two had better get back.' She indicated the clock on the wall. 'If you're not careful you'll be out of work.'

'Oops, got carried away!' Rose grinned and took out her compact to renew her face. 'Just cheer up and stop worrying about a bloody war, you two. It's never going to come to it.' She rose and pulled Nora up. 'Come on or we'll get the sack. But maybe I shan't have to work much longer anyway . . . if Bill's willing to keep me in the manner to which I'm accustomed.'

Nora threw Della a despairing glance as the two departed.

'See you on Thursday,' she shouted after them. She picked up her parcels and rose to leave. Drat all this talk about war! She was looking forward to going home to ice Jerry's birthday cake, then to experiment with sole almondine for dinner. She was quite proud of her cooking now.

At the house, she started in surprise. A police car was parked outside and two policemen stood ringing the doorbell. 'Can I help you?' she offered. 'If you want Mrs Brown, she's deaf, and I'm the only one home during the day.'

'We're looking for a Mrs Davidson,' the elder of the burly policemen said brusquely. 'We've been trying to get hold of her since ten o'clock this morning.'

Della's face drained of colour. 'I'm Mrs Davidson. What's happened?'

'Mind if we come in, Mrs Davidson?' The same man spoke again, this time in a gentler tone.

'Oh, yes.' Della scrabbled for her key with trembling hands. 'But please tell me – what's wrong?'

The younger took the key from her and opened the door before speaking. 'I'm afraid it's your husband, Mrs Davidson. He's dead.'

Della stood still, the blood seeming to rush from her head. The policeman quickly put his arm beneath her elbow to steady her.

'No! No! No!' she screamed hysterically. 'No, God! No!'

'Come on in, missus.' The older man took her other arm, and the pair of them lifted her almost off her feet, half carrying her up the stairs to the flat. 'Let's get you inside, hinny.' Still half carrying her, they eased her limp figure on to the sitting-room sofa.

'No! No!' Della continued screaming. 'Jerry's not dead! He's not!'

'I'll see if she's got any brandy, Mick.' The younger man opened the sideboard door and, in seconds, pressed a glass to Della's rigid lips.

She swallowed, then coughed, opening her eyes. 'How? What happened?' she croaked, forced now to accept reality.

'I'm afraid he jumped off Byker Bridge, missus. It was instantaneous . . . broke his neck. Couldn't have felt no pain,' the older man said gently.

'He . . . he . . . did it himself!' Della's hands flew to her mouth. She felt sick, and the tears that wouldn't come earlier suddenly flowed. 'Oh, God! God! Dear God! Why? Why?'

'Here, missus, have another sip.' The younger man pressed the glass to her lips again.

Della pushed it away. Her sobs stopped and her body felt numb. 'Where is he?' She could hear her voice, but it didn't seem to come from her lips.

The older man cleared his throat. 'He's at the mortuary, missus. We have to take you there to identify him. But first we need some information. We got his name and address from his wallet, but that's all we know.'

'What . . . what do you want to know?' She pressed a trembling hand to her forehead. This wasn't happening. These men would go away. Jerry would come home after work. It was his birthday tomorrow. She'd just bought his present.

The older man shuffled his feet. 'Well, er, was there any reason that you know of?'

'No! No!' she screamed.

'Well then,' the other put in gently, 'he might have left a note for you. They often do. Would you mind if I had a look around?'

She shook her head and pressed her fist to her mouth,

biting her knuckles till they blanched. But she felt no pain.

The policeman disappeared and returned in an instant with an envelope. 'This was propped on the dining-room table, missus. Would you like me to open it for you.'

'No . . . no.' Della put out a trembling hand. She hadn't been in the dining-room today; it must have been there when she got up. Oh, dear God, these men were telling the truth. Maybe if she'd seen the letter earlier she'd have had time to stop him.

The envelope was simply addressed to 'Della'. Shaking with dread, she tore it open. Her stomach heaved as, through blurred eyes, she read the familiar handwriting:

My darling,

I am letting you go free. You deserve a man who can be a real husband to you and a father to your children. I am ashamed of the pathetic figure of a husband I have proved to be.

If I can't make you happy, and I know now that I truly can't, the best thing I can do for both of us is to end this useless life of mine and give you a chance to find happiness.

Please forgive me for the misery I have caused you.

I love you too much to go on making you suffer.
Be happy, my darling, from this day forward.
Jerry

Della threw herself back and emitted a loud wail, the tears shivering on her lashes, the note still clutched in her hand. Dearest God, he had been planning this! That was why he had clung to her so last night. And she had been pleased! Pleased that she thought he was finally beginning to want her sexually, that she must after all be a desirable woman. All these long months she had been selfish enough to feel sorry for herself, had wallowed in her own feelings of inadequacy and rejection, when Jerry was so tortured that he had taken his own life.

The older policeman stepped forward. 'Er . . . do you mind if we take the note, missus?'

'No! *Please, no!* It's private!' Della clutched the letter to her bosom.

'Well, it'll be kept as confidential as possible, missus, but we have to have it for our records.'

Della opened her hand and the letter fluttered to the floor. 'Dear God, dear God!' she repeated, rocking to and fro.

The younger man took out his notebook. 'Do you have any other family, missus? We can get them to come and help you, and they can come to the mortuary with you.'

'My mother,' Della whispered, automatically reciting the address.

He stuffed the letter and notebook in his pocket. 'Well, if you feel up to it now, we can either take you there or go and bring your mother here. She can go to the mortuary with you, or she could even go instead of you if you want?'

'No, no, I'm going,' Della said, her voice like iron. But in a second she broke down again and whimpered pathetically, 'I want to see him.'

As the police car pulled up next-door, Mrs Bowman ran to her front gate, agog with excitement.

Mary answered the knock, her face blanching as she saw Della propped up between two policemen.

'God in heaven!' she screamed. 'What's happened?'

Della threw herself into Mary's arms. 'Oh, Mam, Mam! Jerry's dead! Jerry's dead!'

'No! Oh, dear God, no!' Mary held Della's trembling body tightly to her. 'Come on in, sweetheart,' she coaxed, her own tears escaping despite her effort to control them. 'Come on in and sit down.'

As Mary led Della into the kitchen, followed by the two policemen, Anne came downstairs. Her face paled at the sight. 'Good God! What . . . what's wrong?'

'Jerry's dead,' Mary said in a voice as cold and hard as marble. 'Put the kettle on and get the brandy.' She eased Della's pathetic figure into an armchair and brushed the damp hair off her face, as she'd done so often in times of childish troubles.

The policemen stood, silent and awkward, and Mary absently waved them towards the sofa. She sat on the arm of Della's chair, her arm protectively about her shoulders. 'What happened?' she asked the senior constable. 'Was he in an accident?'

'No, missus.' The man lowered his eyes. 'It was suicide. He jumped off Byker Bridge.'

'God in heaven!' Mary screeched in disbelief. She knelt by the chair and laid her head in Della's lap. 'Oh, my poor lamb! In God's name, why?'

'Because he loved me, Mam,' Della said dully. 'He was afraid to hurt me.'

'Hurt you, my darling?' Mary said, perplexed. 'I don't understand.'

Anne listened in the scullery as she made the tea. She poured the brandy into Della's cup with shaking hands. 'Let me give her this, Mam,' she said, taking charge. 'She can tell us later. Come on, sweetheart, just a sip.' She held the cup to Della's unwilling lips.

'No . . . no.' She pushed away the cup. 'We've got to go to the mortuary.'

'Aye, missus,' the older policeman confirmed. 'You can both come along with her if you like. She's got to identify the body.'

Della prised herself up shakily by the chair arms. 'I'm ready now.'

'Does she have to go in this state?' Mary asked, as she supported Della by the elbow.

'I . . . I . . . want to, Mam,' she whispered. 'Please . . . please come with me.'

'Of course! We're both coming, sweetheart.' Anne took Della's other elbow.

'I'm going to see my darling. I'm going to see my darling,' she repeated in a monotone as they led her out.

At the mortuary, Mary and Anne helped Della out of the car. Her eyes were dry as she muttered, 'I'm here, my darling, I'm here.'

'Look here, constable, can't I go in alone?' Mary pleaded to the older officer. 'This is too much for her.'

'No, Mam,' Della insisted in a cracked voice. 'I want to see my darling . . . I want to see him.'

'All right, sweetheart, all right,' Anne soothed her. 'But we're going with you.'

Della, paper white, said nothing as they escorted her into the waiting room; she concentrated on putting one foot before the other. The policemen spoke to the white-coated man behind the desk who beckoned them all through a door. Della shivered. It was cold, and a strange, unpleasant smell assaulted her nostrils. She thought she was going to be sick and stopped to draw a deep breath.

'Are you all right, sweetheart?' Mary asked anxiously. She felt numb and nauseated herself. 'You can still go back.'

Della shook her head and mechanically moved forward again.

The ghostly, white-coated figure led them into a long room with what looked like large drawers lining the walls. He pulled one out and, still supported by Mary and Anne, Della inched forward.

'No! No!' She howled like a baby as the white-coated assistant pulled back a sheet, revealing Jerry's familiar, rugged face. Della's body stiffened, and she clapped her hand to her mouth as she saw the bruises and grazes around his closed eyes and across his nose. Yet his mouth seemed to smile at her. 'Oh, my darling.' She bent to kiss his lips, but the room spun and she slipped away.

Later, she opened her eyes to see a shadowy, white-capped head bending over her. Anne's and Mary's blurred figures stood at the bottom of the bed.

'You're all right now, hinny.' The nurse felt Della's pulse. 'How are you feeling?'

'Jerry . . . Jerry,' she moaned, as her tortured memory flooded back.

Anne and Mary moved towards her. 'You're all right now, darling,' said her mother, holding her hand.

'We're going to get you straight home,' Anne said briskly. 'Nurse, is she all right to go home now? I'll ring for a taxi.'

'No, you don't need to, hinny,' the plump kind-faced nurse said. 'Two of the drivers are going off duty now; they'll drop you off on the way home. She's not really bad enough for an ambulance, but this one's unofficial.' She stuck her head through the door and yelled. 'Charlie, don't diddle off yet. I've got a patient for you.' She turned to Anne. 'If I know those two, they'll be hooting the siren all the bloody way. They're just in a hurry to get home, luv. Don't get scared.'

Grey and shaking, Della sat between Mary and Anne in the ambulance, deaf to the screeching siren, saying and seeing nothing.

Mary tried to comfort her. 'Nurse gave you some

sedatives, luv. You're going to take one and go straight to bed. You don't have to worry about a thing. The policemen went back to lock up the flat.'

Chapter Twenty-One

Della opened her eyes in her old bed, the reality of Jerry's death rushing back and engulfing her in an avalanche of grief. 'Oh, my darling, my darling,' she moaned into the pillow, which was soon wet from her tears. 'How can I wake up and still be here when you're gone . . . gone? Dear God! Oh, I want to be with you.' She thumped the pillow with her fists and sobbed uncontrollably. 'I can't live without you . . . I can't! I can't!'

Anne stroked her back. 'It's all right, luv. Cry as much as you like.' She had sat by the bed most of the day in order to be there when her sister awoke. Della sat up and clung to her. 'Thank God those pills knocked you out,' Anne said. 'My poor lamb, it's going to be hard for you, but it *will* be over one day. Life will get better again. And you can be assured that Jerry's at peace now.'

'But that's just it,' Della wailed, clinging to Anne. 'He killed himself! How can he be at peace? The church won't let him be buried in consecrated ground. Oh, dear God! And he was such a good Catholic. How could they do that to him, Anne? How? How?' She looked up pleadingly, her face thin and drawn, her whole being racked with intolerable pain.

Anne stroked back the damp hair from Della's blotchy cheeks and tried to console her. 'I don't think

243

it'll make any difference to God, sweetheart. Jerry was a good person. If they won't give him a Catholic burial, then we'll go to a Protestant church. I'm sure it's all the same to God.'

'No! No! It isn't!' Della cried, distraught. 'Once, on a school trip, I genuflected and made the sign of the cross in a Protestant church . . . and the nun slapped me and said it was a mortal sin.'

Anne shook her head angrily. 'That's all a lot of tommy rot, luv! God loves everybody, whether they happen to be born Catholic, Protestant, Buddhist or whatever. He made us all. It's stupid for people to squabble about the right way to find God. He's everywhere, and Jerry's with him at the moment.'

'Oh, do you really think so, Anne?' Della looked only partly convinced. 'Being Catholic's never seemed all that important to me. I mean . . . I have Protestant friends and they're good people, and I'd have married Jerry even if he hadn't been Catholic. Do you really think God will forgive him for taking his own life?' Her eyes begged for reassurance.

'I know it,' Anne said firmly. 'And here's Mam. She'll tell you exactly the same. Nobody's got first rights to God.'

'How are you, sweetheart?' Mary stroked the tousled black hair with trembling hands. 'I didn't know you were awake. Could you manage some tea and toast?'

Della struggled to take a deep breath and wiped her eyes on the sheet. 'Some tea . . . no toast.'

Anne stood up. 'I'll get it, and I'll get you a hankie while I'm at it.'

'Thank God for those pills,' Mary sighed. 'The nurse said you can take a half or a quarter during the day. Do you want to take some more now?'

'What time is it?'

'Two o'clock.'

244

'Oh, I had no idea I'd slept all that time. I thought it was morning.' Della screwed her eyes shut to think clearly. 'But . . . I have to stay awake. The policeman said they'd come back today for a statement.'

'Never mind about that,' Mary said adamantly. 'I can talk to them. Anne's going to the flat for your things. Is there anything special you want?'

'No . . . just some clothes.' Della still tried to clear her fuddled mind. 'But you don't know what to tell the police, Mam. I'll have to talk to them. Oh, God! Do I have to tell them?' Her face crumpled and the tears flowed again.

'You don't have to tell them anything you don't want to – nor anybody else, for that matter,' Mary assured her.

'But people will want to know why . . . and it's so private. It's like betraying Jerry. But I want you and the family to know,Mam. You all knew him and you'll understand. Oh, he was such a gentle person, Mam – you know that. He was so sensitive. That's why he killed himself. He loved me more than he did himself.' She cried out in anguish: 'Oh, how could I have been so selfish and blind? I could have stopped him!'

'No, you couldn't, Della. And you couldn't have known. You're not to blame, do you hear?' Mary's voice was firm but she looked hopelessly at Anne who stood in the doorway with the tea.

'Here, drink this, luv.' Anne held out the cup and laid one of Walter's large white handkerchiefs on the pillow.

But Della waved away the cup. 'It was all his father's fault,' she went on, her voice now grim. 'That man ought to burn in hell for what he's done to his family.'

Mary drew in a breath. So the father had something to do with it. She had never taken to that man.

Slowly, brokenly, the story came out, and Della lay back exhausted with the effort.

'Oh, dear God, what you've been through!' Mary gripped Della's trembling hands. 'Poor, poor Jerry . . . And that bastard! I hope he suffers for this.'

'Don't worry, it'll never get beyond the family, Della,' Anne assured her. 'We'll think of something to tell the police.'

The front door knocker thumped and Anne jumped up. 'That must be them now. I'll talk to them.'

But a few minutes later she returned, ushering Jerry's mother into the room. Mrs Davidson wore a black crepe dress and a veiled black felt hat. She lifted back the veil, revealing eyes as red and skin as pale as Della's. Her elegant features, distorted with pain, looked as if they had somehow been rearranged.

'Oh, my dear,' she said, sitting by Della, who reached up and put her arms round her. They clung together and wept in their shared grief.

After a few moments, Mrs Davidson drew away and tried to compose herself. 'Oh, I feel so guilty! It's all my fault. I had no idea he was still so upset about that awful business.' She paused, twisting her black-gloved hands in anguish. 'I just tried to keep family life going on as normally as possible. And, dear Lord! I was much more concerned for Veronica than for Jerry. If only I'd known how much it had affected him! Maybe if I'd talked to him more about it at the time, I could have spared his suffering. Oh, God, I just hushed it up and said that Daddy was a little drunk and didn't realise he was hurting Veronica. I prayed Jerry would forget about it. I . . . I never dreamed it would torture him so much.' She sobbed again, covering her face with her white lace handkerchief.

Della did her best to console her. 'You weren't to know. You were a good mother to Jerry, and he always loved you. You mustn't blame yourself.' She lay back on the pillow, her shaking hands plucking at the sheet.

Then, suddenly confused, she sat up again. 'But . . . how do you know why he did it? Did the police show you the letter?'

Mrs Davidson shook her head. 'No, they said he'd left you a letter, but they didn't need to show me anyway. William broke down when he heard the news. Oh, dear God!' She ran her hand across her forehead and swallowed hard before continuing: 'He told me Jerry had talked to him the day before . . . that he'd been to the priest, who'd told him he should talk to his father and find out if he'd confessed his sin. And . . . and that if he had, God would have forgiven him, and Jerry must do the same. He said only forgiveness would heal his suffering.' The lace handkerchief fluttered again as she dabbed at her eyes.

'Then why did Jerry kill himself?' Della cried. 'He was a good, forgiving person.'

'William refused to tell him if he'd confessed or not. He said it was none of Jerry's business.' She bit her lip before continuing: 'I've always wondered about that myself. William stopped going to church after that night. But I've never dared to ask him. Anyway, Jerry knew then that his father hadn't confessed and begged him to. But William got angry and they had a row.' She whimpered into the crumpled white lace. 'That was the day before Jerry did it.'

Della's fuzzy mind tried to take in Mrs Davidson's words. Oh, God! She'd been even blinder than she thought. So *that* was why Jerry had been different during the last two days of his life. He'd clung to her because he knew he was going to leave her, and she had selfishly misinterpreted his anguish to suit her own needs. She gave Mrs Davidson a compassionate look. 'I'm to blame as well for not realising what was going on . . . but we couldn't see into his mind.'

'Neither of you can be blamed for anything,' Mary cut

in. 'You both loved him and did what you thought was best for him. What we have to do now is try to preserve his memory. What are we going to tell the police? They said in the paper last night the reason for his suicide was still unknown.'

'I've already told them,' Mrs Davidson said in a stony voice. 'At least, I've told them that he'd had a row with his father the previous day over a family matter, and that Jerry had been very upset. I didn't tell them what the row was about – but not to save William's skin,' she added vehemently. 'I've still got Veronica to think about, and Jerry's memory. The police didn't press me for any more details as there was no doubt it was suicide. And there were witnesses.' She shuddered as the image of Jerry's final moments flashed through her mind. 'They just filed the report that it was suicide while the balance of his mind was disturbed . . . over a disagreement with his father.'

'Oh, thank God!' Della let out a deep breath of relief. 'So Jerry's secret won't have to come out?'

'No, but his father's will,' Mrs Davidson said grimly. 'I'll see to that! I'm leaving him. The whole world will at least know he's a bastard, even if they don't know the details.' She dabbed at her eyes again. 'I don't know how I managed to live with him in the same house all these years. But now I don't have to pretend any more. Jerry's gone . . . and Veronica too, in a different way.' She stood up slowly. 'I'd better be going. I just wanted to see you and comfort you a bit if I could.'

'Oh, you did! Thank you.' Della grasped her mother-in-law's hands. 'I wish I could comfort *you* more.'

'You *are* a comfort, my dear. It's a comfort to know that you and Jerry loved each other so much.' Mrs Davidson turned to leave, pulling down the little black veil to hide her ravaged face.

'Please, won't you stay and have a cup of tea?' Mary

put a restraining hand on the woman's arm.

'No, thank you, dear. I just want to go home and lie down for a bit. I never was a good crier; it gives me a terrible headache.'

'I'll go with you.' Anne jumped up from the other bed where she had been sitting. 'I'm going to the flat to get some of Della's things anyway.'

Mary nodded. 'I'll be here if the police come again. Thank God, at least I know what to say to them now.'

As the front door banged, Della let out a low moan. 'Oh, no. We forgot to mention the funeral. We'll have to do something about it today.'

'No, there's time enough for that tomorrow,' Mary said. 'Now you're going to take a half a pill and get some more rest.'

'Oh, yes, please, Mam. I want to sleep and sleep and never wake up.'

But, at nine in the evening, Della reluctantly opened her eyes from merciful oblivion. Anne sat with her as before, and Walter's and the boys' voices drifted upstairs. Almost fully awake now, she sat up.

'How are you feeling, sweetheart?' Anne asked gently.

Della pressed her hands to her forehead. 'Those pills make me feel funny. My head feels as if it's about to burst.'

'It's all that crying as well, luv. But the sleep and the crying are just what you need at the moment. Mam's made you some chicken broth. Promise you'll take it.'

Della nodded, and Anne called down the stairs to Mary.

In a trice, she arrived with a steaming bowl on a tray. 'Come on, luv,' she cooed, setting the tray on Della's lap.

'Thanks, Mam.' Della looked distastefully at the

broth but decided she'd better please her mother.

Anne waited to deliver her news until Della had put down her spoon, defeated by the remaining broth. She sat on the bed as Mary removed the tray. 'Sweetheart, it's going to be all right. I've been to St Bede's, and Father Ryan said there's no reason why Jerry can't be buried there. He says the final judgement is God's, not his.'

'But Jerry would have wanted to be buried at the Church of the Holy Name – that's his own parish.' Della looked puzzled, though relieved to hear Father Ryan's words. 'Why didn't you go there?'

Anne lowered her eyes. 'I did, Della. I talked to Father Donaldson but he wouldn't hear of it. He's old, sweetheart, and set in his ways. But Father Ryan's younger and more liberal. It doesn't matter which church – at least Jerry will have a Catholic funeral.'

Della's eyes filled again. How could it be that her darling had attended the Church of the Holy Name all his life and yet he was refused a decent burial there? And Father Donaldson *knew* what had driven Jerry to take his own life. It just didn't make sense. Thank God for priests like Father Ryan.

Mary's voice interrupted her thoughts. 'I'm going to give you another pill now, sweetheart, so you can sleep through the night. But this is the last one. Tomorrow you must get up and start to pull yourself together. I've told your dad and the boys to keep quiet.'

'Oh, poor Dad! I haven't even seen him yet, and the boys.'

Mary straightened the bedclothes. 'I've had to practically chain them downstairs to stop them from waking you. Would you like to see Dad now? I don't think he can sleep another night without seeing you.'

Della gulped. 'Does he know everything?'

'Yes, luv, and the boys. We couldn't keep the truth from them.'

'Oh, Mam!' Della's eyes grew wide as a new and devastating thought struck her. 'Dad's job! We shouldn't have told him. He won't want to work for that man now . . . and . . . and he can't afford to lose his job. Promise you won't let him do anything silly about work? Promise, promise, please?'

Mary set her mouth firmly. 'Now, you know I couldn't stop your dad from doing anything he's made up his mind to do. He's handing in his notice tomorrow. He said if he didn't get that bastard out of his sight, he'd end up killing him.'

'Oh, no! Please ask him to come up, Mam. I must talk some sense into him.'

Mary shouted downstairs and a few seconds later Walter tiptoed into the room. He sat awkwardly on the bed and took Della's hands in his work-hardened fists. 'How are you feeling, luv?' he said in a voice gruff with concern.

Della flung her arms round him, tears flowing as he held her in his strong grip. After a few minutes, she pushed him away and pleaded, 'Dad, please don't make things worse by giving up your job. You can't do that to Mam.'

He shook his head. 'I have no choice, luv. I couldn't work for the devil and take his money. I'll be happier back on the dole. But I'll find something else, don't worry. You know work's picking up again.'

'Please, Dad,' she tried again. 'Please don't go back to welding. Please stay on at the office.'

He shook his head once more. 'It's no good, Della. It's out of the question. And stop worrying your head about it; you've got enough to cope with.'

'Dad's right,' Mary's soft voice cut in. 'Now you get some more rest and stop worrying about us. The boys'll have to wait till tomorrow to see you. I think you've had enough for one day. Take this now.'

Della gratefully swallowed the pill Mary held out. She closed her eyes. Tomorrow she must pull herself together. Jerry couldn't have borne to see her like this.

The funeral was held on Friday. Jerry's coffin had been brought to the house the previous day and rested in the sitting-room, covered with sprays of flowers from the family and his mother, and a huge wreath of red roses from Della.

At the mass before the burial, Mrs Davidson sat next to Della, the rest of the family filling the pew. Mr Davidson sat alone in the pew opposite until his brother and sister-in-law arrived and joined him. There were tears in the father's steel grey eyes.

Wearing a new black costume and a large-brimmed black hat, Della got through the service as though in a trance. Only the steady trickle of tears down her pallid cheeks showed that there was life in her body. Throughout the mass her eyes never left the coffin sitting in state on the altar steps.

After the mass, the pall bearers – Michael, Billie, Wally, David, and George, Jerry's best man – carried the coffin to the hearse for the drive to the cemetery. The fleet of cars Anne had hired carried the mourners. It wasn't until they threw the first spade of earth on the coffin that Della finally broke down and knelt over the grave in a paroxysm of grief. Mary and Anne bent over her, gently pulling her away and leading her to the car waiting to return home.

As usual, Mrs Bowman was at her gate as the car pulled up, but the black-clad group ignored her as they walked solemnly down the path.

The table was already laid with sandwiches and pies and the sideboard laden with bottles of sherry and beer.

Anne seated Della on the sofa and handed her a glass of sherry. 'Here, drink this, luv. It'll make you feel better.'

Della sipped mechanically, accepting condolences from each small group as they returned to the house. When Mrs Davidson arrived, Della led her upstairs to her bedroom. 'I'd like to talk to you alone for a minute,' she said. She had always liked this woman, but now there was something stronger than liking that bonded them – shared loss and grief.

'It was a beautiful service, dear. You did well.' Mrs Davidson sniffed as she sat on the bed.

'Anne did it all.' Della sat beside her and took her hands.

'It's a relief that it's all over, I suppose. But seeing him going into the ground is so . . . so final.' Mrs Davidson shuddered.

Della's body stiffened at the memory. She swallowed hard. 'I . . . I wanted to talk to you without any interruptions. Are you still at the house?'

'Only in a manner of speaking, dear. I live there and will have to till I find a flat. I've looked at a couple but they weren't suitable.'

'I'd like you to move in to our . . . my . . . flat. That is, if you'd like to?' Della said. 'I'm staying here. I couldn't go back there. It's already furnished; all you'd have to do is move in. I'd like you to live there and enjoy it . . . and I know Jerry would.'

Moved to tears, Mrs Davidson squeezed Della's hand. 'My dear, I'd like that. If you're sure you don't want to go back?'

'I'm sure. I need to be with my family now.'

'Well, I'll buy the furniture from you, dear, and the rent's reasonable. I shan't be too badly off for money. William's selling out the business to his partner and I've got a share in that, and I've saved up a bit over the years.' She bit her lip ruefully. 'I always thought I'd pass it on to the children.'

Della's ears pricked. 'He's selling up?'

Mrs Davidson nodded. 'Yes, this whole thing's got him down. Even though he deserves it, I can't help feeling sorry for him. He's put the sale in the hands of the solicitor and he's retiring.'

'Oh, if only I'd known! Dad handed in his notice this week . . . and now he needn't have.'

'Don't worry, dear. I know about that. I was going to have a word with your father today, anyway. William only told me yesterday about selling his share, and he said he tore up your father's notice. He claims he was getting tired of the responsibilities anyway and now that there's no one to leave it to . . .' She paused and took a laboured breath. 'It seems that William has some sort of conscience, somewhere deep down. It's a pity it took a tragedy like this to unearth it. But it's too late for *me* now. I wish him no harm, but I could never live with him again. He's going in to the office this weekend to clear out his personal things, and after that his partner takes over.'

'Oh, that's a relief! Let's go down now and tell Mam and Dad.' Della stood up and squared her shoulders. 'It'll be nice to tell them some good news for a change.'

Chapter Twenty-Two

During the weeks following the funeral, Della's emotions died. She felt only a bleak emptiness and saw only a vast blackness stretching before her, which she would have to travel endlessly, dragging her feet through the deep mire, neither knowing nor caring what destination lay ahead. Despite feeling guilty that Jerry would have wanted her to continue going to church, she had been unable to force herself to attend since the requiem mass. At a time when her faith should have sustained her, it had deserted her. Her tortured mind kept asking her how God could be merciful when He let such tragedies happen. Even Jerry's faith had forsaken him at the end, otherwise he could not have taken his own life.

Contriving to keep Della occupied, Mary forced her to help with the housework and cooking, and Anne constantly loaded her with piles of sewing. Since the wedding, word had spread about Anne's talent for dress designing, and she was now working on her fourth order for brides' and bridesmaids' dresses. It enabled her to put a little money aside for Dan's return. Mary had also assigned Della the job of making blackout blinds for the windows and taping up the panes with brown paper strips, according to government instructions.

The endless talk of and preparations for war only served to make Della's outlook even bleaker – not a ray of hope in sight. Although National Service had been introduced that April, it was still peacetime, and she had refused to believe the war would really happen. But now, Wally and David, the two youngest males in the family, had been called up – Wally was in the navy and David in the army – and Walter had joined the ARP (Air Raid Precautions) as a firefighter. Still hoping that the war would be averted at the last minute, Billie had decided to bide his time.

By the end of August, rehearsals had been held for mass evacuation, and Anne had arranged to ship Johnny to Mrs Moynihan who, on the death of her brother, had moved in with her daughter and now lived in a small village in County Durham. Only God knew what might lie in store. The government's decision to prepare for the event of war had stimulated the economy, but nobody thought the cost of another war worth the increased employment.

On the second of September, Walter hustled with the anxious crowd at the newspaper stand and managed to grab a paper. He read it avidly as he walked home. 'Well, this is definitely it,' he said gloomily, as he burst through the kitchen door and flung the paper on the table. 'The buggers have finally crossed the border into Poland. The Poles don't stand a snowball's chance. God in heaven! Tanks and Messerschmitts against horses! The poor sods'll be massacred.' He slumped into his chair at the table. 'I'm telling you, we can't stand back and do nothing, and neither can France, not with the defence treaty with Poland. We'll have to help the Poles, and that means we'll be in it up to our necks.'

Mary, who had listened to Walter's tirade, hands pressed to her mouth and eyes wide in horror, suddenly came back to life. She grabbed the paper and spread it on the table, feverishly devouring the headlines. Anne and Della, who had also been shocked into silence, looked anxiously over her shoulder.

'Please God let something stop them first,' Anne prayed aloud.

Della sat down and stared unseeingly at the floor. What was the point of praying to a God who never listened?

The following day, a Sunday, Anne took Johnny to Mrs Moynihan's. The station was crowded with the first batches of child evacuees. Orderly crocodile lines were shepherded on to trains, many of the children carrying their belongings in makeshift haversacks made of pillow cases, and all with gas masks strung across their shoulders in cardboard boxes. Some cried at leaving their parents, some stood round-eyed and confused by the strange event, while others appeared excited by the new adventure.

What was left of the family sat nervously listening to Chamberlain's speech on the recently acquired wireless. In a flat, uninspired voice, he informed the country that Britain and France had demanded Germany's withdrawal from Poland, and Chamberlain had sent an ultimatum that unless Hitler withdrew at once Britain would declare war. Hitler had ignored the ultimatum. Britain was at war.

Hardly was the broadcast over than the air raid siren began its mournful wail.

Mary screamed: 'Mother of God! Already!'

'Keep your head, woman,' Walter ordered harshly. 'Get into the shelter. That's what it's for!'

They rushed outside and piled into the dank-smelling corrugated iron shelter. Mary, Walter and Della sat on the two makeshift benches down each side, while Billie hunched on the lower bunk at the back, his head bowed to avoid hitting the upper bunk.

Walter was angry. He should have been on duty at the ARP. 'Damn and blast!' he shouted. 'I was supposed to be trained as a fire- watcher by now, and I'm still filling blasted sandbags. Maybe this'll give them a shove.'

'Aye, it looks like this is it,' Billie said. 'People have been saying we'd be the first to get it. It seems they were right. The Germans have been here and seen it for themselves. There's plenty of important targets. I must have been batty to think it still might not happen.'

Della turned on him. 'Can't you see Mam's upset enough? If you can't say anything cheerful, keep your mouth shut.' She was surprised by her own sharp tone. That was the first time since Jerry's death her voice had come out in more than a dull monotone.

'All right! Keep your wool on,' Billie snapped back.

'Stop it, both of you,' Mary ordered tersely. 'And while you're sitting there arguing, do you realise we forgot the gas masks?'

'I'll get them.' Billie made a lunge for the opening before Mary could stop him.

'Dear Lord! He shouldn't have gone out,' she cried. But in seconds he was back, carrying the pile of cardboard boxes that were stored in the scullery. 'In future, everybody keep their own beside them, even in the house,' Mary said grimly.

They sat in tense silence, ears strained, listening for the drone of an engine or the whine of a bomb – but no sound came. Then, what seemed only minutes later, a faint howl began in the distance, gradually growing to a monotonous, unmusical note.

'It's the all-clear!' Della cried.

Mary let out a deep breath of relief. 'Well, it's certainly a more cheerful sound than that awful wailing of the first one.'

'Let's get out of here. I'm not sure whether I'd rather be bombed or suffocated.' Walter made his way out of the opening and helped out the women. 'I'm off to the ARP now. I bet it's bloody chaos there.'

Mary pulled on his arm. 'But, Walter, nothing happened! There's nothing for you to do.'

'Well, at least I'll be there at the ready if the swine come back.' He shook off Mary's grip and marched down the path.

'Who's for a cup of tea, then?' Della enquired automatically as she reached the scullery.

Mary followed her. 'Everybody, I think, luv. I'll help you. I've got to check on that joint anyway.'

When they were seated at the table again, gas masks beside them, Billie was the first to speak. 'Well, this settles it. There's no point in waiting to see if it's a false alarm. They'll be conscripting with a vengeance now. I might as well go under my own steam tomorrow as be called up next week.'

Della's face fell. 'Oh, Billie, that soon!'

'Why aye, what's the difference?' He forced a grin. 'I've been thinking about the air force. Then we'll all have different uniforms. I don't want to look like our David or Wally.'

Head in hands, Mary listened in silent despair.

The following day, Billie joined the air force and Della, now feeling ashamed that she had sat at home and moped over Jerry's death for so long, signed up for courses to qualify to join the ARP. Mary and Anne had encouraged her, glad that at last she would get out of the house and be kept busy.

Anne had decided to remain at home, for the moment anyway, as one of them should stay with Mary during air raids. The first raid had turned out to be a false alarm caused by someone mistaking a flight of British aircraft for an enemy bomber squadron. Everyone was relieved. At least the Germans hadn't started on the North-East as had been feared.

Like most housewives, Mary stood in queues to add

to her stockpile of sugar, flour, tea, and non-perishable items. The air-raid shelter was now equipped with pillows, grey army blankets, and a Primus camping stove. Though risky, it would be welcome during long, cold nights. For inner warmth, Mary had provided a kettle, tins of cocoa and milk, and candles. Still not satisfied that she'd thought of everything, she added biscuits, Mars bars and boiled sweets to the emergency store. Although Della and Walter expected to be working during air raids, provision had to be made for their using the shelter in an emergency.

That evening Della attended her first lecture at the Drill Hall, along with about ten older women and a dozen or so girls of her own age. A similar number of men sat at the opposite side of the crowded room and, despite herself, Della smiled. Just like school again, she thought – the boys separated from the girls.

The middle-aged Drill Sergeant sounded very self-important. This was his first lot of recruits since the war had become a fact. His job was the real thing now. Briefly he spoke of the various branches of the ARP, and Della wondered whether she should become a warden, a roof-spotter or a fire-watcher.

As she left the Drill Hall, a depressing drizzle began to fall. She moved unsurely through the unaccustomed blackness, which the heavily shaded street lamps seemed to emphasise rather than relieve. No warm, friendly lights shone through the blacked-out windows. She shuddered, and then on impulse turned back towards the church. She entered its dim interior, dipped her hand in the holy water and made the sign of the cross before kneeling in a pew near the back.

She prayed aloud: 'Please, God, *do* something this time. Don't let it happen. Please, stop the war now. I'll stop feeling sorry for myself. I'll come back to church. And . . . and I'll forgive Jerry's father. Just, please, don't let my brothers be killed, and please let my mam and dad and Anne and Johnny be all right. Please, God. Please, please, God – no war.'

Tears ran in rivulets down her face while she uttered her childish prayer. As she stood up wearily and made the sign of the cross before leaving, a hand from the darkened pew behind her touched her arm. She jumped, startled. In the dim light sat an old woman holding rosary beads.

'I hope God answers your prayer, hinny,' the old, cracked voice whispered in the still silence. 'We're all prayin' for the same thing. I haven't got any of me own to pray for, I lost them in the last war, so I'll pray for yours, pet. God bless you.'

'Thank you.' Fresh tears fell as Della continued on her way out. Outside the door, she stopped and chastised herself. Hadn't she just told God she'd never feel sorry for herself again? But no, this time she wasn't crying for herself, but for that lonely, sad old woman. She'd lost her family in the last war – the war to end all wars – and now, only twenty-one years later, the country was on the brink of repeating the same insanity.

Forcing her feet to move, she shuffled home as if trudging through sand, deep in thought. Selfish, arrogant, immature creature that she was, praying as she used to pray for special toys on Christmas Eve! Did she really think that God would agree to the ridiculous bargain she had made with him? As if a war could be stopped by her promising God not to feel sorry for herself if she got what she wanted! And while she'd been muttering her infantile, egocentric prayer, that poor old woman, who'd already lost everything, was praying for the rest of the world. Della clenched her fists in her pockets. She must use what energy she had to help others, not waste it on self-pity. Well, she comforted herself, she'd made a start by joining the ARP.

★ ★ ★

She was surprised to find Michael and Ellen seated on the sofa when she arrived home. 'Hello, you two. I didn't know you were coming tonight,' she greeted them.

'We just popped in to see how you all are and to tell you our news,' Michael said.

Della sighed. 'I hope it's good news. We haven't had much of that lately.'

'Well, some of it is,' Ellen said, smiling. 'We're going to have a baby.'

While thinking what a terrible time to bring another child into the world, Della tried to enthuse. 'Oh, that's wonderful, Ellen! When?'

'February . . . I'm just three months. We've been waiting to tell you till we were sure.' She looked just a little plumper than before and her freckles seemed to stand out more than usual against her pale skin.

Della thought she didn't look well. 'All right, that's the good part! What's the bad?' she asked apprehensively.

Michael looked sheepish. 'I'm joining the army.'

'You're leaving Ellen!' Della sat heavily on the sofa arm.

'Aye, I know, but Ellen understands.' Nevertheless Michael gave his wife an anxious look. 'I just wouldn't feel right if I shirked my duty. I mean, now that Billie's done it, I can't be the only one left out. And, anyway, Ellen's going to stay with her mam, so she won't be lonely. And I'll most likely be back before her time's up,' he added with bravura.

'Well, that's all of you off now,' Walter said, lighting a Woodbine. 'I never thought I'd make such a great contribution to the war effort – even Della. How was the ARP then?'

She shrugged. 'A bit disorganised – just an introductory lecture. I didn't really learn much. How was your meeting?'

'Filling bloody sandbags again.' Walter exhaled a cloud of smoke through his nostrils. 'I hope they'll sort themselves out.'

'Anything more on the news?' Della asked.

Michael nodded. 'Aye, the news on the Polish front sounds hopeful. They've recaptured two towns and pushed the Germans back into Germany. But they can't keep that up for much longer with cavalry.'

'But that's not all, Della,' Anne broke in, distressed. 'The Germans have torpedoed a passenger liner just off the Hebrides – one thousand, four hundred civilians going to Canada and no munitions on board. That's not warfare. It's massacre!'

Della looked stunned. 'Are they all dead?'

'No,' Billie volunteered. 'Those that weren't killed in the explosion managed to get into the lifeboats, but they still don't know the death toll.'

Mary stood up from her armchair and braced her shoulders. She couldn't take any more war talk tonight. 'Billie, you should have an early night, you've got to be up early in the morning. You'd better start as you'll have to go on. I'll make some cocoa.'

Della turned a stricken face to Billie. 'You're going in the morning!'

'Aye,' he said cheerfully. 'I had my medical today and I report at seven o'clock tomorrow. Aren't you lucky! Now you can have the big bedroom all to yourself.'

Chapter Twenty-Three

Just before Christmas, Dan and the others were released from prison. After two weeks of loafing about the house, going to the pub or the dog track, and generally getting on everyone's nerves except Anne's, Dan finally announced his intention of joining up.

It was after ten o'clock, and he had just arrived home from the pub. His stocky frame was leaner since his prison stay, and his ruddy face paler but, otherwise, as Mary put it: 'He was as full of himself as ever.'

'I've been talking to Tommy and we're both joining up in the morning,' he said importantly, as the family sipped their late night cocoa.

Anne's face blanched. 'But Dan . . . I . . . I thought you were going to find a job.'

'Aye, I was, but I've changed me mind.' He sat at the table and lit a cigarette.

'But why, Dan? You could get a job now with the war on. You said you could.' Anne's voice shook. Della, sitting next to her on the sofa, took her hand.

'Aye, I could, but I don't want to. I don't want another dead-end job. I want to see a bit of excitement after three bloody years shut away.'

'Excitement!' Mary cut in heatedly. 'Is that what you call it? Going off to likely get yourself killed! Don't you think it's high time you were a husband and father to your wife and child? You don't know what Anne's been

265

through these past three years . . . and now you're
going to run off and leave her again for some – excitement. You're over call-up age. You could do something
for the war effort at home and take some responsibility
for your family.'

'You keep out of it,' Dan snorted. 'It's none of your
business.'

'Our daughter *is* our business,' Walter said quietly,
though his mouth tightened and his eyes bored into
Dan's.

He turned to Anne. 'Will you keep your family out of
this, woman?'

'Please don't shout.' Nervously, Anne stood up.
'Let's go upstairs and discuss it quietly, Dan.'

'Aye, let's get out of here. I'm sick of your family
interfering in our business. But, anyway, there's nothing to discuss. I've made up me mind.' Dan marched
from the room and, as Anne followed, she gave Walter a
pleading look to say no more.

'Well, if he goes, at least we'll have a bit of peace in
our own home again,' Walter said when they had gone.

Mary collected the dirty cups. 'As far as I'm concerned, I'll be happy if he goes tomorrow, but it's Anne
I'm thinking about. God only knows what she sees in the
man.'

'She loves him, Mam,' Della said uncomprehendingly. 'And she's happy with him.' As she uttered the
words, she couldn't help thinking how different she and
Jerry had been together, apart from Jerry's problem, of
course. She dragged her tired body up from the sofa.
'I'm off to bed, now. I've got an early start in the
morning.'

Having completed her ARP training, Della was now
taking driving lessons and day courses in first aid with
the St John's Ambulance Brigade. As well as her ARP

266

duties, she planned to get a day job at a hospital. With so many medical staff in the forces, hospitals were crying out for trained workers.

She had a little under one thousand pounds in the bank – what was left of Jerry's money and the money his mother had paid for the furniture. Della had offered it to Mary and Walter, who had adamantly refused it, though they accepted a weekly sum for her board and lodging.

The so-called 'phoney war' continued. Although rationing had begun, there was no shortage of food in the shops for Christmas and no shortage of gifts to buy. Many of the restrictions imposed earlier had now been lifted – the wireless had resumed live broadcasting instead of records interrupted by news bulletins, cinemas and dance halls had reopened, and there was a general feeling of unreality about the war.

Although pleased that people were beginning to go out and enjoy themselves again, Della restricted her social life to visiting Rose with Nora, or meeting them at the coffee rooms. She looked forward to such a visit to Rose's flat the following evening.

'Hello, luv,' Rose greeted her with a hug. 'Come on in. Nora's just arrived.'

'How are you?' Della returned the hug warmly.

'Not so bad . . . how's yourself?'

Della grimaced as she hung her coat on the hallstand in Rose's elegant two-roomed flat. 'Tired!'

Nora grinned as Della entered the sitting-room. 'You're late! We started without you.' She indicated the glass in her hand.

'We're on gin and lime,' Rose shouted from the kitchen. 'That all right?'

'Fine.' Della threw herself back into one of the velvet armchairs by the fire.

'Here you are, luv.' Rose thrust a glass filled with green liquid into Della's hand.

'Thanks!' Della took a sip. 'Phweew! A bit strong, isn't it?' She placed the glass warily on the side-table.

'Yep! We're celebrating.' Rose grinned and arranged herself comfortably on the sofa.

'Celebrating what?' Della asked.

'This!' Rose proudly thrust out her wrist, which was adorned with a heavy gold charm bracelet.

Della narrowed her eyes. 'Is it real?'

'Of course it's bloody real! And don't give me that famous look of yours. Jerry bought *you* presents before you were married.'

As always when Jerry's name was mentioned, a stabbing pain shot through Della. 'You know that was different, Rose. But anyway, it's your own business.'

'Business! Yes, that's what it's starting to look like,' Nora snorted. 'First of all free rent and furniture, now jewellery – next thing you know it'll be money.'

'Well, I wouldn't say no to that, either!' Rose said with a big smile. 'What's the difference?'

Della ignored the question. 'How *is* lover-boy anyway?'

'Fantastic! Fabulous! What else can I say?' Rose whooped, feigned a swoon, and almost spilled her drink on her white cashmere jumper.

Della thought it better not to mention the new jumper.

'Honestly,' Rose went on, 'I didn't know sex could be so good, and it gets even better every time. Bill's learned a thing or two in his time. And, you know what, I think I'm really beginning to fall in love with him . . . I mean, *real* love, not just infatuation.'

'Oh, Rose, I don't know if that's good or bad news,' Nora moaned.

'What do you mean?' Rose asked defensively.

'You know what I mean. When you love somebody you're more likely to get hurt. You've already been hurt once, and we don't want to see it happen again. We've never met this mystery man, so how can we know if falling in love with him's a good idea?'

'Oh, if that's all then you needn't worry,' Rose said complacently. 'He's a very nice person as well as being dishy and sophisticated and rich.'

Della attempted a second sip of her drink. 'Has he said how he feels about you?'

'Well,' Rose began thoughtfully, 'he says he misses me when he's in Durham, and he says he's never had it so good in bed as with me. That's a good start! I mean, he hasn't actually said anything soppy yet about being in love with me, but things are going the right way. And he's coming up to town more often than he used to. Doesn't that speak for itself?'

Nora indulged her. 'I suppose so. Phil hasn't actually said the three little words yet, but I know he loves me; he's just too shy to say it. I don't see much of him nowadays though, what with his overtime and my ARP duty.' She sighed and sipped her drink. 'We had a long talk the other night and I told him I was thinking of getting a factory job – there's plenty of work for women in munitions and there's more money in it than selling dresses.'

'Ugh!' Rose shuddered. 'You'd get your hands dirty. I'd rather stay where I am. And anyway, it's war work of a sort. Women need to doll themselves up for their morale.'

'Well, Phil's made me think twice about it anyway. He pointed out that if I went on shift-work and overtime we'd never have any time together, so I've decided to stay at the shop. At least I'm doing something useful at the ARP.'

'You're lucky Phil's doing war work, Nora – shifts or no shifts,' Della reminded her. 'At least he's not likely to be called up.' Then, frowning, she turned to Rose. 'Did you know Tommy and Dan are joining the army?'

'No! Since when?' Rose put down her drink in surprise.

'Since yesterday. Anne's very upset.'

'Oh, poor thing,' Nora said. 'The bugger's going to diddle off and leave her again. She might as well not have a husband at all.'

'Sometimes I think it would be better if she didn't,' Della said bitterly. 'He's nothing but trouble.'

'If it was me—' Rose started.

'*Were*,' corrected Della.

Rose ignored her and continued, 'I'd get shot of him anyway. Who wants a man who's nothing but a mill-stone round your neck? I think our Tommy's wife's stupid as well.'

'Well, there's no accounting for love, my mam always says,' Nora said.

Della looked at her watch and sniffed the air for signs of food. 'It's nearly seven o'clock and I'm starving. What are you cooking, Rose?'

She yawned. 'Oh, I couldn't be bothered to cook. I decided to have fish and chips, if you'll come with me. It gives me the creeps going out alone in this bloody blackout.'

'I thought you were going to practise on us so you could cook for Bill,' Della reminded her.

Rose yawned again and stretched. 'Aye, well, I will the next time. But if I start cooking too well, he might stop taking me out to dinner.'

'Oh Rose, you sod! I'm starving.' Nora stood up impatiently. 'Come on then, if we have to go out, let's get it over.'

'Cod and chips three times please – salt and vinegar,' Rose ordered at the fish shop counter, pulling out a half crown from her purse.

Della placed a restraining hand on her arm. 'Rose, put that away. You can't afford to treat us.'

'Who says?' She shrugged off Della's hand.

Della and Nora exchanged glances. Since her family's decline in fortune, Rose had been uncharacteristically careful with her money, and now suddenly she was splashing it about again.

'Are you thinking what I'm thinking?' Nora whispered behind Rose's back.

Della nodded unhappily. Maybe free rent and presents were acceptable, she thought, but somehow money was different. Was this man paying Rose for her services? And, if so, what did that make Rose? It didn't bear thinking about. But she was in love with him, surely that made a difference?

Chapter Twenty-Four

Listening to the news on the tenth of May, 1940, Della little realised how this event would change her life. Even as Churchill took over from the ineffective Chamberlain, the real war began. Hitler invaded Holland, Belgium and France.

A few days after the British retreat from Dunkirk, Della met Nora and Rose at the coffee rooms. She had changed into a blue wool dress topped by her best mackintosh, a present from Jerry. Her hair, released from its uniform cap, fell in loose waves to her shoulders.

Surprised, she saw Rose and Nora at their usual table with two soldiers, the insignia of the Northumberland Fusiliers on their uniforms.

'Hello, luv, you're late,' Rose said with a grin.

Nora's mouth smiled a greeting, but her eyes held a warning look.

The soldiers stood up. 'Allow me,' said one. He offered her his chair and, grabbing another from the next table, squeezed it next to hers. He was strikingly handsome, Della observed as she sat down. Despite the army haircut, his straight, ash blond hair was thick and luxurious, and the neatness of the haircut accentuated his fine bones. She blushed as their eyes met – his dark grey with a serious, almost haunted look.

'Della, this is Paul.' Rose indicated the one in question. 'And this is Andrew.' She fluttered her eyelashes at Andrew, a broad-shouldered, pleasant-faced boy, with laughing blue eyes and a ruddy complexion. His brown curly hair had obviously been attacked by the same barber as his friend's, giving him a clean-cut appearance. He looked more as if he had just stepped off a playing field than a battlefield.

'How do you do?' Della smiled at each of them, but her eyes lingered on Paul. His lean face, although smooth and unlined, had an air of sadness, as if he had seen too much horror for his age. This she estimated to be early twenties.

'How do you do?' the boys replied enthusiastically. Paul's smile was gentle, almost hesitant, while Andrew's seemed to split his face in two.

'I'm afraid we've rather gate-crashed your party,' Paul said, in a soft, educated voice. 'I hope you don't mind?'

'Of course not.' Della lowered her gaze.

'Waitress, another coffee, please.' Andrew bellowed to the same tired-looking, grey-haired woman who had served them coffee over the years.

'Paul and Andrew have just got back from Dunkirk,' Rose informed Della. 'They're on leave, so I thought we'd give them a treat.' She winked broadly. 'When they . . . er . . . accosted us, I opened my mouth to tell them we didn't talk to strange men, but they looked so lonely, I changed my mind.'

'You must be glad to be home after that nightmare,' Della said.

Andrew grinned again. 'You're not kidding! But it's not long enough.'

'How long have you got?' Nora asked.

'Three whole weeks,' Paul replied with a sigh of satisfaction. 'It seems like a heavenly eternity to me. I'm not looking ahead.'

Andrew put down his cap. 'How about you ladies

allowing us to take you for a drink after this? It's a bit
tame to start off our first leave with coffee. A little bird
told me the Douglass has just got its beer in.'

'Sounds fun.' Rose kicked Della under the table to
agree.

'Er, well . . .' she hedged.

'Oh, come on, Della.' Rose gave her another kick.
'You need a break from that sweatshop, and from the
flipping ARP. They'll survive without you if there's an
air raid.'

'All right,' she agreed reluctantly. The boys were both
nice, and both lonely. Why not keep them company for
an evening?

'*I* can't, I'm afraid,' Nora said. 'I'm going to Phil's at
eight o'clock. The poor thing's in bed with tonsillitis.'

Before leaving, the girls excused themselves to go to
the restroom, and Nora jumped on Rose. 'What the
blazes do you think you're doing, Rose, going off with
soldiers? What about Bill?'

'What about Bill?' Rose shrugged as she camouflaged
the freckles on her nose. 'He's in Durham; he never
comes on a Monday. For heaven's sake, Nora, we're just
going to have a drink with the lads, there's no harm in
that.'

'So long as that's all it is, Rose.' Nora's voice was
disapproving. 'You shouldn't be going out with other
men while Bill's keeping you.'

'He's not keeping me,' Rose pouted. 'I still work for
my living.'

'Not the living you've got, luv.' Nora frowned,
rearranging her green felt hat on her brown curls. 'Who
do you think you're kidding?'

Della flicked her comb through her hair. 'Nora's
right, Rose. I shouldn't be going out with them either.
But now we've got ourselves into it, we'll have to go —
just for a couple of drinks and then an early night,

mind you. I'm on duty in the morning.'

They walked to Clayton Street to the Douglass Hotel and made for the picture-panelled bar, only to discover that Andrew wasn't the only one to have got the word about the new beer supply. He pulled a face. 'It seems that little bird told the entire population of Newcastle.'

Undaunted, he and Paul pushed their way through the tightly packed bodies and found standing room in a back corner with space for two against the wall. They left the girls and elbowed their way to the bar, returning triumphantly with four pints of bitter.

'The best we could do.' Paul grinned apologetically as he handed the girls two foaming glasses and took up a stance facing Della.

'That's all right!' Rose reassured him. 'I learned to drink beer at the rugger club.'

But Della had never learned to like beer. 'Thank you. That's fine.' She grasped the handle of the pint mug awkwardly and stared in dismay at the contents. 'But I'll never be able to finish it.'

'Just do your best.' Paul's frank gaze was on her again, but this time his eyes held a slightly amused expression.

Again Della attempted to avoid his scrutiny, feeling even more uncomfortable than before. His body was so close to hers, they were almost at kissing distance. She looked around the room with feigned interest. The bar was noisy, and a thick blue smoke haze hung in the air. This intensified her resolve to make the evening short. The accordionist broke into *Run, Rabbit, Run*, and many of the customers joined in. It was difficult to make conversation.

'Cheers!' Andrew squeezed himself in opposite Rose and raised his glass.

'What do you do in the army?' Rose shouted above the din.

'We're gunners,' Paul obliged. 'We were both at technical college trying to become engineers before the army got us. We'd only done eighteen months. If we're lucky we'll finish when we get out.'

'I work at Binns.' Rose looked up at Andrew from under her eyelashes. 'And Della's a nurse during the day and works part-time for the ARP.'

Della shot her a withering glance. 'I'm not really a nurse. I've only got a St John's Ambulance certificate . . . but I have been thinking I might get my SRN after the war.' Having difficulty holding the heavy mug, she cradled it with both hands and, for the first time, Paul noticed her wedding ring.

'Is your husband in the war?' he asked quietly.

'No . . . he died . . . before the war.'

'Oh, I'm sorry.' His voice was sincere, although there was a look of relief in his eyes.

'That's rough,' Andrew said, 'to lose a husband so young.'

Paul looked more closely at Della. He had sensed there was something more to this girl than she gave away on the surface. She had obviously suffered a lot for one so young.

At the same time, Rose weighed up Andrew. She liked his cheerful smile and sense of humour. The other one was too serious for her liking. She gave Andrew a come-hither look. 'And what about you? Two handsome lads like you home on leave and no girlfriends?'

Andrew's pink cheeks coloured further. 'Oh, well, we do know girls, but nobody special at the moment.'

'I'll get another round before they run out,' Paul offered, noticing Andrew's empty glass. His own was almost finished and Rose was half-way through hers, but Della had only managed a few tentative sips. She put her hand over her glass and shook her head. He smiled.

She watched his tall, slim figure as he made his way to the bar. He was undeniably attractive. But what was she doing feeling attracted to another man only ten months after Jerry? She was shocked at herself. She would excuse herself early.

But the evening turned out to be pleasanter than she had expected. Andrew kept them entertained with an unending stream of jokes and anecdotes, and Della was surprised when the bar tender called 'time'. 'Good heavens!' she said. 'I'd no idea it was so late. I have to go.'

'I'll see you home,' Paul offered.

'Oh, no, you couldn't possibly in the blackout, and you'd never get back.'

'A soldier can always manage to get a lift.' He smiled, undeterred. 'A uniform has its advantages.'

'I'll take you home, Rose,' Andrew offered eagerly.

'Thanks, and if you're a good lad, I might offer you a real drink.' Rose smiled invitingly, squaring her shoulders to show off her bosom, encased in a tight, pointed brassiere under her clinging blue jumper. Andrew's eyes took in the bait appreciatively.

Paul put down his glass. 'We'd better make a move now, before the stampede starts.'

At the bus stop on Grainger Street a grey-painted trolley bus pulled up, its bumpers, fenders and mud-guards painted white to stand out in the dim blackout. Its headlights and interior glowed feebly, total blackout for transport having been abandoned due to a rash of accidents.

They went upstairs and Paul lit his umpteenth cigarette of the evening.

'Do you always smoke that much?' Della asked, at a loss for something to say now that they were alone.

'Since the war, yes. It's my main vice.'

'I'll have one with you,' she ventured, more for something to do than the desire for a cigarette.

'Oh, I'm sorry, I thought you didn't.' He pulled out his packet of Players and held it out.

Della took one and screwed up her nose. 'I don't really, but since I've been working at the hospital the other nurses have tempted me to join them occasionally.' Paul lit her cigarette and she inhaled cautiously. 'The first puff always make me a little giddy,' she admitted.

The ghostly journey was drawing to a close, and Della had to keep her eyes peeled in order to recognise her stop. 'This is it,' she cried, and Paul jumped up, politely descending the stairs ahead of her.

A fine drizzle hung in the air, and Della pulled up her coat collar as they alighted. Paul took her arm and guided her through the blackness, but hardly had they taken a few steps than the air-raid siren sounded.

'Oh, no!' Della wailed. 'And I'm supposed to be at the ARP tonight.'

'Is it far?' Paul asked urgently, as searchlights seared the sky. 'I could come and help.'

'It's about five minutes' walk to the Drill Hall, but I'm stationed at the school now. They park the ambulances in the school yard. That's a bit further.'

'Let's go! You lead.' He put his arm protectively around her waist and ushered her forward in the blackness.

As they neared the school yard, a loud thud and a screech of brakes sounded a few yards ahead.

'Oh, God!' Della cried 'It sounds like another blackout accident. Let's go.'

They hurried on till they came to a dark mass in the middle of the road. A burly male figure stepped out of a car.

'What's happened?' Paul asked as they ran towards him. 'Are you all right?'

'Aye, aye, I think so,' the man said in a hoarse voice, 'but I . . . I hit something.'

'There's a bike, to the right of the car.' Paul pointed to what appeared like a heap of scrap metal in the gloom.

They strained their eyes until Della saw a dark shape sprawled on the road a few yards ahead. 'Here,' she shouted, running towards the figure. 'Are you all right?' But as she knelt by the victim, she knew the question was superfluous. The face was covered in blood, and one arm and one leg stuck out at unnatural angles.

'I . . . I can't move.' It was a young boy's voice.

'It's all right,' Della soothed, removing her mackintosh and laying it over him. 'Don't try to move. I'm going to get an ambulance and take you to hospital.'

'God in heaven!' the car driver cried. 'I hit a lad! Dear God, he must have been thrown ten yards.' He pressed his fingers to his temples in agitation. 'I was in a hurry to get home to the shelter so I was sticking to the white line. He must have been doing the same coming the other way.' He groaned and covered his face with his hands.

'Don't worry,' Paul said. 'It's not your fault, it's this bloody blackout.' He turned to Della. 'You go and get the ambulance. I'll get the car off the road before anybody else cops it, and I'll keep an eye on him.' Taking off his tunic, he placed it over Della's mackintosh. The figure underneath moaned pitiably.

'Right! I should only be a few minutes.' She hurried in the direction of the school.

'Here, take mine an' all.' The driver unbuttoned his coat and handed it to Paul, who laid it on top of the moaning heap.

Paul took charge. 'We'd better get the bike out of the

way first, and then move the car.' He lifted the mangled mess and propped it against a garden wall before peering at the car bonnet. 'It's got a big dent. See if you can get it started.'

The driver climbed in and turned the ignition key. Nothing happened.

'Try again,' Paul urged. Again nothing. 'Once more while I push.' He felt his way along the side of the car to the rear. A heavy Ford, it took every ounce of his strength to inch it forward, but still the ignition made no sound. 'All right, get out,' he said, defeated. 'Do you feel up to helping me push?'

'Aye, I'm all right, mate. I think I just knocked me head a bit on the windscreen. It's that poor lad there I'm worried about.' There was a catch in the man's voice. 'Heaven help me! I hope I haven't killed him.'

He joined Paul at the rear of the car and together they heaved it close to the kerb. Paul, still breathing heavily from the effort, took out his pocket address book. 'I'll stay with the boy; you'd better go and ring the police to move that car and report the accident. What's your name and address?'

'Jack Delaney, 24 Croft Avenue – just a couple of hundred yards away. There's a telephone kiosk at the bottom of the street.'

'Good!' Paul knelt again beside the boy and assured him the ambulance was on its way.

A few minutes later, Della pulled up in an old baker's van converted to an ambulance. She jumped out and opened the back doors for a stretcher. 'How is he?' she called.

'Moaning a lot, poor lad.' Paul ran to help with the stretcher. 'They let you drive alone?' he asked in surprise.

'I told them I had a helper.'

Together they eased the boy on to the stretcher and

gently carried him to the ambulance, Della panting under the dead weight.

'I'll drive! You stay with him.' As Paul made for the front of the van, thuds resounded in the distance and faint lights glowed in the sky. Della quickly climbed into the back of the van and crouched, holding the boy's hand.

'They sound pretty far away. It could be Gateshead,' Paul gasped as he hoisted himself into the driver's seat.

Della made a wry attempt at humour. 'No, it couldn't be. Hitler said if he dropped anything on Gateshead it would be soap flakes.' In the dim light of the makeshift ambulance, she dabbed the boy's bloody face with a damp cotton wool swab. He winced and moaned at each stroke. 'It's all right,' she soothed. 'I'm just cleaning you up a bit before we get you to the hospital so they can see better where you're hurt. We'll be there in five minutes.' As she spoke, more whistles and thuds rent the air.

'Doesn't sound like soapflakes to me,' Paul said grimly. He peered forward, his head almost touching the windscreen, and pressed the pedal down as hard as he dared in the dark.

About a mile from the hospital, the van jerked, then spluttered, then died.

'Damn and blast!' Paul attempted the ignition again – his reward a single shudder followed by silence. 'Looks like the battery's gone.' He banged his fists against the steering wheel in frustration. 'Of all the bloody times!'

'I've had this van before,' Della said miserably. 'There's something wrong with the wiring. They said they'd had it repaired.'

'Repaired, my foot! Is there a torch?'

'Between the seats.' Della gripped the boy's hand as his groans grew louder.

Paul grabbed the torch and jumped out. He lifted the

282

bonnet and, carefully shading the torch with his hand, directed the beam inside. 'Right! Loose connection,' he grunted after a few minutes. 'Could you leave him for a while and hold the torch for me.'

Della smoothed the boy's forehead and spoke casually. 'It's all right. I'm only leaving you for a moment. We've got a loose wire. We'll have you at the hospital in a jiffy.' She jumped out of the back door and felt her way along the side of the van. 'To think I was glad the roads were deserted,' she said forlornly as she took the torch from Paul. 'If only another car would pass, we could get him to hospital.'

'Let's hope another car doesn't pass,' Paul said as he fumbled with the wiring. 'We don't want another accident.'

Della shuddered and gripped the torch more tightly. She realised just how vulnerable they were.

After a few seconds, Paul grunted with satisfaction. 'I think I see it. I'm going to need some pliers.'

'There should be some in the van. I'll get them.' Della shielded the torch and groped between the seats. Miraculously, she found the pliers.

'I'd like to know who repaired this,' Paul said as he grappled with the wiring.

Della sighed. 'It's the same old story. We can't get new parts. We have to keep on re-using the old ones until they give up completely.'

'Got the bastard!' Paul slammed down the bonnet. 'Thanks, Della. You'd better get back to your patient.'

When Della climbed in the back, the moaning had stopped. 'He's unconscious,' she said. 'But it's probably just as well for the moment. At least he's not suffering.'

After delivering the boy to the emergency department, Della climbed into the driver's seat. 'Where do you live? I'll take you home.'

'Oh, no! I'm taking *you* home,' Paul said firmly, grabbing her by the waist and lifting her down. 'Get in the other side.'

'But you'll never get back without a car! Please . . .'

'If you think I'm going to let you drive this wreck home in the middle of an air raid, you're crazy.'

Defeated but grateful, Della slumped in the passenger seat. 'We'll have to take the van back to the school. I'm still on duty.'

'Rubbish! If they've been sitting on their backsides in the shelter all this time, let *them* take over. You've had enough for one night.'

Della gave in. 'All right, but we'll still have to drop off the van first. It's only five minutes' walk home.'

After delivering the van, they hurried home on foot, Paul's arm protectively round her waist. The thuds sounded closer now.

At the house, she led him to the shelter. 'In here.' She fumbled for the torch Mary kept by the opening and climbed down. Paul followed.

'Where's your family?' he asked, crouching on the lower bunk.

Before answering, Della lit the candles and threw a blanket over his blood- and rain-soaked tunic. 'My brothers are all in the war, my father's at the ARP, and my married sister joined the Land Army in Hexham after her son was evacuated.'

'What about your mother?'

'She looks after the old lady next door during air raids. Her husband died at Christmas and she fell to pieces and developed nervous asthma. She has an attack every time the siren goes. My mother's a saint; she doesn't even like the old woman – nobody does. It's ironic! We built the shelter for the family and now there's no family to use it.' As she spoke, Della pumped the Primus stove.

'Here, let me do that.' Paul attempted to rise from his cramped position and hit his head on the upper bunk.

'No, you sit down,' Della said firmly. 'It's temperamental. I know how to deal with it. I'm making some cocoa and there's a tin of biscuits and some chocolate underneath that bunk.'

'Well, you think of everything. I'm starving.' But before he reached for the biscuits he put his blanket around Della's shoulders. 'Your mac's had it.'

She looked down ruefully at the stained mackintosh. 'It goes with the job.'

He got himself another blanket and sat watching her, chewing thoughtfully on a Mars bar. 'You're quite a girl, Della,' he murmured after a while.

She blushed at his tone. 'Oh, everybody's doing what they can,' she said lightly. 'I'm nothing special.' She changed the subject. 'I'm afraid it's condensed milk.'

'That's fine.' He still watched her. Her hair was wet and tousled, her face grimy, her eyes tired, and yet he thought he had never seen anyone so beautiful.

'Here you are.' She handed him a steaming mug and sat beside him.

With his free hand he took hers. 'You're freezing!'

'I'm always cold,' she laughed, withdrawing her hand self-consciously. 'My mam always says I'll get chilblains from standing too close to the fire. Have a biscuit.' She picked up the tin so that he couldn't take her hand again.

He took a shortbread and bit into it while looking at her closely with his fathomless grey eyes. 'I think you're the most beautiful and the most wonderful girl I've ever met, Della.' She concentrated on drinking deeply from her mug. 'Do you mind my saying that?' he asked, suddenly rather awkward. 'I . . . I mean, I know it can't be all that long since you lost your husband . . . you're so young.'

'It's not quite a year,' Della said before again changing the subject. 'Have another biscuit.'

We waved his hand. 'No, thanks. That Mars bar did the trick. Wonderful cocoa, though. I'm warming up from the inside out.'

'That's why Mam insisted on the kettle and hot drinks, but this is the first time they've been useful. We haven't had any bad raids to speak of so far. Please God it keeps up.'

Paul opened his mouth to say something but changed his mind as the siren began to wail.

'Oh, listen!' Della cried, relieved. 'It's the all-clear.'

'Thank God for that.' Paul took a deep breath. 'When we're out there fighting, we think we're the only ones in the middle of it. I see now that it's not so cushy being at home either.' He paused for a moment, his eyes searching hers again. 'I . . . I suppose I'd better go now, then.'

Della put a restraining hand on his arm. 'Would you mind waiting a few minutes? Mam will be putting Mrs Bowman to bed. She'll be back in a minute. I . . . I'd rather she didn't know you were here,' she finished, embarrassed.

'Of course.' He relaxed again and leaned towards her. 'Della,' he began softly, 'I desperately want to see you again. Are you doing anything for the next three weeks? I can't think of anyone I'd rather spend my leave with.'

She laughed. 'The next three weeks! That sounds like a long invitation.'

'I'd like to see you whenever you're free . . . would you?'

'Well, I'm free after six tomorrow.' She smiled. 'Is that all right?'

His shoulders dropped with relief. 'It's a start. I'll work on the rest tomorrow. Shall I come and pick you up?'

'No,' she said hastily. 'Meet me straight from the hospital.'

'The General?'

'Yes.'

'Then I'll meet you outside the main entrance.'

'Oh, I hope that poor boy's all right,' Della sighed.

'Well, however he is, he's a lot better than he would be if you hadn't crossed his path.'

'Sshh!' she warned, as Mary's footsteps sounded down the path. The door creaked open and closed. 'She's inside. You can go now.' Della again felt embarrassed by her childish subterfuge. Why should she feel guilty about being with a man tonight? It wasn't as if they had done anything wrong and, together, they had probably saved someone's life.

Paul bent and kissed her lightly on the mouth. 'I'm looking forward to tomorrow, Della. What time?'

'Time?' she asked, still feeling as though his lips were against hers. 'Oh, yes, I get off at six.' She pulled away and removed the cover from the shelter opening.

Paul climbed out and helped her up, standing for a second holding both her hands. 'Till tomorrow,' he whispered, before disappearing into the darkness.

Andrew helped Rose off the bus. 'You're lucky to live on the moor and so close to town,' he said as they reached her door.

'Yes, it's almost like living in the country.' Rose turned the key in the lock. 'Oh, bother! It's stuck.'

'Let me try.'

She handed him the key. 'It's never stuck before.'

'No, and it's not stuck now either. You forgot to lock it, and you left the hall light on as well. That's not doing your bit for the war effort.' Andrew stepped back politely to let Rose enter first.

Her jaw dropped as Bill's elegant, grey pinstripe-clad

figure loomed in the sitting-room doorway. 'Bill,' she gasped. 'I wasn't expecting you tonight.'

'Obviously not!' His blue eyes were fixed in a steely gaze on the uniformed figure behind her.

'Oh, er . . .' Rose paused, swallowing audibly. 'This is Andrew. He just came in for a cup of cocoa. He's got a long walk home.'

Andrew coughed uncomfortably.

'And where the hell do you think you've been?' Bill demanded icily. 'I've been here since six o'clock.'

Rose wished she could die. 'I . . . I . . . just went out for a coffee with the girls.'

'Well, why don't you bring your girlfriend in?' Bill said in a mocking tone.'

'Oh, Andrew just walked me home because of the blackout,' Rose said lamely, while Andrew shuffled his feet in embarrassment.

'It's all right about the cocoa,' he said, backing out of the door. 'I'll be off now.'

'Oh, thanks for seeing me home, then.' In her haste, Rose almost shut the door in his face.

'I see,' Bill said, returning to the sitting room and pouring himself a whisky. 'So this is what you do when I'm not here.'

'No, it isn't, honestly, Bill.' Rose flung her coat and hat on the nearest chair arm and sat down to get off her trembling legs. 'It's not what it looks like. I *did* go out for a coffee with the girls – I swear it. A couple of soldiers chatted us up and we were sorry for them, that's all.' She gave him a pleading look.

'You stink of beer, woman,' Bill snarled as he stalked past her to the sofa.

'Well, after the coffee rooms we went to the Douglass and had a couple of drinks. We were sorry for them – they were so lonely.'

'And you brought one home so he wouldn't be lonely

all night,' Bill said sarcastically before knocking back his whisky.

Rose was afraid. They'd never had a real row over anything serious, but she knew this apparent self-control wasn't natural to him. Her voice trembled as she explained, 'No, Bill, he was just going to have a drink and then go.'

'Oh, a drink now! I thought it was cocoa,' he spat, returning to the sideboard for more whisky.

'Please, Bill, honestly. I've never been out with anyone or had anyone here, I swear. Please believe me.'

'Give me one good reason why I should.' He returned to the sofa with his glass. Though his face was rigid, his thin black moustache twitched in anger. 'You'd been with plenty before me. How the hell do I know what you get up to when I'm not here?'

At the insult, Rose forgot her fear and shot back at him: 'I don't get up to anything! But nobody would blame me if I did. You leave me on my own too much. All I ever do is see my girlfriends and wait for you to deign to pay me a visit. Why can't we be together all the time, when you're in Durham as well? Then you'd know for sure I wasn't playing around.'

Bill took on the guarded expression he wore whenever she suggested this. 'You know damn' well I live with my mother,' he blustered. 'I could hardly have you living under her roof.'

'We could get married.' Rose pouted, nevertheless pleased that she had reversed the situation, and that Bill was now on the defensive.

'And you know what I think about marriage and all,' he threw at her, rising for yet another drink.

Rose chewed on her lower lip. She was determined to break down his aversion to marriage sooner or later, but her instinct told her now was not the time. 'Well,' she said slowly and deliberately, 'if you don't want to marry me and be with me all the time, you'll just have to run the risk of my finding someone else who does.' She raised her chin and looked into his handsome face, now flushed with anger and whisky. He lowered his steely blue eyes, as he always did when she mentioned marriage, and Rose breathed a silent sigh of relief that she had turned an awkward situation to her advantage. Although the time was not appropriate to push him further about marriage, she could at least close the argument over Andrew. 'Honestly, Bill, I haven't been out with anyone since I met you, and that's the God's honest truth about what happened tonight.'

Bill stared hard into his glass before taking another gulp. He was angry with himself that this chit of a girl had such a hold over him; he didn't want to lose her, but he didn't want any more talk of marriage either. She was right. He'd have to run the risk of her finding someone else. But she might be telling the truth about that schoolboy-faced soldier. He would let the matter drop. 'All right! Let's forget it – this time.' He again emptied his glass.

Emboldened now, Rose sat beside him on the sofa and put her hand on his knee. 'You know I love you, Bill. There hasn't been anyone else in my life since I met you.'

He took her hand. 'Well, just keep it like that,' he slurred. 'I'm not keeping you here for the good of other men.'

'Keeping me?' she queried, remembering Nora's words. 'Is that how you look at it? I thought you were good to me because you love me?' She gazed at him with questioning eyes.

'Well, you know I do.' He eased his arm about her shoulders. 'Why else would I do it? It's easy enough to find girls in Newcastle, especially with a war on. You know you're special to me, Rose.' Again he cursed himself inwardly as he made this admission. He'd never been satisfied with only one girl before. Rose did hold something special for him, and he didn't like the feeling of being so bound to her; he needed her physically as he'd never needed any woman.

'But you never actually say you love me, and you never want to discuss marriage. If you love me, why don't you want to marry me?' Now that she'd won the battle, Rose forgot her resolution not to mention marriage again.

Bill sighed impatiently. 'You know I'm not the marrying type, Rose. I've got all I want with you. And that's that!'

'But it's not enough for me,' she wailed. 'Oh, it *was* at first. It was exciting waiting for you coming, and having our own flat, but now it's just not enough, Bill. I want to be with you more. I spend night after night on my own here.'

'I know, Rose,' he reassured her quickly. 'What if I try to get up to town more often? I came today mainly because I wanted to see you. I just did a little business this afternoon to justify the trip.' He half smiled, chucking her chin and kissing her.

She kissed him back fiercely and he eased her down on the sofa, his hands gripping her breasts through the soft wool jumper till she moaned with pain and pleasure. She unbuttoned his shirt and ran her hands over his hairy chest – he was so manly. All Jim had ever had on his chest was an occasional pimple. Bill pulled up her sweater as she kissed his chest and then, in a second, they were tearing off each other's clothes until they were naked.

'Let's go to bed,' Bill said urgently, picking her up and carrying her to the bedroom.

At that moment the siren sounded.

'Damn and blast!' he cried.

'Oh, let's forget the bloody siren,' Rose said hoarsely, carried away with desire. Bill, equally out of control, laid her on the bed and threw himself over her. The wailing accompaniment and the danger incited their desire and they made love feverishly.

'Oh, Bill, Bill!' Rose cried, as their passion finally mounted, and the weight of his body on hers became limp.

They lay panting and speechless, until he eased himself off her with a groan and lay on his back. 'Oh, God, that was stupid. I got carried away. I had too much to drink. Why didn't you stop me?'

'*I* couldn't stop either,' Rose whispered. 'It was so fabulous to feel *you* instead of a damned sheep's gut – just for once.'

'Well, we can't risk it any more. If I lose my head again, promise me you'll stop me?'

Rose grinned in the darkness. 'You'll have to promise to stop *me* and all. I'd no idea it would feel so different – so marvellous.' She snuggled up to him contentedly and giggled. 'What a way to spend an air raid! And all those poor sods out there sitting shaking in their shelters.' As she spoke, she wondered if Della and Paul had got home before the raid.

That night, Anne and the two other land girls on the farm went to the local, about three miles outside Hexham, with their employer and his younger brother.

The elder, Bob, was a typical farmer – about thirty-five with clear blue eyes, a ruddy complexion, and a moon face below his reddish hairline, which was beginning to recede. The younger, however, looked incongruous in his blue dungarees. He was tall but of slighter build, with dark, mocking eyes, a full mouth beneath his neat, black moustache, and a thatch of black hair. Colin was only three years younger than his brother, but there could have been a decade between them. He was gay and outgoing, his brother serious and shy. Why neither was married was a mystery to all the land girls.

Anne sipped a shandy in the lounge while, in the next room, the two men taught the other girls to play billiards. She couldn't join in the game. Her right forefinger was bandaged from a cut she had received sharpening the kitchen scissors.

Colin's musical country brogue surprised her. 'You look lonely out here. Would you like another drink? How about something stronger than a shandy?'

'No thanks, this is fine. If I drink anything stronger I shan't be able to get up in the morning.'

He sat down and coaxed her further. 'Come on, you need to relax after the day you've put in today. You're one of the best workers we've ever had, you know. And when I first saw you I thought you were just a little sparrow; you didn't look strong enough to wield a soup ladle, never mind a pitch fork.'

Anne smiled. 'My mam always says there's good stuff in little bundles.'

'Aye.' He sat down, weighing her up. 'But it's more than that. You look ten times healthier than you did when you came from the city . . . and a lot bonnier, if you don't mind my saying so. In fact, you're one of the bonniest lasses I've seen for a long time.'

Anne flushed and her blue eyes shone. 'Thank you. I've never had such a compliment.' She was aware that Colin had been watching her for some weeks, and had to admit she felt pleasure whenever she sensed his gaze on her.

'How's your little lad doing?'

'He's fine. I saw him on Sunday. He's thriving in the country as well. Maybe I'm doing the wrong thing bringing him up in Newcastle.'

Colin's eyes held hers. 'And how about the old man? Had any word yet?'

'No,' Anne replied lightly, trying not to show her concern. 'Still no letter and I still don't know where he is. That's just the way he is. He doesn't like writing letters. But I write to him care of Catterick. I know he's not there any more, but they don't return the letters so they must send them on.'

'He's a lucky man to have you to come home to.' Colin's eyes were still on her.

Embarrassed, Anne changed the subject. 'Maybe I will have a drink after all. Perhaps a sherry – if they've got any.'

'Good! I'll have another half as well. They'll be calling time any minute.' He rose and strode on his long legs to the bar.

'Thank you,' Anne said, as he returned and placed a glass of sherry before her. 'I didn't think they'd have any.'

Colin grinned. 'It pays to be a local. I've known the barman since I was a lad. Cheers!' He raised his beer and put it down, saying urgently: 'I've been wanting to ask you for a while, Anne, but it's hard to get you alone with the girls always about. Would you go out with me? I know you're married, but there's no harm in going to the pictures or out for a drink or something. You must get awfully bored spending all your free time upstairs with the girls.'

'Not really,' she said guardedly. 'I've never been one to go out much.'

'But don't you like the pictures?' Colin insisted, his beer forgotten on the table.

'Yes, of course. I just don't go often.'

'Well, it's about time you did. The pictures tomorrow night then? *Alexander's Ragtime Band*'s on at Hexham. It's Tyrone Power and Alice Faye. I bet you can't resist

Tyrone Power?' He grinned and his teeth sparkled white against his dark, weather beaten skin.

Anne melted. 'You've twisted my arm.'

'Good! We'll go straight after tea tomorrow.'

'Hey, you two!' a loud female voice assailed them. It was Nellie – fortyish, plump and still pretty in a blowsy sort of way. Her peroxided hair, showing darker at the roots, was a mass of little curls, which she spent hours crimping every night with curling tongs. Her more than generous mouth was painted a bright crimson, and her eyebrows plucked and pencilled almost half an inch above their natural line, adding a permanently startled expression to her face. She winked as she joined them. 'Not getting off, are you?'

'Of course we're getting off, Nellie,' Colin joked. 'What do you want to go and spoil everything for?'

Nellie grinned at Anne. 'Eey, well, I'm sorry to break up the party, luv, but the others is comin' in a minute. They've had enough o' billiards and it's nearly time anyway. We thought we'd go back to the house and hear the news before we turn in.'

Colin grinned. 'You should know my brother by now. The news'll be over by the time our Bob gives up his billiard cue.'

'Aye, well I prefer darts, mesel',' Nellie said. 'But you can never get near that bloody dart board. Them fellas has been on that game all night.' She indicated the dart score board with a nicotine-stained finger.

'Well, Nellie!' Colin put his arm jovially round her shoulders. 'I can't refuse you anything. Why don't we go back to the house and have a game?'

'You're on!' She stood up and shouted to the others; 'Come on you lot, we're going to have a game of darts at the house. Drink up! It'll be "time" in a minute anyway.'

Through the downpour that had fallen relentlessly all day, the group finally made a dash for Bob's battered old Jowett. Nellie dived into the front beside Bob. 'My turn to sit in the front,' she announced. 'I'm tired of being squashed in the back with them two.'

Beryl groaned as she climbed in the back. 'Bloody rain! I'm sick of it.' She was about Nellie's age but, unlike her, took no trouble to hide it. Her cropped brown hair was turning grey, and her skin, devoid of make-up, had the appearance of crepe paper from exposure to the weather. Only her clear, twinkling brown eyes remained youthful, together with her outlook on life. Her sense of humour never let her down. She hiccuped loudly. 'Ah, well, it's not so bad gettin' soaked outside so long as you're soaked inside first.'

Bob sank heavily into the driver's seat and wiped the windscreen with his sleeve. 'Aye, well, I hope you've dried out inside by the morning. You're not getting any more time off for your so-called head-aches.'

'Aw, stop preachin', man.' Beryl made a face at Bob's back, confident in the knowledge that he couldn't see her.

Anne climbed in next to Beryl, and Colin squeezed in on Anne's side. She was uneasily aware of his proximity and tried to inch closer to Beryl in case he could feel her trembling.

Suddenly the siren sounded faintly in the distance. 'Here we go again,' Nellie bawled. 'I wonder what the buggers is up to tonight. Some poor sods are gettin' it somewhere.' As she finished, a loud buzzing sounded overhead.

'Good God! It's planes!' Anne was unable to control her trembling now, and Colin took her hand reassuringly.

'No need to shake, lass. It's probably our own lads on their way somewhere. There's nowt out here for the Germans, unless they want a field of spring cabbages for their sauerkraut.'

Chapter Twenty-Five

At the hospital the following morning, a consignment of North-East soldiers who had been wounded at Dunkirk were transferred home. Della, wearing her blue uniform dress and starched white cap and apron, moved from bed to bed taking temperatures and pulses and giving bedpans, while the doctors sorted out the more seriously wounded from those who could be treated and returned home. As she reached the fourth bed, a soldier with a heavy bandage over one eye, the rest of his face pitted with small fresh shrapnel wounds, said, 'Hello, Della.'

Startled, she looked at the face more closely – the wide turned-up mouth, the brown, curly hair, one brown eye staring up at her. 'Jonathan!'

'We meet again.' He gave her the same boyish, lop-sided smile she remembered from that first meeting.

'Are you badly hurt?' she asked, picking up his wrist and taking his pulse in a businesslike fashion. She must not be seen wasting time chatting to soldiers while on duty.

'No, I got off lightly,' he replied quietly. 'A bomb dropped only a few feet from my mate. He got the lot; all I got was shrapnel.'

'In your eye?' she asked, concerned.

He nodded. 'They've taken some out already but there's still another piece lodged. I shan't lose my sight completely though, and I've still got the other one.' He grinned again. 'It's going to put me out of the war though.'

'You ought to be thankful for that,' she said briskly, sticking a thermometer in his mouth. 'Do you need a bedpan?' She felt embarrassed at having to do such a personal duty for someone she knew.

He shook his head and grinned even wider, still clutching the thermometer between his straight white teeth.

While Della waited to check his temperature, her eyes glued to her watch, Jonathan took her hand in his. Hastily, she withdrew it and removed the thermometer. 'Just a little high, but they'll be keeping you in for a while with that eye. Doctor will get to you shortly.' She scribbled on the chart at the foot of the bed and turned to the next patient.

'Della, don't go yet,' he said softly. 'I read about your husband. I'm very sorry.'

'Thank you.' She turned to him again, eyes lowered. 'It seems a long time ago now . . . with all this going on.' She indicated the rows of beds and felt an urgent need to change the subject. 'How's Vera?' she enquired, remembering the fur-clad china doll he'd been with at their last meeting.

'She's fine. We're engaged.'

'Congratulations! When's the happy day?' she asked politely.

'Oh, not till all this is over. War's no time to get married and start a family.'

'You're right there.' Della smoothed down her apron. 'If you'll excuse me now, I've got to get on.'

'It's a worthwhile job you're doing,' he said.

'It keeps me busy and makes me feel useful.' She moved again towards the next bed. Sister was giving her a curious look.

'Della!' Jonathan tugged at her hand. 'I know you've

got to get on with your work, but just answer me one question. Will you be on my ward?'

'I never know where they're going to put me next.'

'Well, if you're not on the ward, will you promise you'll come and see me?'

'All right, I promise. But if you don't let me get on now, I'm going to lose my job. Sister's got her evil eye on me.'

At lunch time Della had a bowl of soup at the cafeteria before enquiring at the desk for Jonathan's ward.

'Mr Maddison,' the receptionist repeated, running her pencil down her list. 'No, I don't see him.'

'He came in this morning,' Della insisted. 'It's Maddison with two "d"s. Are you looking in the right place?'

'Ah, *Dr* Maddison!' the girl said, as if a lamp had just been lit in her head. 'He's in staff, D1.'

Della knew Jonathan had gone into medicine but didn't realise he had qualified. She mused as she made her way to his ward: it was six and a half years since that party and he'd been going on eighteen then; he must be twenty-four now and very recently qualified. 'Hello, Dr Maddison,' she said, as she entered his room. 'You didn't tell me you were a doctor now. How are you?'

Grinning, he sat up in bed. 'OK for the moment. They're going to cut me up at three o'clock.'

She stood at the foot of the bed so he wouldn't be able to take her hand again. 'When did you qualify?'

'Just before the army grabbed me. They were civil enough to let me finish. I was hoping to do my internship before I went, either here or at the Infirmary, but I didn't manage it. I suppose I can pick up where I left off now.'

'Having a title certainly has its advantages,' Della remarked, looking around the single room.

Jonathan looked embarrassed. 'I wish they'd just put

me on the ward like everybody else.' He patted the bed for her to sit down.

She ignored the gesture. 'Don't complain. You'll be glad of the peace and quiet before long.'

'How's Rose? It's a shame she and Jim broke up, after all that time.'

'Don't worry, she's doing all right now. She's got a new boyfriend – a rich one. You know Rose!' Della's eyes danced mischievously as she thought how delighted Rose would be when she told her, knowing that the news of her rich boyfriend would reach Jim via Jonathan.

The door burst open and a harassed orderly rushed in with a tray. 'Your meal, Dr Maddison.' She plunked the tray on his knee and departed as fast as she'd entered.

Jonathan grimaced as he surveyed the contents of the two plates – glutinous mashed potato of a greyish hue; a heap of soggy cabbage; anaemic-looking gravy slopped over two slices of what passed for roast beef; and for dessert, a delicacy strongly resembling a suet dumpling drowned in curdled custard. 'Good God! How do they expect people to get well on this? I don't suppose you could smuggle me in something to wash it down?' He gave her a pleading look.

Della smiled as she made for the door. 'There's water by your bed. I've got to go now. I'm back on duty at one.'

'Thanks for popping in.' Another pleading look. 'Will you come again? I'm so bored lying here.'

'Of course. I'll look in tomorrow after your operation. Is there anything you'd like me to bring you from the outside world – apart from alcohol?'

He grinned wickedly. 'Don't be so starchy, nurse. Guinness is good for you.'

At six o'clock, Della changed into the smart beige

costume, white parachute silk blouse and black high heels she had arrived in. Paul was waiting at the main entrance.

'Hello, Della. You look very elegant,' he said shyly.

Della also felt shy on seeing him again. 'Thank you. I see you cleaned up your uniform.'

'I took it to the cleaners and they did it on the spot. I told you a uniform has some advantages.'

'Don't depend on it. What about the conchies?' Della felt her shyness disappearing. 'What shall we do?'

'Whatever you'd like. I expect you're tired after last night and working all day.'

'A bit,' she admitted.

'Then why don't we just have a quiet dinner and maybe a drink afterwards?'

'Sounds wonderful! I'm starving.'

'I know a little place down by the Bigg Market. It's not fancy, but I know it's still open and they serve good food.'

'I haven't had a meal out since before the war. Anything will be a treat.'

'There must be a bus due with all these people waiting,' Paul said hopefully as they reached the bus stop.

Della smiled at his innocence. 'Not necessarily! It's obvious this is your first time home since the war. All the services are deplorable now. But we still manage to get about.' As she spoke the trolley bus glided towards them.

'Upstairs?' Paul asked, taking her elbow and guiding her among the jostling passengers.

'Anywhere! So long as we can get on.'

On the platform, the conductor tried to control the eager crowd. 'Two left upstairs,' he yelled, placing his arm behind Della and Paul.

'That was lucky, and two together.' Della flopped

gratefully into the vacant seat at the back. It had been a hard day.

Paul sat beside her. 'Would you like one?' he offered, taking out his cigarettes.

'No thank you. Maybe later.'

'Fares, please,' the conductor bellowed as he climbed the stairs.

Paul fished in his pocket, but the beaming, wizened old man waved his hand in a gesture of dismissal. 'Nah, mate. Yours is on the bus company.'

'Er, thanks.' Paul was visibly embarrassed. 'I think I'll wear civvies from now on. I don't want special treatment.'

As they walked from the bus stop to the Bigg Market, Paul stopped outside an off-licence. 'Hang on a minute.' He disappeared into the shop.

Della, surprised to see the shop open at all, was even more surprised when Paul reappeared waving a bottle wrapped in brown paper.

'The restaurant's not licensed,' he explained, 'and Andrew tipped me about the shop. His uncle owns it. It's only Merrydown cider, but it's got a kick in it.'

'But can you do that – take your own, I mean?'

He grinned broadly. 'I just changed my mind about wearing civvies.'

The restaurant was small and intimate with clean white tablecloths, though the decor was shabby. They sat at an empty table in a corner and Paul placed the bottle on the table. The waitress, a large formidable-looking woman with an impatient expression, loomed over them with two menus.

'We can't serve drinks here,' she announced on seeing the bottle.

Paul smiled disarmingly. 'But we're not asking for drinks – just two glasses.'

She shrugged. 'What the hell! Why not? You might

as well enjoy yourself while you can.'

'Thanks.' Paul gave Della a triumphant look.

'Well, you certainly have changed your tune,' she rebuked him, smiling.

'Only because I want to make a toast to the most beautiful girl I've met since last night.'

The menu was simple and homely. Both chose Irish stew and trifle, afterwards sipping the last of the cider contentedly.

'Did you find out anything about the boy last night?' Paul asked, looking at her over the rim of his glass.

'Yes, I checked first thing this morning. He's got a nasty head wound, a broken arm and a broken leg, but they say he'll pull through.'

'Thanks to you,' he said with admiration in his eyes.

'And to you.' Della blushed under his gaze. 'I could never have fixed that wire.'

He changed the subject. 'Would you like coffee here and then we can go for an after dinner drink somewhere?'

'Yes, please,' she answered, already feeling a warm glow from the cider.

After coffee, they went to the Long Bar, opposite the station. It was quiet and dimly lit, unlike the cacophony and crowds of the Douglass the previous evening.

Della looked quizzically at Paul. 'You've been asking questions about me all evening. What about you?' She sipped the brandy he had set before her and coughed.

Paul smiled apologetically. 'Sorry it's not Courvoisier. I hope it's not for cooking only.'

'It's still better than beer.' Della grimaced and continued to probe relentlessly. 'You know, when people ask too many questions about others, it usually means they don't want to talk about themselves.'

'There's not much to tell, and what there is isn't very interesting,' Paul said, pulling a face. 'I don't want to

bore you but, if you insist – I was the youngest of eight.
My mother had me when she was forty-five and the
others were all working, so I was spoiled rotten. Their
money helped to put me through school – I went to the
Royal Grammar,' he explained. 'None of the others had
the advantage of a decent education, so they were all
determined I should. My mother worked in a fish shop
to help out. Dad was a fitter; he's retired now. I always
did a paper round, and I worked in the fields or at the
cannery during the holidays. After I left school I worked
at Camel Laird's for a couple of years as an apprentice
engineer and decided to speed up the process by going to
technical college. I'd saved up a bit by then. I was born
and brought up in Fenham, and there I still live. That's
it.' He picked up his glass. 'The rest you know.'

'You're ambitious,' Della observed.

He looked serious for a moment. 'You could say that.
I feel I owe it to my family to make a success of myself
after all they did for me, and I'd like to pay Mam and
Dad back financially in their old age.' As if to close the
conversation about himself, he looked at his watch. 'It's
almost time. Would you like another drink?'

'No, thank you. I'd better go now.'

'At your service.' He jumped up eagerly, ignoring the
remains of his drink.

The night air was cool as they walked from the bus
stop to Della's house, but tonight the sky was brilliant
with stars instead of search-lights.

At the gate, she stopped. 'Thank you for a wonderful
evening, Paul. I . . . I'd ask you in for coffee, but
Mam'll be waiting up for Dad. He's at the ARP.'

'That's all right. I've had coffee already anyway. But
I'd love another cup of cocoa and a Mars bar,' he added
softly. 'I thoroughly enjoyed our nightcap last night.'

She hesitated, then chuckled. 'You mean in the
shelter?'

'Why not? We ought to put it to some good use. And you couldn't refuse a uniformed man a cup of cocoa, could you?' He grinned and his white teeth flashed in the dark.

Della gave in and opened the gate. 'All right, but we'll have to be very quiet.

'I feel like a naughty schoolgirl,' she whispered, suppressing a giggle as Paul climbed into the shelter and helped her down.

He flashed the torch while she found the candles and lit the stove. As she finished, he sat munching on a Mars bar.

'My mam's going to wonder where all her stocks have disappeared to.'

'No problem,' he muttered with his mouth full. 'Just tell her it was the little boy next-door.' He stuffed the empty wrapper in his pocket. 'Now the evidence is hidden. But we left tracks last night; we forgot to wash up.' He indicated the dirty mugs on the floor where they had left them.

'Don't worry, there are two more clean ones. I'll have to sneak them in and wash them when Mam isn't looking.' Della gave up trying to suppress a smile. 'You know, I wish I *had* been a naughty schoolgirl. I must have missed out on a lot of fun.'

'It's not too late. Why not sin and have a Mars bar?'

'No thanks! That trifle finished me. The cocoa will be ready in a few minutes.' She smiled again, it suddenly occurring to her that she smiled a lot when she was with Paul. Her gaze returned to the kettle, which as yet showed not a single puff of steam.

'Why don't you come and sit down?' Paul said softly. 'You look as though you're saying your prayers down there on your knees and, anyway, you know a watched pot never boils.'

Obediently, Della eased herself up and joined him on

the bunk. He took her hand and his voice was low as he said, 'You don't know how much I've enjoyed this evening, Della.'

'I did, too,' she said cautiously, aware of the blood rising to her face.

Paul's serious eyes were intent on her flushed face. 'I'm in love with you, Della.'

She opened her mouth and closed it. 'Paul . . . I . . .' she attempted again, but he pressed his forefinger against her lips.

'You don't have to say anything. I know it's sudden. I don't expect you to feel the same way about me, but I just had to tell you. I have so little time; I don't want to waste a moment of it.'

He kissed her gently on the mouth, and she felt the same delightful tremor pass through her as on the previous evening. The splutter of the kettle interrupted them.

'I'll get it,' he said, pulling away and turning off the stove.

Della still sat motionless when he rejoined her and kissed her again, this time holding her gently in his arms. She felt the warm flush to her face spread all over her body. It was like a fire in her blood. She kissed him back, and their lips crushed together as she returned his embrace. He moaned and held her tighter, his hands exploring her back, her shoulders. She melted into him, caressing the rough cloth of his uniform, the back of his neck. And then his tongue forced her lips apart. She gasped. What was he doing? But the warm intimacy of their joined mouths made her head spin and she returned his kiss, her body throbbing. Was she going crazy?

'Oh, Della, Della.' He laid her back on the bunk and leaned over her. 'I never thought anyone like you would happen to me.'

Suddenly his lips were on hers again, and she felt the weight of his chest. His mouth travelled over her face, her throat, and she thought she'd explode with pleasure. What in God's name was she doing? She hardly knew this man! And so soon after Jerry! She tried to raise herself, but his mouth was back on hers, tenderly yet insistently, his tongue exploring hers once more. She felt powerless to resist. Nor could she stop him as, still with his mouth on hers, he gently undid her blouse buttons. She felt his hands glide over her underslip and slide beneath her brassiere. Moaning with pleasure as his fingers caressed her nipples, she made no attempt to stop him, but began undoing his tunic, his shirt, her hands exploring his hard chest.

He raised himself a little, then lifted her shoulders gently, pulling off her jacket and blouse. She didn't resist, and he laid her back before tearing off his tunic and returning to her, gently drawing her slip and brassiere down to her waist.

'Oh, my God, you're lovely, Della,' he said in a choked voice as he gazed at her white skin, tinged with the glow from the candlelight.

He buried his head in her bosom and kissed her, moving slowly to her nipples. She uttered a cry as he kissed first one, then the other, first gently, then wildly, until the pleasure became almost a pain. She moaned and thrashed her head on the coverless pillow. She had never felt anything like this before. Her whole body screamed out to his. Was this the war madness people talked about? Nothing seemed to matter except her desire for him. He kissed her on the lips again with bruising fierceness, and she frantically tugged off his shirt. The feel of his body against hers heightened her passion and she clutched him fiercely.

He murmured her name and fumbled with her skirt

buttons, while his lips travelled slowly down between her breasts to her waist.

She moaned louder and felt Jerry's name almost issue from her lips. 'No! No! This is crazy!' She sat up abruptly.

Paul took her trembling body in his arms and soothed her, his voice hoarse. 'What's wrong, Della? It's all right. I won't do anything you don't want me to.'

She pressed her head against his chest, almost sobbing. 'I've never felt anything quite like this before,' she admitted, as he held her tightly. 'I'm afraid of myself.'

'Don't be afraid. I'd never do anything to hurt you,' he murmured, brushing her forehead with his lips.

'I'm sorry, Paul. I'm so confused. It was awful of me to let you go on like that.' She buried her head in his chest.

'I thought it was wonderful,' he said, stroking her hair.

'No, I mean, it *was* wonderful. It was so wonderful I had trouble stopping you. And I . . . I . . .' She burst into tears.

'Oh, my Della, what's wrong?' He lifted her chin and looked closely at her. 'I'm sorry if I've made you unhappy.'

'It's just that . . . that . . . I've never done it before,' she finally blurted out, her body shaking with sobs.

His hands stopped in the act of stroking her. 'But you were married,' he said unbelievingly.

She shook her head against his chest. 'It wasn't a real marriage.'

He drew in a breath and, tipping her chin, looked at her in astonishment. 'You mean you never made love with your husband?'

She bit her lip and shook her head again. 'I wanted to, but he couldn't . . . But I loved him.'

'Oh, Della,' he murmured incredulously, cradling her

again and rocking her. 'Poor Della. I had no idea. I'm sorry. I didn't mean to barge into your life and upset you.'

'No, no, you're not upsetting me,' she protested, and then half smiled as he stroked her wet cheeks. 'I mean, it's a good upset. I've got to put that part of my life behind me, I know. It's just that it's difficult . . . it's so sudden.'

He stroked her cheek tenderly. 'I know, I rushed you; I'm sorry. But I feel as if I've known you for ever . . . and there's so little time ahead for us.'

Della silenced him almost harshly. 'Don't say that! We've got almost three weeks . . . and you'll get more leaves.'

'Yes,' he murmured, bending to kiss her gently. 'You'd better get dressed now.' He picked up her blouse and jacket from the floor. 'It was selfish of me to keep you up when I knew you were tired.'

Silently, they dressed and stole out into the dark. 'Don't see me to the gate. Go straight in.' He kissed her lightly, and then said urgently, 'You *will* see me tomorrow, won't you?'

'Of course,' she found herself saying without hesitation.

'Six o'clock, then. And, remember, I love you,' he whispered into her ear before disappearing into the darkness.

Chapter Twenty-Six

The following day at the hospital was frantic. Because of four new admissions, Della fell behind in her rounds. She worked through her lunch break and didn't sit down until three o'clock, when she had a cup of tea in the staff room.

At five-thirty Sister took pity on her. 'Why don't you go now, Nurse Davidson? We can get along without you for half an hour,' she said in her crisp, authoritative voice.

Della, emptying her umpteenth bedpan of the day, sighed gratefully, 'Oh, thank you, Sister.' Sister was known to be a firm disciplinarian; this was out of character, Della thought as she retreated to the rest-room. She splashed her face, brushed her teeth, and put on a dab of lipstick before changing into her blue tweed skirt and blue twinset, throwing over her shoulders a loose, swing-back grey jacket. She didn't really need it now, but she would before the evening was out. The weather was finally turning spring-like.

Her watch said twenty minutes to six. She had time to see how Jonathan was doing before she left.

She knocked peremptorily on the door and burst in. Vera sat on the bed, looking very fragile and beautiful in clinging pink crepe, her blonde hair immaculately waved and curling over her shoulders. She stared at Della for a second before recognition dawned.

'Oh, I'm sorry. I didn't know you had visitors,' Della said to Jonathan before turning to the girl. 'Hello, Vera.'

'Hello,' she returned, taking in Della from head to toe.

'You remember Della, don't you?' Jonathan said easily. 'Nice to see you, Della. I missed you at lunch time.'

'I worked through lunch, that's why they let me off early.'

Vera took Jonathan's hand possessively as she appraised Della again, saying in a deep, resonant voice that belied her delicate appearance, 'I didn't know you worked here.'

Oblivious of the tension in the room, Jonathan grinned. 'Della's a budding Florence Nightingale.'

'Not quite,' she corrected him modestly. 'I just popped in to see how the patient was doing.'

'Thanks. I'm bored silly. But the shrapnel's out. I should be out of here in a couple of days.'

Della put on her businesslike voice. 'Well, that's good news. I'll check on you before you leave. Bye, Vera, nice to see you.'

'Bye,' Vera returned with a guarded expression on her face.

Della closed the door with relief. That's a possessive female if ever I saw one, she thought. But she needn't have any fear I'm after Jonathan.

She didn't have long to wait at the entrance. Paul arrived early. He took both her hands and kissed her in greeting. 'You look wonderful, as usual.'

'Thank you. And I see you're wearing your uniform, as usual. Have you changed your mind about it?' Della teased.

He grimaced. 'Not really. I got out my best suit and the moths had got at it. There's no point in buying another now, so I'm afraid you're stuck with a Tommy.'

'I like you as you are.' She tucked her arm in his and he hugged her to him as they strode to the gate.

'What would you like to do?'

'First I want to sit down and have a glass of cider,' Della said with determination, 'and then I want two helpings of Irish stew and trifle. I've hardly sat down or eaten all day.'

'You've got your wish,' he said. 'I can't think of anything nicer, although I think you should be adventurous and try something different.'

Half an hour later, armed with a bottle of cider, they entered the restaurant. The same waitress greeted them. 'Well, you must have liked your dinner last night.'

'Thank you. We certainly did.' Paul placed the bottle on the table and grinned up at her. 'And we enjoyed the cider.'

'You'll get me shot,' she said with mock firmness.

After homemade shepherd's pie and treacle tart, followed by coffee, Della sighed with satisfaction. 'Mmm, I feel almost alive again. That was wonderful.'

Paul looked at her with concern. 'They shouldn't let you work that long without eating. It's not human.'

'Maybe not, but it's good for the waistline.'

'There's nothing wrong with your waistline, Della,' he murmured, taking her hand across the table.

'Thank you.' She lowered her eyes. 'What shall we do now?'

'There's a Cary Grant picture on at the Haymarket. I've forgotten the title, but I assume you like Cary Grant. We could just make the second house.'

Della smiled. 'Do you know any girl who doesn't like Cary Grant?'

In the cinema she tried to relax, but the touch of Paul's hand in hers was too disturbing. She felt restless. He shifted about in his seat also. His arm slid round her shoulders, and her whole body tingled with his proximity. She gripped his hand harder.

'Let's go,' he whispered, about an hour before the end.

She nodded in the dark, and silently they inched their way along the aisle.

Outside, Paul hailed a passing taxi.

'Paul, what are you doing?' Della remonstrated. 'What's wrong with the bus?'

'Nothing – if you like long rides.'

He stopped the taxi at the bottom of the street and they walked to the gate. Without a word, they made their way to the shelter. Paul silently climbed down and helped Della, closing the entrance after her.

She didn't even pretend to light the stove, but sat on the bunk waiting for him to join her. 'Oh, Della,' he murmured, kneeling and taking her in his arms. He kissed her tenderly at first and then with growing passion. 'Della – oh, Della,' he murmured again, before he once more forced her lips apart and explored her mouth. The intimacy of the kiss made Della's head reel.

He groaned and eased her jacket off her shoulders. She was hardly even aware that he'd taken his lips off hers when she realised they were both naked. Tonight, she knew this was Paul making love to her, not Jerry.

His head was bent in the dark under the low shelter roof – they hadn't even bothered to light the candles – and gently he eased her on to the bunk, leaning over her until almost his full weight was on her. He kissed her lips again, then her breasts, and she felt the same exquisite pain she had experienced the night before.

'Oh, God, Della, wait a minute, I want to see you,' he said huskily, groping for his trousers on the floor and fumbling for his lighter. By the small flame he found the candles and lit them, casting warm shadows on Della's body. Reverently, he kneeled beside her, worshipping her with his eyes as he traced the lines of her thighs with his fingertips. Della drew in her breath at the sight of his muscular body. She pulled him down, feeling the length of his nakedness over hers. She shivered with anticipation. His hands searched her body and she squirmed with delight, at the same time exploring him with her hands.

He fumbled on the floor for his jacket and groped in the pocket. She cried out as he eased away from her, but his weight was back on her in a second.

'I love you,' he whispered, kissing her tenderly as he merged his body with hers, slowly, gently. She gasped with pleasure and he stopped, breathing heavily. 'Am I hurting you?' he asked hoarsely.

'No, no, no . . . don't stop.' The moment was unreal. Della closed her eyes with the intensity of her feelings, and in one delightful, incredible moment, she felt she could experience no more pleasure than this. She felt their bodies moving together until she cried out. In the dark interior of the shelter, she saw flashes of purple and gold, and he uttered a final cry, before his full weight fell on hers.

Afterwards, they lay, limp and breathless. Della had no idea how much time had passed when Paul turned on his side with difficulty in the narrow bunk, pressing himself against the cold, corrugated iron wall that they had been oblivious of until now. She grabbed the two blankets from the floor, placing one behind his back and pulling the other over them before nestling in his arms. The world stopped as they lay in silent contentment.

'Della,' he whispered finally, grazing her mouth with his. 'You're wonderful. How could I be so lucky?'

'I didn't know it would be so marvellous,' she breathed.

'And I didn't hurt you?' he asked anxiously.

'I . . . I . . . prepared myself for my honeymoon.' She tried not to let the memory spoil her present happiness.

'My poor Della,' he said, holding her tighter.

'Oh, Paul, I don't want you to go away.' She clutched him fiercely. Now the prospect of the end of his leave filled her with dread.

He pressed his finger against her lips. 'Sshh! Let's just live in the present. I never thought life could be so good as it is at this moment. Don't let anything spoil it. We'll be together every minute you're free.'

'Oh,' she said miserably. 'I have to go to the ARP tomorrow evening.'

'Then I'll come with you.' He grinned. 'They won't object if I'm in uniform.'

'Talking about your uniform reminds me,' she teased. 'Do you always keep those things in the pocket?'

He laughed wickedly. 'Of course! Army issue! They come with the uniform.'

'You fibber!' She giggled and nuzzled his neck.

Reluctantly, he eased her from him. 'I hate to be the one to say it. I'd like to keep you here all night, but you'd better get some sleep or I'll be meeting a walking corpse tomorrow.'

'What time is it?'

He screwed up his eyes to look at his watch. 'Twenty to twelve.'

'Good God!' She sat up with a start. 'My mam'll think I've disappeared off the face of the earth. I've hardly been home the past few days.'

Unwillingly, she crawled from the bunk and sorted out the mess of her clothes. He sat up watching her, his eyes still drinking in her nakedness. 'I can't believe I'm here with you like this,' he whispered.

She threw his shirt at him. 'Well, you are, but not for much longer. You can't stay here all night or someone's

318

bound to see you in the morning.'

'I could stay here till you come back to me tomorrow,' he chuckled, putting on his shirt. 'I could happily spend my entire leave here.'

'So could I,' she said softly. 'Where shall we meet tomorrow? I usually eat at the hospital and go straight to the ARP when there's a meeting.'

'Well then, I'll see you at the hospital as usual. We can still eat together.'

'But the canteen's only for hospital staff,' Della protested.

'And who's going to refuse a man in uniform – especially if he walks with a limp?' Paul said with a straight face as he buttoned his shirt.

'You and your ruddy uniform,' she giggled, throwing his jacket at him.

Chapter Twenty-Seven

Paul's leave passed all too quickly. He met Della after work, and they spent every free moment together, making rapturous love in the air-raid shelter every night.

On their last evening, sipping their drinks in the little pub near the restaurant, they were both quiet and thoughtful, looking at their watches, waiting for darkness, impatient to disappear underground to their private world.

'I know you don't want to talk about it,' Della burst out suddenly, 'but I can't go on like this – pretending it's not going to happen.' Her eyes brimmed with tears as she looked at him.

'Don't cry, Della,' he soothed. 'That's exactly why I don't want to talk about it. It just makes it even worse.'

Her voice quavered as she asked, 'When will you know where you're going?'

'Probably when I report tomorrow. I saw Andrew today and he's heard rumours about sending reinforcements to the colonies – could be Singapore or Burma.' He shrugged. 'But there are all sorts of rumours at the moment.'

'That far!' Della swallowed hard. 'You'll write to me immediately so I know where to write to you?'

Paul had deliberately avoided this subject, but now he knew he must deal with it. He looked straight at her.

'Della, I don't want you to write to me.'

'Not write!' she cried, aghast. 'You mean you're just going to go away and leave me and forget me . . .' Her voice trailed off in disbelief and more tears escaped, trembling on her eyelashes.

'You know I couldn't possibly forget you, Della, ever. It's just that I don't know what's in store for me. I don't want to ask you to wait for someone who might never come back, or . . . might come back in pieces. I've seen too many lads with girlfriends pining away for them at home, pinning their hopes on an all too often non-existent future. I don't want you to do that, Della. I want you to get on with your life in the meantime. Believe me, if and when I do come back, you'll be the first to know.'

'Won't you even write occasionally, just to let me know you're all right?' she begged.

He shook his head firmly. 'If I write at all, you'll always be waiting for a letter, and if one doesn't arrive you'll worry. I don't write to my family either for that reason. So long as they never hear from me, they don't have to panic.'

She clenched her fists under the table, her nails biting into the palms. 'I don't understand.' She shook her head and drew a deep breath. 'Do you mean that this was just a wartime romance? That we can pretend it never happened?'

'Idiot,' he murmured, taking her hand. 'This has been the most wonderful experience I've ever had – the romance of a lifetime for me. I never want it to end.'

'But you *are* ending it,' she protested, the tears on her lashes trickling slowly down her cheeks.

He pulled out his handkerchief and tenderly wiped her face. 'I'm not ending it, my darling Della. I'm just postponing it till I get back. You'll never be out of my mind, but I can't ask you to put your life in cold storage while I'm away. You've already had one tragedy with your marriage – that's enough. I run the risk of another man snapping you up in any event,' he added wryly, 'letters or no letters.'

'Never! I could never love anybody else now.' Her lower lip trembled as she stammered, 'How . . . how could you even think that?'

'Sshh,' he murmured. 'Promise me, if I don't come back, you'll find someone else to love. There's too much love in you to go to waste, Della.'

She took the handkerchief he still clutched and blew her nose noisily. 'Find someone else?' she repeated numbly, closing her eyes. 'That's the second time in my life a man's said that to me.'

'Oh, my darling, don't look on the black side. There's every chance I'll come back. For me, staying out of your life while I can't share it is just a sort of insurance . . . in case anything happens.' He looked at her imploringly.

She gulped in air, then stood up. 'Let's go now, please.'

When they reached home it was dark, and they made their way silently to the shelter. Although wearing a wool jacket, Della sat shivering on the bunk as Paul lit the candles.

'Are you cold?' he asked tenderly.

'No, I've just got the shivers.' She didn't tell him the reason – that she was thinking this might be the last time they would make love.

He joined her and took her urgently in his arms. She responded desperately, and he made love to her tenderly, yet more completely than ever before.

At midnight Della reluctantly looked at her watch. 'You're the one who's got to get up in the morning. We'd better go,' she said in a dead voice.

They dressed in silence. This time she walked with

him to the gate, where he took her in his arms and kissed her and held her as if he would never let go. Then, with a catch in his breath, he muttered, 'I love you, Della.' She stood, numb, as he dropped his arms and turned away abruptly.

Before entering the scullery, she wiped her eyes and pinched her cheeks, praying that Mary and Walter would be in bed. But the light was on in the kitchen. She'd forgotten it was Anne's day to visit.

Mary gave her an anxious look. 'Hello, luv. Did your boyfriend get off all right?'

'He leaves first thing in the morning,' she replied with tight lips. 'Hello, Anne. Sorry I'm so late. I forgot you'd be here.'

'That's all right.' Anne also looked at her with concern.

The family knew Della was seeing a soldier on leave, but she had told them no more than that. Nevertheless, from her constant absences from home for the past three weeks, it was apparent this wasn't a casual affair.

Mary rose from her armchair. 'I've got the kettle hot for some cocoa. Dad's gone to bed, but we waited up for you.'

'Thanks, Mam.' Della took Mary's chair and warmed herself by the fire. She always felt chilled to the bone when she came inside from the damp shelter, yet she never noticed the cold when she was with Paul. 'How's Johnny?' she asked Anne mechanically.

Anne's eyes glowed. 'He's thriving! And Mrs Moynihan's looking much better since she moved in with Molly and the kids. She needs a lot of activity around her.'

'Here you are,' Mary said, carrying in a tray with three mugs.

Della stood up. 'Here, have your seat back, Mam.'

'No, you stay there. You look frozen and exhausted. I'll sit on the sofa.'

'How's work, Anne?' Della asked, knowing that they could see she was upset and trying to keep the conversation away from herself.

'Fine! I'm getting more muscles every day,' Anne smiled. 'And I've brought some new potatoes, a lettuce, a cucumber, and – wait for it – a leg of lamb. Colin gave it to me because I worked a bit late last night. He's very good to me.'

'He sounds nice,' Della said. Colin's name seemed to come up more and more frequently on Anne's visits.

'You must be sad your boyfriend's gone?' Mary cut in, unable to pretend any longer. She was worried. Why had Della been so secretive about this man?

Della spoke calmly. 'Yes, I am. I'll miss him.'

'But you'll see him on his next leave.' Anne tried to comfort her, but knew that words weren't enough.

'Yes . . . whenever that is.' Not wishing to discuss Paul's departure any further, Della asked, 'Any more news from the boys?'

Mary answered cheerfully. 'Yes, a letter from David. He doesn't say much, just that he's fed up and footsore, and some pieces of the letter have been cut out. He still can't say where he is, and it was a War Office post mark.'

'It's time I caught up on some letter writing.' Della put down her mug on the hearth, wishing she could include Paul on her list. 'I'll write to them all tomorrow. I'm going up to bed now, if you don't mind, I'm very tired.'

'Of course, luv,' Mary said. 'I'm getting worried about you. And you're losing weight as well. I wish you'd eat more and get more rest.'

'Night, Mam.' Della kissed Mary on the cheek. 'I'm going to sleep late tomorrow.'

Anne yawned and stood up. 'I'm coming up as well. What a wonderful thought! I can sleep in too.'

Upstairs in the bedroom they once again shared on Anne's visits, they undressed silently, put out the light and climbed into bed.

'Night, Anne,' Della said, turning her face into the pillow.

'Night, luv.' Anne turned over, but both were aware that sleep wouldn't come easily. As Anne had expected, soon she heard muffled sobs in the darkness. She got up and stroked Della's back, which was shaking under the blankets. 'You really love him, don't you, luv?' she said softly.

Della rolled over and reached for Anne's hand. 'Yes,' she whispered. 'I . . . I thought I could never love a man again after Jerry. I couldn't believe it was happening to me, and now . . . he's gone. Why do the men I love keep on leaving me?'

'But he'll come back, luv, and you'll write. It's not like Jerry. Don't say that.' Anne switched on the lamp and sat on the bed.

Della shook her head. 'No, he won't write and he won't let me write to him. He doesn't want me to pine for him while he's away, in case he doesn't come back,' she sobbed.

'Oh, Della, he'll come back. You must have faith.' Anne tried not to show her surprise and prayed silently it wasn't simply this man's way of ending the affair.

Della dried her eyes on the sheet and took a deep breath. 'You're right, Anne. We keep our faith that the boys and Dan'll come back. It's just another waiting period. I seem to spend all my life waiting,' she said ruefully, thinking of the years of waiting to marry Jerry, and then the long months of waiting for him to be able to be a real husband to her.

'You've had a bad time, sweetheart. But it'll get over.'

Anne tried to sound reassuring.

Della was now sorry she'd heaped her grief on Anne. 'Oh, I'm so selfish! I shouldn't burden you with my troubles. You've got plenty of your own . . . and Dan doesn't write to you either.'

Anne's voice was bitter when she replied: 'Not for the same reason, though. He's just too lazy to write and too selfish to care.'

'Anne!' Della sat up in surprise. 'I've never heard you say a bad word about Dan. What's wrong?'

Anne plucked fluff from the blanket. 'It's just that I see him more clearly now since I've known Colin,' she confessed.

'Are you . . . in love with Colin?'

'I think so,' she whispered. 'He's only taken me out a few times for a drink or to the pictures, and he's never done more than hold my hand or kiss me on the cheek. He knows I'm married. But I can't help comparing him with Dan. He's so nice, and gentle, and fun to be with. And . . . and I know he likes me a lot. When I'm with him he makes me feel so important. He treats me like gold – makes me feel good about myself.' She bowed her head. 'That's one thing Dan never did.'

'Oh, Anne, Anne! Dare I say it, but I'm glad! It's time you had someone in your life who appreciates you.'

'But what about Dan? I feel so guilty about him,' Anne said miserably. 'How could I stop loving him just like that, just because another man comes along?'

Della took Anne's hands and said firmly: 'I think it's time you stopped feeling guilty about Dan. Do you think *he'd* feel guilty if he met someone else? Oh, Anne, I know it's awful to advise you to forget about your husband, but I think it would be wonderful if you loved someone else who could make you happy. You could hardly say Dan's been a good husband to you.'

Anne looked up and stared at the wall as she spoke. 'I

admit he's made me very unhappy at times, but I thought I loved him despite everything.'

'Well, you're a saint if you can love a man who beats you, who's a thief, who's completely selfish, who treats you like a servant, and who doesn't give a jot about his own son!' Della burst out. 'You know I could go on and on, Anne. I never thought I'd be able to say these things outright, but it's high time. You're wasting your life on Dan.'

'I know that now,' she said slowly. 'But it could never come to anything with Colin. I'm married to Dan.'

'It doesn't matter! Leave him!' Della exhorted. 'Nobody would blame you, and I know the whole family would be relieved.'

'But what about Johnny?'

'What *about* Johnny? Dan's never been a real father to him anyway.'

Anne sighed. 'I know you're right, Della. I suppose I'm just scared. And what would people say? We could never get divorced.'

'I don't see why not. Dan doesn't give a jot about his religion, and I don't honestly believe that God would want you to stay with a man who makes you miserable just because you made a mistake when you were nineteen.'

'Oh, I don't know,' Anne said cautiously. 'But it makes no difference anyway till after the war.'

'And in the meantime why don't you give Colin a chance? If it turns out that you love each other, it doesn't matter if you've got a marriage certificate or not.' Della hesitated for a second before admitting, 'Paul and I have made love and made each other happy, and we're not married.'

Anne's eyes widened. 'You *did*!'

'Yes, and it was wonderful, it couldn't possibly be wrong. I never dreamed I'd think this way. Maybe it's the war . . . I don't know. But whatever it is, I'm glad. I think the most important thing in life is that people be happy and don't hurt one another, not that they conform to man-made laws.' As she spoke the words, Della realised that meeting Paul had a lot to do with the way she now thought.

Anne smiled. 'You're beginning to convince me. I'll just see how things go with Colin for the moment but, even if they don't work out, I suppose it's a good thing that I'm finally seeing sense about Dan. I'll just have to work out that problem when the time comes.' She kissed her sister. 'And now I think it's time you got some sleep. I'm glad you found Paul.'

'And I'm glad you found Colin. Goodnight, sis.'

'Goodnight, luv.' Anne switched out the lamp and climbed back into bed.

On Monday evening Della met Nora and Rose at the coffee rooms. Rose greeted her caustically. 'Well! Look what the wind's blown in! So you've finally decided to honour us with your presence.'

Della looked apologetic as she sat down. 'I know. I'm sorry I haven't made it the past couple of weeks, but I thought you'd understand.'

'Paul?' Nora enquired cautiously.

Della nodded.

'Are you in love with him?' Rose dared to ask.

Della nodded again.

'And is he in love with you?' Nora pressed gently.

Another nod. 'I know what you're thinking – so soon after Jerry. A rebound! A wartime romance!'

Nora patted her friend's hand. 'No, I think it's wonderful. You need someone in your life again and, remember, Jerry wanted it for you as well.'

'And I think it's wonderful, too,' Rose said warmly.

'It would be if he didn't have to go away.' Della

picked up the menu and stared at it sightlessly in a desperate search for distraction. She felt close to tears again. 'How are you both doing?' she asked.

'Well, I'm fine and so is Phil, but Rose is in the dumps.'

'What's wrong, Rose?'

'I'm late,' she answered dully.

Della drew in her breath. 'How late?'

'Ten flipping days.'

Della looked at her anxiously. 'Does Bill know?'

'No.' Rose's lower lip quivered. 'I don't want to scare him till I'm sure.'

'Have you ever been late before?' Della's voice was worried.

'Nope.' Rose bit her still quivering lip and shook her head. 'Except once when I'd had a temperature of over a hundred when I had flu. But I haven't had a temperature this time.'

Nora made a vain effort at reassurance. 'I'm sure it's just a fluke, luv. You're always so careful.'

'That's just it,' she moaned, 'we got carried away one time, and that was three weeks ago. I know because that was the night Andrew took me home and there was an air raid.'

Della broke the ensuing glum silence. 'Why don't you tell Bill? At least you wouldn't have to worry alone.'

'I'm going to tell him if nothing's happened in a couple of weeks. By then I'll know the worst,' Rose answered dejectedly.

The waitress finally interrupted them. 'Just coffee please,' Della said.

Nora was depressingly realistic. 'What will you do if you are?'

Rose thumped her fist on the table. 'Well, that bugger had better marry me, hadn't he?'

Della and Nora exchanged glances but said nothing.

★ ★ ★

Five days later, Rose made sandwiches while waiting anxiously for Bill to arrive. She'd felt totally miserable and alone for days and had decided not to wait any longer to confront him with her fear. From the kitchen, she heard a male voice on the wireless and ran to the sitting-room to hear the news.

After the announcement she returned dejectedly to the kitchen. Italy had declared war on France and Britain. She shuddered. The war was definitely going to be a long one now. What a day to break her own news to Bill! But she had to do it. She couldn't go on worrying alone any longer; she needed his comfort and support. Her heart skipped a beat as she heard his footsteps on the landing.

She ran to the door and stretched to embrace his tall figure. 'Hello, luv. Have you heard the news?'

'Yes. Mrs James downstairs caught me on the way up about some rising damp in her kitchen. I heard it on her wireless.' Bill threw his trilby on a chair and flopped on to the sofa. 'Bloody Ities!' he spat. 'Licking Hitler's boots! They don't seem to realise the days of the Roman Empire are over. All they're good for now is shooting little birds and making spaghetti.'

Rose, anxious not to embark on a discussion of the war that would delay her own news, poured him a whisky and herself a gin and lime, announcing as she did so, 'I made you some paste sandwiches.'

Bill glanced distastefully at the plate of wizened sandwiches, the bread separated by a thin brown line of dubious origin. 'No, thanks. You know I can't stand meat paste, and anyway I've already eaten.' He leaned back in the sofa, his glass in his hand.

Rose sat nervously beside him clutching her own glass tightly. She must get this over with quickly, she thought, taking a large gulp of her drink. 'Bill, I've got some other news for you as well.' She looked straight at him. 'I . . . I think I'm going to have a baby.'

He slammed down his glass on the side-table and looked at her aghast. 'Are you sure?'

'I'm over two weeks late, and it's never happened before. It must have been that night when we didn't go down to the shelter,' she said miserably.

'Good God! That's all I need!' Bill pressed his hand against his forehead.

'All *you* need!' Rose shot back at him, shocked. 'Bill, *I'm* the one who's having it!'

His eyes slid away from her before he muttered, 'Well, there's plenty of time to do something about it.'

'You mean have an abortion?' Rose cried in horror.

'What else do you think, woman?' he shouted, running his hands through his hair in agitation.

'But if I *am*, it's *your* baby. Why can't we get married like other people and just have it? I mean, I never wanted to have a baby, but now that it's happened, surely that's the best thing to do?'

Bill shook his head. 'I've told you a dozen times, Rose. I'm not the marrying kind. You knew that from the start. You can't say I didn't warn you.' He picked up his glass and drained it before stalking to the sideboard to refill it.

Rose watched his elegant back with wide, frightened eyes. 'Bill, you know I never planned it. We're both responsible.'

'I'm aware of that,' he snapped, returning to the sofa and throwing himself down angrily. 'Don't worry! I'll see to my responsibilities. I'll pay for everything.'

'I wasn't thinking about money,' Rose said dully. 'I thought this would make you feel different about getting married.'

'Well, you thought wrong! I know someone who'll do

the operation, if necessary. But give it at least another couple of weeks to be sure.'

Rose gasped in horror. 'You . . . you mean you want me to go to one of those awful back-street women?'

'It's a man and he's a doctor,' Bill corrected her. 'At least he used to be a doctor. He knows what he's doing.' He drained his second whisky in a single gulp and got up for a third.

Rose stared into her glass and her voice was flat when she finally spoke: 'So you've been through this before?'

'No! He happens to be a friend of mine, that's all.' Bill threw himself back on to the sofa. But after a moment, he took her hand and wheedled, 'Look, if it's true, in a couple of weeks it'll all be over and you'll forget it ever happened.'

'*You* might, you mean,' Rose said bitterly, withdrawing her hand and getting up to refill her glass. She faced him from the sideboard. 'Do you love me, Bill?'

'You know I do. For God's sake don't let's go through all that again.'

'Yes.' Rose sighed in resignation, sitting down beside him again. 'I think you do in your way. I suppose I'll just have to settle for that.'

'That's my girl,' Bill said with obvious relief. He put his arm about her shoulders and, as usual, Rose felt herself melt at his touch.

'Oh, Bill, I love you, you rotten sod!' she cried into his chest.

He put down his glass and held her in his arms. 'It'll be all right. I'll see to everything,' he soothed, kissing her softly at first, then with gathering passion.

She pushed him away and looked into his eyes for a second before repeating miserably, 'Oh, you're such a sod, Bill!' And then she clung to him, this time returning his kiss.

Chapter Twenty-Eight

The second day in June, Della was waiting in the queue at the canteen when a voice behind her spoke. 'Can you recommend something edible?'

She turned, surprised. 'Jonathan! What are you doing here?'

He grinned widely. 'I have to eat, the same as everyone else. I'm working here now.' In place of his eye patch, he now wore a pair of horn-rimmed spectacles. 'They've taken away my white stick,' he joked.

Della smiled. 'You look very distinguished in glasses.'

'The right lens is plain glass. I thought a monocle might look too pretentious.' He flashed his grin again.

They inched slowly up the queue. 'Which department are you in?' Della asked.

'I'm a sort of roving aid at the moment. I'm doing my internship, so it should help me to get a broad view.'

'Well, the first thing you'd better learn is to avoid the gravy,' Della warned as they reached the counter. She slopped a spoonful of mashed potatoes on to her plate.

'And how about the sausages?' he asked, pronging two anaemic, undercooked sausages.

'We're only supposed to have one each. And they're always half raw. But you needn't worry about eating raw meat; it's anybody's guess what's in them, except for bread.'

Jonathan dropped a sausage on to each plate, and

Della obliged with the peas. 'May I join you?' he asked, following her without waiting for an answer and squeezing beside her at the end of one of the trestle tables.

She looked sideways at his handsome profile. 'How's Vera?' she asked politely, not caring a fig how she was.

Jonathan swallowed a piece of sausage and grimaced at the taste. 'She's all right. How's your soldier boyfriend?'

Della looked up from her plate, her face colouring. 'How did you know about him?'

'Easy.' He smiled, the pupils of his eyes growing large and dark. 'I used to watch you meeting him every day after work. Remember, I had a private room with my own window.'

'It strikes me nothing's private in this place,' she snapped.

He looked uncomfortable. 'Oh, Della, I wasn't spying on you. I was just bored and spent most of my time looking out of the window anyway.'

Della relented. 'I don't know how he is. He's gone back now.'

'Nice-looking chap.'

'Yes,' she agreed. Why was it she always felt she was sparring with Jonathan rather than holding a conversation? Was it because of what his family had done to her mother, or was it because he was getting rather too self-assured as he got older? There was something almost cocky about him. Funny she hadn't noticed it earlier.

Doggedly sawing away at his sausage, Jonathan felt her gaze and looked up. Again, the colour travelled to Della's face. She pushed her meal away half eaten and rose. 'I have to be back at one, never mind that I got off late.'

Jonathan stood up politely. 'It was nice to see you, Della. Maybe we can dine in style again tomorrow.'

She made no reply but smiled as she turned to leave.

Later that afternoon, Sister summoned her in a steely voice: 'There's a telephone call for you, Nurse Davidson.'

'For *me*?' Della cried, amazed and dismayed. Something must be wrong for anyone to ring her at the hospital.

'Sorry, Sister,' she gulped, as she ran anxiously past her to the office. With trembling hands, she picked up the receiver. 'Hello.'

'Della! Oh thank God I've got you. It's Rose.' The voice sounded strained and distant. 'Listen, I'm ringing you from work. I can't talk. Can you meet us outside the shop tonight?'

'Yes, but what's wrong?' Della asked, though she guessed what it must be.

'I'll tell you when I see you.'

'All right! I'll be there shortly after six.' The phone went dead.

Sister was outside the office as Della left. 'Sorry, Sister,' she said meekly.

'You know private phone calls aren't allowed?' Sister snorted.

'Yes, Sister, but it was an emergency. I'm sorry.'

'It sounded to me more like you were making arrangements with someone.'

'Yes, they were arrangements about an emergency,' Della replied lamely.

The air-raid siren terminated the conversation. 'Glory be to God!' Sister cried. 'In broad daylight!' Then she resumed her formal voice and ordered: 'Go and help Nurse Jones. See that all the patients have their gas masks, and then stay and keep them calm. I'll join you in a minute. I have to look in on Ward 12 first.'

Della ran to the ward, where Nurse Jones was already

taking the patients' gas masks from their cases and placing them on their beds where they could reach them. 'I'll help,' Della offered, starting on the opposite row of beds.

'So Jerry's decided to pay us a visit in daylight,' old Mr Watkins in the first bed observed unnecessarily.

Della flinched, still sensitive when the Germans were referred to by Jerry's name. She snapped at him. 'They're Germans not Jerries, Mr Watkins.'

'Jerries, Germans, Huns, swine . . . what's in a name? Anyway, our lads'll be able to get a better look at the buggers in daylight. They'll blast them to smithereens.' He chortled loudly and brought on a coughing attack. Swiftly, Della sat him up and held a glass of water to his lips.

'Mr Watkins,' she remonstrated, 'please lie still and keep calm. We don't want to have to deal with you and the Germans at the same time.'

'Aw, go on with you,' he wheezed. 'Let a man have a bit o' fun while he can.'

'Aye, let the poor old bugger alone,' Mr Bryant from the next bed said with a wide grin. 'This calls for a sing-song.' With that he sat up and began a solo version of *Rule Britannia*, which the rest of the ward soon picked up. Nurse Jones and Della joined in. But the voices died as the sound of droning engines began, followed by the inevitable sinister thuds.

'By God, they're close!' Mr Winfield cried, getting up to look out of the window. 'It sounds like they're gettin' it in the middle of the town.'

Mr Bryant disagreed. 'Nah, the buggers seem to be all over the place. But they're not right overhead, at least not yet.'

With shaking hands, Della administered a Felsol powder to Mr Watkins, who was now having a full-blown asthma attack. He lay back on his pillow and continued to gasp for air for a few seconds, before his breathing began to slow down. He nodded his thanks.

Nurse Jones approached, her thin face white and her pop eyes popping more than usual. 'I'm sorry, but I've got to go to the lav, luv,' she said urgently. 'I've had the runs all day. Can you manage on your own for a few minutes? Mr Jackson needs a bed pan.'

Della nodded and made for the sluice to get a bed pan. When she returned and pulled the screens round Mr Jackson's bed, the ward was silent, ears straining, waiting for the next thud. She gave the bed pan, then automatically checked on each patient. But her mind was on the noise out there. It seemed an eternity before the all-clear sounded. At the same moment Sister returned.

'Well, thank God that's over. Sorry I couldn't make it earlier. I had an emergency next door. Everything all right here?'

'Yes, Sister.' Della's shoulders sagged with relief. 'Would it be all right if I went for a cup of tea now, Sister?' she ventured hopefully. 'I missed my tea break.'

'All right,' Sister said almost kindly, 'go off to the canteen and listen to the wireless. See if there's any news. But be back in ten minutes.'

As she made her way to the canteen, Della felt physically and emotionally exhausted. The large room was crowded and there was a lot of speculation as to what exactly had been hit, but the wireless continued to broadcast *Music While You Work*.

She returned feeling slightly revived after the tea, but with no positive information. Gradually, however, word filtered through about the first major raid of the war on the North-East. The targets had been Newcastle and Jarrow and the figures so far were nine people killed and ninety injured, though they were still digging victims out of devastated buildings. It seemed that a bomber attempting to destroy the Tyne High Level Bridge had hit the Spiller's Flour Factory instead. Della thanked God that the West End had not been hit but was worried about Nora's family in Jarrow. She wondered if Nora would be there when she met Rose.

At six o'clock, Della got wearily on to the bus, listening to the passengers' varying accounts of the raid. But at least the buses on this route were running, she thought. And there was no evidence of damage on the short ride down Westgate Road and Grainger Street, where she alighted.

Della was relieved to see Nora with Rose outside the shop. Her family must be all right. Rose's freckles stood out on her chalky white face which she hadn't bothered to make up. Her hair straggled over her shoulders instead of shining in the fashionable victory roll she had recently adopted. There was something terribly wrong for her to be seen out like this.

Nora greeted Della glumly, giving a sidelong glance towards Rose, who stood silent. 'Hello, luv. Let's go and have a coffee first and a sandwich or something. My stomach's got the heebie-jeebies after that raid, and Rose needs to eat something.'

'Have you heard from your family? Are they all right?' Della asked Nora.

'Yes, they're all right, thank God. Mam phoned the shop. The street next to us got it, though. I was going to go home to see if there was anything I could do at the ARP but we've got an emergency here as well. Rose is in trouble.'

Della searched Rose's blanched face. 'You still haven't started?'

Rose shook her head. 'No, and it's worse than that. I hate that bastard!'

'Why? What's he done?' Della asked, alarmed. All

Rose needed now was to fall out with Bill.

'The sod's married,' Nora announced before putting her arm in Rose's and coaxing her gently, 'Come on, luv. First we're going to get some food inside you.' She turned to Della who stood with her mouth open. 'She hasn't eaten a bite all day. Come on.' Della took Rose's other arm and they set off for the coffee rooms.

'Oh, Rose, you poor thing!' Della cried. 'Are you positive he's married? How did you find out?'

'Yes, I'm positive,' Rose said miserably. 'I had to ring Fraser's of Durham this morning about an order, and I came across a William Fraser on the same page in the book so, out of curiosity, I rang the number. He always told me he wasn't on the phone, the sod! And all those rotten lies about living with his mother!'

'But why do you think he's married just because he's on the phone?' Della asked.

'It's a lot more than that, you ninny!' Rose turned on her almost angrily. 'A little kid answered, and I thought I had the wrong number, but a woman took the phone from him. It certainly wasn't an old woman's voice and there were more kids' voices in the background.'

Dismayed, Della pressed her. 'So what did you say?'

Rose swallowed hard and continued in a monotone: 'Just to make sure it was the right number, I asked if she was Mrs Fraser and she said she was, so I said I was one of her husband's tenants from Newcastle calling about a leaky pipe. She said he'd be in town tomorrow and asked for my name. That did it! I put the phone down.' Rose swallowed again. 'I mean, there couldn't be two William Frasers in Durham who own property in Newcastle. That's why I decided to ring that so-called doctor friend of his for an appointment tonight. I couldn't bear the thought of this . . . thing . . . growing inside me another day. I was stupid enough to think that if I hung on a bit longer he might soften about getting married.

Ha, ha! That's a laugh,' she finished bitterly.

'Oh, Rose!' Della helped her up the stairs to the coffee rooms as if she were an invalid.

Nora ordered three coffees and cheese sandwiches, while Rose sat with her head in her hands.

'I'll come back and stay with you tonight, Rose,' Della offered.

'Won't your mam worry if you don't go home?' Despite her protest, from the tone of Rose's voice she was grateful.

Della chewed her thumbnail and thought for a moment. 'I could ring the Drill Hall and ask someone to go round and tell her.'

'Oh, you're an angel,' Rose said thankfully.

'There's nobody I could ring or I could stay as well,' Nora said.

Della shook her head. 'There's no need, Nora. You can tell them at work tomorrow that you saw Rose tonight and she wasn't well. Say she might be off for a couple of days.'

The coffee and sandwiches arrived, and Della and Nora persuaded Rose at least to drink her coffee. Thus fortified, they walked down the Groat Market towards the Quayside. 'I know it's somewhere near Trinity Church but I haven't got a map,' Rose said miserably.

After taking several wrong turnings and passing two bomb sites, they finally found the house, or rather what appeared to be the back entrance to a warehouse. Despite the mild evening, Della shivered as she knocked hesitantly on the battered door of the grimy brick building. Presently, the door creaked open a couple of inches and a woman's voice came through. 'Who is it?'

'I've got an appointment,' Rose said in a cracked voice. 'I'm Bill Fraser's girlfriend.'

The hinges creaked further. 'Oh, aye, come in.' As the door opened wide to let them enter, they found themselves in a dimly lit passage, a dilapidated staircase covered in worn brown linoleum leading to a landing. The woman, now revealed in the light as elderly and at least four stones overweight, waddled to the staircase and laboriously climbed the creaking steps. The girls followed nervously.

The woman showed them to an outer office, furnished with an ancient, ink-stained desk and four rickety wooden chairs. 'Sit yoursel's down.' She indicated the chairs and disappeared into an adjoining room.

'Oh, God,' Rose moaned. 'I don't think I can do it.'

'It'll be all right,' Nora soothed doubtfully. 'He's a doctor, isn't he?'

'Was,' Rose corrected her.

The adjoining door swung open and a middle-aged man dressed in a soiled white coat appeared. His eyes were bleary, his mouth loose, and his thinning brown hair plastered to his scalp with too much Brylcreem.

Rose suppressed a shudder, and Della took her hand.

'Miss Johnson?' the man enquired, eyeing the three of them.

'That's me.' Rose walked shakily towards him.

'How do you do?' He held out his hand. But as Rose returned the handshake, she noticed his black-rimmed finger nails. She bit her lower lip as she stepped into the room.

Nora and Della exchanged worried glances. '*How do you do?*' Nora mimicked. 'How does he bloody well think she's doing?'

The door to the office closed. But only a few seconds later it burst open again and Rose appeared, screaming hysterically: 'No! I can't! I won't! No! No!'

'Stop that noise,' the woman growled, following her out. Nonplussed, the white-coated doctor stood in the doorway.

'Let's get away from here,' Rose begged, her eyes

round and luminous in the dim light.

The three were out of the door and down the stairs almost before the woman had reached the landing. 'Mind you keep quiet, and shut the door,' she growled again. 'And don't think you can come back here no more.'

Outside, Rose broke down and sobbed. 'I just couldn't. The bed was dirty, and he had all sorts of horrible-looking instruments on the table. And I bet they weren't clean either.' She laboured for breath. 'But . . . but you know the funniest thing. I don't think I could have gone through with it – clean or dirty. I must be going stark, raving mad.'

The two girls put their arms round her. 'I don't think you are, Rose,' Della said.

'Me neither,' Nora agreed. 'Come on, let's get you home now.'

Back at the flat, Rose flopped on to the sofa while Nora poured her a gin and lime.

'Ta, luv.' Rose took the glass and stared into the empty fire grate.

Nora and Della sat on either side of her, saying nothing. Finally, Rose drew a deep breath and broke the silence. 'Well, I've done it now, haven't I? Who'd have thought that plucky little Rose would rather have a baby than have an abortion?'

'I think it takes more pluck to do what you're doing,' Della said, squeezing Rose's hand affectionately.

'Me, too, luv,' Nora agreed.

Rose emptied her glass and stared into the grate. 'I wonder what Bill's going to say tomorrow when I tell him?'

'He can't force you to go through with it. It's your own body,' Nora said fiercely.

'And it's his kid,' Della added practically. 'He's got

the money. He can afford to keep it, and you.'

'Yes, that's what I've been thinking since I got the screaming hab-dabs at that filthy place.' Rose still stared at the grate. 'I can't believe he sent me there; I could have died. But who would have believed I'd even consider the alternative of having a kid? It seems little good-time Rose has had her good times for a while. Thank God I don't care a bugger what people think.' She twirled her empty glass with shaking hands, before throwing back her head and mewling like a frightened kitten: 'Oh, who am I bloody kidding? I don't want to be an unmarried mother. I want to be Bill's wife.' She laid her head back on the sofa, tears trickling down her face. 'What a hell of a mess I'm in!'

'You're a survivor, Rose,' Nora encouraged her. 'Whatever you do always turns out all right in the end.'

Della nodded. 'Nora's right. I'm going to stay tonight anyway. Nora, you'd better be going or you'll never get home. Here's the Drill Hall number.' She fumbled in her bag for her address book and wrote on a page before tearing it out.

Nora stood up. 'Thanks. I'll use the kiosk on the corner if it's working.' She bent and kissed Rose on the cheek. 'Keep your pecker up, luv. I'll see you at work.'

After Nora's departure, Rose spoke: 'I'm scared, Della.'

Della took her hand again. 'I'm sure it'll all work out in the end, luv.'

'But I'm scared either way, you see.' Rose concentrated on scraping off the red nail varnish on her left thumbnail. 'I'm a coward. I just couldn't bear the idea of those instruments inside me, and I can't bear the idea of having a baby either. Oh, if only something would happen like in the pictures. Maybe I could fall downstairs or something.' Her voice broke and more tears oozed down her cheeks.

'Don't talk rubbish, Rose.' Della shot her an alarmed glance. Rose could be stupid enough to try something like that. 'Come on, it's time you got some sleep. You'll feel better after a good night's rest. Will you ring Nora at the shop after Bill's been? I'll ring her there to find out how you are. The old dragon won't stand for another phone call on the ward.'

Rose sniffed and nodded dumbly before rising and making for the bedroom. After helping Rose into her nightdress and into bed, Della undressed to her under-slip and flopped beside her, her exhaustion finally giving way to a fitful sleep.

Rose lay wakeful most of the night and got up to make Della tea the following morning. However, she willed herself to sleep through most of the day; she didn't want to think any more until Bill arrived.

At five o'clock, she got up, had a bath, and made another pot of tea. At six o'clock she heard footsteps on the landing.

'Hello, beautiful!' Bill appeared in the sitting-room doorway. 'How are you feeling? Anything happened?'

'How do you think I'm feeling? And, yes, something's happened. But not what you bloody well think!' Rose put down her teacup and stared at him with something like loathing in her eyes.

'What are you looking daggers at me like that for?' he objected, flinging himself down in an armchair. 'What the hell's up now?'

'*You*, that's what's up!' Rose flung at him. 'And I was stupid enough to believe your lies. Did you also tell your *wife* you weren't the marrying type, nor the father type?'

Bill's handsome face turned white and his eyes narrowed. 'What are you talking about?' he muttered defensively.

'I spoke to her yesterday on the telephone, so don't

try to deny it,' Rose said slowly and deliberately, almost enjoying his discomfiture.

'I see . . .' A faint flush crept up from his neck towards the pallor of his face. 'I . . . I'm sorry, Rose.'

'Sorry? So am I!' she spluttered, trying to keep back her tears. She didn't want him to see her losing ground. 'I'm sorry about the wife! I'm sorry about the children! I'm sorry about that filthy "doctor" you sent me to! I'm sorry that you obviously don't care a bugger about me! But, most of all, I'm sorry that I believed all your damned lies!'

Bill sat next to her on the sofa and took her hand. But Rose pulled it away.

'You know I love you, Rose. I can explain.' He spoke in almost a whimper. 'But first tell me what happened. Did you have it done?'

'No, I bloody well didn't have it done,' she spat at him. 'And, for your information, I'm not going to. I'm not going to let that filthy man carve me up and maim me for life. I'm going to have it. How do you like the idea of being a daddy again? From what I gather you've got quite a brood already. One more can't make much difference.'

Bill's face stiffened. 'You can't, Rose. Be sensible!' He spoke sharply, but then paused and added in a relieved tone, 'You mean you're going to have it adopted?'

'I haven't decided what I'll do with it yet – suffice to say that I do know I'm not having a filthy abortion to please you. And whatever happens, the kid'll be your responsibility. Maybe your wife would like another one,' she jeered. 'Tell me about her. Is she as pretty as I am? Is she as good in bed? Do you love her as much as you say you do me?'

'Rose!' he snapped. 'Stop it! I . . . I didn't know I would get so stuck on you. It was just fun at first, but

347

after a while I began to need you.'

'So I was just fun, was I, and you got stuck on me?' Rose taunted. 'And was your wife "just fun" at first, and did you "get stuck" on her . . . and your kids? But as the fun seems to have worn off now, why don't you divorce her and marry me, if you *need* me as much as you say?'

'Rose, stop it! It *is* possible to love more than one person at once, you know.'

'So you *do* love her?' Tears squeezed through Rose's closed eyelids.

'No. At least not in the same way as I do you.' He took her hand again. 'I couldn't leave her and the children; they need me. They're my responsibility. I could never upset their lives like that. But I want you, Rose.'

'So you want to have me in bed, and you want *her* to have your children and cook your dinners. Is that it?' Rose sniffed and wiped her eyes with the back of her hand.

'No, no. I didn't plan it that way, Rose. In fact, I didn't plan it at all,' Bill insisted, taking her in his arms.

Rose resisted his embrace for a second before giving in and sobbing on his chest. He held her and stroked her hair until her sobs gave way to little hiccuping breaths.

Finally, she pulled his handkerchief from his jacket pocket and blew her nose. 'God, what an idiot I am,' she sniffed. 'I still love you, Bill Fraser, even though you've made a fool of me – and her – all this time. I take it that she doesn't know about me?'

'Of course not,' Bill snapped, losing control. 'And there's no reason why she should.' But he checked himself and resumed his wheedling tone. 'Look, Rose, we haven't got a real marriage. She hasn't wanted it since the last kid was born. So, you see, you can't blame me for wanting you.'

'You mean she won't sleep with you and yet you want to stay married?' Rose said, her eyes wide in surprise.

Bill felt confident now that he was winning her over. 'I've told you, Rose,' he said quietly, 'she's my wife and the mother of my family, and they're all my responsibility, that's all.'

'What are we going to do now then?' Rose shrugged. She was capable of doing just about anything to keep Bill, but breaking up a family was a terrible thing to do.

'Nothing,' he soothed, caressing her cheek, now certain of his victory. 'If you're determined not to have an abortion, I can't force you. I know it's risky. If you want to go through with it and have it adopted, I can't stop you. I'll take care of everything.'

'Money.' Rose sighed. 'Money makes life so easy, doesn't it? I never wanted to have a baby. You know I can't stand kids. But now I'm not sure if I want to have it adopted. I agonised over it all night long – first I thought yes, and then I thought that this thing inside me is part of you and me.' She rubbed her brow in confusion. 'Oh, I'm so mixed up.'

'Don't worry!' Bill said confidently. 'You're a sensible girl, Rose. When you're feeling better, you'll know it's the best thing for both you and the kid.' To end the discussion he kissed her damp cheek and travelled slowly towards her mouth.

'Oh, I wish I didn't love you,' she murmured before submitting to his kiss.

Anne waited outside the car for Colin while he went to get the keys from his brother. Her freshly washed hair glistened golden in the sunlight and her eyes reflected the blue of the sky.

Colin swung his long legs out of the house and opened the car door for her. His handsome face was newly shaven, his moustache neatly trimmed. Anne thought he looked like Clark Gable.

'Well, here's to an exciting night at the local,' he declared.

'It's enough excitement for me,' Anne said softly.

'You're looking very pretty tonight. I like girls in summer dresses. Blue suits you.'

'Thank you.' She drew her white cardigan about her shoulders. 'I think I was optimistic about the weather.'

It was a Tuesday evening and quiet at the pub. They sat, he with a pint and she with a shandy, discussing the events of the day. Suddenly, impatiently, Colin took her hand across the table. 'I'm sick of talking about work, Anne. I think it's time we came out with it. You know I'm in love with you, don't you?'

Anne lowered her eyes. 'Yes.'

'And you are with me, aren't you?' he said forcefully. She raised her eyes this time. 'Yes.'

'Then, for God's sake, why are we both pretending we're just friends! It doesn't fool anybody at the house.'

'I know.'

'Look here, Anne, you've just admitted you love me. That must mean you don't love your husband any more, then?'

She nodded. 'I know that.'

'Then why on earth are we pretending we don't love each other? There's no point in avoiding the subject any longer. Let's be together while we can.' Colin's work-toughened hand gripped hers tightly. 'We'll deal with the future when we come to it.'

'Oh, Colin, I feel guilty about letting Dan down, even though I know I don't love him any more.'

'A fat lot of good guilt'll do either you or me. Come on.' He stood up and tugged at her hand.

'Where are we going?' she asked, grabbing her cardigan from the back of her chair.

'Anywhere! Out of here!'

Once in the car, they fell silent. Colin parked about a mile from the house, where a grassy meadow led down to the stream. He led her to the bank and threw down his jacket for her to sit on. Silently, she obeyed, heady from the new certainty that he loved her. The sweet, pungent smell of the damp grass mingled with Colin's musky odour as he took her in his arms and kissed her tenderly. Anne was lost. She had never been kissed this way before. She was powerless to stop him when his kisses travelled down her neck to her throat, even when he undid her dress. She cried out with pleasure when he gently kissed her bare breasts, and tenderly she unbuttoned his shirt. Both naked, they didn't even notice the cool night air. Anne felt like a bride, making love for the first time.

Chapter Twenty-Nine

When invasion loomed as France fell to Germany and Churchill refused Hitler's offer of peace with Britain, Walter left the ARP to join the newly organised Local Defence Volunteers. He trained to fight the Panzers in the streets with an assortment of weapons, including pitchforks, pikes, broomhandles and shotguns.

Gloom prevailed everywhere. Mary had to queue for over two hours at the local grocer's, ration books in hand, to acquire three sets of the emergency rations issued to every citizen. She shook her head in despair at the meagre supply of baked beans, corned beef, sugar and other staples.

In place of playing children, pillboxes dotted the beaches, linked by the ubiquitous barbed wire. They were also erected in unlikely spots in the country where people had hitherto felt safe. Anne worried about Johnny. There was no way of knowing where he would be out of danger.

But the Battle of Britain came and went. Aided by radar, the RAF inflicted crippling casualties on the Germans. By 17 September, Hitler had postponed indefinitely his invasion of Britain, and the nature of the German attack had changed to aerial bombardments of London and other industrial cities.

Della constantly wondered where Paul was, and how he was. A recurring nightmare haunted her: covered in blood, he stood on one side of a deep, wide trench and she on the other. He held out his arms to her and she tried to leap the gap, but fell into nothingness and awoke in horror. She had volunteered for extra duty at the hospital, necessitating giving up her ARP activities. Her only respite was Monday evening at the coffee rooms with Rose and Nora. This Monday, she waited for them. The weather being unusually cold for September, Rose wore a heavy swagger coat to conceal her pregnancy.

'Rose! That thing makes you *look* pregnant,' Della laughed. 'And you're hardly showing yet. Even *I'd* look pregnant in it.'

Rose flung the coat over the back of a chair and sat down. 'What the hell! It's fashionable anyway.'

Despite the war, Nora had never looked prettier. Her happiness with Phil glowed in her eyes. She flopped into a chair. 'How are things, Della?'

'The same . . . busy.' Della stifled a yawn.

'Any word from the boys?' Rose enquired, knowing better than to ask if there had been word from Paul.

'Yes, a letter from Wally, and this time it had a Malta postmark. It was dated six weeks ago. He says he's got a nice suntan, and that's about it. But Mam was relieved to hear from him. She worries about him the most, being in the navy. I'm worried about Michael, though,' she added, frowning. 'Even Ellen hasn't heard from him since before Caroline was born, and that's three months now.'

Rose looked down at her belly with disgust. 'Maybe I should talk to your Ellen to find out more about giving birth. I'm getting more squeamish about it every day. God, I'm going to be a nervous wreck when the time comes.'

'Rose,' Nora chastised, 'you're supposed to be glowing with excitement and full of joy when you're expecting.'

'I'm too busy feeling sick,' she retorted.

'Oh, come on, you look as fit as a fiddle,' Della scolded. 'Stop feeling sorry for yourself. You've made the decision and you've got to stick with it.' Then she added more gently, 'How's Bill?'

Rose's face softened. 'Quite amazing, really. I can't believe he's been so considerate since I've been in the family way. He's staying in town about three nights a week now.' She paused and her voice choked. 'Aw, bloody hell, I just wish he could live with me all the time. Being expectant's getting on my nerves, especially now I can't even get out of the house to go to work. And I'm beginning to look like a sack of spuds,' she added in despair.

'Come on, luv,' Nora broke in cheerfully. 'At least you've got no money worries. Most girls in your situation would have that to deal with as well.'

'Yes, count your blessings, Rose,' Della said. 'Have you thought any more what you're going to do?'

'Yep,' she said decisively. 'I've made up my mind and that's it. I'm going to give it to anyone who'll have it. In fact, I've made an appointment with an adoption agency next week. I must've been barmy to think I might keep it. I've had enough of the little bugger already, and it's not even here yet. I'm just not cut out to be a mam. I was born to be a lady and live the good life.' Suddenly, her face cheered up. 'That reminds me! Bill got two tickets for Sadler's Wells at the Theatre Royal next week and he can't go. Who'd like to come with me? It's *The Barber of Seville*. I've never been to an opera.'

'Why don't *you* go, Della?' Nora coaxed. 'You never go anywhere these days, and I've always got Phil to go out with.'

'What night is it?' She looked half interested.

'Saturday.'

'Oh, I shouldn't really. Anne's coming home on

Saturday night and I only see her once a fortnight.'

'Aw, come on, Della,' Rose wheedled. 'You can see her afterwards and on Sunday.'

Della gave in. 'All right. I've got a half-day this Saturday as well – the first for two months.'

Saturday arrived and Della returned home from the hospital looking forward to her free afternoon and evening out. She stopped dead as she entered the kitchen. Mary and Walter sat holding hands on the sofa, both red-eyed.

'Oh, Mam!' Della ran to her. 'What's wrong?' But as she asked the question, she knew what sort of answer it would be.

'It's Wally,' Mary moaned.

Della noticed a telegram on Walter's lap. She sank to her knees beside them both. 'Dead?' she cried.

'Aye,' Walter said through clenched teeth, 'and all for nowt. It was on the news the other day, but we didn't know our Wally was in it then. He was on the *Royal Oak* when it was torpedoed. For God's sake!' he shouted to the ceiling. 'It was a World War I ship – no bloody use to the Germans anyway. All they got out of it was over eight hundred lads' lives – our Wally's among them.'

Della closed her eyes to stop the room from spinning. Tears squeezed through the closed lids. Dear God, Wally was gone! 'How do they know? Did they find him?' she shrieked, refusing to accept the news.

'No.' Mary shook her head, and her shoulders sagged as if someone had dropped a sandbag on them. 'They haven't got the divers or equipment for a search. But he was on the crew list.'

Della put her head in Walter's lap and sobbed, while he stroked her hair with his hard hands. Eventually, he eased up her head. 'Why don't you sit with your mam a bit and I'll make you both a cup of tea? If I don't do something, I'll go out and punch the first person I see.'

At any other time, Walter's offering to make tea would have been followed by derisive laughter. This time, Della simply sat on the sofa and put her arms round Mary, burying her tear-stained face in her shoulder. Mary's eyes were dry now as she held her daughter and stared unseeingly at the wall. 'You'll have to go out for the rations first,' she said mechanically to Walter. 'We're out of tea and sugar.'

Della discarded her plans for the day and, when Anne arrived, the family were seated round the supper table with glum faces.

She knew immediately something was wrong. 'Oh, God! Who is it?' she whispered.

'Wally's dead,' Della said softly, rising to put her arms round her sister. They clung together and Della sobbed anew with Anne. Mary automatically rose to get another cup.

'My little baby brother!' Anne howled, as Della led her to a chair. 'I used to change his nappies. It was only yesterday . . .'

'Come on, lass,' Walter interrupted her roughly, rising and striding to the sideboard. 'Never mind the teapot, Mary. What we all need is a large brandy before bed. Then maybe we can get something like a night's sleep.'

In bed, Anne stared at the ceiling in the dark. 'Della,' she ventured.

'Yes,' came the muffled reply.

'Oh, Della, I feel so ashamed,' she went on in a voice choked with anguish. 'I've got to confess to someone.'

'What's the matter, Anne?' Della's body stiffened. She simply couldn't take any more bad news tonight.

'It's just that . . . when I heard about Wally . . . I

found myself wishing it had been Dan. Isn't that awful?' she said brokenly.

'Oh, sweetheart!' Relieved, Della got up and sat on Anne's bed, taking her hand.

'You, see,' Anne continued, 'it would have solved my problem with Colin. We're in love, and we've made love, and I want to stay with him always . . . but I can't because of Dan. Dear God! As if being unfaithful to him isn't enough, now I'm wishing him dead. What's happening to me? I used to love him!'

'It's all right, Anne. Stop tormenting yourself. I'm sure it's a normal reaction.' Della half lied, unable to assess the truth. 'I felt guilty about falling in love with Paul, even though I still loved Jerry, or at least his memory.'

Anne swallowed the lie gratefully. 'Oh, do you think so, Della? It's just that it's so awful thinking about the future. I can't bear the thought of Dan making love to me after Colin. In fact, I know now that Dan never did make love to me. He used me, and I was stupid enough to be happy just to please him. I had no idea what real love could be like – I mean, to have a man who loves you and wants to please you, not just possess you.'

'Poor Anne,' Della soothed. 'Take your chance at love while you can, sweetheart. God knows, Dan's made you suffer enough in the past. Just take it day by day and deal with the future when you get to it. That's what I'm trying to do. It's the only way I can keep my mind off Paul.'

Anne's sobs abated. 'Poor you,' she said penitently. 'Here am I pouring out my troubles to you, and Colin's safe with me. You don't even know where Paul is.' She took a deep breath. 'You're right! We've got to learn to live for the present. The future doesn't bear thinking about.' But she broke down again. 'Oh, Wally! There's no future for him. I can't believe we'll never see him again . . . never laugh at his jokes . . . never hear him whistling as he walks down the path . . .' Her voice trailed away as she began to cry again.

'Oh, please stop, Anne,' Della begged, covering her face with her hands and breaking down also. The two wept until exhaustion finally overtook them.

Chapter Thirty

In early March, 1941, Sister approached Della in the sluice, her face stony. 'A telephone call for you – and it had better be an emergency.'

Della dropped the sheets she was rinsing and fled to the office. 'Hello,' she squeaked apprehensively.

'It's me, Rose,' a voice at the other end gasped. 'I'm in the telephone kiosk down the road. I think it's coming.'

'You know I can't come now.' Della kept her eyes on the door in case Sister returned but guessed that she was listening in the hall anyway. 'I gave you the midwife's number. Have you rung her?'

'No, I wanted you to come first,' Rose wailed.

'Don't be silly! Ring that number and then Nora. I'll come straight after work.'

'Nora's not at the shop,' Rose whimpered. 'She's not well. I tried her first because I knew you'd moan about getting telephone calls at the hospital.'

Della softened. 'All right. Just do as I tell you and I'll see you as soon as I can.'

Mercifully, the corridor was clear as she made a hasty exit. She checked her watch – four-thirty. With luck, she could be there in a couple of hours.

She left the hospital promptly at six, a wool headscarf tied under her chin to ward off the stinging sleet that slapped her face. But, after the particularly savage snowstorms of the previous month, the sleet was almost a relief. At least the buses were running again.

She stopped dead as she passed the main entrance. A tall, lean, khaki-clad figure stood on the steps, his back to her. Paul! Her heartbeat quickening, she ran towards him. 'Paul! Paul!' He turned. She stood rooted to the spot. 'I'm sorry,' she mumbled. 'I thought you were someone else.'

'That's all right,' the owner of the strange face assured her. 'We all look alike in uniform.'

She trudged forlornly to the bus stop, her heart still thumping. Oh, if only Paul would write, just one letter, so that she'd know for sure he was still alive.

It was close to seven when she arrived at the flat, two buses having passed by full. The midwife opened the door. 'How is she?' Della asked anxiously.

The matronly, grey-haired woman, though not exactly misshapen, looked as if she had been designed and made in a hurry by a careless craftsman. She put her hands on her wide hips and shook her huge head, booming. 'All right! She's making a song and dance about nothing. The pains are still eight minutes apart and it's a perfectly normal birth. Anyone would think she was the first woman in the world to have a baby.'

Della smiled as she stepped over the threshold. 'I'm sure Rose thinks so.'

'You go in and shut her up, and I'll make us all a cup of tea. It's going to be a while yet.'

'If there's anything to eat in the house, I'd love a sandwich,' Della called after her as she hung up her sodden coat in the hall. 'I haven't eaten yet.'

'Oh, Della! Thank God you're here!' Rose screeched from the bedroom. 'I'm going to die!'

'No, you're not, you idiot. Everything's going perfectly fine,' Della assured her as she approached the bed. 'You're just being a baby.'

'I don't even want to see it,' Rose howled. 'I've never resented the little bugger more than I do at this moment.'

'Rubbish!' Della snapped. 'You're going to have to look after it for the first few days at least.'

'Oooowwww!' Rose shrieked in answer, as another pain grasped her.

Four hours later Rose screamed for the last time.

'Oh, it's a girl and she's beautiful!' Della cried, as the midwife turned the slippery little body upside down and spanked it. It let out a wail its mother could have been proud of.

'A girl!' Rose lay back, gasping. 'Let me see her.'

Giving Della a knowing look, the midwife held up the baby to Rose.

'Oh . . . I want to hold her.' Rose's voice was hushed, shocked.

'Not yet,' the midwife snapped. 'I've got to clean her up and wrap her up first. Do you want her to catch her death of cold? And I'll have to clean you up and all. You've still got more to come, you know.'

Della ran to the kitchen for a bowl of warm water and she and Rose watched open-mouthed as the woman deftly dunked the little body, miniature arms and legs flailing. At last she patted her dry and wrapped her in a fresh towel.

'Oh, come to Mammy, baby,' Rose cooed, nervously taking the tiny bundle in her arms. 'Oooh, isn't she lovely? And she's got my hair!' she cried joyfully.

Della and the midwife exchanged glances. 'Well, I'm going to get a bottle ready,' the latter announced, making to leave the room.

'Can't I feed her?' Rose begged.

'Not if you're giving her away. She'll have to get used to bottles from now on.'

'Don't talk rubbish,' Rose said irritably. 'Who said I was giving her away? Now show me how to do it.'

'Aw, *my* mistake!' The midwife gave Della a sly smile. 'I could have sworn you said you were having her adopted. And what about all those tins of baby milk in the cupboard? I suppose they're to put in your tea.'

Rose grinned. 'They will be now. I couldn't possibly give her away. She's so beautiful – just like her mammy.' She cradled the now silent bundle to her breast, while the midwife showed her how to hold and feed her.

'Now she won't get milk at first,' she instructed, 'but what she gets is good for her.'

Enthralled, Della watched Rose's amateurish attempts to feed the infant who, after much coaxing, eventually suckled noisily. She stood up and announced happily: 'I'm going to have a drink to celebrate. I've just won a shilling!'

'What for?' Rose asked without interest, intent on watching the baby.

Della kissed Rose's forehead. 'Nora and I had a bet on you.'

'Silly buggers,' Rose muttered, momentarily taking her eyes off the baby. Then she grinned. 'I think I'll call her Rosemary. That's half her mammy's name.'

'That's nice,' Della agreed. 'Let's drink to Rose-mary.'

Della sipped her drink happily, while Rose, finally over the birth and cleaned up, beamed at the sleeping infant in her arms. But her grin faded as the air-raid siren whined. 'Hell's bells! Eleven-thirty!' she shrieked. 'You can set your bloody watch by them. I'm not risking staying up here with her. Can one of you take her and the other one give me a hand?'

The midwife wrapped the baby in wool blankets from

the cot, while Della helped Rose out of bed and into a warm coat. Grabbing her own wet coat, she eased Rose's exhausted body gently down the stairs to the shelter. The two occupants of the other flats in the house moved over to make room on the bench. The siren stopped. Rose's teeth chattered loudly. They were going to be bombed.

Huddled in the cold, they listened to the drone of planes, like a swarm of hornets buzzing towards them.

Rose asked the midwife nervously, 'Did you turn off the gas?'

'Aye, I remembered,' the woman grunted. 'Now, here, you take her.' She handed the baby to Rose, who clutched it to her breast protectively. She wanted to rock it to comfort it but was unable to move, squeezed in as she was between her companions.

The old man from the attic flat shone a torch. 'I brought the cards,' he said cheerfully, fumbling in his pocket.

'Put out that torch, Jack,' Mrs James, the ground-floor tenant hissed. 'Save the batteries, man.' But in the brief light she had noticed the baby in Rose's arms. 'Eey!' she exclaimed. 'So you've got the bairn already. What is it?'

'A girl,' Rose answered proudly.

'Eey, that's nice, luv,' Mrs James said warmly. 'I heard a commotion up there, but I had the wireless on. I thought you were a bit far on for you and Bill to be hanky-pankying. I bet you're glad it's all over, hinny.'

Rose nodded in the dark.

The planes were overhead now, sinister silhouettes among the stars, the wings washed in sparkling silver moonlight. 'I suppose they'll be making for the Quay as usual,' Jack said.

But at that moment a bomb fell close by. They heard a

whine, a thud, then the shelter walls rattled, followed by the sound of splintering glass.

'God almighty! That one was close!' Rose hugged the baby to her breast with shaking arms.

They listened to the engines droning. Were they going to the coast? And then it started. Della gritted her teeth. They sounded almost overhead. The barrage of bombs was loosed, shock upon shock. Would it never end?

Mrs James prayed aloud: 'Our Father, which art in heaven . . .' Della took the woman's hand and gripped it comfortingly.

A fire engine's bell rang in the distance. The bombs stopped for what seemed like minutes, then started again. The group was silent now. Mrs James had stopped praying, and the baby, who had started whimpering earlier, had fallen asleep despite the fracas.

Then, as suddenly as they'd started, the bombs stopped again. The all-clear still hadn't sounded. Della patted Rose's knee. 'It seems that's it for tonight.'

'I don't care! What are those alarm bells ringing for? I'm not budging till the all-clear goes,' Rose whispered feebly. She felt weak. She thought she was going to faint.

Suddenly there was an almighty bang. 'So that's why they didn't sound the all-clear,' Jack hissed low, as though the enemy might hear him.

They all held their breaths, waiting for another bang. None came. A single plane phut-phutted in the sky, and Della daringly stuck out her head into the night. 'I think it's been hit.'

'Watch out, then.' Jack pulled her back into the shelter. 'That's a bomber, not a fighter. It might dump its cargo on us.'

Della's mind raced. Was the plane going to crash on top of them? Would the pilot bale out? If so, enemy or

not, she must do what she could to help, but where to
find an ambulance? Another blast! The stray plane had
crashed. The sound of shattering glass again splintered
the air. Then silence.

Mrs James prayed again, and Rose clutched Della, the
baby between them until, after what seemed an eternity,
the all-clear sounded.

Rose groaned with relief. 'Oh, thank God for that!
What a night to bring a bairn into the world.'

'I think we can go out now.' Della poked her head
through the opening again. 'Watch where you put your
feet. Mind the glass.'

'Here,' Jack said, passing her the torch.

Della shone it quickly on the sodden ground and, for
a second, on the ground-floor windows. 'Yes, some of
the windows have had it. But you'll have to wait till
morning to check for any other damage; you can't use
the torch any more tonight.'

The midwife again took the baby, and Della helped
Rose upstairs. 'I feel as if all my innards are coming
out,' Rose gasped, as laboriously she climbed the
steep flight.

Once inside, they discovered that most of the windows had shattered. Fragments of glass crunched under
their feet. Della carefully moved the bedroom blackout.
The sticky paper had held the larger pieces in place, but
cold draughts blew from all directions.

Rose collapsed on the bed, still wearing her coat,
while the midwife set the baby in her cot, draping a
blanket across the wooden rails to cut down the draught.
'Well, that's that! There's no point in trying to get home
tonight. You've got two lodgers, Rose.'

'Thank God for that,' she sighed wearily.

'I'm going to go out and see if anyone's been hurt,'
Della announced.

'You're a blithering idiot,' Rose said, though her

voice betrayed her admiration. 'And anyway, you can't see a thing out there.'

'No, but I can hear. Where's your torch?'

'In my handbag on the hall table.' Rose still shivered and clutched her coat round her. 'But don't flash it around or you'll get a fine. I read in the paper an old man had a coughing fit and lost his false teeth. He lit a match to find them and got fined, poor old sod.'

'I'll be careful. I'm not stupid,' Della reminded her.

Outside in the pitch blackness she could see nothing. A quick flash of the torch here and there showed only splintered glass and fallen bricks and tiles. She walked down the street, shouting, 'Anyone there?' No replies came. And then she saw the narrow slits of light from the headlights of a car or van. She flashed her torch for a second and the van pulled up. 'Are you all right, miss?' a male voice enquired.

'Yes,' she said, inching closer to the van. 'I just came out to see if anybody was hurt. I'm a St John's Ambulance nurse.'

'Nah, so far it looks like everybody got into the shelters in time,' the voice replied. 'It was lucky we had enough warnin'. God has mercy on us sometimes. Me mate and me's ARP and he's first-aid. We're checkin' things out. You go on home, miss.'

'Well, I'm at number twenty-seven, if you need any help,' Della volunteered, nevertheless grateful for the chance to sleep. She was on overtime duty the following day and the entire week.

'All right, hinny, we'll come for you if we need you,' the man assured her.

After a warming cup of tea in the kitchen, Della boiled the kettle again to fill the hot water bottle the midwife had left out for her. She flashed the torch cautiously round the sitting-room. The blinds and curtains, flapping furiously when she left, were now anchored to the window sills by books. The midwife lay curled up on the sofa wrapped in blankets, her coat thrown over the top.

Della crawled into the empty half of Rose's double bed, still wearing her indoor clothes and clutching the hot water bottle.

'Was anybody hurt?' Rose asked wearily.

Della stifled a yawn. 'It doesn't seem like it. But there's a lot of damage. Sorry if I woke you. Are you feeling all right?'

'Mmmm,' Rose murmured. Then, silent for a moment, she reached for Della's hand. 'Thanks for being here, luv, for the baby coming and everything. I'm scared silly in air raids. I'll have to keep a stiff upper lip now that I've got her to look after.'

'If I know you, you will,' Della encouraged her.

Rose let out a long breath. 'My God! I'll never forget the ninth of March – Rosemary's birthday and the worst raid we've had yet. They say things always happen in threes. What else?'

'Nothing. Go to sleep now.'

'Would you ring Bill tomorrow and tell him?' Rose's voice shook, giving away her nervousness. 'He's under William Fraser in the telephone directory. If his wife answers, just hang up and try again.'

'Of course,' Della assured her softly. 'You're not worrying about him, are you? Surely he can't stop you from keeping the baby.'

Rose hesitated a moment. 'It's just that I don't know how he'll take it.' She paused again before adding adamantly, 'But I'm keeping her, whatever he says.'

'I'm sure he'll understand.' Della tried to sound convincing. She still hadn't met Bill, still didn't know what he was really like, except for what Rose had told her. It must be hard on her to have to keep her lover secret, especially now.

They both lay silent, unable to sleep. Della closed her eyes. Occasionally, her thoughts were interrupted by the clang of a fire engine or the ominous sound of falling rubble. She pulled the blankets over her head and eventually dozed off, but Rose continued to stare into the blackness.

The baby awoke several times during the night, and Della was exhausted when she dragged herself up at six o'clock, careful not to wake Rose, who now slept peacefully. She tiptoed into the living-room, broken glass crunching under her feet. The midwife still slept. Envying the sleepers, she went to the bathroom and removed her crumpled clothes. She needed a warming bath, but they had forgotten to relight the boiler after the air raid. Shivering, she made do with a frigid wash. Cold, damp air still blew into the flat through the sides of the anchored curtains. She must at least tell Bill about the windows, even if his wife did answer the phone.

After grabbing a cup of tea and a piece of bread, she picked her way through the glass and rubble to the telephone kiosk. A heavy fog, coupled with the bleak early morning light, created an eerie atmosphere. But, so far as she could see, all the houses still stood, though most without windows and many with gaping holes in roofs or walls. A batch of ARP and Home Guard workers, the new name given to the Civil Defence Volunteers, were clearing up the debris.

Across the road, Della noticed a dark, tangled mass on the verge of the moor. A plane! Oh God, that close! 'Did anybody survive?' she asked one of the workers, a tired-looking man about her father's age.

'Nah, the crew must've been dead before they hit the ground. The fuel tank exploded in mid-air,' he informed her.

Della shuddered. 'Was anyone else hurt?'

'Aye, an old couple were late getting to the shelter and

they got hit by flying glass, but as far as we know that's all. Lucky for these folk they live on the edge of the moor. Most of the bombs landed across the road. If there'd been houses opposite, it would have been a flaming mess.'

Della thanked him and continued towards the telephone kiosk – not a single window left in it. Opening the door with difficulty over the mounds of glass, she stepped gingerly inside and picked up the receiver. Dead! She might have known. She'd have to telephone from the hospital.

Still shivering, she crossed the North Road to the bus stop. Half an hour later, not a single bus had arrived. Dear God! Were they not running? How would she get to the hospital? She'd walk into town. Perhaps they would be running there. She pulled her coat, still soaked from the night before, more tightly about her. The early morning light had trouble penetrating the fog, making it difficult to distinguish the puddles left by the previous day's sleet from the black, wet ground. She gave up trying, ignoring her soaked feet.

About a hundred yards further, she stopped and gasped. A trolley bus lay on its side, a gaping hole in the road beside it and scorched and twisted metal and debris everywhere. A crew of workmen were picking up the litter and dismantling the huge, charred vehicle. A lorry lay in wait, no doubt to haul the debris away. Della gazed in horror at the overhead lines straggled across the road, and the dark stains spattered on the ground near the overturned bus. Although used to the sight of blood, she felt her stomach turn over. This had been a major tragedy.

'Watch your step, miss,' one of the men warned her, as he dragged towards the lorry what had once been an upholstered bus seat but was now a bare mass of twisted metal frame and springs.

'Are the buses running further down?' she asked him, her voice coming with difficulty. There was no point in asking if anyone had been hurt.

'Aye, they're startin' at the Haymarket,' the man puffed.

'Thank you.' She walked on in silent despair. How many more people had to die before it would end?

Finally arriving at the hospital three-quarters of an hour late, Della hurried straight to the telephone kiosk. At last, she heard a ringing sound. A woman's voice answered, but Della was not to be put off. 'May I speak to Mr Fraser, please? I'm one of his tenants.'

'Just a moment.' Silence, then a man's voice.

'Hello.'

'Mr Fraser, I'm a friend of Rose's,' Della explained hurriedly. 'She's had a baby girl.'

'I see. Thank you for letting me know.'

'That's not all,' Della interjected before he could hang up. 'You'd better go to the house anyway. It was damaged in an air raid last night.'

'How much damage?'

'I'm not sure – windows and some tiles and loose bricks, but I don't know what else.'

'Was anybody hurt?'

'An elderly couple and the passengers on a trolley bus,' she replied tartly, noticing that he'd enquired about the property damage first.

'I'll go over today. Thank you.'

The receiver went dead. Della sighed with relief that he'd see Rose that day and fix up the windows. Nevertheless, she felt uneasy about this man as she made her way hurriedly to her ward. He hadn't asked how Rose was. But, she rationalised, it would have been difficult for him in front of his wife. She wondered what his reaction would be to Rose's change of heart. Well, she consoled herself, from experience she knew that if Rose wanted something she usually got it. And surely he couldn't refuse to let her keep her own child? He *could* refuse to support it though – and Rose. She couldn't survive on her own. No! She mustn't be so negative. So far, he hadn't refused Rose anything she wanted.

She approached Sister's closed office door and braced herself before knocking. Now for it.

At one o'clock, Bill arrived at the flat. Rose lay on the sofa, wearing a wool dressing gown with Bill's dressing gown over her. Mrs James had been up and down the stairs all morning after the midwife had left and had taped newspapers over the living-room windows to shield the draught. The fire glowed and the baby slept peacefully in her cot.

Rose felt emotionally and physically drained as well as apprehensive about telling Bill her news. Had Della been able to get him? she wondered. A key turned in the lock. Thank God! She looked up eagerly as Bill entered the room. 'Are you all right?' he asked, looking searchingly at her.

'Well, I've felt better.' She tried to grin, but instead her face crumpled and she wept.

He took her in his arms. 'Stop blubbering, it's all over now.'

Rose allowed herself the comfort of his strong arms for a few moments before pushing him away and indicating the cot with her head. 'Don't you want to see your baby?'

Bill stood up and peered at the sleeping, wrinkled face and the red hair. 'She's like you,' he muttered awkwardly.

'She's got your nose.' Rose attempted a light tone, but her voice broke as she burst out, 'I'm keeping her, Bill. I can't let her go!'

He straightened up and stared at her in disbelief, his face turning an unflattering shade of magenta. 'That's a sudden change of mind, isn't it?' he snapped.

'Oh, Bill!' Rose bit her lip, and tried to stem a new flood of tears, to no avail. 'As . . . as soon as I saw her and held her, I knew I couldn't give her away.'

He slumped into an armchair and stared at her angrily. 'You must be out of your mind, woman! Do you realise what you're letting yourself in for? It's a responsibility for a lifetime, you know – not just having a baby to play with while it's little. And you'd be tied down twenty-four hours a day. You couldn't stand that, Rose.'

'I know all that, Bill,' she cut in impatiently. 'I'm not daft. I know I've acted stupidly before in my life, but not now. And Mrs James said she'd look after her whenever I wanted.' Her voice softened and fresh tears glistened on her lashes, today untinted by mascara. 'I didn't know how much I'd love her, Bill.'

As always when perplexed, he ran his hands through his hair. He must change his tactics, he realised. 'You obviously haven't given a thought to *me* in all this, have you, Rose? Do you think I want to be stuck with another kid – a bastard?'

'Bill!' Rose reacted with disbelief. 'She's our baby! How can you call her that? If you have no feelings for her, then you can't have any for me. I'm keeping her, whatever you say, you unfeeling sod!' Through her tears she saw the muscles in his cheekbones tighten, but he said nothing, half turning from her. 'Bill,' she entreated, with guile now, 'it won't make any difference to how I love you, but I need her as well. I didn't know it would feel like this being a mother. I promise I'll let Mrs James look after her whenever you're here. I'll keep her out of your way as much as possible. She won't be a nuisance, I promise . . . and I know you'll grow to love her in time.'

Bill stood in front of the fire with his back to her,

hands on the mantelpiece and head bent, deep in thought. 'You couldn't keep her on your allowance without getting a job,' he said at last, 'and I'm not giving you any more.'

Rose resumed her defiant tone. 'I don't care, Bill. Mrs James will look after her during the day, and I'll have her the rest of the time.'

'And what about me?' He reeled round to face her. 'Whenever I come here you'll be taken up with the kid. The place'll be littered with dirty nappies and it'll keep us awake wailing half the night. Don't you think I get enough of kids at home? I come here for a bit of peace.'

'I thought you came here to be with me, Bill,' she said quietly.

'I do, and you know it. That's the whole trouble. You're taking advantage of that,' he said in a low, level voice. He cursed himself inwardly for needing this chit of a girl so much when he could have any fancy-piece he wanted. 'All right,' he said reluctantly, his voice betraying his defeat. 'I can't stop you from keeping her, but let's get one thing straight. I want her out of sight whenever I come here. And what the hell good is it to me if you're at work when I come during the day? You won't have to work. I'll increase your allowance. But that doesn't mean I'm acknowledging her as my kid, mind you,' he added quickly. 'She's entirely your responsibility.'

As she listened to his words, Rose's mouth fell open. She closed her eyes to think. Had she gained a victory? A partial one, maybe, although she was hurt by his rejection of the baby. But the sudden change of plan had come as a shock to him; surely he would come round in time? And, in the meantime, she would have the baby most of the time, and she wouldn't have to leave her to go to work. Yes, she must agree to his terms for the moment. She couldn't bear to lose either of them. This was a good start, she finally persuaded herself. He would change his mind eventually about seeing his own baby. 'All right, then, if that's how you want it. It's a compromise, I suppose.'

'Good. Now that's settled I can get on with my business,' Bill said coolly. 'I have to check this place out and then check down the road.'

Rose opened her mouth to speak, but before the words came out, he had turned with military precision and marched from the room.

Chapter Thirty-One

That December, the Japanese bombed Pearl Harbor. Anne groaned as she put down the newspaper. Now the Americans were no longer simply 'helping out' the Allies with supplies; they were in the war. 'Well, we may no longer be alone in the war,' she said to Colin, 'but now it's getting bigger. Will it ever end?'

'Aye, God only knows! But worrying your head won't end it, lass. You've had a hard enough day. Try to relax a bit before bed.'

Colin's brother was out for the evening, Nellie and Mavis were in bed, and Anne and Colin had a rare moment alone in the cosy farmhouse kitchen. Of late they had given up the pretence of waiting until the girls were asleep before Anne sneaked into his room. They were all grown-ups and everyone knew what was going on anyway. What's more, nobody cared. The motto of the day was, enjoy yourself while you can.

'Would you like some cocoa before bed?' Anne asked.

'Aye, luv, that'll do. I'd rather have a stiff brandy to forget the news, but there's not much left.' Languidly, Colin stretched out his length in the easy-chair before the roaring fire, his boots drying on the hearth and his feet resting on the high brass fender.

'I'll put the kettle on and then get ready for bed.' Before going upstairs, Anne set the blackened kettle on the trivet, easing it over the flames with the long brass poker. A few minutes later she returned wearing felt slippers and a wool dressing gown, her warm winceyette nighty underneath. Her face, shining with health, glowed in the firelight as she took the tin from the mantelpiece and spooned cocoa into two mugs. As they sat at either side of the fire sipping their cocoa, Colin gazed at her affectionately. 'Did I ever tell you, you're a very beautiful woman, Anne?'

'Yes, but I'll never get tired of hearing it.' A contented smile started slowly at the corners of Anne's mouth but stopped as the door knocker thumped impatiently. 'Oh, no! Who can that be?' She sighed with disappointment, their precious few moments alone interrupted. 'I'm not dressed. You go!'

'It's probably somebody lost his way in the dark,' Colin said, padding to the hall in his stockinged feet.

As he opened the door, a male voice slurred: 'I'm looking for me wife.'

'Well, you won't find her here, mate!' Colin attempted to shut the door.

On hearing the voice, Anne ran into the hall to escape upstairs – too late. Dan saw her and jammed his foot in the door.

'So she isn't here, then?' he rasped, flinging the door back in Colin's face. He attempted to shut it again, but Dan's body blocked the doorway. Anne trembled on the bottom stair, her earlier healthy glow now a parchment mask.

'Cosy little set-up you've got here, eh?' Dan sneered. 'Aren't you going to invite me in?' He leered at Anne, taking in her dressing gown and slippers. It was evident from his bleary eyes and his voice he'd had a lot to drink.

'Why didn't you let me know you were coming?' Anne whispered shakily.

'What! And spoil the surprise!' Swaying in the doorway, Dan surveyed Colin. 'A double surprise, eh? I gathered when you stopped writing there was something up.'

'You'd better leave my house,' Colin ground out through his teeth.

Dan raised his chin pugnaciously. 'Not without my missus.'

'Let him in.' Anne gave in quietly, returning to the kitchen. Pushing Colin roughly out of his way, Dan followed her. But Colin was close on his heels.

'Very cosy,' Dan sneered again, surveying Colin's boots on the hearth and the two mugs of cocoa. 'Just in time for a bedtime drink, am I? So this is what a soldier can expect when he comes back from the war.'

'You'd better know now she's not going back to you,' Colin said quietly, stepping between them in front of the fireplace.

'Oh, isn't she now?' Dan glared across him at Anne. 'Why don't you let her speak for herself?'

Her voice shaking with the effort, Anne dived straight in: 'He's right, Dan. I . . . I want a divorce.'

'A divorce, eh? Hold on a bit, lass.' As Dan made a slight movement towards her, Colin clenched his fists, at the ready, but Dan's eyes were fixed on Anne. 'You can't just get rid of your old man like that, you know. We're married, remember? And we've got a bairn. Even if I wanted to give you a divorce, which I don't, who do you think would get the bairn – its whoring mother or its poor, wronged, soldier father, risking his life to fight for his country while its mother turns into the tart of the town?' His mouth curled into a malicious grin, his eyes victorious.

Anne's shoulders dropped, as if someone had loaded a sack of potatoes on to them. 'Well, I didn't think you'd agree to a divorce, Dan,' she said, her voice still shaking. 'But I'm not coming back to you, whatever happens. I just want you to leave me alone – and Johnny too. You never wanted him before, and you only want him now to spite me.'

'Aye, I can pay you back with Johnny all right,' he snarled, making towards her again.

Colin faced Dan squarely. 'Don't you lay a finger on her.'

'So . . . the protective type, eh?' Dan mocked, his features now contorted with anger. He lunged at Colin. 'We'll see how protective you are.' His fist shot out and slammed into Colin's face. Colin recoiled, then regained his balance and threw a punch at Dan's chin. The blow slowed Dan down for a second, but now both his fists hammered into Colin, wherever he could hit him. Dan had the advantage in weight, but Colin in agility. He dodged the blows and grabbed Dan round his neck, squeezing until Dan's face turned purple. He grasped wildly at Colin's hands in a futile attempt to free himself.

'For God's sake, stop it, Colin!' Anne shrieked. 'You'll kill him.'

But no sooner were her words out than Dan used his brute force. He raised his knee sharply into Colin's groin. He slid to the floor, groaning. Labouring to recover his breath, Dan leaned over the crouched, agonised figure and in seconds was on his knees, his hands round Colin's neck, forcing up the bent head, forcing Colin up on his knees. 'Fornicator!' he yelled, as he pressed his thumbs hard into Colin's throat.

Anne, petrified and speechless at the sight of Colin at Dan's mercy, suddenly came to life; she grabbed the poker and dealt Dan's bent back a blow through the heavy uniform cloth. 'Get off him!' she screamed as she raised the poker again. But Dan was too quick for her. He let go of Colin's neck and awkwardly pushed himself up, whirling round on Anne in an attempt to grab the poker from her shaking hands. But Colin grabbed Dan's right foot and yanked it off the floor before he had regained his balance. Dan tottered and fell backwards with a scream of rage, before his head struck the fender. He lay quiet, his bloodshot eyes bulging.

'Dear God!' Anne screeched. 'Is he dead?' Her eyes were like huge glass marbles.

Still winded, Colin dragged himself up. He looked at Dan's face and bent to feel his pulse. 'God in heaven!'

As he spoke, Nellie and Mavis hurtled into the room. 'We seen it all,' Nellie shouted, her pencilled eyebrows arched in amazement almost to her hairline, her bleached hair tied up in rag curlers. 'We heard the rumpus and came down. I was just going to run over to the Browns to ring the police when he conked out.'

Colin put his arms round Anne, who shook wildly. He struggled for breath as he attempted to soothe her: 'It's all right, luv. He can't hurt you any more now.'

'It was self-defence,' Beryl assured them, her brown eyes popping in her wrinkled face. 'We both seen it.'

A car pulling up outside indicated Bob's return. 'Thank God,' Colin whispered. 'Bob can drive to the Browns and ring the police.'

'What the hell—?' Bob started as he entered the kitchen.

'It's Anne's husband,' Colin said lamely, still with his arm round her. 'He came to get her, and when she wouldn't go, he went for her. I tried to stop him, and we had a fight. He hit his head on the fender.'

Bob whistled through his teeth. 'God almighty! Don't touch him. I'll get the police.' In seconds, the door slammed behind him.

Nellie lifted the rug in front of the sideboard where the key was hidden. 'I think you two could do with a brandy. I think we all could.'

'Eey, Nellie, you dark horse!' Beryl said. 'How did

you know where the key was hid?'

'Never mind now,' Nellie snapped, pouring four generous brandies. 'Here, hinny.' She handed a glass each to Anne and Colin, both still standing stupefied beside Dan's body. 'And get away from there and sit down.'

'I . . . I'd better get dressed,' Anne muttered. 'It'll look bad if I'm in my night clothes.'

'Well, we're in our dressing gowns, pet,' Beryl soothed her. 'And you were upstairs with us in bed when he came. Colin called you down, and then all the uproar started. Isn't that right, Nellie? He went for Anne and her boss tried to protect her.'

'Aye, that's what happened, luv,' Nellie confirmed. 'You've got nothing to worry about. Colin was down here by himself. I'll just wash up these mugs.'

The front door creaked and Bob returned. 'They're on their way,' he said, sitting down heavily at the table.

Beryl joined him. 'We were just saying how it happened, Bob. Anne was in bed with us when her husband came, and Colin called her down.'

Bob ran his fingers through his thinning hair. 'Aye, whatever you say.'

Beryl continued. 'And we all knew he had a history of beating his wife – and a prison record.'

'Aye, I know all that,' Bob said irritably. 'Colin's my brother, isn't he? Do you think I'd be daft enough to tell the police they were having an affair?'

Anne sat at the table, her head in her hands, her shoulders still shaking. 'Dear God!' she sobbed. 'I wished him dead, and now he is.'

'Then what are you crying for, you ninny?' Nellie said firmly. 'He was a rotten lot and you're well shot of him.'

A few seconds later, the police arrived, closely followed by an ambulance. In a daze, Anne related the story, as amended by Nellie and Beryl. At first the inspector was cool and polite, but after the body had been removed, he put his hand on Anne's shoulder. 'It's all right, missus. We'll take care of everything now. If you and your boss would just come down to the station tomorrow morning and make a formal statement, we'll see to the rest. But,' he hesitated awkwardly, 'neither of you can leave here until the investigation's over.' Anne looked startled, and he went on kindly: 'There's not much doubt it was an accident, and self-defence, and you've got two witnesses. Your boss here's lucky.' He nodded towards Colin.

'Thank you,' Anne said, still trembling as she showed him out.

On her return from the police station the following morning, Anne wrote a letter home.

Dear Mam, Dad and Della,
I can't come home on Saturday. Dan's dead. He had an accident. He found me here and had a fight with Colin. It ended up that Dan fell and hit his head on the fender.
Please don't worry about me. I'm all right, and everyone is being very kind to me.
With luck, it should all be sorted out by next week and I'll be going to Mrs M's to see Johnny. Could you all come?
I'm longing to see you, but I must see Johnny as well to tell him about his dad.
Honestly, I'm all right. I still feel shocked, but you'll be pleased to hear that I'm also relieved. I stopped loving Dan a long time ago. You were right about him all the time, but I was too blind to see it.
I love you all,
Anne

Mary drew in her breath as she read. Without emotion,

she announced: 'Dan's dead.' Walter grabbed the letter and, stunned, Della read over his shoulder.

'Well,' Walter said at last, 'it's never good news when a young fella dies, but I have to be honest, I'm not all that sorry about this one.'

'Me neither, I'm ashamed to say,' Della said.

Mary sat at the table in a daze. 'It means Anne can have a chance of a decent life, and no more beatings. I hope she finds someone else.'

'She already has, Mam,' Della said quietly. 'But she'll tell you about it herself now. She didn't want to upset you with her problems before, but with Dan gone, there won't be any more trouble.'

Mary nodded knowingly. 'It's Colin, isn't it?'

'She really loves him, Mam, and he treats her well.'

'Well, that'll be a novelty for her,' Walter muttered, helping himself to more tea.

Mary picked up the letter, folded it, and put it back in the envelope. 'Still, I can't believe we're all so cold about it.'

'We'd be hypocrites if we weren't,' Walter said honestly.

'Dad's right, Mam,' Della agreed. 'We shouldn't pretend what we don't feel. I have to go now. I'll be able to go to Mrs M's with you on Sunday.'

Anne arrived first at Mrs Moynihan's and the frail old woman greeted her at the door. 'Eey, me poor bairn,' she hollered, in a voice as strong as ever. 'I got your letter. How you feelin', hen?'

'Just a bit shaky still,' Anne replied, returning Mrs Moynihan's hug. 'It was a shock, but I'm not going to pretend that I'm mourning him.'

'Good for you, lass!' Mrs M boomed. 'Come on in and have a cup o' tea. Our Molly's got the kettle on ready, and Johnny's in the back yard with the other

384

bairns. You can leave him there for a bit.'

'Hello, luv,' Mrs Moynihan's daughter greeted Anne in the cosy kitchen. 'Eey, I'm sorry about your Dan.' Her blue eyes were sympathetic in her still pretty face. Her dark blonde hair, just beginning to turn grey at the temples, was tied up in a scarf. But, despite the greying hair and unflattering turban, her face still had a youthful appearance. Her strong cheekbones and determined jawline she had definitely inherited from her mother.

'Well, you can be sorry for *him* if you like but not for me,' Anne said firmly. 'I'm not going to pretend any more. It's a blessing for Johnny and me.' She hung her coat and headscarf on the back door and sat at the kitchen table, placing her large shopping bag beside her.

'Aye, I must say you don't look bad on it, hinny,' Mrs Moynihan observed, joining her.

'How are *you* feeling, Mrs M?' Anne enquired with concern.

'Can't complain, hen. The best thing I ever did was move in with our Molly and the bairns. I think me biggest problem was that I was lonely after me brother died. I love havin' the bairns around. It takes you out o' yoursel', if you know what I mean.'

'I know,' Anne said, noticing that the old woman's hands were more swollen and distorted than ever. 'You never complain, do you?'

'Eey, what's the point? Complainin' doesn't make no difference to how you feel, and it only makes them around you miserable.'

Molly smiled as she poured the water into the pot. 'One of these days she'll die, swearin' she's as fit as a fiddle.'

'I hope our Johnny isn't too much for you,' Anne said anxiously. 'When all this has died down, perhaps I could take him on the farm with me?'

385

Mrs Moynihan shook her head. 'Not on your nellie, hinny. We'd miss him. Right little ray of sunshine he's been lately.'

'You've both done wonders with him,' Anne said gratefully. 'I've warded off telling him about his dad, but I'd better get it over with before the others get here. I asked Mam and Dad and Della to come today. I hope you don't mind.'

'Mind, hinny!' Mrs Moynihan's voice was joyful. 'Eey, do you hear that, Molly? Though what in the world are we goin' to feed them with?'

Smiling, Anne dipped into her shopping bag. 'I've brought a dozen fresh eggs, two loaves of Hovis, two tea cakes, and some home-made strawberry jam.'

Molly's eyes widened. 'Eey, and I was goin' to make a bacon hotpot. We can have bacon and eggs and fried spuds instead.' She set the teapot on the table. 'I'll get Johnny in before I pour your tea, luv. Would you like us to leave you alone?'

'No, it'll be better if you stay . . . please.'

'Whatever you want, luv.' Molly opened the door and yelled, 'Johnny! Your mam's here.'

He bounded in and threw himself at Anne. 'Hello, Mam,' he greeted her happily.

'Hello, monkey face! Have you been behaving yourself?' Anne hugged him to her until he pulled away.

'Aye, I got nine out of ten for arithmetic last week, and after Christmas I'm going to secondary school.'

'I know, pet.' Anne sighed and pulled out the chair next to her. At eleven, Johnny considered himself too big to sit on her lap. She took his hand and forced herself to deliver the news. 'Do you miss your dad very much?'

Johnny screwed up his freckled nose thoughtfully. 'Not very much. Uncle Jimmy's more fun anyway.'

Anne squeezed his hand. 'Would you miss your dad if you could never see him again?'

'Well . . . I suppose so.' Johnny stared at the table and kicked the chair leg.

Anne put her arm round him and told him softly, 'Well, luv, he won't be coming back any more.'

'Did he get killed in the war?' Johnny asked, round-eyed.

'No, not exactly. He had an accident when he came home on leave.'

'Oh . . .' Johnny was evidently disappointed.

'But he *was* a soldier. He did fight for his country,' Anne reminded him, defending Dan's memory.

'Aw, I know all that, Mam,' Johnny said impatiently. He looked thoughtful for a moment, then screwed up his face in distaste. 'Ugh, does that mean I'll have to go to the funeral and all that?'

'No, luv. That's all over. I waited till I could tell you in person.'

'That's good,' he said, relieved. 'Can I go out to play again now? Andy and me's playing marbles.'

'Yes, if you want to.'

He slid from the chair and darted off.

'Well, that didn't seem to bother him much,' Mrs Moynihan gasped in disbelief. 'I think that bairn sees more than we give him credit for.'

But Anne continued to defend Dan. 'Well, he's barely seen his father since he was six – first prison, then the war.'

Molly nodded. 'Aye, I know. But I still think me mam's right. And I think you should be glad it didn't upset him much.'

'Much!' Mrs Moynihan cried. 'It didn't upset him a bugger if you ask me. Eey,' she added, shaking her head, 'but you never know with bairns, do you?'

'Oh, well, whatever,' Anne sighed, pouring the tea. 'Let's just be grateful he took it so well. I'm glad I got it over with before everybody comes.'

Chapter Thirty-Two

By mid-1943, even Walter was more optimistic about the war.

'Things are looking up at last,' he said almost cheerfully. 'Now that we've flattened the Ruhr, the swine are committed to other fronts.'

Mary passed his porridge over his newspaper. 'It's wonderful to have a few more peaceful nights. Do you think this will mean the end of the Battle of Britain, then?'

'Aye, it's got to soon. They can't keep it up here and save their skins elsewhere.'

'Thank God for that,' Mary sighed.

'Thank Churchill not God, woman,' Walter grunted.

Della stood up to leave. 'I'm off now. Bye.'

'Try to take it easier today, luv,' Mary said anxiously. 'You look done in before you start.'

'Yes, Mam.' Della smiled weakly as she left. Despite the hopeful news, she was war weary – weary of her menial duties at the hospital, weary of waiting for the end, and, most of all, weary of hoping and praying for Paul to come home.

She consoled herself that life was getting better for everyone she loved. It must be her turn soon. There had been no more bad news about the boys since Wally's death, and, the scandal of Dan's accident having died down, Anne and Colin were engaged. Rose had gradually wheedled Bill into allowing the child to be around in his presence, and she delighted in her role of mother to Rosemary, even nurturing the hope of having a brother or sister for her one day, if only she could talk Bill into it. Nora and Phil, now married, had rented a flat in one of Bill's properties near Rose's.

On the bus, Della pondered on her own existence. Why was it that other people's lives continued to move along, war or no war, when hers had stopped? She was tired of waiting for life to begin. She felt stuck in the quagmire of the war, unable to pull herself out and move forward. Life was marching past her.

As the bus pulled up outside the hospital, she pulled a face at the government sign on the window: 'Is your journey really necessary?' She wished hers weren't.

At the ward, she discovered she had been transferred to wards 5 and 6. Jonathan looked up from his desk as she entered the new office.

'Well, good morning! Are you going to be one of *my* angels of mercy from now on?'

'Seems like it,' she replied dully.

'That's nice. But let me warn you about Sister.'

Della raised her eyes to heaven. 'Not another one?'

'Afraid so! They seem to be a special breed.' Jonathan wiped his spectacles on his handkerchief and squinted his brown eyes at her approvingly.

Avoiding his gaze, she turned to go. 'Well, I suppose I'd better report to Sister.'

'She's not on the ward,' Jonathan grinned. 'I saw her going into the ladies'.'

Smiling, Della sat in the visitor's chair. 'Well, I'm not going to disturb her there. How's work?'

'Mmmm, hard but satisfying.' He put on his clean glasses and looked at her again. His eye appeared completely normal now, despite some loss of vision, but his handsome face was still slightly pockmarked from the shrapnel. Funny how men can still look attractive with scars and glasses but women can't, Della mused.

'How's Vera?' she asked. It was some time since she had seen Jonathan.

He lit a cigarette. 'Fine as far as I know.'

'What do you mean, "as far as you know"? You don't sound much like a prospective bridegroom.'

'Well, to tell the truth, I'm not. I haven't seen her for a while.'

Della looked surprised. 'I'm sorry. I didn't realise. When did you break up?'

'Oh, a couple of years ago.' He shrugged. 'And you needn't be sorry. It was best for both of us. How's your boyfriend?'

Della looked at the floor. 'I still don't know.'

'Then I think you need cheering up. How about coming to the pictures with me tonight? Walt Disney's on, and the Three Stooges, and I hate to go to the pictures by myself. Some strange woman might accost me in the dark.' His face was serious, but his eyes betrayed a smile.

'Thank you, but I can't.'

'On duty I suppose?'

'No, I'm busy,' she lied.

'Then we'll make it tomorrow night.'

She hesitated before answering. 'I—'

'And don't tell me you're busy tomorrow,' he interrupted. 'Just keep me company at the pictures and enjoy the film. You don't have enough fun, and neither do I. Everybody needs a good laugh these days.'

Della loved Walt Disney. 'All right,' she agreed uncertainly. Surely the past wasn't important now? She didn't need her mother's permission to go out with a man any more. And, besides, Jonathan knew about Paul and was just being friendly.

'Splendid!' Jonathan looked suitably pleased.

As the door creaked and Sister returned, Jonathan grinned disarmingly at the stern face. 'Well, I'll be off now, Sister. You've got a new recruit. Try to be nice to her. She's a friend of mine.'

The following evening, at five past six, Jonathan waited outside Sister's office. Della had changed into a deep pink cotton dress and high-heeled sandals.

'You look like a fresh strawberry,' he complimented her. 'Nice to see you out of that uniform. And it's a nice change to see frankly bare legs. I don't know why girls paint those awful stockings on them.' He paused in thought and chuckled. 'Quite a change from those thick school things and lace-ups you wore the night I first met you.'

Della pulled a face. 'You beast! You noticed! And you still remember.'

'Of course! I remember everything about that night,' he said quietly. 'I watched you camouflage your feet with your dress every time you sat down, and I watched you when you sneaked out to meet your father – without make-up.'

Della grinned. 'And I thought I'd been so clever in my subterfuge.'

He took her arm and guided her towards the car park. Despite herself, she was looking forward to an evening's entertainment. Jonathan was right. She didn't go out enough. She settled herself comfortably in the passenger seat of his little Austin 7. It was wonderful not to have to rely on the vagaries of the buses. 'How do you manage for petrol?' she asked.

'I get my ration, plus doctor's allowance . . . and occasionally a present from a grateful patient.' He grinned mischievously, turning the key until the car rattled into action.

As they left the hospital behind them, he let out a long

sigh. 'What a relief! No more broken bones, appendicitis, ulcers, measles, diphtheria or gonorrhoea for one day – sad how the latter's increased since before the war,' he added thoughtfully. 'War makes people throw caution to the wind, I suppose. Prostitutes are starting as young as sixteen. Did you know, the percentage increase in VD since before the war—'

Della interrupted him, 'I don't think I want to.' She screwed up her nose. 'We're out for an evening's enjoyment, remember.'

'Sorry, you're right.' Jonathan turned an apologetic smile on her. 'No more shop talk. Now for a slap up meal before the cinema.'

'A slap up meal! Where on earth do you think we'll find that?'

'At my flat. Where else? I've been saving up my rations.'

'You! Cook!' Della exploded into laughter.

'What's so funny about that? When a man lives alone and likes to eat, he has to cook. But I enjoy it anyway, it's my relaxation after work.'

She endeavoured to straighten her face but was still amused at the prospect of Jonathan in the kitchen. 'This should be interesting,' she spluttered. 'What's on the menu?'

Unperturbed, he replied seriously. 'You may laugh now, but how would you fancy a bacon omelette, new potatoes and garden peas, followed by cheese and biscuits – and, to wash it down, a nice bottle of wine from my well-stocked cellar.'

'You're kidding! New potatoes and garden peas! Where from?'

'A grateful patient.'

'I wish my patients would show their gratitude like that,' Della sighed. 'All I ever get is their heartfelt thanks.'

'Ah, but I perform such miracles on them, a mere thank you wouldn't suffice.' He turned to look at her. 'Are you still going to train as a nurse when the war's over?'

'Yes, it's the only thing I want to do with my life now.'

'What about getting married and having babies?' he asked frankly.

Della blushed. 'Oh, maybe that too, but the war's done a lot for women. They've proved now they can bring up children and have a career as well.'

'You're right about that, but they'll be in for a fall when the men come back and push them out of their jobs.' He glanced sideways at her. 'Except for nursing, of course. They'll always want women for that.'

'Don't you believe in progress for women then?' she asked, surprised. 'I'd have thought you'd be more enlightened.'

'Oh, I believe in it all right,' he assured her. 'I think every woman should be able to make a free choice about her life; it's just that I doubt there'll be enough jobs to go round both sexes after the war, and men will have preference as the breadwinners.'

'That's true,' Della admitted. 'But it's also true that there'll be an awful lot of work to do to put the country right. That should create jobs, at least for a while.'

'Yes, for a while maybe. Just imagine – women builders and navvies! Almost as funny as a man in the kitchen, eh?'

He pulled up the car outside a Victorian terraced house in Fern Avenue. 'Same house I lived in as a student,' he explained, 'but now I've got the ground floor instead of the attic. The landlady likes me for some reason.'

'I can't imagine why,' Della laughed, as he ran round the car to open her door.

The flat was large and airy, and comfortably though sparsely furnished in a man's style: a dark brown rexine three-piece suite, a plain green carpet, and a walnut sideboard and drop-leaf dining table and chairs.

Jonathan indicated the sofa. 'Please sit down.' Della sat in an armchair.

'And what would you like to drink before dinner?'

'You mean there's a choice!'

'I confess, I raid my parents' cellar whenever I go home. There's enough there to last a lifetime.'

'How *are* your parents?' Della asked politely, not really caring to know.

'All right. I don't go home much – just duty visits. There's still no love lost between us, but I'm the only son they've got left at the moment, so I have to play the role.' Jonathan pulled out bottles from the sideboard as he spoke. 'Let's see, I've got sherry and port and—'

She stopped him. 'I'd love a sherry, please. And I'm sorry, Jonathan, I haven't even asked how your brothers are.'

'James was shot down over Germany,' he said soberly, handing her a glass. 'His mates saw his plane go down and his parachute didn't open.'

'Oh, I'm sorry,' Della commiserated, experiencing again the ache of losing her own brother.

Jonathan poured himself a sherry and went on: 'Charles is still flying. They both flew as a hobby before the war, so they automatically became pilots.' Sitting on the sofa, he stared into his glass thoughtfully. 'It's funny, Charles used to love the cushy life at home, and now he's risking his neck every day out there. He'd just about had his fill of the folks before he left. Father still rules the estate like a school master, and Charles was getting tired of waiting to take it over. He always wanted to expand and modernise it.'

'Did you never want to go into the business?' Della asked curiously.

'Nope,' he said adamantly before raising his glass. 'Cheers! You know I could hardly wait to leave home. I even hate to visit, but they *are* my parents, and I feel I owe them for my education and career.' He turned the subject around. 'Does your mother know you're out with me this evening?'

Della shook her head. 'No, I didn't think it necessary to tell her. I'm old enough to choose my own friends now.'

He quirked his eyebrows. 'How the years fly! But you look just the same as you did at fourteen. In fact, even prettier.'

Della laughed, pleased and embarrassed. She searched for a distraction. 'I thought you said we were going to eat. I'm starving.'

Jonathan drained his glass and stood up. 'Right you are! Dinner's on the way. Would you prefer to relax in here or watch the cook at work?'

'I must see this.' Della grinned. 'I've never seen a man in the kitchen. My dad can't even make a cup of tea.'

She leant against the door of the tiny kitchen as Jonathan bustled about getting food from the larder. '*Et voilà!*' he cried triumphantly, placing three large brown eggs on the bench. 'None of that powdered stuff in this establishment.'

Della's eyes widened. 'Fresh eggs!'

'I choose my patients very carefully. This one keeps hens.'

She watched, impressed, as he deftly prepared the meal, afterwards helping him set the table in the living-room.

'Please be seated, madam,' he said, pulling out her chair. 'Dinner will be served presently.' He disappeared into the kitchen and returned, setting two heaped plates

on the white tablecloth before disappearing and returning again, this time waving a bottle of Bordeaux, which
he uncorked with a flourish. He filled two glasses. Della
picked up hers and sniffed it cautiously.

'Don't worry, it's the real thing – no tea-leaf plonk for
my parents. Some of their stuff is older than I am.'

'I suppose we should drink to your parents then,' she
said reluctantly.

'Not on your nellie! To us!' Jonathan clinked his glass
against hers. 'And to an evening off.'

After the meal, Della put down her knife and fork.
'That was wonderful! Thank you. Do you do this often?'

'As often as you'd like,' Jonathan replied, his voice
flippant but his eyes serious.

She looked down at her empty plate, deciding she'd
better sort this out before he got any wrong ideas.
'Look, Jonathan,' she began, flushing with embarrassment. 'You know that we could never be any more than
friends. And, anyway, you also know I've got a boyfriend.'

'So what?' he said lightly. 'Is there any law that says a
man can't cook for his friends? And, besides, it makes
me feel less guilty about accepting bribes if I can share
the spoils.' He fixed his eyes on her before saying
seriously, 'Della, I enjoy your company, that's all. I
promise.'

Della blushed even deeper. 'I'm sorry if I read
anything into it that wasn't there, Jonathan. It's just that
I didn't want to lead you on. I'd feel like a tease.'

He grinned and his voice was flippant again. 'You can
tease me as much as you want. And now, would you like
coffee before we go? Afraid I've only got Camp.'

She smiled, relieved that she'd made their relationship plain. 'I can stand Camp.'

After the cinema, Jonathan drove her home, the headlights feebly emitting the regulation cross of light through their black paper covers. His hand accidentally brushed against her leg as he changed gear, and Della shifted uncomfortably in her cramped seat, her colour rising in the dark. She disliked the tingling sensation that surged through her. Was it possible to feel physical attraction for one man when you were in love with another? Rose's words about sex all those years ago flashed through her mind: 'Once you've had it, you can't do without it.' Was Rose right? Was she just missing sex? Jonathan was undeniably an attractive man. But she was madly in love with Paul. No, it was ridiculous! She wanted sex with Paul because she loved him. She didn't love Jonathan.

At the house, he helped her out of the car and escorted her to the gate, where he stopped. 'I see you've lost your gate. Force of habit! I was just about to open it for you.'

'Yes, it went to the scrap iron effort, together with most of Mam's pots and pans.'

'Oh, well, it's a make-believe world,' he said gaily, going through the motions of opening the invisible gate and closing it carefully after Della had passed through.

'Thanks for a lovely evening, Jonathan. I enjoyed myself.'

'So did I. When are we going to do it again?'

'When are you getting your next supply of black market goodies?'

'Tomorrow.'

Della's smile was lost in the darkness. 'I'm on duty. How about one evening next week? We can decide later.'

'Whatever you say. See you in the morning.'

As Della walked down the path, the engine started. She did feel more cheerful after an evening out. Jonathan was nice, despite his parents. Something on her mam's side must have rubbed off on him. And if she had felt herself stirring at his touch, surely it must be normal – though she would see that it didn't happen again. As she let herself into the house, she wondered vaguely why he didn't have a real girlfriend. But it was none of her business.

Chapter Thirty-Three

A week later, Mary greeted Della cautiously as she returned from work. 'Hello, luv. Did you go out with Rose and Nora?' She stirred a pan of soup in the scullery while Walter read the paper at the table.

'No, I went to the pictures with a friend from the hospital,' Della answered evasively. There was no point in worrying her mother about Jonathan again.

Mary followed her into the kitchen, a wary look on her face. 'There's a letter for you on the mantelpiece.'

Della whirled round and picked up the envelope propped in front of the clock. Her heart sank. It had a local postmark. But who would write to her? The envelope was in a shaky, spidery hand. Inside was a note in the same hand, and another envelope with her name and address written in bold letters. She scanned the note first. Oh, God! It was a Fenham address:

> 28 Baycroft Avenue
> Fenham
> 15 June 1943

Dear Della,

Our Paul left this envelope for you and asked us to send it if anything happened to him. We got a telegram today to say that he's missing, believed dead. I wasn't quite sure whether I should send it now or wait till we hear more, but his dad said I'd best send it anyway.

I understand you're a special friend of his and I know that you'll be praying along with us that he'll come back safe and sound.

God bless you,
May Conway

As she read, Della's face turned grey.

'Is it from Paul?' Mary asked fearfully.

'His mother,' Della whispered, sitting down slowly on the sofa. 'He's missing.'

'God almighty!' Walter cried. 'Not another one!'

Della opened the second envelope slowly, her hands shaking and her eyes glazed with tears. Through a blur, she read:

My Darling Della,

I hope you will never receive this letter, but I need to write it. If anything happens to me, I want you to know that I loved you, and that meeting you was the most wonderful thing that ever happened to me. My mind is full of the unforgettable memories you created, and these will keep me going until my time comes, or until I come back to you. I pray it's the latter, but if not, please don't weep by my grave.

Thank you for the most wonderful three weeks of my life.

Paul

The note fluttered to the floor as Della covered her face with her hands. A low moan escaped through her clenched teeth. Mary threw herself down beside her and put her arms round her. 'Oh, my God! Not Paul?' Her tears flowed as freely as Della's as she rocked her and patted her back as if winding a baby.

'He's missing, believed dead,' Della groaned.

Raising his eyes to the ceiling, Walter bellowed, 'Dear God, how many more times? What the bloody hell do you think you're doing up there?'

'That's enough, Walter,' Mary said. 'Why don't you make her a cup of tea?'

'No, we've still got some brandy. I think it's called for again.'

Della knelt slowly and picked up the letter, pressing it to her wet cheek – the second letter from the dead she had received in her short life. 'No, no!' she cried aloud. 'He *will* come back.'

After work the following day, Della took the bus to Fenham, asking the conductor to tell her when they reached Baycroft Avenue.

'This is your stop, miss,' he yelled up the stairs where she nervously smoked a cigarette to calm her nerves. The street turned out to be much like her own – a long row of semi-detached council houses that the architect had spent little time designing and the council little money on building. Drab and featureless, the only 'decoration' was the drainpipes running down the front walls. Most of the small front gardens had been turned into victory gardens, the only blooms the monotonous green tops of vegetables.

At number twenty-eight, she rapped tentatively on the knocker. A frail old woman answered, her grey hair neatly covered with a matching hairnet. The thin face was lined and careworn but the hazel eyes were still bright.

'Mrs Conway?' Della enquired.

'Aye.'

'I'm Della Dolan, Paul's friend.' Tears started at the sight of Paul's mother.

'Oh, hinny, come on in.' Mrs Conway's eyes filled as she spoke.

Della followed her down the dark passage to the small kitchen, crammed with the usual armchairs, sofa and dining suite. It was comfortable and cheerful. An old man sat by the empty fire grate.

'This is Della come to see us – Paul's friend,' Mrs Conway told her husband.

He stood up and took Della's hand. Tall and slim, though now his back was stooped, he had an air of elegance. And despite his lined face and thinning white hair, Della could see that in his youth he had been as handsome as Paul.

'How do you do?' she said formally, feeling lost for words.

Mrs Conway indicated the other chair. 'Sit yoursel' down, hinny. Would you like a cup of tea? I'd just put the kettle on before you came.'

'Thank you.' Della sat, tears coursing down her cheeks. 'Thank you for sending me Paul's letter.'

'Aye, that was the least we could do, luv.' Mrs Conway set cups and saucers on the yellow seersucker tablecloth.

'Paul was our youngest,' the old man said, shaking his head in disbelief.

'*Is* our youngest,' his wife corrected him firmly. 'We haven't heard that he's gone yet and, unless we do, he's still alive, do you hear?' She set the milk jug firmly on the table. 'Sorry we've got no sugar, hinny. Can you take it without?'

Della nodded.

'Aye, his mam's right,' the father sighed. 'We should look on the bright side. It's just that our Paul always had this feeling he wouldn't come back. He talked to me about it but not his mam. Now I'm starting to believe him.'

'I know.' Della twisted her hands in her lap. 'He didn't actually say it outright to me, but I knew what he felt. He was prepared for it.'

Mrs Conway carried in the tea pot. 'Aye, he always was an uncanny sort of lad for his age – very knowing, if you know what I mean. I had him when I was forty-five, and they say old mothers have old children.' She poured three cups of tea and handed one to Della.

'Thank you,' she said gratefully. She hadn't had a cup of tea since breakfast.

'Would you like some ginger snaps with it, luv?' Mrs Conway asked.

Della shook her head. 'No, thank you.' She didn't want to eat the old people's rations.

Mrs Conway handed her husband his tea and sat on the sofa with her own. 'Funny, isn't it? Life goes on!' She lifted her cup with a shaking hand. 'Here we are just drinkin' our tea, and we don't even know if our bairn's alive or dead.' Her face puckered and she broke down and sobbed.

Della relieved her of her cup and sat beside her, taking her hand. 'Wherever he is, he said he wanted us to get on with our lives,' she soothed.

'Aye, that's what he said, hinny.' The old woman sniffed and took a deep breath.

'I just wanted to meet you and to let you know that I'm praying for him to come back as much as you are,' Della told her gently, her own grief seeming less important now that she had someone else to comfort. 'Did they say any more in the telegram – where he went missing, or what happened . . . anything we could hang on to?'

The old man removed the empty pipe from his mouth. 'He was in Tunisia, hinny, tryin' to get the Germans and Italians out. The telegram just said that he went missing during the course of battle, believed dead.

They didn't give us anything to go on – just what his mam told you in her letter.'

'But if they haven't found his body, he could still be alive. You *will* let me know if you hear any more?' Della implored.

'Why, of course, flower.' Mrs Conway wiped her eyes before squeezing Della's hand. 'It's nice of you to come and see us.'

'I would have come before, if I'd known where you lived. I'm so glad I've met you. Paul and I had such a short time together, he didn't meet my parents either.'

Mrs Conway nodded. 'It's all right, hinny, we understood.'

'Aye,' her husband said. 'You were a right Godsend, coming along when you did. He was really cut up when he came home and found out Margaret was married with a bairn. You really helped him get over it.'

'Margaret?' Della felt her stomach lurch.

Mrs Conway gave her husband a look that told him to shut up. 'That was his last girlfriend, luv. It was all over and done with before he met you. He didn't find out till he came home that she'd got pregnant and married somebody else while he was away. We didn't know where to write to him, or we'd have prepared him for it. But he fell hook, line and sinker for you anyway, so it was all for the best in the end.' She patted Della's hand in reassurance.

'He didn't tell me about her,' Della said in a flat voice. She closed her eyes. Had Paul fallen in love with her on the rebound?

'Well, no reason why he should tell you, luv,' Mrs Conway said. 'It was all over before he met you and, from that first night, he just hung around the house with us old fogies, waiting for half-past five when he could go out to meet you. We knew you must be a special lass.'

'Thank you.' Only half comforted, Della managed a

smile. 'You have a special son, too.' She squeezed Mrs Conway's hand again and stood up. 'I'm on duty tonight, I have to go now. I just had to see you and thank you for the letter.'

The woman eased herself up slowly. 'Eey, come and see us any time, luv. We're really pleased to know you and to know that you think so much of our lad.'

Returning down the cheerless street, Della bit her lip to hold back another rush of tears. Why hadn't Paul told her about his ex-girl- friend? Could it have been that he still felt something for this Margaret? No. Surely, he couldn't have been in love with another woman and made love to her the way he had? Maybe she shouldn't have told him so much about Jerry. Maybe he hadn't wanted to know about her past either. Well, she reasoned, neither of them was a child; it was only normal that they should have their own pasts, and if he hadn't wanted to tell her about his, that was his business.

She sighed as she reached the bus stop. Seeing Paul's parents was like history repeating itself. It was a long time since she'd seen Jerry's mother; she must pay her a visit too. She'd thought she could never love anyone else after Jerry, and yet she had. No! She still did. Paul wasn't dead. And he *did* love her.

Jonathan greeted her the following morning. 'Did you see Paul's parents?'

Della nodded.

'Any more news?'

She shook her head. 'Only that he went missing in battle in Tunisia. There's still hope he might be alive.'

Jonathan took both her hands and looked into her eyes. 'Look, I know you're upset, and that's exactly why I think you should come to the pictures with me again. It'll help to take your mind off your troubles. Life must go on, you know. I'm off for a week but I'll be back next Friday. I'll see you here at six.'

Della removed her hand. His words 'life must go on' echoing in her head, and then Jerry's words: 'From this day forward.' 'I don't know about "life going on". Mine is always about to start, but it never actually gets going.'

Jonathan took her by the shoulders and spoke firmly. 'Your life is going on now, Della. If you don't make the most of it, you've only got yourself to blame.' Then he said more gently. 'I insist you come out with me next Friday and throw off this cloud of gloom, at least for a few hours. Doctor's orders!'

Despite herself, Della smiled and gave in. 'Whatever you say, doctor.'

'Good! How about *Seventh Heaven*? It's on at the Odeon next week.'

'Again, whatever you say.'

'I like acquiescent patients.' He grinned. 'See you on Friday, then. And I'll see what culinary delights I can find in my larder.'

Della signed herself in, neatened her cap, took a deep breath, entered the ward. Another day.

The following Friday, Jonathan was waiting when she arrived at six. Della had removed her precious black stockings and changed into a simple floral cotton dress, a white cardigan slung over her shoulders. The sun had shone almost constantly for two weeks, not that she'd noticed it.

'You look smashing as usual.' Jonathan surveyed her approvingly and took her arm.

Della hastily withdrew it. 'Jonathan! What about Sister?'

'What about Sister?' He quirked his eyebrows. 'You mean she might get jealous?'

'You know what I mean, you idiot. People will get the wrong impression.'

'Well, if people want to get wrong impressions, let them,' he said firmly, taking her arm again. This time Della gave in.

At the flat, she relaxed in an armchair while Jonathan poured two sherries. 'To your health!' He held up his glass and added: 'And happiness.'

'And yours,' she responded.

'Thanks, but I'm doing all right. It's *you* we've got to work on. First, for your health, I think I can rummage up a nice piece of cod, mashed potatoes, and peas fresh from the tin, followed by cheese and biscuits.'

'Cheese! Your entire ounce for the week!' she mocked.

Jonathan gave her a sly smile. 'You should know better than that. Another grateful patient! This one keeps goats.' He stood up, emptying his glass. 'And after we've seen to your health, we'll improve your state of mind with a large dose of Hollywood's latest escape for war-torn Britain.'

'Your medicine doesn't sound too bad, doctor.' Della leaned back in the chair and surveyed him. 'You're looking well after your week's holiday. Where did you go?'

'Well, it wasn't exactly a holiday. My mother was ill. I went home. The doctor didn't think she'd last, but she's still hanging on. Remarkable woman, my mother.'

'Oh, I'm sorry.' Della felt penitent. Here was Jonathan trying to cheer *her* up, and he had problems of his own. 'What's wrong with her?'

'She had a heart attack,' he said matter-of-factly. 'Funny thing, she's spent most of her life pretending to be ill; she thrived on the extra attention it brought her. Yet now that she's genuinely ill, she doesn't want to see anyone. I kept Father company, though, and helped him sort out some estate problems. He knows she won't last long.' Della saw the muscles in his cheekbones tighten as he went on: 'I feel sorry for him. He's aged a lot lately, and the estate's getting too much for him. Ironic, isn't it? Now that he *wants* Charles' help, he can't have it.'

'You wouldn't change your mind about running the business?'

'Never!' He shook his head fervently. 'It's a nice old place, but I could never give up medicine.' He placed his glass on the sideboard. 'Do you want to watch the chef at work again or sit and put up your feet.'

'Mmmmm, the latter, if you don't mind.' With a sigh, she kicked off her sandals and rested her feet on the fender.

Jonathan excelled himself in the kitchen and, after the meal, they drove to the Odeon. Della felt mellow from the wine and food. But she cried throughout most of the film. Watching the newly married hero and heroine, despite poverty, living in ecstasy in their seventh-floor flat (their private 'seventh heaven') made her feel her loss and aloneness even more.

'Would you like to leave?' Jonathan asked, as she sniffed audibly for the umpteenth time.

'No.' She shook her head in the dark. 'It's lovely.'

He chuckled and settled back in his seat, handing her his handkerchief.

'I'll never understand women,' he teased, as he led her out of the cinema. 'So that's your idea of having a good time!'

'It was a beautiful film,' she protested, 'and very moving.'

'Yes, it was. But I think next time we'll make it Walt Disney again. I took you out to cheer you up and I'm taking you home all red-eyed.'

'All the same, I did enjoy it.'

Jonathan opened the car door for her and Della crossed her legs awkwardly under the low dashboard, striving to keep as far as possible from the gear lever. She still felt uncomfortable about her physical reaction to his touch on their previous outing.

At the house, Jonathan escorted her to the gaping gateway. 'I insist you take this medicine at least once a week from now on,' he said with mock firmness. 'I don't want my staff cracking up and getting ill on me.'

'Thank you, Jonathan. You're right. I do feel better for having got out of myself a bit.'

'Next week then. See you tomorrow.' His voice retreated into the darkness and she heard the car start up. He *was* pleasant company, she mused as she walked down the path.

Opening the door, she heard laughter in the kitchen and saw an airforce blue uniform jacket hanging on the peg on the scullery door. 'Billie!' she shrieked, running joyfully into the room.

'Wehey! Our Della!' Billie jumped up from the sofa and picked her up, swinging her like a child.

'But you weren't due till tomorrow,' she gasped as he put her down.

'Aye, we were lucky. Our last mission was cancelled so we got off a bit early.' He took both her hands and looked down at her. 'Mam told me about your boy-friend. I'm sorry, luv.'

She bit her lower lip. 'Thanks.'

'This is my mate, Joe.' Billie dropped her hands and, for the first time, Della saw a large figure in an American uniform seated on the sofa. He stood up politely. Billie went on, 'And this is my little sis, Della.'

'Pleased to meet you, Della,' the voice drawled.

'How do you do?' She smiled politely as he engulfed her hand in his huge grasp.

Billie beamed. 'It was too far for Joe to go home to California for six days, so I dragged him along with me. I told him that Newcastle's got the prettiest girls in the country.'

'I see he wasn't wrong.' Joe spoke softly for an American, his grey eyes on Della.

She looked up at his good-looking, chiselled face. Good Lord! He was huge – at least six foot two or three. She turned to Mary and Walter at the table. 'Hello Mam, Dad. What a lovely surprise! Have we got anything to celebrate with?'

Billie's blue eyes twinkled as he made for the sideboard, just a little unsteadily. 'Don't worry, Joe's taken care of that. We've already had some, but there's always room for more.' Brandishing a bottle of bourbon, he wobbled to the table.

Della smiled affectionately at her brother. 'I can see you've had some already. What is it?'

'It's American whiskey,' Joe informed her. 'I hope you like it. They don't supply us with Scotch.' He was seated again on the sofa. Della sat at the table.

Billie carefully poured her a glass. 'Here you are. Drink up! It's on the American government.' He handed her a glass with unsteady hands and turned to his parents. 'Come on Mam, Dad, have another. You don't get a chance like this every day.'

Mary smiled and put her hand over her empty glass. 'Some people know when they've had enough, but I'm sure your father would like some more.'

'Aye, why not?' Walter said ungraciously, holding out his glass.

Mary threw him a look. 'And wait till you see what else Joe's brought,' she said, handing round a tin of sugared almonds. 'More than a whole month's worth of our sweet ration, a whole pound of processed cheese, two tins of biscuits, fresh bananas and tinned peaches and, wait for it, *real* ground Kona coffee.'

Della smiled at Joe. 'That's very kind of you.' She sniffed her glass cautiously and grimaced. 'But if you don't mind, I think I'll swap this for the coffee.'

'It's an acquired taste.' Joe grinned, showing a set of perfect white American teeth.

Maybe it was all the milk they drank as people said, Della thought, admiring his smile, or maybe they just had better dentists. He looked like a Hollywood film star. She smiled back at him. 'I'll make some coffee, then. Would you like some?'

Joe waved his hand in refusal. 'No, thanks. I brought all this stuff for you. I hate to consume my own gifts.'

'Nonsense!' Mary silenced him. 'I think we'll all have some.'

While the women made the coffee, the bourbon finally loosened Walter's tongue. He had been unusually quiet since Billie had arrived with his American friend. 'So how long have you been stationed at Norwich with our lad, then?' he asked Joe.

'Almost eleven months, sir, but I've been in the Air Force eighteen months. I went through pilot training in Texas first.'

'Oh, aye.'

Joe couldn't make out Walter's tone and went on uncomfortably, 'My first bomber mission was from Norwich, though. Eighteen months ago, I had no idea I'd be over here bombing Jerry, but it feels good to be doing something useful at last.'

'Aye, *at last*,' Walter repeated meaningfully, and Billie, despite his happy state of inebriation, realised his father was getting ready to round on Joe.

'Oh, come off it, Dad,' he said. 'The lads have nothing to do with government decisions. They came when they were told to. I wouldn't have been in a hurry to fight somebody else's war either.'

Taken off guard, Joe flushed and cleared his throat. 'I'm sorry you feel like that, sir.'

'Aye, well, we could have done with your help earlier, you know that. But Roosevelt didn't want to get involved, not till the Japs dragged him in with Pearl Harbor.'

In the scullery, Mary pricked up her ears. 'Listen to your father.' She frowned at Della, who had just set the coffee pot on the stove. 'He's getting on his Yankee hobby horse again, and to that nice boy. Go in and shut him up.'

Della pulled a face and returned to the kitchen. 'Dad,' she said sweetly, 'the lid on the biscuit tin's stuck. I can't budge it. Would you come and have a try?'

Walter rolled his eyes as he stood up. 'Helpless women,' he muttered on the way out.

But Della grinned and the tension was broken. 'Don't take any notice of Dad,' she said to Joe. 'He's really a very nice person when he's not talking about the war. We try to keep him off the subject.'

'I see,' Joe said. 'I know what he means, though. A lot of us over there thought we should have got our feet wet earlier.'

'Well, you're here now, and that's all that matters,' Della said, sitting again at the table.

Billie looked proudly at Joe. 'Aye, and when he did get his feet wet, he jumped in the deep end. He's a bloody good pilot, aren't you, Joe?'

'Aw, Billie,' he began, intent on studying his large, highly polished black shoes.

But Billie persisted. 'I was there on his first mission. Our lads were in number one plane and Joe and his mates had to fly on our left wing without any friendly fighter support. Our target was an ammunitions factory near Stuttgart. We thought we'd hit it but couldn't be sure because of the cloud, and then the radio said, "Fighters at seven o'clock". They were so close, we could almost have stuck out our hands and touched them – two bloody twin-engines. But our Joe here kept his nerve.'

'Billie, that's ancient history,' he protested.

But Billie was carried away. 'Even with all the flak flying, he dived and aimed his guns. He punctured one of the buggers till it looked like a sieve and then – bang! It exploded into a ball of fire and fell right on the target we thought we'd hit. It was like Guy Fawkes night, even through the cloud. Boom, cracker, boom, cracker, boom!' he bellowed. 'Then the explosives set one another off. The sky was lit up like twelve o'clock noon. The second fighter got the heebie-jeebies and turned tail. Our Joe was the hero of the mission.'

'Not the next day,' he laughed, embarrassed by Billie's reverent tone.

'What happened then?' Della asked, curious, though knowing she was supposed to steer this conversation away from war.

'Oh, jeez, it was nothing,' Joe protested, shifting uncomfortably in his seat. 'I was a dumb novice exceeding my orders, that's all. I just saw those sons-of-bitches and I knew I could get them, so I went for it. The Lieutenant Colonel wasn't too pleased with me but, because by a fluke the plane I'd hit fell on the target, they let me off with a warning.' He shrugged modestly. 'That means I have to watch out for my ass in future.'

Della smiled at his American invective.

'That was no fluke!' Billie argued. 'That was bloody good aim, and you know it.'

'Beginner's luck,' Joe insisted.

Mary arrived with the coffee and cups on a tray, followed by Walter, now looking suitably contrite. Mary had obviously reprimanded him in the scullery.

'I'm looking forward to this,' she declared as she poured the rich black liquid. 'Have you ever tasted Camp coffee, Joe?'

He pulled a face. 'Yes, ma'am, at the base.'

As Della handed round the cups, Joe noticed her bare legs. He began awkwardly, 'I, er, brought some nylons for the ladies. They're in my bag upstairs.'

'Nylons!' Della could have kissed him. 'Oh, you shouldn't have done that,' she protested feebly.

He grinned. 'Why not? I don't wear them myself.'

'That's kind of you, Joe. Thank you,' Mary said, delighted.

Billie smiled ruefully. 'Joe makes me look stingy. All I've got for you is my last month's sweet coupons.'

Again, Joe looked uncomfortable. 'Please, I hope you don't mind my giving you gifts. I mean, I know that some of the British think we Yanks like to talk and act big. It's just that, well, I've got things you need that I don't . . . and I've got no one else to give them to.'

'That's all right, lad.' Walter took the cue to make a circuitous apology. 'We're not too proud to accept.' He raised his coffee cup. 'Nice coffee.'

'Thank you, sir.' Joe's face relaxed. Suddenly he felt comfortable with this British family.

Chapter Thirty-Four

Billie and Joe were at the table when Della trailed down to breakfast. She started in surprise. 'Good Lord! You scared me. Why are you up so early when you're on leave?'

'It's kind of hard to break the habit,' Joe said.

Billie slurped his tea and grinned. 'I'm going to show Joe the sights today, and I thought we'd go to the Oxford tonight. Fancy coming?'

'No thanks!' Della grimaced, joining them at the table. 'I'll be too tired after work, and I don't feel like dancing anyway.'

But Billie was not to be put off. 'Oh, come on, our Della. You need to let your hair down once in a while.'

'It would be great if you'd come, Della,' Joe encouraged her.

'Aw, don't be a spoilsport,' Billie grumbled. 'I thought we could get a crowd together and go for a drink first. Do you know any nice nurses at the hospital?'

'They're all married or have boyfriends,' Della said, feeling a pang of exclusion.

'Rose isn't married,' Billie reminded her.

'No, but she's got a boyfriend *and* a baby, don't forget.'

'That shouldn't stop her having a night out,' Billy persisted. 'From what I hear, she hardly ever sees that old geezer anyway.'

Della smiled at Billie's tenacity. 'You always had a sneaky pash on Rose, didn't you, Billie?'

'Well, I always thought she was attractive, but I could never afford her in a million years. And anyway, I've got a girlfriend at the base – she's a WREN. I just thought some female company would be nice, and Joe hasn't got a girl.'

'Oh, a WREN, eh?' Della teased, spreading margarine on a slice of bread. 'What's she like?'

'Nice.' Billie's fresh face cracked into a wide grin. Though since the war he looked thinner, he hadn't lost his boyish sparkle.

'She's great,' Joe interjected. 'I was sorry Billie got to her before I did.'

'Good Lord! You're all up!' Mary suddenly appeared in her dressing gown. 'I thought you'd want a lie-in on your leave.' She glanced at the table. 'And look what you're having. Bread and margarine! We can do better than that, war or no war.' She marched into the scullery and returned triumphantly with a packet of corn flakes and a bottle of milk. 'If I'd known you'd be a day early I'd have got the rations yesterday. But I've got a surprise for tonight.'

'We were just trying to talk Della into coming with us to the Oxford tonight,' Billie said, draining his teacup.

'Why not, luv?' Mary turned to Della. 'It'll do you good to have some fun.'

'I went out last night,' Della hedged.

'But you don't go out enough,' Mary insisted, setting cereal bowls and a cup and saucer on the table. She poured herself tea. 'It would take you out of yourself to go dancing for a change.'

Della gave in. 'I suppose I'll get no peace till I say yes. I'll ring Nora at the shop to see if she and Phil want to come, and she can pop down and ask Rose; she only lives a few doors away.'

'Whoaho! Wait till you get a load of Rose!' Billie nudged Joe knowingly. 'Della and I are being faithful, so we'll be stuck with each other. You'll have the field to yourself, Joe. She's just your type – a cuddly red-head.'

'I thought she was taken,' Joe said, nevertheless looking interested.

'Not really! She's got an older boyfriend who's never around, and a kid. But I can't see that stopping Rose from enjoying herself.'

'Wally!' Della reprimanded him. 'Rose still likes a good time, but that's all. She's good company. I don't get home till half-past six, so the earliest I can eat, change, and get into town would be eight. I'll tell them to meet us at the Eldon. Does that make you happy?'

'It sure does,' Joe said.

Della stood up. 'I've got to get dressed. Have a nice day seeing the sights, such as they are, and try to avoid the bomb sites.'

Della arrived home at twenty minutes to seven. Mary had kept dinner waiting and they embarked on the minuscule piece of pork she had wheedled out of the butcher, accompanied by apple sauce and mashed potatoes, and followed by Joe's gift of cheese with cream crackers.

'That was real good, Mrs Dolan,' Joe said appreciatively as he finished. 'I was beginning to believe what the Americans say about British cooking.'

'Nothing wrong with British cooking,' Walter interjected. 'You've just got to marry the right woman and stay out of restaurants.' He leaned back in his chair, satisfied. 'Now how about some more of that American coffee?'

'Not for me. I have to change.' Della darted from the room, returning twenty minutes later. Her appearance was arresting: her black hair glistened on her shoulders,

turned under in a fashionable page-boy with the help of
Mary's curling iron; her face glowed with a light touch
of make-up and her lips glistened a bright red. Her
topaz dress skimmed her body, and her legs shimmered
in Joe's nylons.

He let out a low whistle, and Billie shot him a glance.
Joe flushed, then smiled awkwardly. 'Sorry if that's not
done here, but it's a mark of appreciation back home.'

Mary laughed. 'I wish someone would do it to me.'

'You've had your day, woman,' Walter snorted.

The Eldon was crowded. Della shuddered as they
entered. Why had she suggested meeting in a crowded
pub? It brought back the memory of that similar night
with Paul. Rose, Nora and Phil were seated at a small
table for four. Della introduced Joe, who immediately
fascinated everyone with his American smile – especially
Rose, who eyed him with her usual blatant appreciation
of handsome men.

'Why don't we find somewhere quieter?' Della
shouted over the din.

'Good idea!' Phil agreed. He looked stockier than
ever, having gained weight since his marriage. His
frank, good-natured face already showed a tendency to
jowls. It was obvious Phil was a man you could count
on. Nora, her arm through his, glowed with happiness.
She looked very pretty in a blue cotton dress. Rose,
however, had gone all the way. She wore an emerald
green silk dress that reflected her eyes, the sweetheart
neckline cut outrageously low, even by Rose's stan-
dards. Her bright hair was turned up at the front in a
fashionable roll, the rest hanging in burnished waves to
her shoulders. She looked as if she had just stepped out
of a glamour magazine. Joe noticed, and everyone
noticed Joe noticing.

'Let's try the Dun Cow,' Phil suggested. 'It's not as

grand as this but it'll be less crowded.'

Billie teased Joe. 'It's a famous local haunt for prostitutes, if you get desperate.'

'That doesn't seem likely,' Joe replied, staring openly at Rose, who fluttered her eyelashes and ran the tip of her tongue over her lips before flashing him a smile.

Della wondered if she'd done the right thing in inviting Rose. 'Let's go, then,' she said.

The Dun Cow was much quieter, though the old-fashioned red wallpaper and carpet had seen better days, and an aroma of spilt beer hung in the air.

'First round's on me,' Billie declared.

'Gin and tonic, please,' Della said, glad to sit down at the first empty table. She'd been on her feet all day and wasn't relishing the thought of dancing the night away.

'For me too, please.' Rose tilted her chin and smiled coquettishly at Joe, even though Billie was buying the drinks.

'And me!' Nora slyly raised her eyebrows at Della, who had also witnessed Rose's smile.

'I'll help,' Joe said, following Billie to the bar with Phil at the rear.

'Wow!' Rose popped her eyes exaggeratedly. 'He's gorgeous! He looks like Gregory Peck. And what a size! I could go for him in a *big* way.'

'You made that pretty obvious,' Della remarked. 'What about Bill?'

'What *about* Bill?' Rose snapped. 'I haven't seen the bugger for a week.' Then her voice softened. 'His wife's ill.' She sighed heavily. 'It's times like this that bring it home to me. I'm just the second string to his bow.' She took out her compact, dabbed at her nose, examined her face, then flicked the compact shut angrily. 'And next week he's going to London. His mother was bombed out and, now that the worst of it seems to be over, he's going to buy her a house further out of the city. He's an incurable businessman. He can't resist cheap property. Nobody wants to buy a house that might be a heap of rubble the next day – except Bill. He's a risk-taker. But, anyway, I suppose his mam does need somewhere to live.' She paused and chewed on her lip. 'Oh, I know he's good to me, but his other family takes him away from me so much. Sometimes I feel like an outcast.'

'Well, luv, you knew that in good time to get out of it,' Nora reminded her.

'I know. I made my own bed and now I've got to *die* on it. But I'd die happy if only he could be there to share it with me more,' she added with a touch of her old humour.

'Is that what you miss?' Della asked, thinking of her own loneliness and her physical reaction to Jonathan's touch.

'Oh, not only that,' Rose replied, slightly irritated. 'I miss his company as well, and Rosemary misses his visits. Lately I've been thinking twice about having another one. I thought a brother or sister would be company for her, but I'm not sure that it's fair to have two of them without a father.'

'You've got a good point there,' Della said. 'I didn't want to interfere with your plans when you were so keen on the idea, but I did wonder about the wisdom of having another one. How is Rosemary?' she added.

'All right. Mrs James is looking after her. I'm glad you asked me out. I feel like having a good time tonight . . . I suppose partly to spite Bill for neglecting me this week.'

'Here you are.' Billie placed the girls' drinks on the table, while Joe and Phil brought the beer.

'Your brother's persuaded me to try the local brew,' Joe announced, looking suspiciously at his pint of dark brown ale.

Della noticed that he went out of his way to sit beside Rose.

Billie winked as he squeezed in beside Della. 'Newcastle Brown! We'll see how these Yanks can hold their booze.'

'Aye, you'd better be careful with that stuff,' Phil warned. 'It's dynamite, and you're too big to carry home.' He sat next to Nora and raised his glass.

Joe followed. 'Well, bottoms up, as you say. But you forget I'm a hardened bourbon drinker. Beer's kids' stuff.'

Rose held up her gin and tonic. 'To Billie and Joe and a wonderful leave for both of them.'

Joe gave her the full benefit of his smile. 'I can't complain about the way it's starting.' He took a draught from his glass. 'Jeez!' he spluttered. 'This stuff's *beer*? It tastes more like oxtail soup, and it's about the same temperature.'

Billie rose to the defence of English beer. 'I'd rather have warm oxtail soup than cold dishwater like that Yankee rubbish you drink. This stuff grows hairs on your chest.'

'I bet he's already got them,' Rose giggled. But she caught Nora's eye on her and changed direction. 'Where are you from, Joe?'

'California?'

'Oh, I'd love to go to California,' she breathed ecstatically, 'all that sunshine and all those wonderful beaches you see on the travelogues at the pictures.'

Joe laughed. 'I'm afraid it's not all like the parts you see in the movies. We have our slums and eye-sores as well.'

'Whereabouts in California, Joe?' Nora asked.

'San Jose, not far from San Francisco.'

'Ooh, I've always wanted to go to California,' Rose repeated.

'Then why not? After the war! It would be my pleasure.' Joe's gaze held Rose's for some seconds before he added, 'You're all invited.'

'Thanks, but where'd we get the money from?' Phil said, practical as always.

Rose pulled a face. 'We can dream, can't we?'

'Looks like we're ready for another round,' Joe said, noting several empty glasses.

Phil stood up. 'I'll help.'

'Ooh,' Rose said to Billie after the two had left, 'your friend's dishy. Has he got a girlfriend?'

'Not a special one – at least not over here. Let's just say he doesn't go short of female company when he wants it.'

'I'll bet,' Nora said. 'He's charming, too. Is he always like that or does he just put it on in female company?'

'Nah!' Billie shook his head. 'He's popular with the lads and all. He's just a nice all-round fella.'

When Joe and Phil returned, Joe raised his glass with a grin. 'They didn't have bourbon, so I settled for another cup of soup.'

'Have you ever had an English gin and lime, Joe?' Again, Rose put her eyelashes to work.

'Can't say I have.'

'Well, we'll all go back to the flat after the dance and I'll treat you to a *real* English drink.' She gave him an inviting look, running her tongue over her lower lip provocatively.

Della and Nora looked at each other. Nora raised her eyes in silent despair, then shrugged and grinned. Della grinned back. At least Rose was more like her old self tonight, and that meant she was happy.

At the dance hall they found a table near the floor, Della and Nora positively refusing to stand around looking as if they were cattle for sale. The band played Benny Goodman. Joe was in his element. 'Would you like to dance?' he asked Rose eagerly.

'Sure would,' she imitated him as she jumped up in an unladylike fashion. In seconds they were spinning around on the dance floor.

'I think Rose's made a hit with Joe,' Billie observed belatedly.

Della smiled. 'I think Joe's made a hit with Rose, too . . . so long as he remembers she's tied up.'

'I could be wrong,' Phil said, 'but I don't think Joe would let that bother him much anyway.'

'Oh, what the hell!' Nora swore uncharacteristically. 'It's about time our Rose had a bit of fun. I know she loves Bill and all that, but he never takes her out where they can be seen, and it's against her nature to closet herself up the way she's been doing. If Bill wants to keep her, he'd better start thinking about that.'

'Do I closet you up?' Phil asked.

'No, you ninny. But do you realise we haven't been to a dance since we were married? How about asking me?'

'I'm afraid I'm not up to *that*.' Phil indicated Joe and Rose, jiving wildly. Rose had caught on quickly, as she always did to new dances.

'Go on! Give us a laugh,' Della said. 'And you, too, Billie. Why not ask that blonde girl over there? She looks lonely.'

'Not my type. And, anyway, I'm keeping myself pure for Nancy. I'll stick to you, sis.'

'Good Lord! This WREN must be serious,' Della declared. 'In that case, I give in. Can you jive?'

'No.'

'Neither can I. Come on. *And* you two.' She challenged Phil and Nora. 'I dare you.'

The four trekked on to the floor, holding each other tentatively and swaying until *In The Mood* finally lived up to its title, and soon they were gyrating as wildly as

Joe and Rose, if not as expertly. They all sat down, breathless, when the music stopped.

Rose, fanning herself with her hand, fell into her chair. 'Oh, I do declare, sir,' she began in her best Southern belle accent and finished in Geordie, 'you're a bloody good dancer, Joe.'

Joe smiled, imitating her, 'Well, ma'am, as you locals would say, you're not so bad yoursel', hinny.'

'I don't know what we'd do for films and dance music without the Yanks' exports,' Billie said, his face still pink from his efforts on the dance floor.

'And that's not all they export,' Rose remarked, smiling at Joe.

He looked pleased. But, while Della was still glad to see Rose enjoying herself, she was worried. Joe was only here for a few days. What if Rose got entangled with him and lost Bill?

Joe broke into her thoughts. 'May I have the pleasure?' The band struck into *We'll Meet Again*, and the plump, ageing singer attempted to fulfil her fantasy that she was Vera Lynn.

Della smiled at Joe. 'Thank you. This is more my pace.' She felt dwarfed by his size. He was an incredibly graceful dancer for such a big man. The last man who had held her in his arms on the dance floor was Paul, she thought sadly.

'Penny for them?' Joe interrupted her reverie.

She told only half the truth. 'I was just thinking what a good dancer you are.'

'Well, that's very flattering, but it can't have been that or why would you look so sad?' His dark eyes looked at her intently.

'All right, I was thinking that the last time I danced like this was with my boyfriend, Paul.'

'Billie told me about him. I'm sorry,' he said softly. 'I hope you hear soon.'

'Thank you.' She bit her lip.

'I understand you didn't know him very long. It must have been very special.'

She nodded. 'It was.'

'He's a lucky man.'

'Is or was?' Della said, biting her lip again to stop the tears, but despite her effort, disobedient droplets oozed on to her lashes.

'I'm sorry, I shouldn't have brought it up,' he said, concerned at her distress.

'It's all right. I have to face up to it. It's just so awful not knowing either way.'

'At least there's a chance,' Joe tried to comfort her. 'You've got to keep on hoping.'

'What about you?' Della wanted to change the subject. 'Have you got a girlfriend at home?'

'Well, I was dating when I left, but it's hard to keep up a romance when you're six thousand miles apart.'

The music stopped and he escorted her back to the table.

Rose had just returned with Billie, and Nora and Phil sat holding hands like new lovers.

Almost immediately, the band and the singer started again. This time it was *I'll Be Seeing You*.

'Billie,' Della coaxed, 'why don't you go and ask a girl to dance? You don't really want to be stuck with me all evening.'

He grinned. 'I told you! I'm being faithful. I'd much rather dance with Nora. I know I'm safe while Phil's around.'

Joe silently took Rose's hand and she floated off with him, while Phil and Della looked at each other knowingly. Phil lit a cigarette and exhaled heavily. 'I hope Rose knows what she's doing.'

'Me, too,' Della sighed. 'May I have a cigarette? I'd like to sit this one out. My feet hurt.'

Phil fished in his pocket. 'He seems like a nice fellow. But he's here today and gone tomorrow. I hope she doesn't mess things up with Bill for the sake of a roll in bed with a handsome Yank.' He offered her a cigarette and struck a match.

She inhaled and sighed again. 'I think we should all know by now that Rose will do what she wants to, whatever we or anybody else thinks about it.'

She smoked her cigarette, idly watching the dancers – some uniformed men, some middle-aged men, and some young boys. The women outnumbered the men by at least five to one and many danced together for lack of partners.

Suddenly her eye caught a handsome couple on the floor. Jonathan! He was dancing with a very shapely brunette, her tight skirt concealing none of her curves. He held her close. When they turned, Della saw that the girl was strikingly beautiful. The classic lines of her face were shown off by her simple backswept hairdo, the long, dark hair anchored by a lace snood in a heavy coil on the nape of her neck. Della's stomach jumped and she felt an unpleasant emotion shoot through her. Was it jealousy? Why on earth should she be jealous? Jonathan was just a friend. And she was the one who'd made that plain. So he *did* have a girlfriend after all! As the dance ended and the couples dispersed, she turned her back to the dance floor. She felt disconcerted. Why did she not wish Jonathan to see her?

Afterwards, she avoided dancing, claiming legitimately that she was tired after a day on the ward. She tried to keep her eyes off the dance floor, but couldn't resist an occasional peek. Twice she saw Jonathan dancing with the same girl. They jitterbugged very well and made a stunningly attractive couple. Well, Jonathan's private life was none of her business. After all, there was no reason why he should have told her he had a girlfriend.

The rest of the evening continued pleasantly until Rose looked at her watch. 'Bloody hell! Eleven o'clock! I've got to go. Mrs James doesn't like to be kept up late.' She stood up. 'You lot stay on and enjoy yourselves,' she said miserably, directing her glance at Joe.

'I'll see you home, Rose,' he offered quickly.

Her face glowed again. 'Oh, really! Thanks, Joe.' Then she added unwillingly, 'But you'll miss the last bus home.'

'No problem.' He waved his hand to dismiss the idea. 'There'll be cabs, won't there?'

'If you're lucky,' Billie grinned. 'But you always are, you bastard! Don't worry. We never lock the door.'

Joe addressed Nora and Phil. 'It was nice to meet you. Perhaps we can do this again. See you two later then,' he nodded to Della and Billie as he tucked Rose's arm in his. As they left, Rose winked over her shoulder.

Billie grinned. 'Well, it seems she forgot she invited us *all* back? They all fall for Joe.'

Rose had avoided talking about her personal life on the dance floor but, on the bus, she knew she must prepare her ground. 'I have a little girl, you know,' she began tentatively.

'I know.'

'Her father keeps her and visits her, but we're just friends now. He's got another girlfriend and I go out with other boyfriends occasionally, but nothing serious.'

She glanced sideways to see his reaction and sighed inwardly with relief. His expression hadn't changed. He had swallowed her lie. She went on more cheerfully, 'Have you got a girlfriend at home?'

'I was dating before I left,' he said enigmatically.

Rose wondered if that meant he still had a girlfriend

but decided she'd better not pursue the matter.

'We're almost there,' she said. 'I don't live far out of town.'

'What's your little girl's name?'

'Rosemary, half after her mammy.' Rose tried to study his handsome profile with a sidelong look, but he turned and caught her glance.

His gaze held hers for some seconds before he asked: 'Is she like her mommy?'

'The spitting image.'

'Then I'm bound to like her.' He smiled down at her.

Rose felt the same thrill she'd felt all evening whenever Joe had smiled at her. God, this man was exciting! But what about Bill? Well, Bill wasn't around for her, she thought almost angrily. This man was here, and he obviously liked her. 'Next stop's ours,' she announced, rising.

He helped her off the bus and took her arm in the blackness. Angry shouting and the sound of scuffling came from a police box nearby.

'What the hell's going on?' Joe asked.

'Saturday night!' Rose said matter-of-factly. 'The police pick up the drunks every night, but Saturdays are the worst.'

Joe dropped her arm. 'I'd better go. Maybe I can help.'

Before Rose could stop him, he had marched ahead to the police box. 'Can I help, sir?' she heard him ask as she followed him quickly.

'Nah, it's all right, mate,' a cheerful voice replied. 'I've phoned the station and the Black Maria's on the way. He's just had one over the eight, that's all.'

'Bloody interferin' Yanks!' the drunk yelled, attempting to lunge at Joe. But the policeman had the man's arms firmly pinned behind his back. The drunk hiccupped loudly, then leaned against the box for support.

'Yanksh go home,' he slurred, before spitting in Joe's direction.

'Don't take any notice of him, lad,' the policeman said. 'We're glad you're here.' As he spoke, two dim crosses of light approached them. 'This is me mate now. Thanks for offerin' anyway.'

'You're welcome,' Joe said, and Rose, who had been standing nearby, approached him and took his arm. She felt ashamed of some of her fellow countrymen's attitude towards the Americans.

But Joe ignored the drunk's insult, apparently used to such treatment. 'I really admire your bobbies,' he said as they walked on. 'I think it's great the way they just walk their beat and carry a stick. Back home that drunk would have had a gun in his ribs.'

'I'm sorry about what he said,' she said quietly. 'We don't all feel like that, you know.'

'I know,' he assured her. 'And it doesn't bother me any more. I still think this is a great country. But I'll never get used to this god awful blackout.'

'It's funny. You get used to anything in time,' Rose sighed, 'even the bloody war. I feel as though it's always been wartime.'

'Yeah, you Brits are hardy people,' Joe said with admiration. 'Back home the folks are too used to the soft life. It's been an education for me coming over here.'

Rose laughed. 'Oh, yes. We're famous for our stiff upper lips, remember? Mine's getting stiffer by the day.' She stopped in front of the house. 'We're here, and we might even get in if I can find my key.' She fumbled in her bag and groped for the key. 'Now, the next trick is to find the keyhole. First time lucky!' She pushed open the creaking old door and closed it behind them, turning on the hall light. 'I'm on the ground floor now. I used to be upstairs, but this has an extra bedroom. The old lady swapped with me because the rent upstairs is cheaper. The house belongs to my parents, so I get it rent free.' Another lie jumped out. It was one thing letting Joe know that Bill paid for his child, but she couldn't admit that he kept her as well. She turned on the sitting-room light and Joe looked around approvingly.

'Nice place.'

'Thanks. Sit down and I'll be back in a minute. I have to get Rosemary from Mrs James.'

A few minutes later she returned carrying a large, still bundle. 'She's asleep,' she whispered. 'I'll get her into bed.'

'Let me help.' Joe stood up and took the dead weight from her, peering at the sleeping face. 'She *is* like her mommy,' he said softly. 'Beautiful.'

Rose glowed with pleasure. 'Thank you.' She led him into the small bedroom and he gently lowered the bundle into the cot. 'You're very good at it,' she remarked, impressed by his huge gentleness.

'I like kids. I was the eldest of four. My mom always moaned that she wished I'd been a girl.'

'Well, I'm glad you're not.' Rose took his arm and led him back to the sitting-room. He threw himself down on the sofa, his endless legs stretching almost to the fireplace.

'Would you like coffee or something stronger?' Rose asked lightly. Now that they were alone in the flat, she found herself shivering inside.

'Can't say I'm gone on English coffee,' he admitted. 'Anything else would be fine.'

'Whisky?'

'Great!' As he spoke, Joe's blue-grey eyes followed her movements towards the sideboard.

Rose poured two whiskeys and handed him one, dissolving into the sofa beside him. She knew she should have sat in a chair, but she hadn't played coy with him so far and she wasn't going to start now.

'To the most wonderful evening I've had since I can remember,' he toasted solemnly.

She looked at him from under her eyelashes. 'It's not over yet.'

Joe was silent for a moment, and when he spoke his voice was hushed. 'I sure was lucky to meet you on my first night on leave, Rose.'

He took her hand and a wild thrill ran through her. She had to swallow hard before she could speak. 'Here's to your leave,' she said breathlessly.

As he bent and kissed her gently on the lips, Bill's image flitted through her mind. For a fraction of a second, she hesitated before returning his kiss. Why the hell not! Life was short! Joe put his glass on the side-table and, pulling her closer, kissed her harder this time. She responded in a daze. This man made her feel weak all over; her body was already crying out for him. He was incredibly exciting and different. He removed the glass from her hand and placed it with his own. Rose lay back, eyes closed, waiting for that kiss again. It came, gently at first and then with increasing pressure. She wound her arms about his neck and clung to him. She wanted him and he wanted her. Why in heaven's name pretend? And, besides, he knew she wasn't a virgin.

His hands began to explore her body and she tugged at his uniform buttons, then his shirt. They were both in a hurry. He lifted her. 'Where's the bedroom?' he asked urgently.

'Through there,' she whispered, indicating with her head. He carried her through, laying her on the bed gently and undressing her. She helped him until she was naked, and then lay, hypnotised, as he flung off the remainder of his clothes. Frantically, they discovered each other's bodies with eyes, hands, and lips, until they could wait no longer, and he threw himself over her. He was everything she'd thought he'd be. She cried out in ecstasy, and he let out a final low-pitched moan. As though in a trance, they lay in silence.

Rose drank in the smell of his hair. It smelled fresh and clean and different from Bill's – no Brylcreem, she thought vaguely. A wail from Rosemary's room brought her back to reality. 'Oh, no!' She forced up her limp body. 'I'd better go to her. We must have woken her.'

A few minutes later she returned. 'She's all right. She woke up and her bunny was on the floor. She can't sleep without him.' She lay back on the bed and Joe took her in his arms almost reverently.

'That was the most marvellous lovemaking I've ever known,' he whispered unbelievingly.

'Me too,' she breathed.

He ran his fingers through her hair. 'I guess we just go together well. You're a fascinating girl, Rose. You don't pretend. I find that very refreshing.'

'That's my trouble,' Rose sighed. 'I can't pretend even when I want to. But I didn't want to tonight anyway.'

'I sure am glad,' he murmured, pulling her closer and tracing his fingers down her back.

'Watch out! Any more of that and I might attack you again,' she grinned impishly.

'Go ahead. You have my permission – only this time attack me more slowly, please. I'd like to savour your delights this time.'

Rose was thoughtful for a moment. She'd better not pretend about this either. She began slowly, 'Joe . . . I appreciated your being so careful, even though we got carried away. But I have got some things.' She felt awkward saying this, but he seemed unperturbed.

'That's great! I'll be more prepared next time. I wasn't expecting such a wonderful time tonight.'

'Do you think I'm too fast?' she asked apprehensively.

'Nope!' He grinned widely in the half-light. 'Not so long as I can keep up! Go and get those damned things and we'll take it nice and slow this time.'

'Joe! You know that's not what I meant,' she insisted, desperately needing to know if he thought her too 'easy'.

He ignored her remark and joked: 'It's like dancing. I like the fast, lively ones . . . *and* the slow, smoochy ones.'

'You daft bugger!' she laughed, her worry forgotten.

'Is that a compliment?'

'Definitely.'

'Good! Now just do as you're told, honey, and get those things. You can't keep a guy waiting for ever.'

In a flash, Rose was up. Afterwards, cradled in Joe's arms, she asked reluctantly, 'Do you have to leave, Joe?'

He groaned. 'I wish I didn't, but it would be considered American bad manners if I deserted my hosts.'

'Aw, Billie would understand,' she wheedled.

'Gee, you don't think I worry about Billie, do you? I just don't like to be rude to his mom and dad; they've been so kind to me. But tomorrow night maybe I can make up an excuse.' He paused before asking anxiously, 'You *are* free tomorrow, aren't you?'

'I'm free whenever you are,' she said without hesitation.

'Thank you, ma'am. I sure am glad you don't mess around. I've only got six days.'

'I know,' Rose said quietly. 'There's no time for playing games, even if I liked them.'

Chapter Thirty-Five

Della jumped in surprise as Rose appeared in the hospital canteen the following Monday. 'Rose! What on earth! How did you get in here?'

'Never mind that. I'm here,' Rose giggled, sitting opposite.

Della put down her spoon, happy to ignore the remainder of her semolina pudding. 'Whatever for, you ninny? You'll get me into trouble. You know visitors aren't allowed.'

'I just had to talk to you and I didn't dare ring you and, anyway . . . I want to ask you a favour.'

Della gave her a suspicious look. 'All right! What do you want? It's something to do with Joe, isn't it? And, while we're on the subject, what's going on with Joe? He's hardly been at the house since Saturday night. Billie told Mam he'd met a girl at the dance, but she doesn't know it's you. We had to swear Joe to secrecy.'

Rose bit her lip. 'I know, Joe told me. Thanks. Lord knows, your mam doesn't approve of me as it is.'

'No, you're wrong, Rose. She didn't approve when you were flirting around with Tom, Dick and Harry but, since you decided to keep the baby and settle down, you've gone up in her estimation. We just thought it better not to let her know you're playing fast and loose again.'

'But I'm not, Della,' Rose retaliated. 'I'm not just

flirting around with Joe. I've really fallen for him.'

'You didn't need to tell me that. I think the entire dance hall knew it on Saturday.'

'But I mean *really* fallen,' Rose persisted. 'I'm in love.'

'Oh, Lord, Rose.' Della groaned in despair. 'What about Bill? Joe's only here for a few days. For heaven's sake don't do anything silly. How would you live without Bill's help?'

Rose looked crestfallen. 'Oh, I knew you'd say all that, and don't think I don't know it. I just don't know what to do, Della. I'm really crazy about Joe, and he is about me. It's incredibly marvellous when we're together. It's too late now. I can't just pretend I never met him.'

'I suppose you mean you're good in bed together?' Della said stonily.

'Out of this world!' Rose sighed, missing Della's censorious tone. 'But it's much more than just sex, honestly! And I swear he's as much smitten as I am.'

'Well, why did you come to see me, Rose?' Della was becoming impatient. 'It's obvious you've made up your mind you're going to go on seeing him anyway. I know you're clever, but how the devil are you going to sleep with two men at once, especially when you're half living with one of them? That's stretching it, even for you.'

Rose drummed her fingers on the bare wooden table. 'That's just it. Bill won't be back until after Joe leaves. I've got to see Joe while he's here, Della. I know I might never see him again after that, but I've at least got to have the memory.'

'And what if Joe does come back? What if he wants you to write to him? How could you even write to one lover while another one's keeping you?' Della clasped and unclasped her hands in agitation. 'Look, Rose, you know I'm not a prude, but there *is* a limit. I'm worried about what might happen to you if Bill finds out.'

As she met Della's gaze, tears welled in Rose's eyes. 'I know I'm being an absolute bitch, but I honestly can't give Joe up. If nothing comes of it, Bill won't get hurt. You know – what the eye doesn't see, the heart doesn't grieve.' She tried to smile but her lips only twitched.

'And what if something *does* come of it?'

'I'll just have to deal with that when the time comes, if at all,' Rose answered dolefully. 'I'm not stupid, Della. Joe's so handsome, wherever he goes girls are going to chase him. I know he could easily forget all about me. And, if he does, then *I'll* be the only one who gets hurt. And I'll deserve it.'

Puzzled, Della searched Rose's face. 'But how do you feel about Bill in all this? I mean, I thought you loved him.'

'I did . . . do . . . oh, whatever.' Rose wrinkled her forehead in confusion. 'It's not impossible to love two men at once, you know, Della. I mean, I feel a lot for Bill. I'm very fond of him, and he's the father of my child.' She gave Della a pleading look. 'But what I feel for Joe is different. He makes me feel more alive than I've ever felt before and—'

'I hate to disillusion you, luv,' Della cut in as kindly as she could, 'but I seem to remember you saying something very like that about Bill when you first met him. Don't you think it could just be the initial excitement, and when it wears off you might feel the same way about Joe as you do about Bill now?'

Rose shifted uneasily in her chair. 'Knowing me, you could be right, but this time I feel different. It's funny, isn't it? You tried to warn me off Bill when I first met him, and again when you found out he could never marry me. And now I've met a young, single fellow who could marry me, and you're warning me off him in favour of Bill – life's strange.'

'Oh, luv!' Della took Rose's hand across the table. 'It's only because Joe's so . . . so . . . tenuous. I mean, he's here today and gone tomorrow, but Bill's always going to be there to take care of you and Rosemary. I hate to think what you'd do without him?'

'I know exactly what you're saying,' Rose replied, unmoved.

Nevertheless, Della persevered. 'Look, you know I'd like nothing better than for you to meet a nice boy who would marry you and be a father to Rosemary – but an American airman on a few days' leave?' Her voice rose in consternation. 'Be sensible, Rose. Don't jeopardise what you've got with Bill for a flash-in-the-pan.'

'You don't know that he's a flash-in-the-pan.' Rose's mouth set in a stubborn line. 'And, anyway, even if he is, I'm too far gone to turn back now.'

Defeated, Della shrugged. 'I don't know why you even bothered to come for my advice. You never take it anyway.'

'But I need a favour as well,' Rose ventured, unnaturally timidly.

Della smiled, despite her concern. 'All right! What now?'

Encouraged, Rose went straight to the point. 'Can you lend me some clothing coupons?'

'What!' Della's eyes boggled. Even for Rose, it took some nerve to ask for such precious possessions.

'I swear I'll pay you back when I get my next allowance. But I'm all used up, and I need a new dress. I feel so dowdy in my old things when I'm with Joe.'

'Dowdy! You! Rose, *now* you're really being stupid. You've got more fabulous clothes than a Hollywood film star.'

'Aw, but I've had most of them since before the war,' Rose complained. 'I need something new to make me feel different. I have to look my best when I go out with

440

Joe – so many girls give him the eye. People used to look at *me* when I was out with a man, but now it's Joe who catches their eye first.'

'Oh, you poor thing! That must be a blow to your ego,' Della said drolly. 'All right. I've got enough left for a dress. What do I need a new dress for? I spend most of my life in uniform anyway, though I don't know why you prefer utility rubbish to your fabulous pre-war things.'

'But I'm so bored with them! I want to wear something new. Oh, I knew you'd say yes, Della. You're a gem! I'll pay you back – cross my heart, God's honour, hope to die, and all that.'

Della grinned at the childish promise. 'Rose, you're an idiot. I hope you never grow up. But you don't think I carry them around with me, do you? You'll have to go and get them. And, while you're there, ask Mam to give you the pair of nylons on my dressing table. Joe gave us two pairs each. I know he'd have saved some for you if he'd known you then.'

Rose screeched with joy. 'You angel! You've made my day! I can go to the shops this afternoon while Mrs James has Rosemary.'

'Does she know what's going on?' Suddenly Della looked concerned. Why hadn't she thought about the neighbours before? What if they talked?

Rose lowered her eyes. 'Not exactly. I told her Joe's my American cousin, and his wife asked me to look after him while he's on leave.'

Della tut-tutted. 'Do you really think she's that daft?'

'Well, either she is, or she just likes me.' Rose hinted at a smile. 'Besides, I found out from Bill that she used to be a professional. Her husband was one of her clients. So who's she to moralise about me? She doesn't give a hoot what I do, and she loves minding Rosemary. I like the old girl,' she finished, the smile spreading to a huge grin.

'I'm not surprised.' Della returned her grin. 'But what about the old man upstairs?'

Rose dismissed the question with a wave of her hand. 'Oh, the old geezer's all right. He's got a soft spot for me because I flirt with him a bit. He'd never say anything bad about me to Bill.'

'I hope you're right.' Della stood up. 'I'm back on duty at one. Give Mam my love and have a nice time shopping.'

Returning to the ward, Della wondered how much longer Rose's luck would last. So, she thinks it's possible to love two men at once? she thought. She was fooling herself. And yet, she reminded herself with discomfort, she had fallen in love with Paul less than a year after Jerry's death and, even though she loved Paul, she had felt stirrings of jealousy on seeing Jonathan with his girlfriend at the dance – and those physical feelings when he had touched her. Was it simply human nature to be emotionally (or sexually) fickle?

She had no more time to brood on the subject. Two orderlies wheeled a new patient back from the operating theatre into the ward.

'Quick,' Sister ordered, handing Della the drip. 'Take this and get him into bed. The children's ward's full.'

Della took the drip and looked down at the face, swathed in bandages. The white sheet covering the body was flat where the legs should have been, and only a bandaged stump jutted from the right shoulder. 'My God! What happened?' she asked the orderlies.

'Twelve-year-old lad,' one of them answered. 'He was playing with his brother on a bomb site in Copeland Terrace, near Manors Station. They found an unexploded bomb. He's the lucky one. His brother was blown to smithereens.'

Della felt sick. 'Lucky! Poor little mite!' She took a deep breath and steadied the hand holding the drip. Though trained not to let her emotions interfere with her work, her eyes filled as she gazed in horror at the small torso, the only remaining limb the left arm. How much longer would this insanity last? And the poor mother! One son dead and one who'd be better off dead, all in a matter of seconds, all because of human greed for power. She suppressed a shudder as the orderlies transferred the little body to the bed. After attaching the drip carefully to the stand, she covered him gently with the sheet from the stretcher before running for a frame to keep the weight of blankets off his wounds.

On her return, the man in the next bed sat up, his face a study of pity. 'What in God's name happened to the bairn?'

'Unexploded bomb.' She bit her lip as she draped the sheet and blankets over the frame.

'God help the little lad,' the man sighed.

'He hasn't been much help so far, has he?' Della snapped before hurrying out, head down. It wouldn't do to let the patients see her crying.

Jonathan didn't appear at the hospital until Wednesday. His mother had suffered a second, and fatal, heart attack. He'd gone home for the funeral. His office door was open and Della greeted him. 'Hello, Jonathan. I was sorry to hear about your mother.'

'Thanks,' he replied, buttoning his white coat.

'How's your father taking it?'

'Not very well. In many ways it was a strange marriage and yet there was a bond between them. He's drowning his sorrows in booze, and his gout's bad, but he won't listen to sense. The estate's becoming too much for him.' He fished in his pocket for his handkerchief and cleaned his glasses. 'I tried to talk him into hiring a manager but he won't hear of it – principally the money, of course; he hates parting with the stuff.' He leaned back in his chair and looked ruefully at the pile of papers that had accumulated on his desk. 'Anything interesting been happening?'

'A lot, unfortunately – four new patients, one of them a twelve-year-old boy, Robby. There were no beds in the children's ward but they're transferring him tomorrow. Even *you* are going to find this one hard to take. That's his report.' Della pointed to a sheaf of papers on top of the pile.

Jonathan picked it up, glanced through it, and let out a low whistle. 'The Manors bombing was two years ago. How the hell can they let a bomb go undetected all this time?'

Della shook her head hopelessly. 'I'm just going to say hello to Robby before I get started. I brought some sweets for him.'

'Watch out, nurse,' Jonathan said. 'You've got enough of your own troubles; don't take on your patients' as well.'

'Wait till you see Robby.' Della's eyes misted. 'And he's such a cheerful little chap.'

Jonathan looked at her closely. 'I think it's time for another dose of Hollywood for you. It's obvious you've been missing your treatments.' He smiled wryly. 'And I could do with a tonic myself. How about tomorrow night?'

Tomorrow – only his second evening back. Why wasn't he seeing his girlfriend? Maybe she was away or worked in the evenings? Maybe he did still need company? Well, so did she, so why not? 'It sounds lovely,' she said, 'but my brother's leaving tomorrow. He's been on a few days' leave. I should stay with my mam; she's going to be miserable.'

'Friday, then?'

'All right.' So he was free on Friday, too! It must be a long-distance love affair.

'Good! I stocked up with goodies from home. I'll surprise you.'

'You always do.'

As she left, Della wondered if his girlfriend knew he was taking out another girl? She'd surely find it hard to believe they were just friends.

On Wednesday afternoon, tears trickled down Rose's cheeks as she made fish paste sandwiches while Joe played with Rosemary in the sitting room. Rose sniffed and wiped her eyes with the back of her hand; he was so marvellous with Rosemary – like a two-year-old himself. How on earth was she going to live without him now? And what was she going to do about Bill? Both questions had nagged at her for days, but she had refused to seek any answers until she was forced to. Their time together had been too short and too precious to spoil by talking about a non-existent future.

She carried in the tea and food on a tray. 'Lunch is ready, such as it is. But I managed to get some minced beef for later. I thought I'd try my hand at hamburgers to give you something to remember me by.' She managed a smile.

'Thanks, honey, but I said I'd be at Billie's by three to pick up my things, and his mom's having something ready for us. It's only polite to say goodbye to them.' Joe picked up two sandwiches, gave one to Rosemary and sat her on his lap.

Head down, Rose poured two cups of tea and a cup of milk for Rosemary. She didn't want Joe to see her face as she sought to control her feelings. He was leaving so early! This was the last couple of hours they'd have together. She plunked Rosemary on the floor by the coffee table, removed the sandwich and carefully placed the cup in her chubby hands.

'No milk! Tea!' Rosemary pouted.

'All right.' Rose mollified her, unable to deal with a tantrum now, of all times. She compromised, pouring a few drops of tea into the milk. Rosemary was satisfied.

'She pouts just like her mom,' Joe chuckled. 'She's a cutie, just like her mom, too. I'd like to pack you both in my kitbag.'

'I wish you could,' Rose said fervently, joining him on the sofa with her tea. 'We're both going to miss you, Joe.'

'I'm going to miss you too, baby.' He picked up his cup and grinned. 'You put milk in my tea again.'

'Oh, sorry, I wasn't thinking.' Rose made to get up.

'Don't bother! I'm even beginning to like it. You might make a Tommy out of me yet.' Joe sipped the tea and looked at her. 'You're not eating.' He handed her the sandwich plate.

She took one mechanically, bit into it and chewed slowly, then threw it on the table with a grimace. 'I'm not hungry, and I can't stand fish paste anyway.'

Having finished her milk, Rosemary climbed back on to Joe's knee, the remains of her sandwich in her fist. 'No fish paste!' She imitated her mother before throwing the sandwich to the floor.

'Rosemary,' Rose chided wearily. 'Get down and pick that up, and leave Uncle Joe alone. He's trying to eat.'

'No! Uncle Joe! Up, up, knee, knee!' Rosemary insisted, pouting again.

Joe settled her in his lap. 'Tell you what, kid, if you eat *my* sandwich I've got some American candy for you, and you can have it in bed while I tell you a story before your nap.'

'Crafty bugger!' Rose smiled despite herself. 'Admit you don't like fish paste either.'

He grinned as Rosemary eagerly grabbed the sandwich and crammed half of it into her mouth, her cheeks bulging. 'Does anybody?' he asked.

'Rosemary, you'll choke yourself,' Rose admonished, as the child attempted another bite. 'Swallow first.' Rosemary swallowed hard and, undaunted, pushed the remaining crust into her mouth with the palm of her hand.

'Bribing my daughter with sweets,' Rose said affectionately. 'You're too soft with her.'

'But I do know how to get her out of the way when I'd rather have her mommy in my lap.' Joe tousled Rosemary's dark red curls and swung her on to his shoulders. 'OK, now for candy and a story and then a nice *long* nap. Promise Uncle Joe you'll make it nice and long.'

Rosemary screamed with delight as he marched her into her bedroom.

As soon as he was out of sight Rose's tears flowed again. She blinked hard and looked in the mirror above the mantelpiece. Blast! Her mascara! And her eyes were red! With her handkerchief, she scrubbed at the dark smudges under her eyes, patted her cheeks to bring some colour to them, and ran her fingers through her hair. She certainly didn't look her best for Joe today.

She washed up until he returned, stealing behind her in the kitchen and putting his arms round her waist.

'Is she off?' Rose leaned back against him and closed her eyes.

'Yeah, one down, one to go,' Joe grunted, lifting and swinging her round to the door. Rose buried her face in his neck until he gently laid her on the bed. He undressed her slowly and lovingly before throwing off his own clothes and lying beside her. They held each other for some time, he stroking her hair, she pressing her face into the curve of his shoulder, savouring his familiar musky odour. Slowly, tenderly, they made love. The bitter sweetness of their bodies meeting for the last time was almost unbearable and, afterwards, silently they held each other again.

At length Joe interrupted Rose's poignant thoughts. 'I'm going to miss you, hon,' he murmured softly, brushing her forehead with his lips.

'Oh, Joe!' Rose clutched him tightly. 'I don't know how I'm going to live without you.'

'I'll be back whenever I can. And I'll write whenever I can.' He kissed her forehead again. 'And I'll be waiting for your letters, impatient as hell.'

'I'll write every day.' She bit her lip. 'But, Joe, you'll be careful, won't you? You won't do any more stupid brave things like that escapade Billie talks about?'

'Don't worry, baby, I'll keep my ass covered,' he chuckled. 'And you keep yours covered – it's such a great little ass.' He stroked her buttocks tenderly.

Rose managed a smile, a very fond smile, but as it lingered her lips quivered.

'Come on, honey, don't look so miserable,' Joe coaxed, kissing her softly. She clung to him and he kissed her more fiercely. This time they made love frantically, as if it would indeed be the last time.

Chapter Thirty-Six

One unseasonably cold Saturday evening in August, the fire flared with an old chopped up kitchen chair to conserve the coal ration for winter. Mary, Walter and Della were listening to Tommy Handley in ITMA when Anne arrived with Colin.

Walter turned off the wireless and hailed Colin with pleasure. He could always count on a good discussion or friendly argument with Colin.

'Anyone would think I was invisible.' Anne smiled as the men greeted each other, delighted as always that Walter and Colin got on so well.

Mary hugged her and bustled to the scullery. 'Yes, we might as well not be here when those two get their heads together. Sit down, luv, and I'll put the kettle on.'

'There's a bag on the bench, Mam,' Anne called after her as she flopped beside Della on the sofa. At the table, Colin and Walter were already deep in conversation.

Della gave the men a warning look. 'Now don't you two start on war and politics till we've told them the news.'

'What news?' Anne's eyes widened with excitement. It was obviously good news.

Walter opened his mouth to speak, but Della silenced him. 'Please, let me tell them, Dad.'

'I don't flipping care *who* tells me,' Anne said impatiently. 'Get on with it.'

'David's coming home on leave,' Della announced.

Anne's mouth fell open with surprise and delight. 'When?'

Della was about to speak, but Walter got in first: 'Probably next week. He's going to send a telegram when he knows for sure. We got a letter today. He's just got back from Sicily.' He picked up the remaining half a Woodbine from the ashtray and lit it; smoking half a cigarette at a time helped to eke out his ration. 'Aye, it's a good job the Ities didn't put up much of a fight. If the Jerries hadn't held out so long he'd have been home weeks ago.'

Colin smiled without humour. 'Aye, thank God we got the buggers out and put Mussolini behind bars. Hitler's next on the list.'

'That's a wonderful thought,' Mary said feelingly as she returned with the tea.

Anne's face glowed. 'Oh, how marvellous to see David! It was wonderful to see Billie, even if it *was* only one day. Colin had him driving the tractor – the stingy bastard even makes my guests work.' She patted Colin's shoulder affectionately as she got up to go to the scullery. 'You forgot the goodies, Mam. There's a packet of ginger snaps, and I made a chocolate cake to celebrate. We've got some news as well.'

'Don't tell us!' Della shrieked. 'You're getting hitched!'

Colin shrugged in exaggerated helplessness. 'Aye, she's finally twisted my arm.'

'Oh, that's wonderful!' Mary cried, kissing Colin on the cheek.

Anne returned with the ginger snaps and chocolate cake. 'We decided we've waited long enough. And anyway, we don't care if people gossip. The whole town sees us out together, so what's the difference?' She cut five portions of cake. 'And you needn't ask where the sugar came from – nor the other stuff in the bag. Colin's been up to his wheeling and dealing again. He's doing a roaring trade with the butcher, and guess what?' She paused dramatically. 'We've got half a turkey for tomorrow.'

'Turkey!' Mary's eyes popped. 'I won't ask what you had to trade for that, Colin.'

Colin looked at her innocently. 'That's right! Ask no questions and you'll be told no lies.'

'In other words,' Walter put in, 'button your lip, woman.'

'Yummy!' Della swallowed slowly, savouring the chocolate treat. 'When's the happy day going to be?'

'We're starting the banns tomorrow and we'll get married as soon as they're up.' Anne sighed happily. 'Oh, I hope David's home by then. That would be the best wedding present I could ever have . . . except for Wally,' she finished. Her eyes brimmed at the mention of his name.

Walter shook his head. 'Aye, well, I suppose we should thank God we've still got three left. Some families are worse off.' He crammed the last of his chocolate cake into his mouth and, seeing Mary's face begin to pucker, changed the conversation. 'Nice cake,' he said with his mouth full. 'Are we rationed to one piece?'

'Help yourself.' Anne dried her eyes with the back of her hand. 'I told you, it's a celebration.' She turned to Mary, who was still trying to hold back her tears. 'We only want a small do, Mam: just Colin's family and Nellie and Beryl, our family, and Muriel and Cath. I haven't seen them for donkeys' years.' Anne's face saddened as she thought of her old friends who had helped her through so many bad times with Dan, but she smiled and looked affectionately at Colin. 'And, of course, Mrs M and Molly, and Rose and Nora and Phil.'

'Don't worry about food, Mrs Dolan,' Colin grinned. 'I'll use my connections.'

Mary exhaled loudly. 'Well, that's a relief.'

'Are you going to have a white wedding?' Della asked, handing round the ginger snaps.

'Of course not, you ninny,' Anne laughed. 'I'm past that, thank goodness. I've seen a costume in Binns I rather like, but I'd have to scrounge some extra coupons.' She looked expectantly at Mary.

'Not mine,' she said adamantly, though unable to suppress a smile. 'How many do you need?'

Anne jumped up and hugged her. 'As many as you've got.'

'I gave the last of mine to Rose,' Della moaned.

'The little minx! I can guess why.' Anne pulled a face, and was about to say more but changed the subject when Della shot her a silencing look. 'I'll have to make everything. I can copy the one I liked in Binns for less than half the price. And I need to make Johnny a suit.' She gave Mary a concerned look. 'Johnny's coming to us after the wedding. Mrs M's going to be upset when I tell her.'

'Well, it had to happen some day.' Mary refilled the teacups. 'It'll be nice to have him back with you, luv.'

'I wanted her to do it ages ago,' Colin said. 'But she wouldn't while she was still officially a Land Army Girl; she's always too worried about what people think.'

'You know it wasn't only that,' Anne corrected him. 'It wouldn't have been fair on Nellie and Beryl. They've got kids as well, and we couldn't have had them all there.'

Walter lit another cigarette almost with reverence. 'Aye, it'll be good for him. And make sure you make him work for his keep. He always was a lazy little bugger, like his dad.'

As always, Anne jumped to Johnny's defence. 'Dad,

you know he's getting better since he's been with Mrs M. I know he *did* have a lot of his father in him, but he's growing out of it, and Colin will be a good influence on him.'

'I know, luv,' Mary reassured her. 'He never had a real father, even when Dan was alive. It's the best thing that could happen to him.'

Walter agreed sombrely. 'Aye, you brought that bairn up on your own, and now our Ellen's doing the same. Our Michael's going to be a stranger to his own kid when he gets back.'

'Any more word from him?' Anne's eyes suddenly lost their sparkle.

Della nodded. 'Ellen came round last Sunday. She's had another letter, but no mention of a leave. She doesn't know where he is; the letter was censored so much it looked like a paper doily.'

'Aye, well, there's good and there's bad to it,' Walter muttered, rising. 'I wouldn't have minded if I hadn't seen my lot till they were grown up.' He put his hand on Mary's shoulder. 'I'm off to bed now, luv. Goodnight you lot.'

Mary smiled and patted his hand. 'It's just as well they know you're a rotten liar, Walter Dolan.'

Later, in bed, Della confided in Anne. 'I . . . I went out with Jonathan again last night,' she began hesitantly.

'Again? Getting regular, isn't it?' Anne's voice came muffled through the blankets.

'I know, but he's got a girlfriend as well, so there's nothing in it.'

'Did he tell you he's got a girlfriend?'

'No, I saw him with her at the Oxford when I went with Billie and his friend. The funny thing is, I was jealous when I saw them together. I don't know what's getting into me, Anne. I mean, I still love Paul. Why in the world should I feel jealous of Jonathan?'

'Mmm.' Anne chewed her lip thoughtfully. 'Sounds to me as if you're getting fond of him again.'

'No, I'm not,' Della returned firmly. 'How could I be? I don't want him. I've told him I don't want him. It's established that we're just friends . . . yet I had such a stupid childish feeling when I saw him with another girl. I felt as if she'd taken my toy away from me.'

'And he's still asking you out even though he's got someone else? It sounds fishy to me, luv. Maybe she was just a one night stand.'

'It didn't look like it the way they danced together.'

'Well, if he still wants to take you out and you enjoy his company, you go,' Anne urged. 'Jonathan's a grown man; he knows what he's doing.'

'But I'm not sure *I* do, Anne. I mean, I feel funny about being jealous.'

'Aw, stop worrying your head, luv. It's probably a normal reaction. I remember once just after I'd ditched Tom, I saw him on the Lonnen with another girl. I felt furious and hurt, even though I'd broken it off. And the next time I saw them together I had just met Dan, and I was so pleased that I was with a handsome fellow.' Anne chuckled. 'One in the eye for Tom I thought. Feelings aren't always rational, you know.'

'But you were eighteen then,' Della persisted. 'I should know better by now.'

'Well, some parts of us never grow up.' Anne yawned. 'If I were you I'd stop worrying about it and get some sleep.'

Della sighed with relief. 'You're right, I suppose. Goodnight, luv. I'm so happy for you and Colin.'

'Me, too. Goodnight, pet.'

A moment's silence ensued before Anne's voice penetrated the dark again. 'By the way, Billie told me about Rose and his friend. What's going on?'

'Oh, she's got herself into a real conundrum. She's madly in love with him. You almost let the cat out of the bag tonight. You know it's better not to tell them about Rose's escapades.'

'What about Bill?'

'She claims she's still fond of him.'

'What's she going to do then?'

'God knows! And I'm too tired to worry about it at the moment.'

On Monday Della went to the coffee rooms as usual. She felt tired and hungry. It was raining heavily and two buses had passed the stop full.

Rose sat alone, her face a mile long. 'I thought you'd never come,' she grumbled.

'I couldn't get on a bus,' Della snapped, dumping her soaked mac and headscarf on a chair. 'And stop looking so pokerfaced! Just tell me the worst. I take it you've seen Bill.'

Rose nodded. 'He came over on Saturday. Oh, it was awful.'

Della looked surprised. 'You told him about Joe!'

Rose shook her head glumly. 'I couldn't. I'd thought about it every minute since Joe left. One minute I decided *yes* and the next I decided *no*. But something Joe said to me just before he left made me think. He told me to keep my ass covered, or something like that.' She smiled wanly. 'And I know what a mess I'd be in without Bill and so would Rosemary, so I decided just to carry on for the moment as if nothing had happened. But I'm not such a good liar as I used to be.'

Despite Rose's miserable face, Della giggled. ' "Keep your ass covered",' she repeated in amusement. 'I suppose that's the American way of saying keep your knickers on. It didn't take him long to size you up, did it?'

'It doesn't mean that,' Rose flashed back. 'If you want to know, it means look after myself.'

'Ooops! Sorry I spoke.' Della tried to suppress her smile. 'Well, if you didn't tell Bill, what happened that was so awful?'

'Oh, I just couldn't be my usual self with him. I mean, I was glad to see him and all that, but I couldn't go to bed with him. I told him I had a headache, but he knew something was up. He's no fool. And he knows I'd have to be on my death bed before I'd say no to sex, especially when I haven't seen him for over a week.' Rose rested her chin in her hands and stared glumly at Della.

'So what now?'

'I'll just have to play it by ear and hope it gets easier. I mean, I *am* still fond of him.'

Nora joined them apologetically. 'Sorry I'm late.' She threw her wet coat over Della's and sat down.

Della gave her a resigned look. 'You've missed Rose's news. I suppose I'll have to sit through it again.'

'Don't worry! Phil and I got it all last night. She came over and parked herself on us for three hours. I suppose she's been so full of herself she hasn't told you *my* news.'

'I forgot,' Rose muttered.

'Of course you would! You're so bloody wrapped up in your own affairs.' Nora shook her head hopelessly, but patted Rose's hand. 'Sorry, luv. I know you've got good reason to be preoccupied.' She turned to Della with dancing eyes. 'Guess what! I think I'm expecting.'

Della hid her misgivings about starting a family in wartime and adopted a pleased expression. 'Oh, marvellous, Nora! Are you sure?'

'Well, I'm only a week late, but it's never happened before.'

'Where's that bloody waitress?' Rose cut in irritably. 'I've been here over ten minutes.'

'Stop being such a pain, Rose,' Della scolded her. 'Can't you at least congratulate Nora?'

'I already did,' she said ungraciously. Then her eyes filled with tears. 'Oh, hell! Don't take any notice of me. I know I'm a pain in the arse. Let's go to the Eldon and have a drink. I need something stronger than coffee.'

'Rose, you know Della and I hate going to pubs without a man,' Nora groaned. 'It looks as though we're on the lookout.'

'What the hell if it does! Don't be so bloody old-fashioned.' Rose stood up to make it plain the decision was made.

'All right! Let's go.' Nora gave in. 'She'll be better with a drink or two in her, anyway,' she said to Della by way of encouragement. 'She ruined last night for me. I'm not going to let her do it again.'

Della followed obediently as they made a dash through the downpour to the pub. It was as crowded as usual, even for a Monday, although they found a table against the back wall.

'I'll get them,' Rose offered. 'What do you want?'

'A shandy, please.' Nora took off her coat.

'And one for me,' Della said. 'Give me your coats and I'll hang them up.'

She hung the coats on the rack in the entrance and made her way back through the throng to the bar. Rose would need help with the drinks. She didn't notice the appreciative male glances that followed her.

'Della!' A voice startled her from behind.

She turned. 'Jonathan! Hello.'

'I didn't know this was one of your haunts,' he said.

'It's not. I'm just here with Rose and Nora for a drink.'

'Well, why don't you all join us?' Jonathan inclined his head towards a group seated at two tables pulled together.

Della recognised his friends from the dance, two doctors from the hospital, a man she'd never seen before, and three women, including the ravishing brunette. Tonight, her dark hair, glistening wet, curled around her face and fell loosely halfway down her back. And the neckline of her simple blue dress plunged to reveal a cleavage that rivalled Rose's. Now that Della could see her close up, she guessed that she wasn't English. The face was stunning, the single small defect of the strong features being a slight curvature of the nose, though this only served to give her an exotic, Arabian look.

'Did you hear me?' Jonathan shouted over the din.

'Oh, yes, I did, sorry. Thanks, but I have to go in a few minutes. I'm on duty tonight.' It was a lie, and Jonathan knew Monday wasn't usually a duty night. 'One of the other girl's is ill.' Another lie.

'That's a pity,' he said with evident disappointment. 'See you tomorrow then.'

Della nodded and edged her way towards Rose. Damn him! He even wanted to introduce her to his girlfriend. She couldn't imagine the brunette appreciating that. And she'd feel guilty meeting her in any case. Even though she and Jonathan were only friends, she did take up some of his free evenings.

She rescued one of the three glasses from Rose, hissing as they pushed through the crowd, 'I'm going in a minute.'

'What for? You've just got here!' They reached the table and Rose plunked down Nora's shandy and her own gin and lime.

Della sat down and hastily swallowed half her shandy. She muttered with her head down as if Jonathan could read her lips, 'Jonathan's over there with his friends.' She indicated the direction with her head. 'He's asked us to join them and I said I was on duty.'

'Oh, you rotten spoilsport,' Rose complained. 'What did you say no for? It would be fun.'

'He's with his girlfriend,' Della snapped. 'And I don't want to meet her.'

'Which one?' Nora peered curiously in the direction of the two tables.

'Which one do you think?' Della replied almost angrily, 'The beautiful brunette, of course!'

Rose surveyed the girl, then made a little exploding noise with her lips. 'Now that's what I call competition!'

'I'm not competing for Jonathan!' Della retorted, aware that she sounded childishly belligerent. She took another gulp from her glass and passed it to Nora. 'Here, you finish it. I said I was going, so I'd better.'

Rose drew in her breath as Della's back view disappeared into the crowd. 'There's something funny going on with that Jonathan friendship, if you ask me. Why else would she go on like that just because he's got a real girlfriend?'

'Ask me!' Nora said, equally puzzled.

As Della silently paddled through the puddles to the bus stop, she asked herself the same question.

Chapter Thirty-Seven

Four weeks later the wedding day arrived. Anne had never looked so happy. It was a simple affair at St Bede's, Anne dressed in a copy of the cream costume she had seen at Binns and Colin in a blue serge suit. Mary wore the lavender outfit she had worn to Della's wedding, and Della, once again, reluctantly wore her going-away costume.

David's short leave had come and gone, but Michael had arrived unexpectedly three days earlier, so the day was as perfect as it could be under the circumstances. A fine drizzle hung in the air, but it didn't detract from the happy occasion.

Sitting in the same pew she had sat in at Jerry's funeral, Della felt a mixture of emotions: thanking God Anne's second marriage would be happier than her first, and wondering if her own life would ever be happy again. Would she ever stand at that same altar with Paul?

Bob, the best man, stood rigidly, the back of his neck fuchsia with embarrassment. As the priest recited the wedding vows: 'To love and to cherish . . . from this day forward', Della closed her eyes. Jerry's words reverberated through her head. A choked sob escaped her, and Mary took her hand. She knew her daughter was weeping for reasons beyond the moving words of the wedding vows.

When the guests returned to the house, Della was glad to help Mary and Walter attend to them. There wasn't a single paste sandwich on the table. Colin had been true to his word, providing a bacon joint, a chicken, tinned salmon, and fresh produce from the farm. They had raided several off-licences to stock up with drinks; alcohol was easier to obtain than food. Michael had saved his sweet coupons for months, and the children's eyes glowed as they surveyed the dishes of caramels and boiled sweets.

After attending to the guests' immediate needs, Della joined Mrs Moynihan and Molly on the sitting-room sofa. Johnny sat on the arm munching a chicken sandwich, the sulky expression on his face looking uncomfortably like his father's.

'Hey, Johnny, cheer up,' Della chided, half jokingly and half warningly. 'This is a wedding, not a funeral.'

His thirteen-year-old voice cracked back: 'What's the difference?'

'Don't take no notice of him, hinny,' Mrs Moynihan said. 'He's just in the dumps because he's going to miss having the lads to play with.'

Della tried to coax him. 'But there are boys your age at the Smiths' farm. And you can ride the tractor . . . and there's a horse.'

'Aw, I know all that. But I still don't want to go,' Johnny grumbled. 'I want to stay with Mrs M and Molly.'

'You'll like it even better at the farm,' Molly said sharply, 'and you'll be with your mam. Don't you dare sulk over her today.'

'Aye, and I'll be with Colin an' all,' Johnny pouted.

'But you like Colin,' Mrs Moynihan said, more as a command than a statement.

Johnny kicked his feet against the sofa. 'He'd be all right if he wasn't always telling me what to do.' He paused and added belligerently, 'And he's going to make me work in the fields.'

'Johnny!' Della chastised him sharply. 'Don't talk about your Uncle Colin like that. He's very kind to you. You'll have to work full-time when you leave school next year, and would you rather work on a farm or in a factory? That's what it comes down to nowadays.' She added more softly, 'The farm will partly belong to you one of these days. Doesn't that make you feel proud?'

Johnny looked as though he had suddenly tasted something sour and kicked the sofa again in answer.

'Johnny!' Mrs Moynihan's tone brooked no argument. 'If you don't behave yoursel' an' be nice to your mam an' your Uncle Colin, I won't let you come back to see the lads no more, an' I won't let them go to see you neither.'

'You wouldn't!' Johnny shouted in disbelief.

Molly backed up her mother. 'Oh, yes, we would. So straighten your face and be nice to your mam and Colin – or else,' she threatened enigmatically. She smiled at Della. 'Lads! God played a dirty trick on me giving me four. I wish they'd been girls.' She poked Johnny in the chest affectionately, though her voice was stern. 'So if you want the lads to come to see you, you'd better keep your nose clean. Do you hear?'

'Aw, I hear you all right,' Johnny muttered, kicking the sofa again. But Mrs M and Molly smiled at each other.

These women certainly knew how to handle Johnny, Della thought. Hopefully, with Colin to back her up, Anne would also be more strict with him. She patted Mrs Moynihan's knee affectionately and, for the first time, noticed how much worse the arthritic ankles were. They overflowed the sides of her men's black shoes. 'How are you feeling, Mrs M? Are your feet bothering you?' She looked with concern also at the swollen and distorted hands.

'Why aye, hen, everythin's botherin' me.' Mrs Moynihan grinned, showing her two broken front teeth. 'But what you can't do nowt about, you don't shout about.'

Molly shook her head sadly at Della, who tried to sound more cheerful than she felt. 'You're a tonic, Mrs M. I wish some of your attitude would rub off on me.'

'Well, why not, hinny? Life's a bugger! The only way to deal with it is to kick it up the backside and punch it in the nose.' She looked thoughtful for a moment before bellowing with laughter and poking Della's thigh. 'That's probably why me hands and feet are so bad now – I've done that much kickin' an' punchin' in me life.' She guffawed again at her own joke, and Della broke into an affectionate smile. She wished she could be more like Mrs Moynihan. 'I suppose I'd better circulate.' She went to join Anne, who stood by the window talking to Rose and Nora. 'How does it feel to be a married woman again?' Della asked, hugging her from behind.

Anne sighed with happiness. 'Wonderful!'

Rose raised her sherry glass to Anne and Nora. 'To the new bride and the new mother-to-be.' She sipped the sherry and added wryly, 'Maybe one of these days it'll be my turn.' Belatedly remembering Della, she said softly, 'And yours, luv . . . may Paul come back safely.'

'Thank you,' Della whispered, feeling a stab of pain on hearing Paul's name. No one mentioned him any more, knowing that if there'd been any word they wouldn't need to ask. She stifled a sigh. 'Heard any more from Joe?'

'Not since last week. He just said he's fine and still covering his ass.' Rose managed a smile.

But Della recognised the pain behind the smile. 'And how are things with Bill?' she asked softly.

Rose replied in a resigned voice, 'The same – ticking

over. I'm still glad to see him when he comes. I'm not complaining.'

'Well, *I'm* complaining,' Nora gasped, screwing up her face and thrusting her sherry glass at Rose. 'I'm going to be sick!'

Rose nudged Della as Nora made a dash for the stairs. 'So now she knows what it's like,' she gloated, 'after all she had to say to me about the joys of being preggers.'

'I'd give anything to be sick again,' Anne said. 'We're going to try now, war or no war. At my age I can't afford to wait any longer.'

Rose looked thoughtful. 'It's funny, isn't it? When my mam was thirty-three I thought she was an old woman. Strange how our ideas about age change as we get older. Why don't you try tonight, Anne – your wedding night? Oh, how romantic!' She feigned a swoon.

Anne smiled. 'I'd hardly call it romantic. We're staying at the Queen's Head at Morpeth and going home tomorrow. Johnny's in the same room or it would have been twice the price. We'll spend the day there tomorrow and go home in the evening. A day out will be a nice way for Johnny to get to know Colin better.'

'Phweew! Some honeymoon!' Rose blinked rapidly, hardly believing her ears.

But Anne smiled again. 'My life's going to be a honeymoon, Rose, and I'm excited about taking Johnny back with us. It's been hard seeing him only once a fortnight.'

Della felt a chill on hearing the optimistic words. She prayed Johnny wouldn't spoil Anne's and Colin's happiness.

Michael approached them, carrying three-year-old Caroline. He looked older and thinner, his uniform hanging loosely about his body, but his bright eyes and wide smile hadn't changed. 'Would you mind taking her to the lav?' he asked Della apologetically. 'She wants to go but the door's locked and somebody's puking their guts out in there. I can't find Ellen, and Nellie and Beryl are screaming at me to help them louse up the car.' He grinned mischievously. 'They're trying to put half a kipper in the engine and they can't get the bonnet up.' Only then noticing Anne in the group, he clapped his free hand over his mouth. 'Oops! I've put my foot in it! You didn't hear that, Anne. You're not supposed to know.'

'Don't worry!' she consoled him with a grin. 'I won't spoil your fun. By the time it starts to cook we'll be out of town anyway. So long as you promise no tin cans and bog rolls.'

'Cross my heart,' Michael lied.

Surprisingly, Rose relieved Michael of Caroline, saying, 'Go on! You get on with your monkey business. I'll take her out to the garden. I never thought I'd get used to ka-ka,' she muttered as she lugged Caroline away.

Anne looked at her watch. 'Six o'clock! I suppose I'd better freshen myself up and get Johnny ready. Where's Colin?'

'Last time I saw him he was talking to Dad in the kitchen,' Della said in amusement. 'Or, rather, Dad was talking to him, as usual. I'll tell him it's time.'

Making her way through the throng of guests, Della noticed Mrs Bowman clacking away to Mrs Moynihan. No doubt she was bleating about her asthma or her offspring's neglect, her only topics nowadays. Mam was such a softy for inviting the old crow, she thought fondly. Poor Mrs Moynihan! But if anyone could handle Mrs Bowman, Mrs M could.

She rescued Colin from Walter and, within five minutes, the battered old Jowett was crammed. Colin was dropping off Bob and Nellie and Beryl at the bus station on the way.

The guests hooted and cheered at the car, on which Nellie and Beryl had done a wicked job with tin cans and newspaper streamers.

Good-naturedly, Colin clattered to the end of the street before removing the decorations. Anne smiled secretly at the thought of the kipper. She'd let Nellie and Beryl think they'd got away with it until they dropped them off.

On Monday Della awoke with a stuffed nose and a slight sore throat. Her body felt as heavy as a sandbag as she trailed down to the kitchen. 'I think I'm getting a cold,' she squeaked to Mary.

'You sound like it.' Mary looked at her closely. 'And you look peaky. Why don't you go back to bed?'

Della blew her nose. 'Oh, I'll shake it off once I get going. It's just a little cold. There's a lot worse than that where I'm going. And anyway, Nancy's having her wisdom teeth out today. Sister'll have a fit if two of us are off.' She ate half a bowl of cornflakes and sipped half a cup of tea. It hurt to swallow.

'You'd better eat more than that, lass, if you're going to do a day's work,' Walter said, finally looking up from his paper. His uncanny ability to read while missing nothing that went on had always been a family mystery.

Della stood up and rumpled his hair affectionately. 'Dad, you're turning into an old woman. I'll have something at tea break.' She made a quick exit.

'Morning,' Jonathan shouted as she passed his office. 'How did the wedding go?'

Della paused outside his door. 'Very well,' she replied hoarsely. 'Everyone had a good time. How was your weekend?'

'So, so.' He looked at her curiously. 'Are you all right?'

'Oh, I've just got a bit of a cold. It's nothing. Don't worry, I'll be careful not to breathe on the patients,' she croaked over her shoulder as she disappeared down the hall.

By mid-morning, exhausted, Della had a cup of tea in the staff room but couldn't manage anything solid. Wearily, she returned to the ward. She had three more bed baths to do. 'Morning, Mr Brown,' she greeted her third patient listlessly. Maybe she should have stayed in bed. Whatever this thing was, she wasn't shaking it off as she'd hoped.

Mr Brown beamed at her. 'Mornin', nurse! Rub-a-dub-dub time, is it?'

'Afraid so.' Della attempted to drag the screen round his bed. It seemed to weigh a ton. She stood, smiling wanly at the fourteen-stone paralytic and wondering how on earth she would manage to turn him over, when Jonathan started his rounds.

'Nurse Davidson!' He addressed her sharply. 'Would you please go to my office and wait there till I've finished my rounds? Get Nurse Jones to take over.'

'Yes, doctor,' Della replied meekly.

It was almost an hour later before Jonathan returned to his office, but Della had been glad to sit quietly. 'Now, let's get to you,' he said, employing his professional voice. 'Open your mouth.' She obeyed. He pressed a spatula against her tongue and shone a light down her throat, peering in closely and grunting before sticking a thermometer under her tongue. When he finally spoke his voice was firm. 'How long have you had this?'

'Jush today,' Della lisped, clutching the thermometer between her teeth.

Jonathan felt her pulse. Without speaking, he removed the thermometer, glanced at it and replaced it on the tray by his desk.

'What's my temperature?' Della squeaked, feeling ridiculous.

'A hundred and two. Undo your apron, and your dress.'

Reluctantly she did so, not looking at him. Thank goodness he hadn't mentioned her slip and brassiere. She knew her face must be scarlet.

'Cough!' he ordered. She obliged. 'Again!' She obliged again. Then she felt the cold steel on her chest, travelling under her brassiere and slip. She could feel her heart pumping in embarrassment.

As Jonathan withdrew the stethoscope, Della hurriedly buttoned her dress. 'What's the verdict?' She avoided his gaze.

'Head back.' He ignored her question and poked a swab up her nose. 'What have you been in contact with recently?' He removed the swab and smeared it on to a culture dish.

'I helped out on the children's isolation ward on Friday.' The frightening thought struck her. 'Do you think I could have picked up something there?'

'Too early to tell exactly. Any aches and pains?'

'All over,' she answered miserably.

'No rash?'

She shook her head.

'It could be 'flu. But I don't like the look of that throat.' Rummaging through the medicine cabinet, he produced two bottles, one red and one a revolting shade of brown. He placed them on his desk, adding a bottle of aspirins. 'Gargle with the red one every four hours and take two teaspoons of the brown one every four hours – and two aspirins every four hours,' he added firmly.

'Dr Maddison, I can read labels,' Della admonished, smiling despite her misery.

Jonathan ignored her remark. 'I'm taking you home.'

'But you're on duty.'

'Even a doctor has to eat. I'll take an early lunch.' He flashed her a smile as he changed from his white coat into a casual tweed jacket. 'Dr Simpson can cover for me anyway. Come on,' he ordered, taking her elbow.

Della shook it off, though not ungratefully. 'Please, no! I can manage.'

Jonathan shrugged in resignation. 'I know! What would Sister think? Well, I don't give a damn what Sister thinks! But if it makes you happy, I'll keep two steps behind you – your royal consort.'

Della sank gratefully into the car seat, shivering though the day was mild. Jonathan pulled her cloak more tightly about her and covered her knees. Her head felt fuzzy, and she was surprised when she realised they were driving down the next street to hers. She shuddered as she saw an all too familiar sign in a house window: 'Diphtheria is Deadly', and, a few doors further, the 'ID' sign that indicated an infectious disease in the house, probably scarlet fever, she thought. But, she consoled herself, they were mainly children's diseases.

Jonathan pulled up at the house. She'd hardly noticed the journey, he'd been unusually silent. But she hadn't felt like talking either. He helped her out of the car and supported her by the arm down the path.

'Jonathan, please,' she begged, realising he wasn't going to leave her at the gate. 'I can manage from here. Thank you for all you've done. I'm very grateful. I promise I'll be a good patient and follow doctor's orders.'

'I need to make sure about that,' he replied firmly, knocking on the front door.

Oh, God! Della was about to beg him again to leave when the door opened.

Mary's hand clapped to her mouth in dismay. 'Dear Lord! What's wrong with—'

But Jonathan cut in reassuringly. 'It's all right; she's

just got an infection – probably 'flu. I'm the doctor on her ward. I was passing this way to go home anyway so I gave her a lift.'

'I'm fine, honestly, Mam.' Della tried to sound convincing as she attempted to heave her weak knees up the two stone steps. Jonathan helped her.

Mary stood back, her face like granite. 'Oh, thank you, doctor. Bring her in here.' She led him to the kitchen. He still supported Della who, at the earliest opportunity, disengaged herself and sat on the sofa.

Jonathan produced the two bottles and the aspirins from his jacket pockets and repeated the instructions to Mary. 'And keep her warm to sweat out the fever.'

'Thank you, doctor. It's very kind of you—' Mary started, but Della interrupted her.

'I wish you wouldn't talk about me as if I weren't here. I'm feeling much better now. I promise I'll take my medicine and go up to bed. Thank you for the lift, doctor,' she added dismissively.

Jonathan glanced at the clock on the mantelpiece. 'Goodness! Is that the right time? I must be off.'

But Della's glance had followed his to the clock. A white envelope stood propped against it, where Mary always put the post. The scrawling handwriting was familiar. Della gulped, painfully, forgetting Jonathan's presence. 'Is that for me?'

Mary gave Jonathan a helpless glance before replying. 'Yes, dear, but it can wait till later. You go up and get into bed and I'll bring you your medicine.'

But Della had already prised herself out of the chair and feverishly torn open the envelope. She read, transfixed:

30 August 1943

Dear Della,
   We just got word today from the War Office

that our Paul's body's been found in the desert. We wanted you to know straight away. It seems he went quick, thank God. A bullet went right through his chest. They sent us his wallet. That's how they identified him. It had a photo of you in it.

They said they thought it better to give him a military funeral over there. His body's lain there that long, like. They sent us their sympathy and condolences. Lord have mercy on us! Is that what we get for bringing up a lovely lad – sacrificing him to our country?

As we can't have a funeral, we're having a memorial service at the Church of Jesus Christ on Sunday, and we're having a headstone made. We know you'll be there mourning with us.

Come to the house first, about half-past ten. As you know as well, hinny, the waiting was so awful that in a funny sort of way it's almost a relief that that part's over.

God bless you for loving our son.

Our love and prayers.

May and Bill Conway

The letter slipped from Della's shaking hand as she crumpled in a heap on the floor. Jonathan swiftly bent over her and laid her flat. He loosened her dress buttons and slipped his hands behind her to undo the tight brassiere before taking her pulse. Mary stood immobilised.

'Have you got any smelling salts?' he asked, tight-lipped. But at the sight of Mary's distraught face, he added kindly, 'Don't worry, she's only fainted.'

Mary ran upstairs, returning with a bottle of Dr MacKenzie's which Jonathan waved under Della's nose. Her eyelids fluttered and she moaned. Slowly, she opened her feverish eyes wide.

'You're all right,' he said. 'You fainted.' He picked her up and laid her on the sofa, commanding Mary over his shoulder, 'Bring a cold, damp flannel.'

In a flash Mary obeyed, and he dabbed the cloth over Della's face before laying it on her forehead.

'Paul's dead,' Della groaned to herself.

'I know, luv,' Mary said softly, desperately wanting to take her in her arms, but knowing she must let the doctor take care of her. 'I guessed it when I saw the envelope. If I'd known you were coming home ill, I'd have kept it from you.'

'No, I had to know . . .'

Jonathan waved a silencing hand. 'You must get some rest now, Nurse Davidson. You can talk later.' He looked at Mary. 'I'll help you to get her up to bed.'

Della tried to stand, but he swept her up as if she were a child. His tall, slim body was surprisingly strong, and he followed Mary upstairs to the landing with little apparent effort.

'In here, doctor.'

Jonathan laid Della gently on the bed. He undid one shoe and Mary the other.

'Is she wearing anything tight besides her brassiere?' he asked.

'No, she doesn't wear roll-ons.'

'Better to leave her in her clothes for now. She's in shock.' He eased the blankets from under her and covered her gently. 'Would you mind getting me the brown bottle and the aspirins? She'll have to wait till later to gargle.'

Mary disappeared and reappeared in seconds, watching as Jonathan administered the medicine and tablets with professional skill. Della, in a half-trance, eyes dry and staring, submitted weakly and swallowed when ordered.

Jonathan spoke quietly to Mary. 'The medicine and fever will help her to sleep, but she'll need sedating.' He inclined his head to the stairs and Mary followed him down.

'I haven't got my bag with me but I'm going back to the hospital this afternoon. I'll drop something off this evening on my way home and see how she is.'

'Thank you, doctor. That's very kind of you.' Both gratitude and fear showed in Mary's eyes.

Jonathan smiled reassurance. 'It's my job, Mrs—' He cut himself short. He'd been about to address her as Mrs Dolan.

'Dolan,' she obliged. 'Davidson's Della's married name.' She shook her head miserably and held on to a dining chair for support. 'It seems to be true that it never rains but it pours, doctor. Now she's got to deal with grief and illness together.'

'Well, at least the illness will take the edge off the grief for the moment. She's going to be partly out of it with that fever for a few days anyway.'

Mary put out her hand. 'I can't thank you enough, Dr—'

Jonathan hesitated. 'Simpson,' he lied, his colleague's name coming easily as he returned her handshake. He hated to deceive Mary, but Maddison wasn't a common name. Why risk stirring up more complications for Della when she had enough to deal with already? 'I'll be back early this evening. I'll see myself out,' he said, making for the hall.

'Thank you again, doctor,' she said gratefully.

Mrs Bowman peered through her sitting-room lace curtains as the tall young man with the sombre face drove off in the little red car. At six-thirty she was back at her post when the car drove up again.

Mary answered Jonathan's knock. 'Oh, hello, doctor. Please come in.'

'Hello, Mrs Dolan. How's the patient?' He employed his best professional, cheerful manner.

'Not good, doctor, not good.' Mary shook her head as she led him down the hall. 'She's dozed off and on, but when she wakes up, she just keeps on whispering her boyfriend's name. Her voice sounds very hoarse. I think she's losing it.'

Jonathan followed her up to the bedroom. Della's eyes were open, but they looked like two small brown glass beads in her flushed face.

Mary looked at her with pain in her eyes. 'The doctor's here to see you, luv.'

'How're you feeling?' Jonathan sat on the bed.

'Awful.'

He opened his bag and withdrew a thermometer, placing it gently under her tongue and noting that her lips were cracked and dry. He checked her pulse, removed the thermometer and glanced at it. A hundred and three!

Mary looked on anxiously. 'What is it, doctor?'

'It's up a bit more.' Jonathan took a spatula and torch from his bag, gently opening Della's mouth and pressing down her tongue. She gagged. 'It's all right – only for a second.' He shone the torch quickly down her throat.

She gasped for breath as he withdrew the spatula.

'How are the aches and pains?'

'Terrible,' Della lisped through her cracked lips.

'Well, it seems you've got yourself a nice dose of 'flu, Nurse Davidson. Your culture seems all right. For the moment, we'll just stick to the treatment, but I'll pop in every day.' He delved in his bag again. 'You should sleep all right, but I've brought you some sedatives. You can take one every four hours if you feel very bad, but try not to take them if you don't need them.'

Della nodded her thanks.

'I'll look in on you again tomorrow.' Jonathan rose

abruptly, and Mary followed him downstairs.

For once, Walter's newspaper lay unopened beside him on the table. Mary introduced them, 'This is my husband, Walter Dolan, and this is Dr Simpson.'

Walter nodded towards a chair. 'Please have a seat, doctor.'

Feeling awkward, Jonathan sat down. Much as he'd like to get to know these people, he must keep this meeting brief and businesslike. He felt a fraud, deceiving them.

'How is she, really?' Mary asked warily.

Jonathan smiled. 'You didn't believe me then?'

'Well, yes, but—'

'It's all right, Mrs Dolan,' he cut in. 'I admit I *was* worried at first that it might be diphtheria or scarlet fever, especially as she helped out on the children's isolation ward. But she isn't showing any of the other symptoms. There's no rash, and her culture was fine. It's just a bad case of 'flu.'

He looked directly at Mary, noticing for the first time that, despite her worried expression and a few streaks of grey in her bright auburn hair, she was still a very beautiful woman. 'I don't mean to minimise it,' he went on. 'It seems like a very nasty strain, and there's always the danger that it could lead to pneumonia, but your daughter's a strong girl. I'll pop in every day, just to keep an eye on her.'

Walter, who had been listening quietly, spoke up. 'It's very good of you, doctor, but we don't like to trouble you any more. We could always call our own doctor.' From his tone it was evident that he liked this quiet-voiced, refined young man.

'I always like to be responsible for my own staff,' Jonathan replied, adding jokingly, 'That way I know they're in good hands.' Then his voice sobered. 'And I know she's got other problems at the moment that could possibly affect her progress.'

Mary ran her hand over her brow in despair. 'I read the letter, doctor. They found her boyfriend's body, but it was too late to send it home. The parents are holding a memorial service and having a headstone erected on Sunday. She insists on going. Will she be well enough by then?'

Jonathan shook his head. 'Not unless she has a miraculous recovery and, besides, she shouldn't mix with other people for at least a week.'

Mary sighed. 'Well, she's done most of her mourning already anyway; she's been dreading this for a long time.'

'Yes, I knew her boyfriend was missing in action. The sedatives should ease her grief temporarily, but I don't want her to continue with them too long. Some mourning is necessary; it's a natural healing process.' Jonathan glanced at the clock. 'I'd better be going. I'll be here at the same time tomorrow.'

Mary managed a smile. 'Thank you, doctor.' She showed him to the front door and looked at the handsome face and into the kind brown eyes. 'I'm very grateful for all you've done.'

Jonathan looked embarrassed. 'I'm only doing my job, Mrs Dolan, and I love it. No need for thanks.'

Mary watched him walk down the path, his back straight, his gait self-confident. Such a handsome young doctor and such a nice man, too, she thought as she closed the door.

Jonathan's mind was on his cousin as he walked to his car. Despite the hardships in her life, she hadn't lost her air of breeding, and her husband certainly commanded respect. He seemed a personable, self-confident man, though not of an overbearing personality. Jonathan sighed as he turned on the ignition. No wonder their daughter was so special.

Chapter Thirty-Eight

By Friday afternoon Della felt well enough to lie downstairs. Mary had insisted that having more company and listening to the wireless would be therapeutic. Della shuffled in on shaky legs and flopped, exhausted, on to the sofa.

'I told you to wait for me to help you.' Mary placed a pillow behind Della's head and covered her with a blanket.

'I've got to move sometime.' The fever having now subsided, Della's face was chalk white, her cheeks hollow.

Mary gave her a worried look. 'I'm starting the dinner now.'

Della closed her eyes. *Music While You Work* droned in the background. Work! She felt as if she'd never be able to work again, yet longed for activity to keep her mind busy. In all her waking moments, Paul never left her thoughts. The horror of it! His poor body lying there all that time. She shuddered. No! She must stop dwelling on that. But she was determined to go to his memorial service no matter what.

Mary carried in a bowl of potatoes. 'It's nice to see you downstairs again, luv. I'll peel these in here to keep you company.'

'Mam, I think I'll be well enough to go to the service on Sunday,' Della attempted feebly, anticipating her mother's reaction.

'Stop talking rubbish, sweetheart.' Mary's tone was firm but her eyes were sympathetic. 'Just look at you! You can't even get down the stairs by yourself without collapsing.'

'But I'll be better by Sunday,' Della persisted, causing Mary to use her last line of defence.

'You heard what the doctor said. Would you want to pass it on to all those people?'

Still, Della persevered. 'But I could stand at the back and keep away from everyone. I just want to be there.'

Mary was adamant. 'No, luv, it's out of the question. I'll order the wreath tomorrow, and Mr and Mrs Conway should have my letter by now. They'll understand. You can go and see them and visit the headstone as soon as you're well enough. And Dr Simpson will have to decide when that is.'

Della cringed. Though grateful that Jonathan had tried to protect her from any more problems, she felt guilty about deceiving her mother.

Mary plopped the potato she'd peeled back in the bowl and spoke softly: 'Do you think Paul would have wanted you to get out of your sick-bed just to prove you're mourning him?'

Remembering the words in his letter: 'Please don't stand by my grave', Della gave up the argument.

Suddenly Richard Dimbleby's voice broke through the music on the wireless. 'We interrupt this programme to give you a news bulletin. Today, the Anglo-American forces swept across from Sicily to the mainland, gaining a strong foothold. Only the German army retaliated. Fighting is still going on—'

A knock on the front door diverted their attention. Mary stood up, wiped her hands on her apron and removed it before answering the door. 'Oh, hello, Dr Simpson.' She greeted Jonathan with pleasure. 'They've just announced on the wireless – the Allies have invaded

Italy, and the Italians didn't even retaliate.'

'That's good news,' he said. 'It looks like it won't be long before they're on our side. A pity it took them so long to get the message.'

They hurried to the kitchen, by which time *Music While You Work* had resumed.

'What else did they say?' Mary asked Della.

'Only that they would keep us informed. It seems that's all they know at the moment, or at least all they want us to know.'

'More likely the latter.' Jonathan looked closely at Della. 'Downstairs, eh? Feeling better?'

'Yes, thank you, doctor. You're early.'

'I had to leave early . . . some personal business.' He took the thermometer from his bag and inserted it under Della's tongue. She submitted docilely. As usual, she felt like a child as he examined her.

Jonathan took her pulse. 'Now, let's have a look,' he said in his brisk bedside manner. He glanced at the thermometer. 'Still up a bit, but nothing to worry about so long as you behave yourself.'

'She was talking about going to the service on Sunday, doctor,' Mary said.

'She should know better than that.' Jonathan bent over Della with a spatula. 'Open wide!'

Della bristled. They were talking about her as if she weren't there again. 'I wish you'd stop treating me as if I were ten years old,' she snapped when Jonathan removed the spatula.

'Good!' He grinned infuriatingly. 'You sound much better today.' Thoroughly enjoying himself, he turned to Mary. 'Just watch her temperature and continue the medicine, Mrs Dolan. I'm going out of town for a few days, so I'll pop in on Tuesday.'

Glowering at him, Della got her revenge. She turned her gaze on Mary. 'Would you please tell the doctor that

I shan't be home on Tuesday? I'll be out of quarantine by then. And would you please see him out?'

Mary looked flustered, but Jonathan gave her a reassuring smile. 'It's all right, Mrs Dolan. I'll see myself out.'

'Oh, doctor, I'm so sorry—' she began. But he interrupted her as he turned to leave.

'Please don't be! I'm delighted to see her more like her old self.'

On Tuesday, much against Mary's will, Della got up to visit Paul's parents and to lay some flowers at the headstone. Still feeling weak, she gave in to Mary's insistence that she go with her and that they take a taxi. On the way, Della prayed that Mr and Mrs Conway would be at home and, when they arrived at the house, Mary kept the taxi waiting just in case.

But Mrs Conway answered the door. 'Why, hello, hinny.' Her eyes welled with tears. 'Are you better?'

Della nodded dumbly and they hugged, weeping together. Mary joined them, carrying the bouquet of yellow roses she had bought for Della that morning.

'This is my mam,' Della sniffed.

'Pleased to meet you.' Mrs Conway held out her hand.

'I'm very sorry about your son.' Mary took the woman's shaking hand and dispensed with formal introductions.

'Thank you, hinny. Come on in.' Mrs Conway led them down the hall. 'His dad's out. I persuaded him to go to the club for a pint. He's just sat around moping ever since we got the news.' In the kitchen, she indicated the sofa, automatically going to the scullery to fill the kettle. 'Would you like tea or coffee?'

'Tea, please,' Mary said, sitting down.

'I'll help.' Della followed the old woman into the scullery.

'Aye, hen, it's funny isn't it?' Mrs Conway sighed as she filled the kettle. 'Like I said in my letter, it's a sort of relief in a way to know for sure.'

Della nodded. 'I . . . I know what you mean.'

'Are you feelin' better now then, luv?'

'Yes, thank you, but this is my first day up, so my mam insisted on coming with me.' Della took cups and saucers from the dresser through to the kitchen, setting them on the table with trembling hands.

'Aye, we'll go after tea. It's St Nicholas's Cemetery. It's not far. Can you manage the walk?' Mrs Conway called through from the scullery.

'Of course.' Della joined Mary and took her hand. 'Thanks for coming with me, Mam. I do feel shakier than I thought.'

'You're going straight to bed when you get home. I'll be embarrassed if we're not there when the doctor arrives.'

'Stop worrying, Mam. We'll be back by then. And he doesn't need to see me any more anyway.'

'Well, I think he's been very kind to you, and very patient,' Mary insisted. 'You should be grateful to him.'

'Oh, Mam, he's just doing his job,' Della lied. She was embarrassed by Jonathan's kindness and knew he was doing much more than his job.

Mrs Conway arrived with the tea. 'I'm sorry, I'm out of sugar. It all went at the reception after the service.'

'We're used to doing without it now,' Mary assured her.

'Aye, aren't we all?' the old woman sighed, perching on the edge of an armchair.

Della looked at the worn, sad old face and pity stabbed through her like a knife. 'I was very upset that I couldn't come to the service. How did it go?'

'Eey, it was very nice, luv.' Mrs Conway's lips trembled. 'All his family was there and all his friends that aren't away in the war.'

'Have you other sons in the war?' Mary asked, feeling a sympathetic bond with this woman.

'No, only Paul.' She shook her head sadly. 'The others are a lot older, Paul comin' so late, you see. But they're doin' their duty at home; they're all in munitions.' She looked at Mary, who had put her cup down on the sofa arm. 'More tea, hinny?'

Mary shook her head. 'No, thank you. We'll have to get a move on. I have to go for the rations when I get home and that'll mean at least an hour in the queue. I'd hate to miss the doctor.'

Mrs Conway glanced at Della. 'I thought you were better, hen? But you still look peaky.'

'She's not well enough to be out today,' Mary said. 'We'd better get moving. I want her back in bed by five o'clock.'

'I'll just get me cardigan, then.' Mrs Conway stood up slowly, with the effort of old age. 'Warm day for September, eh?'

But by the time they reached the cemetery a fine drizzle fell, making the warm, humid day even heavier. Della's legs felt like lead.

'This is it, hinny.' Mrs Conway pointed to a newly erected white headstone, an array of wreaths and flowers on the ground in front. 'Funny to have a headstone without a grave, isn't it?' The old woman broke down and sobbed, and Mary put a comforting arm round her.

Kneeling by the stone, Della read the inscription through blurred eyes: 'In loving memory of our dear son, Paul John Conway, who died fighting for his country. 27 May 1926–June 1943.'

'We didn't even know the day he died,' Mrs Conway whimpered, 'so we just had to give the time we heard he was missin'.' Mary gripped the shaking old shoulders more tightly.

'Oh, Mam! I forgot to bring a vase,' Della cried in dismay.

'Just throw that lot out, pet.' Mrs Conway pointed to a vase of wilting carnations. 'They've about had it anyway. And I know he'd rather look at your flowers.'

Della emptied the vase in the waste bin nearby and refilled it at the tap. Reverently, she replaced it in front of the headstone and carefully arranged the fresh yellow roses and ferns. 'I promise I won't stand by your grave again, my love,' she whispered. 'But I must this once. I hope you can smell the roses.' She stood up, blinded by tears.

Mary put a steadying arm round her. 'Come on now, luv, you've had enough,' she coaxed. Della allowed herself to be led away.

Mary left Della at the house while she went to the telephone kiosk. 'The taxi will be here in a few minutes,' she announced on her return.

'Eey, well, it was nice of you both to come,' Mrs Conway said. 'Your Della and my Paul would have made a lovely couple.' As more tears flowed, she gripped Della's hand, and Della's face crumpled again.

Mary sat biting her lip, words of comfort failing her, when the taxi hooted. She stood up hastily, glad to get Della home and back to bed as soon as possible.

'I'll come back and see you,' Della whispered as she hugged Mrs Conway one final time.

'God bless you both,' the old woman said as they took their leave.

'And you, too,' Mary replied as she helped Della into the taxi. 'Brigham Gardens,' she ordered the driver.

'Right you are, missus.' He stepped on the accelerator and turned at the same time. Mary hung on to Della as they rocketed through the traffic. But, mercifully, the drive took little more than five minutes.

'That'll be two bob, missus,' the driver said.

Mary gave him a half-crown and waved him off as he fumbled for change. Just getting home was worth twice the price.

'Thanks, missus.' He grinned, pleased with his large tip.

Back in the kitchen, Mary helped Della on to the sofa, and pulled up the blanket. Della sank back gratefully.

First banking up the dying fire, Mary collected a shopping bag from the scullery and poked her head round the kitchen door. 'I'm going out for the rations. I hope I'm back before the doctor arrives.'

'Aw, Mam,' Della moaned. 'I hope you're not. I'm tired of you both treating me like a child.'

Mary ignored the remark. 'Try to sleep.'

Della didn't need to try. Her eyelids closed immediately and she fell into a sleep of the dead until the doorbell awakened her. She glanced at the clock. Half-past five! It must be Jonathan. Thank goodness Mam wasn't back. Now she could give him a piece of her mind. She rose sleepily and trudged to the door.

Jonathan beamed at her. 'You're up, I see. And dressed! You must be feeling better?'

'Yes, I am. You really don't need to come any more. I mean . . .' Della realised how ungrateful she sounded, and repented. 'I really do appreciate all you've done, but I don't need to take up any more of your time. I've been out today. I should be all right for work in a few days.'

'I think I'm the one to decide that.' Jonathan used his professional voice, but his eyes smiled. 'Are you going to let the doctor in?'

Della relented and led him to the kitchen. She sat at the table.

'You don't look as good as you pretend.' Jonathan scanned her face.

'It's just been a bit of an emotional day,' she confessed. 'I went to see Paul's mother and took some flowers to his headstone.'

Jonathan sat next to her and took her hand but didn't feel for her pulse. 'Oh, Della, you weren't well enough for that,' he said softly.

'I had to get it over with,' she whispered. 'It's like the end of another chapter. Funny how my life seems to have such short chapters.' Her lip quivered and self-pity took over. She clenched her teeth to gain control, but his sympathy broke her down and tears started.

He let her hand go and gave her his handkerchief.

'Thanks,' she mumbled, dabbing at her eyes and drawing a deep breath. 'I'm sorry! I didn't mean to let go like that. You didn't come here to listen to my troubles.'

'But I want to, Della, if it helps to talk about it. I want to help you in any way I can.'

'You're so kind to me, Jonathan,' she sniffed, handing back his handkerchief. 'I don't deserve it.'

He replaced the handkerchief in his top pocket. 'That's a matter of opinion . . . though I admit you've been a bit of a bitch since you've been ill.' A trace of a smile touched his lips.

'I know, and I'm ashamed of myself, Jonathan. It's just that I felt so awful about deceiving Mam like that, and I suppose I took it out on you.'

'I felt bad about it, too. Your mother's a wonderful woman. I hated lying to her.' His voice held an unusual note of sadness.

'Jonathan, tell me truthfully,' she said earnestly. 'Are you being so kind to us to try to make up for what your parents did to Mam?'

'No,' he answered honestly. 'I'm being "kind", as you call it, because I like you, and your mother. I enjoy your company and hers too.' Avoiding her eyes, he looked at his watch. 'I'd better just check you over, and then – perhaps – I'll sign you off.'

Della submitted to his brief examination obediently.

'How's your temperature?'

'Normal.'

'All right, I'll take your word for it. You can come back to work on Monday. But if I see you on that ward before then, I'll send you straight home. I have to go now; I'm on duty tonight. I've got a lot of lost time to make up.'

'You mean you came all this way just to see me, and you're going back to work?' Della asked unnecessarily.

'I have to take a dinner break.'

Suddenly Della clapped her hand over her mouth, guilt overwhelming her. She was so wrapped up in her problems, she'd forgotten to ask about his. 'Jonathan, I'm sorry. How thoughtless of me. I haven't even asked how *you* are. I didn't like to mention your personal affairs in front of Mam, but I guessed something was wrong at home. Is it your father?'

Jonathan nodded. 'He's had some gallstones removed. He was lucky to come through it at his age. The doctors were worried about the anaesthetic. But it's only a matter of time before he kills himself with over-indulgence anyway.'

'I'm so sorry,' Della said sincerely.

Jonathan clicked his bag shut and stood up. 'Don't be! He's had a good life in his own way, and he's made it to seventy-four.' He strolled towards the door. 'Glad to see you looking better. See you on Monday.'

Della followed him. 'Thank you, Jonathan,' she said, genuinely grateful.

'What for?' He turned and waved as he reached the car.

Chapter Thirty-Nine

In early June the following year, Della stared out of the hospital lobby window, hypnotised by the monotony of the rain cascading down the panes in an unrelenting curtain. It was her weekly evening out with Jonathan and he had been called to an emergency. Eager to escape the smell of disease and disinfectant, she had decided to wait for him here. She looked forward to the evening ahead. Though she hated to think about it, she wondered how much longer their friendship could go on. She'd seen him leaving the hospital with the same brunette only the previous week, so their affair was obviously still blooming. Although several times she'd been tempted to ask him about his girlfriend, she had thought better of it. If he didn't want to discuss his private life, she wasn't going to push him. And, anyway, she thought bitterly, she didn't want to hear about his love affair.

'Sorry I'm late.' Jonathan's voice startled her out of her trance.

'Oops! Don't creep up on me like that!' Della jumped up and smiled in greeting.

'Hang on.' He placed a restraining hand on her shoulder. 'I've got an umbrella in the car.'

Dashing out into the deluge, he returned soaked but triumphant, brandishing a decrepit umbrella.

She ducked under it, avoiding the broken spokes, and

they plodded to the car. Della's feet squelched in her high-heeled sandals. 'I never thought I'd miss weather forecasts so much,' she panted as she climbed into her seat.

'Well, if they tell us, they also tell the enemy. Would you rather get wet or get bombed?' Jonathan closed his door and threw the sodden umbrella into the back seat.

'I know,' Della sighed. 'Sometimes I wonder if life will ever be normal again.'

'Well, my sweet, you're about to have a perfectly normal evening, so stop complaining. Just pray the engine's not soaked.' Miraculously, it ticked over at the first attempt. He turned on the windscreen wipers.

'What's on the menu?'

'Spam, spuds, salad, and bread and butter pudding, followed by *The Grapes of Wrath*. I confess I had some pâté de foie, but it was beginning to smell unfriendly, so I ate it for breakfast.' Jonathan peered through the small triangle of clean glass, his nose almost touching the pane as he inched out of the car park.

Della smiled. 'Spam! That's not up to your usual standard, Jonathan. I might as well have gone home.'

'Ah, but would you have a bottle of claret with which to wash it down at home, you ungrateful hussy?'

'No, nor Steinbeck to follow. I adore Henry Fonda,' she admitted happily.

As they reached the flat, Mrs Boyd, the upstairs tenant, bumped excitedly downstairs, her rolls of flesh bouncing with each step. 'Have you heard the news?' she panted as she neared the bottom. 'The British and American forces have landed on the beaches at Normandy.'

'Mrs Boyd, I could kiss you.' Jonathan grabbed the large woman and did just that, afterwards dancing a jig with her in the hall. 'Now we'll shove those bastards back where they belong.'

'Aye, and I know where that is,' Mrs Boyd puffed.

Jonathan let her go, smiling, while she struggled to regain her breath.

'Is that all they said?' Della asked.

'Aye, that's all.' Mrs Boyd held on to the banister for support. 'I wish they'd tell us more.'

'Military secrets, Mrs Boyd,' Jonathan reminded her. 'Remember, "Careless words cost lives". Would you want the Germans to know what we're up to?'

Della's shoulders slumped with relief. 'That's good enough news for me for the moment. Let's see if there's any more on the wireless.'

'Aye, I'd better go back and all. Jack'll be home any minute for his tea.' Mrs Boyd heaved her bulk up the stairs by the banister.

Inside the flat, Jonathan hung their damp jackets on the hallstand while Della sank into an armchair in the living room and kicked off her soaked shoes. As usual, she allowed herself to be spoiled while Jonathan poured two sherries. He switched on the wireless, hoping for further news bulletins, and Della found herself humming in accompaniment to the Andrews Sisters' rendering of *You Are My Sunshine*.

He handed her a glass and sat opposite her, raising his own, 'To the liberation of the Frogs! Now I've got two good reasons to celebrate. I was thinking of having a small party on Saturday anyway.' He paused before adding, 'You're invited.'

Della sipped her sherry to gain time to think. 'What's the celebration . . . and who'll be there?'

'An old school chum's coming home on leave, and it'll just be a small group of close friends.'

'The people you were at the pub with that time?' she asked with forced casualness, knowing her question must sound strange. But she had to know.

Jonathan looked surprised. 'Yes. Fancy you remembering!'

So, his girlfriend would be there. Della felt a tight sensation in her stomach. No doubt she would be expected to partner his school friend. 'Thanks, Jonathan, but Anne and Colin and Johnny are coming on Saturday, and I haven't seen them for ages.' Her refusal was polite but unconvincing.

'Aw, Della, you can see them any time. How long is it since you went to a party?' Although Jonathan's voice was jovial, his brown eyes regarded her seriously through his spectacles. 'Please come. The only friends you ever see besides me are Rose and Nora. You're turning into a hermit, Della. It's time you met new people, made new friends.'

So he *did* want her to meet his school friend! He was trying to make a blind date for her. She considered the thought painfully. But curiosity and common sense overcame her. She would go, if only to find out what was really between Jonathan and this girl. If it was serious, she would definitely stop seeing him and put an end to this emotional attachment she'd begun to feel for him.

Jonathan smiled as he got up to refill their glasses. 'For goodness' sake, woman, how long does it take you to make up your mind to accept an invitation to a party?'

As she watched his tall, slim figure move to the sideboard, Della felt a jolt of jealousy. He would be dancing with that woman at the party, holding her close. The thought was painful, yet she heard her voice saying quietly: 'All right, thank you. I'd like to come.'

'Good!' He beamed as he handed her another glass. 'I'll probably make it about eight o'clock. I can give you a lift from work if you like.'

'No,' she said quickly, 'I'll have time to go home and see Anne and thc gang first. Thanks anyway.' They never arrived before nine, but she planned to wash her hair, have a long soak and a face-pack. She wanted to look her best before confronting Jonathan's girlfriend.

'Well, now that's settled, I'd better start on that Spam if we're going to make it to the Haymarket in time.'

'I'll help,' she offered. They had become quite a good team in the kitchen by now.

While she soaked in the bath before the party, Della forced herself to think rationally about the evening ahead. Yes, she admitted, she must put an end to this. She had become much too fond of Jonathan over the past few months, and she had no right to. Firstly, she had made it plain from the beginning that they could never be any more than friends and, secondly, he had a girlfriend. Perhaps seeing them together would help her put him out of her mind – and out of her life. She was simply getting silly, romantic feelings about him because she saw so much of him. It would be a good idea to ask for a transfer at the hospital, too.

After spending an hour in the bathroom and in her bedroom, she surveyed herself in the wardrobe mirror. Despite the stimulating effect of the face-pack, she still looked pale. Another dab of rouge would remedy that. For the rest, however, she was pleased with what she saw. For a change, she had tied up her hair in rag curlers, and now it fell in soft curls to her shoulders. The red crepe dress she had bought for the occasion with the last of her clothing coupons, though demurely cut, clung to her figure, and the high-heeled black shoes and nylons (the latter, courtesy of Rose, who had received another parcel from Joe) added the final touch of glamour. She grabbed her black patent bag and a light wool jacket and ran downstairs.

'What's going on?' Walter put down his book in surprise on seeing his daughter dressed to go out on a Saturday evening.

'Just a small party Joan's giving,' Della lied, hating herself for this never-ending deceit. The 'friend from the hospital' she had been going out with every week she had finally been forced to call 'Joan'. Only Anne was in on her secret.

'You look lovely, sweetheart.' Mary glowed with pride. 'I'm so glad you're going out.'

'Thanks, Mam.' Della hugged her warmly. 'Sorry I'll miss Anne and the gang, but I'll see them tomorrow.'

She hurried to the bus stop. After ten minutes she checked her watch. Eight o'clock! She'd intended to be late, but not this late. Quarter of an hour later, a bus glided to the stop. She arrived at the flat forty minutes late, nervously patting her hair into place as she rang the bell.

Jonathan opened the door. 'Della! I thought you'd changed your mind. Come on in.' He stood aside and ushered her into the hall.

'I know, I'm sorry I'm late. I think the buses are on a go-slow.' Della's voice sounded squeaky, but he didn't seem to notice.

'Never mind, you made it! And your hair looks nice. I'm afraid we're all a couple of drinks ahead of you, but you can have fun catching up. Let me introduce you first.' As he took her jacket and hung it on the hallstand, Della's knees began to wobble. But she managed to maintain outward calm as he led her into the crowded living-room. Immediately, she spotted the brunette, sitting on the sofa beside a pretty blonde girl, a man she vaguely recognised beside them on the sofa arm. The three chatted animatedly.

'I'm going to cut this down to size,' Jonathan announced loudly over the cacophony of music and conversation. 'Everyone, this is Della Davidson, an old friend of mine.' He led her to one of two couples standing by the sideboard and waved his hand towards a tall, pale young man in airforce uniform, a tiny chestnut-haired girl by his side. 'This is Maureen Brown and my old school chum Dick James – her fiancé and our guest of honour.'

So he hadn't invited her to escort his friend, Della realised with a shock. Instead she was going to be a gooseberry! Which was worse? She croaked a casual 'Hello' which the two reciprocated before Jonathan turned to the other couple, a well-dressed, thin girl who looked like a model, and a middle-aged man whom Della recognised as a doctor from the hospital.

'And this is Joyce Laidler and her husband Greg,' Jonathan said. They smiled acknowledgement and Della forced a smile back.

Jonathan then eased her towards the blonde girl on the sofa. 'This is Marian Carrington, her other half's in the gents. And, lastly, Miriam Greenberg and her husband, George.' He gestured to the brunette and the familiar-looking man who now stood up politely.

Della swallowed hard and, in confusion, mumbled 'Hello' to all three, who returned her greeting.

George grinned at Jonathan. 'You dark horse! Where've you been hiding her?'

Jonathan's words rang through Della's head like church bells: 'Miriam and her husband, George'. She closed her eyes for a moment to gather herself together. Her knees felt weaker than before, and she was grateful for Jonathan's arm as he guided her to the kitchen. Her head spun with confused thoughts. So Jonathan had invited her as *his* partner. Miriam wasn't his girlfriend! Della felt like shouting for joy.

In the kitchen, Jonathan smiled at her apologetically. 'You deserve a drink after all those introductions. What'll it be?'

Della straightened her shoulders and smiled back at him with new confidence, still enveloped in a warm glow. 'I'll have a gin and lime, please, if you've got it – a strong one.'

'I think we can manage that. My friends have donated generously.' He rummaged among the array of bottles on the table, poured a liberal glass and handed it to her.

She raised the glass. 'To your friend, Dick.'

'Hold it.' He stalled her, pouring himself a whisky. 'And to my prettiest guest.'

Della flushed with pleasure. 'Thank you, Jonathan, but you underestimate Miriam. She's very beautiful.'

'Yes, she is. George is a lucky man. After ten years of marriage and three kids, they're still like a couple of honeymooners.' He looked into her eyes as he spoke and, instead of evading his gaze as usual, Della looked squarely back at him, a smile on her lips. But inwardly she chastised herself: George and Miriam had been married ten years! God, how stupid she'd been, jumping to conclusions like that!

'I suppose we'd better join the party,' she suggested, her tone giving away her reluctance.

'Right! I'm supposed to be the host.' Jonathan also sounded reluctant. He sensed a warmth in her tonight that he would have preferred to enjoy more privately.

The gramophone was playing *Lilli Marlene* and most couples were dancing on the little square of carpet in the centre of the room; only Miriam and George sat on the sofa.

Almost shyly, Jonathan asked, 'Would you like to dance?'

Della nodded and allowed herself to be taken into his arms. They moved gently to the lilting sadness of the music, Jonathan holding her at a respectable distance. 'Do you realise it's over ten years since we danced together?' he said softly.

'At Rose's cousin's party,' Della filled in unnecessarily.

'You were the only girl I wanted to dance with,

despite the schoolgirl shoes and stockings.'

Della laughed, delighted. 'Jonathan, will you ever let me forget that?'

There was a new softness in her voice that encouraged him. He drew her closer. 'You're a better dancer now.'

'So are you.' The feel of his body against hers was unnerving. She was glad when the record stopped.

'I'd better see to that.' Unwillingly, he let her go. 'I put your drink on the sideboard.'

'Thank you.' Della retrieved her glass and helped herself to a *vol au vent* with an unidentifiable filling. She sniffed it cautiously.

'Sardine mousse,' a throaty female voice informed her. It was Miriam. 'I only know because I made them myself. I'd recommend something else.'

Della noticed a slight foreign accent. 'It smells interesting,' she said, taking a nibble.

'Well, you're braver than I am.' Miriam smiled, revealing flawless white teeth. 'I'm going to stick to Jonathan's cheese spread canapés.' She cast Della an inquisitive look. 'So, you've known Jonathan a long time, then?'

'Yes, ten years.' Della quickly volunteered her answer. Though not knowing why she should divulge such personal information, something about Miriam seemed to draw her out.

Miriam inspected a canapé and, deciding against it, replaced it. She looked again at Della. 'We met when he first worked at the hospital. George is a paediatrician there. Jonathan's been a good friend to us ever since.' She traced a slender red-tipped finger over her high forehead, smoothing back a stray strand of hair, while her dark eyes smiled over Della's shoulder. 'Here comes the man himself.'

Jonathan approached with a wide grin, having just

put *Run Rabbit Run* on the gramophone. 'That ought to liven them up a bit,' he chuckled.

Miriam pouted prettily. 'Oh, Jonathan, I was just about to ask Della if I could borrow you for a dance. It's not exactly dance music.'

'But it's very appropriate, don't you think? According to the news, the rabbits are running all over the place.'

'Oh, let's not talk war, please.' Miriam's face looked pained as she took Jonathan's arm. 'Let's dance anyway.' She turned to Della. 'Jonathan's my stand-in dancing partner. George's got three feet. I promise I'll only steal him for this one.'

Jonathan allowed himself to be led away, and Della's eyes followed them. They glided across the floor, undeterred by the ungainly marching beat of the song. She sipped her drink, feeling almost weightless, and was about to sit down when Marian, the blonde girl, approached with a dark-haired young man. 'Della, you haven't met James, my husband.'

'How do you do?' They greeted each other simultaneously.

He took her hand and held it in a hard grip. 'I see Jonathan's doing his duty with Miriam. May I have the pleasure?' He noticed Della's quick glance at Marian. 'Don't worry,' he assured her. 'Marian's glad to get me off her hands once in a while.'

'Off my feet would be more accurate,' Marian smiled.

Della knew they had rescued her because she was standing alone. Though she appreciated their consideration, tonight nothing mattered. She was with Jonathan! James took her in his arms and began wheeling her around in all directions. Della suppressed a smile; she knew now what Marian had meant.

The record stopped and Jonathan put on another. But James still held Della in his grip. After a few crackling sounds, the strains of *I'll Be Seeing You* emerged, one of

Della's favourites. James began his manoeuvres again, but Jonathan rescued her, tapping James on the shoulder. 'Sorry, mate, you've got your own girl; this one's taken.'

The words sent a warm feeling surging through Della's veins, and she submitted happily as Jonathan took her over. This time he drew her close immediately and she melted into him. 'You're very different tonight, Della. If I'd known, I'd have invited you to a party long ago,' he joked.

'It's not the party. I *feel* different tonight.' She had no intention of wasting any more time with Jonathan by being coy, and she knew from the way he danced with her that he felt the same as she. He held her tightly, their bodies swaying, their feet hardly moving.

'Della,' he whispered into her ear, 'you don't know how long I've dreamed of holding you like this.' He gripped her tighter round her waist. 'I can't believe it. You're like a butterfly emerging from its chrysalis.' But then he looked down warily at her upturned face. 'You're not going to wrap yourself up in your old cocoon again tomorrow, are you?'

'No,' she replied softly. 'I've thrown it away.'

'Well, thank God for that.' He drew her close again.

A round of applause interrupted them and they looked around: Jonathan surprised, Della embarrassed. The music had stopped and they were the only couple on the floor. Flushed, Della broke away from him.

'We hate to break it up,' George shouted jovially, 'but the record stopped at least three minutes ago.'

Unabashed, Jonathan grinned. 'Spoil-sports! Whose party is this anyway? You mind your business and we'll mind ours.' He took Della back in his arms. 'Somebody else see to the bloody gramophone.'

James obliged, and the ear-splitting sound of the *Hokey Cokey* filled the room.

'Some friend!' Jonathan shouted as the others laughed and joined them in a circle. But, as Della dutifully obeyed the chorus and put her right foot in and her left foot out, she was still aware of Jonathan's closeness.

'I need a drink after that,' he said. 'Time for a break.' He put on another record, and the poignant strains of *When They Sound The Last All-Clear* affected everyone. They sat down, some on the floor, and joined in the words: 'Oh, how happy, my darling, I'll be'. Jonathan pulled Della up by the hand. 'Come and help me refill the glasses.' Wordlessly she followed him, noticing on the way that Miriam was crying.

'Miriam seems upset,' she remarked when they reached the kitchen.

He lit a cigarette. 'She has more right to be upset about this war than any of us. She's a German Jew. She came over here when she was eighteen to learn English and met and married George within six months.' He paused in the act of setting bottles on a tray. 'Her family used to visit her and she them, but she hasn't heard from them since 1940. A neighbour wrote to tell her they were rounded up and taken away, but no one knows where.'

'Oh, the poor thing.' Della sat down, overcome with pity. To think she had envied Miriam!

'Yes, it's hard to lose a mother, father, and three younger brothers all at once.'

'But surely when the war's over she can try to find them . . . and they know where *she* is,' Della said with forced optimism.

Jonathan shook his head solemnly and stubbed out his cigarette. 'The fact that they know where she is is what worries her. She knows they would have got in touch if they possibly could.' He lifted the now laden tray and she opened the door for him. 'All right, chaps, refills all round.' He moved a plate of stale sandwiches on the sideboard to make room for the tray. 'It's self-service from now on. I'm going off duty.'

The record had just stopped and George got up. 'I'll take another whisky for Miriam. That song always upsets her.'

'Sorry, I should have thought.' Jonathan poured a large whisky. 'I'll put something cheerful on and dance with her.' He chose *In The Mood*, and she took his proffered hand, though her eyes still glistened with tears. After a few slow steps, Jonathan gently swung her round. She responded, and soon the pair were jiving like professionals, Miriam's flared black skirt swirling almost to the top of her shapely thighs.

Della and George remained by the sideboard and watched them, Della remembering the last time she had seen them dancing to that tune. Suddenly she felt George's eyes on her. 'If I didn't know those two better, I could easily become a jealous husband,' he smiled, knocking back his whisky.

Was he trying to reassure her? 'They dance well together,' she said lightly. She *felt* light. She knew Jonathan would be coming back to her, and that to him, Miriam was simply his friend's wife.

A tap on her shoulder made her turn. Dick grinned down at her. 'Care to buggy, baby?' he drawled, attempting an American accent.

'Sure, handsome! But I think the word's "boogie".' He jived well and, thanks to Joe's lessons, Della managed to keep up with him.

The evening passed too quickly as everyone grew more inebriated. Jonathan and Della managed only two more dances together. Miriam was the first to give in, pulling George up from his armchair and removing the umpteenth whisky from his hand. 'Come on, George. We've got to go now.' She turned to Jonathan. 'His mother's looking after the children and we can't keep her up after midnight. But it was a wonderful party.

Thank you, Jonathan.' George rose to his feet a little unsteadily, and Miriam shook her head at Della in simulated dismay. 'This is why I learned to drive.'

The others took the cue. It was a noisy leave-taking, and Jonathan leaned against the doorpost as the cars pulled away. 'Phweew,' he whistled under his breath. 'My landlady could throw me out for less than this.'

'They certainly all had a good time.' Della turned to go inside, but he grabbed her hand and pulled her back.

Just look at this.' He pointed upwards.

Della followed his gaze. The moon, full and opalescent, surrounded by stars, looked like an expensive brooch set against the blue-black velvet display in a jeweller's window. 'It's beautiful,' she whispered as he put his arm round her waist and pulled her close. She shivered slightly. 'I know it's silly, but it makes me feel sad – it's so short-lived.'

Jonathan looked down at her sympathetically. 'It's finished one cycle and it's about to start a new one. What's sad about that?' He guessed what she was feeling. 'Life doesn't run in a continuous straight line, Della. There are always beginnings and endings and new beginnings. Let's go in now.' He took her hand and led her to the living room.

Now that she was alone with Jonathan, Della suddenly felt nervous. She withdrew her hand. 'I'll help you clean up,' she offered, picking up dirty glasses.

He took them from her and put them back on the coffee table. 'I don't care if they stay there for a week,' he said firmly, taking her by the shoulders and kissing her softly on the mouth.

Della's nervousness evaporated as his lips touched hers, and she felt a sudden glow. Though not her first kiss, it might as well have been for the excitement that filled her. It was a new and yet familiar excitement, as if they had kissed before in another lifetime. Jonathan felt her response and drew her to him, exploring her mouth with all the intensity of the pent-up yearning of ten long years. She clasped her arms about him, her own desire matching his, until he pulled away, breathless, his eyes searching hers. 'I can't believe this is happening. I'm almost afraid to know why.'

She put a restraining finger on his lips. 'Don't ask now,' she murmured, reaching up and kissing him, first on the lips and then down to his neck. He moaned with pleasure then sought her lips again, holding her tenderly but firmly as together their passion rose.

At last, Della pushed him away and, wordlessly, held out her hand. Jonathan gathered her into his arms and carried her to the bedroom, setting her down near the bed. By the dim glow of the bedside lamp, he undressed her slowly and expertly, kissing each new area of her body he revealed. Della moaned with pleasure. Mutual, unspoken longings took over, and he laid her on the bed. Without embarrassment, she watched as he threw off his clothes, affectionately wondering if he would take off his spectacles. She smiled as he removed them and laid them on the bedside table.

He knelt on the bed and devoured her with his eyes. 'God, you're beautiful, Della,' he breathed as he lowered his head to her firm breasts. His lips caressed her nipples, and she was transported from the confines of her body. She felt so happy she was almost tearful. He moved his lips down her body until she could bear the pleasure no longer and pulled him back, exploring him with her hands. He lay, abandoned to her touch, groaning as if in pain until, finally, he knelt over her. His voice was hoarse as he whispered: 'I've wanted you so much for so long, I want to make this last for ever.'

He took her slowly and tenderly. Della revelled in the joy of their union, tears stinging her eyes. He was a gentle and perceptive lover. She felt throbbingly alive, her nerve endings bare, her pulse beating throughout her body. She knew why he wanted this to last for ever. And then the force of his desire began to mount, become almost fierce, and she cried out as the tension between their bodies finally rose to a crescendo.

'Oh, Della, Della, I love you so much,' Jonathan moaned as he finally fell, limp, beside her. She drank in his words but couldn't speak as they lay together in the after-glow, slowly coming back to reality. He rested on one elbow and looked down at her almost with disbelief. 'Dare I hope that this means you love me, too?' he asked haltingly.

'Yes, yes, I do.'

He drew in a breath and held her to him, closing his eyes to savour her words before he could speak. 'Oh, my darling Della! If you don't want to tell me any more, that's all I need to hear. But you can't blame a fellow for being stunned by this suddenness – after all this time.'

'I want to tell you. I owe you an explanation for the way I've treated you. I think I loved you from that first night,' Della said hesitantly, 'or at least I had a gigantic schoolgirl crush on you. I was devastated when my parents wouldn't let me see you, but I was fourteen, Jonathan – I couldn't go against their wishes. I pined for you and it hurt more every time I saw you – when you insisted on following me around. I tried to put you out of my mind because I knew it was impossible to see you and, eventually, Jerry came along.' She sighed deeply. 'He was so nice, he was easy to love, and he loved me. This time it seemed right, and my parents approved.' She swallowed hard before going on. 'But, as you know, our marriage didn't have a story-book ending.'

'I know, and I was sorry, but I dared to hope that after you'd got over it I might stand another chancc.' Jonathan's eyes were full of sympathy as he stroked her forehead.

Della looked at him, puzzled. 'But by then you were engaged to Vera. Even if I had been looking for a replacement for Jerry, which I wasn't, I couldn't possibly have considered any man who was in love with someone else.'

Jonathan groaned. 'You don't know how ironic that is. I was fond of Vera; she was a very nice person. Pretty though she was, she didn't even appeal to me physically at first, but she grew on me. I felt more for her than any other girl I'd ever taken out. She wanted to get married and have children, and I thought it would be a good marriage, that I could make her happy. That was when you and Jerry were married, remember? By then I'd lost all hope of you.' He paused, digging up painful memories. 'Then, after Jerry's death, when I was in hospital and you were so cool and distant, I knew I still didn't stand a chance. Even so, that day when you barged into my ward and Vera was there, I wanted *you* to stay and *her* to go. I realised then it would be unfair to marry her, still feeling the way I did about you. I thought about it all that night and broke it off the following day.'

'You broke it off with Vera because of me – even then! But I didn't know that.' Della was incredulous.

'Why should I have told you?' Jonathan stroked her damp hair from her forehead. 'My God! If I'd thought then that it would have made any difference, you'd have been the first to know.'

'And then I met Paul . . .' Della's voice trailed off.

'That's right!' Jonathan managed a grin. 'You can't blame a chap for feeling unwanted, can you?'

'But, you idiot, I thought then that you were still with Vera. I simply didn't give you a thought as a prospective boyfriend, even if I'd been looking for one. I've told you, I don't tread on other people's grass.' Della paused, searching for words. 'And when Paul was missing, as you know, I waited for him to come back . . .' Tears misted her eyes. 'Though I didn't know it at the time, his death finally released me.' She looked into his eyes. 'I'm not going to lie to you, Jonathan. I loved Paul too.'

'I know you did, my sweet.' He stroked her cheek. 'And I wouldn't have it any other way. You love easily, though not indiscriminately, and I love you for that. I'm sure Jerry and Paul were both very special people.'

Della nodded sadly. 'They were, Jonathan, and they'll always be a part of me. But I began to realise after Paul's death that I had to put those episodes of my life behind me. It was sad, but I had to do it.' She managed a half-smile. 'In a funny sort of way, Rose taught me that.'

'Rose taught *you* something!'

Her smile grew into a grin. 'Yes, Rose! We were thirteen when I met her at school, and the first time she came to my house she was horrified to see my teddy bear still sitting on my pillow. Of course I didn't take him to bed with me then, but he'd given me so much joy and comfort over the years that I didn't want to part with him, so I kept him out where I could still see him.'

Jonathan squeezed her hand affectionately. 'That sounds like you.'

'But I realised Rose was right. My time with Teddy was over. I had to let him go. I cried half the night before I did it,' she confessed, 'but the next day I put him in the cupboard under the stairs. I didn't just throw him away, mind you. I put him in a box, and I dust the box whenever I clean out the cupboard.'

'You're adorable,' Jonathan whispered, brushing her cheek with his lips.

But Della went on: 'What I'm trying to say is – it's sort of the same with Jerry and Paul. My time with them is over, but I could never throw them out of my mind.' She hesitated and looked at him closely. 'It's like what you said tonight about the moon – about one cycle ending and another beginning.'

He smiled. 'I was trying to persuade you to start again, not all that subtly, I suppose. You were obviously warming towards me tonight, and I was full of hope. But I couldn't understand the sudden change.'

Della giggled. 'I'm almost afraid to tell you this part, but I had actually decided not to see you again after tonight and I was going to ask for a transfer at the hospital.'

'But why, Della? Why?' Jonathan shook his head, puzzled. 'You're such an enigma.'

'I thought you were in love with Miriam,' she confessed, 'and that you were inviting me for your old school friend.'

'Miriam!' Jonathan laughed loudly. 'Whatever made you think that?'

Della defended herself. 'Well, it's only natural. I saw you last summer at the Oxford, and you danced with her most of the evening, *and* I've seen you with her several times since.'

'Well, if you have, George's always been there,' Jonathan said in disbelief.

'But I didn't know he was her husband . . . and he wasn't there when you gave her a lift home from the hospital last week.'

A satisfied grin spread over his face. 'So, you've been spying on me . . . and since last summer. Does that mean you've felt something for me all that time?'

'Sort of.' Della smiled deliberately coyly. 'But it's grown an awful lot over the past few months.'

Jonathan exhaled loudly in amazement. 'Well, you could have fooled me!'

'But I couldn't show it. How could I let you know I loved you when I thought you were in love with someone else?'

'And if I didn't care about you, why on earth would I

have bothered with you at all? Accepting your ration of a once a week friendship and playing the perfect gentleman! God! It was all I could do to keep my hands off you. I kept telling myself I was a fool, and I suppose I was.' He paused and sighed. 'But seeing you in any capacity was better than not seeing you at all. I must have a masochistic streak.'

'But I honestly thought you just liked me as a friend,' Della protested. 'Though I did wonder where your girlfriend was when you were with me.' The bed shook with Jonathan's laughter, and Della joined in. 'I suppose it *is* funny in retrospect.'

'Funny! That's hardly the word.' Jonathan chuckled, but immediately became serious. 'Damn and blast! To think of all the time we wasted playing silly games with each other!'

'We can make up for it now.'

'What a marvellous idea!' He gathered her once more in his arms and kissed her tenderly, then with increasing pressure. They made love again and, now that their love was truly acknowledged, they gave without seeking and yet received more than they gave.

Afterwards, they lay back on the pillows, spent and silent, until Jonathan voiced what had as yet been unspoken but was on both their minds. 'Della, I'm not going to let you get away from me this time. What are we going to do about your parents?'

'I knew you'd be thinking about that. So was I,' Della admitted. 'I'm twenty-four years old and able to make my own decisions now. I'm going to tell them the truth tomorrow.' She paused, tracing his profile with her fingertip. 'Besides, Mam knows you now and likes you. My mam's honest. I don't deny it'll be a shock at first, but I know she'll admit that she was wrong to prejudge you because of your parents.'

Jonathan frowned. 'I felt rotten about deceiving her

when you were ill, but I feel even worse now.'

'You did it for me, don't feel bad about it.' Della snuggled into him. 'Anyway, even though it *was* under false pretences, the fact that she's met you, and likes you, should make it easier when I tell her tomorrow.' She tried not to let her voice give away her misgivings.

Chapter Forty

Della stretched and glanced at the alarm clock. Ten o'clock! She'd never slept that late in her life. She closed her eyes again, the events of the evening before enveloping her in a rosy glow. Jonathan had dropped her off at the bottom of the street at four-thirty and walked her to the gate. Her heart quickened at the thought of seeing him again that evening. And then she returned to the present. She would have to tell Mam and Dad straight away. She blanched at the prospect but, with determination, swung her legs over the bed and flung on her dressing gown.

Hearing voices in the sitting-room, she deliberately went to the kitchen first and had tea and cereal. She needed some sustenance before embarking on her confession. Ten minutes later, she entered the sitting-room where Mary, Walter and Anne were reading the Sunday papers. 'Morning,' she said as casually as she could. She joined Anne on the sofa and kissed her on the cheek. 'Nice to see you, Anne. Where are Colin and Johnny?'

Anne gave her a quizzical look before replying. 'Hello, luv. Johnny wheedled Colin into taking him for a row in Leazes Park. Colin's just butter in his hands now.'

'What's got into you this morning?' Walter grunted, glancing at his watch. 'It's more like afternoon.'

Mary looked at her closely. 'I gather you had a good

511

time at the party. We didn't hear you come in.'

'It was late. I tried to be quiet.' Della fidgeted with her dressing gown cord.

'Well, how was it then?' Anne again searched her sister's face for any secrets it might betray.

But Della's expression remained neutral, despite her churning stomach. 'It was a wonderful party. And I've got something to tell you all.' Abandoning the dressing gown cord, she twirled a strand of hair between her fingers. 'I'm going out with the doctor who treated me when I was ill.'

Mary lowered her newspaper to her lap, a delighted expression on her face. 'That nice Dr Simpson! That's wonderful! I thought he had his eye on you, what with all that special treatment he gave you.'

Della cringed. Now was the time. 'His name's not Simpson, Mam. It's Maddison – Jonathan Maddison. I'm sorry we had to keep it from you before, but I wasn't going out with him then – at least not like I am now.'

Mary's face drained of colour. 'That was *Jonathan Maddison*!'

'I'm sorry, Mam.' Della lowered her eyes. 'Jonathan hated deceiving you, but he didn't want to cause any trouble for me. And there was no point in telling you the truth then, anyway. He was just a friend.'

Mary's newspaper slid unnoticed from her knee to the floor. 'A friend? I thought you just worked with him.' She ran her fingers across her forehead in an uncomprehending gesture.

'I did, Mam . . . and I still do.' Now came the next confession: 'But he's the friend I've been going to the pictures with every week – on a friendly basis only,' Della added quickly. 'He had a girlfriend, or at least I thought he had until last night.'

Walter, who at first had listened with only half an ear, finally realised that this was no casual conversation.

512

'Wait a minute! That Dr Simpson was your mam's cousin?'

Mary grew impatient. 'Yes, Jonathan Maddison, Walter. He's the doctor who came here. I wish you'd learn to listen.'

Walter looked puzzled, his brow furrowing as he slowly recollected the incident. 'That cousin lad she wanted to go out with when she was a kid?' His voice rose in anger as he turned to Della. 'But you weren't allowed to see him! Do you mean to say you've been deceiving your mam all this time?'

'Oh, I know, Dad, and I'm sorry.' Della looked down at her slippers. 'But I didn't think there was any point in upsetting Mam when he was only a casual friend.' Please, God, don't let this turn into a row, she prayed silently.

'Casual friend! Then what is he now?' Walter demanded angrily.

'Don't shout at her, Walter.' Mary spoke calmly, having regained her composure.

'We love each other,' Della said, forcing her gaze to meet her father's.

Anne, who had kept out of the discussion lest she give herself away, took Della's hand in encouragement.

'This is a lot to take in at once.' Mary looked squarely at Della, though her expression showed no anger. 'So, your friend Joan was Jonathan Maddison, and Dr Simpson was Jonathan Maddison too!' She shook her head slowly. 'I'm not applauding you for lying to us, but I can understand why you did.'

'I'm sorry, Mam,' Della began again, but Mary silenced her with a wave of her hand.

'I think you've apologised quite enough. It's my turn now. I have something to be sorry about. I'm sorry I judged that young man by his family without even knowing him.'

Della jumped up and put her arms round Mary. 'Oh, Mam!' was all she could get out before she burst into tears.

Mary held her, and Della sat on her lap like a child. 'There's nothing to cry about, luv,' Mary sighed softly. 'I can't deny I don't like the fact that you lied to me, but I suppose I'd have done the same in your place.'

Della felt euphoric with relief. 'Oh, Mam, I *knew* you'd understand.'

'Well, I doubt I would had I not met him,' Mary admitted, '*Dr* Maddison! I didn't know he was going to become a doctor.'

'Neither did he when we first met, Mam.'

'I'd never have guessed in a million years he was a Maddison.' Mary lowered her head as painful memories surged through her mind. Then she looked up, her mouth twisting into a wry smile. 'Who'd have thought those two would have a nice son like that?'

'Aye,' Walter conceded. 'He's a nice fellow all right. Your mam and I both liked him.'

'Oh, I knew you did. I knew it would be all right in the end.' Della rose from Mary's lap and hugged Walter, then sank down beside Anne again.

Mary looked pained. 'Yes . . . in the end. But if it hadn't been for my stupid prejudice, I'd have given him a chance when you first met him. You really fell for him then, didn't you, and he fell for you?'

'It was probably only a schoolgirl crush then, Mam.' Della smiled to console Mary. 'I'd probably have outgrown it.'

'No, knowing you, I doubt it. And *he* didn't outgrow it, did he? He's been carrying a torch for you all these years.' Mary moaned, passing a hand over her forehead. 'If only I hadn't interfered, I might have saved you a lot of pain.'

Della again tried to comfort her. 'Don't say that,

Mam! I'm beginning to believe in fate now. I think we were meant to go our separate ways for a while – sort of like walking along different predestined paths, full of twists and turns, until they join to form a straight road ahead.'

Walter snorted. 'I never thought my daughter would turn into a philosopher. But you might be right. And it makes *me* feel better to hear you say that, an' all,' he added uncomfortably. 'I went along with your mam as well, without giving the lad a chance.'

Anne spoke at last. 'For heaven's sake, you lot! Why don't you stop going over all your past mistakes and concentrate on the present? I want to know all the news.' She looked at Della expectantly. 'What happened last night to make you finally find the "right path", as you call it?'

'Well, you know it wasn't only last night.' Della turned to her parents in explanation. 'I told Anne, but I was afraid to tell you. I've been falling in love with Jonathan for a long time. I didn't allow myself to admit it until long after Paul's death. But after I'd got over my mourning, I began to feel alive again – mostly thanks to Jonathan,' she added affectionately. 'He forced me to go out and enjoy myself. At first it was only friendly on my part. I thought he had a girlfriend anyway. But it wasn't until last night – when I found out the "girlfriend" was his friend's wife – that I let Jonathan know how I felt about him. And it was like a miracle when I discovered he felt the same about me.'

'Bloody idiot!' Anne swore out of character. 'I've been telling her for months he must be crazy about her to do what he does for her. I know he's a nice fellow, but there are limits to what people do for friends.'

Mary's face had resumed its natural colour, but she still looked stunned. 'What's going to happen now?'

'Well, we didn't discuss it last night, but I know we'll

515

get married – probably soon.' Della smiled wryly. 'We certainly know each other well enough by now to dispense with the courting period.'

'I hate to bring it up,' Mary said reluctantly, 'but what about his family? Won't there be problems there?'

Della knitted her brow in thought before answering. 'To tell you the truth, we were so concerned about *my* family's reactions that we didn't even discuss *his*. But there's only his father left now, and an elder brother in the Air Force.'

'Oh!' Mary's hand flew to her mouth in surprise. 'What happened to his mother? And there was another son.'

'His mother died of a heart attack,' Della explained. 'And his brother was a pilot; he was shot down over Germany.'

Walter lit a cigarette and exhaled heavily. 'Well, from what I know, I'd say good riddance to *her*. But I'm sorry to hear about the son.' He looked at Mary. 'And stop putting a spoke in the wheel, woman. The lad's old enough to deal with his family and to marry the girl he chooses. If any man turns up his nose at our Della for a daughter-in-law, I'll punch it right through to the back of his head.'

Ignoring the rebuke, Mary remained silent for a moment. Only *she* knew exactly what Joseph Maddison was like. But she kept her thoughts to herself. 'How *is* the father?' she asked curiously.

'Failing fast, according to Jonathan.' Della kicked off her slippers and tucked her feet under her, all the time watching Mary's face closely. 'Apparently he's aged a lot since the mother died. Jonathan's concerned about him, but he *is* in his seventies.'

Her expression impassive, Mary said nothing. But then, brushing the thought of her Uncle Joseph aside, she stood up and smiled. 'I think, after all this excitement, I'd better get back to reality and make some lunch. Colin and Johnny will be home soon.'

Anne sighed impatiently. 'Mam, sit down a minute. If I didn't know better, I'd think nobody cared about *my* good news. Della doesn't know yet.'

'Oh, luv, I'm sorry.' Mary sat down again. 'It's just that Della's news was so surprising. You know we're just as happy about yours.'

'I know what you're going to say!' Della turned an excited face towards Anne. 'You're expecting!'

Anne grimaced. 'Aw, you spoilt it. I thought it would be a surprise.'

'Oh, Anne, that's wonderful! You've waited so long for this. When?'

'I'm just over a couple of weeks late. But I'm sick in the mornings already, so I'm pretty sure. Colin's like a cat with two tails.'

Mary stood up again. 'Well, now that all the good news is out, do I have permission to make lunch?'

Anne grinned. 'Yes, you're free to go. I'll help. And you'd better get dressed, Della. It'll be afternoon soon.'

Della soaked in the bath, the tension of the morning flowing from her body as if a dam had burst. She could hardly wait for six o'clock to tell Jonathan the good news.

The evening was cloudy and humid. Waiting outside the hospital entrance, Della felt blanketed by the air, as if a clothes line of damp washing were blowing against her.

Jonathan was only a few minutes late, but his face looked tired and drawn, though when he spotted Della the downward line of his mouth curved upward into a delighted grin. He took her squarely by the shoulders and kissed her. 'I've missed you,' he said.

'Jonathan!' Della pushed him away, blushing but delighted. 'Not here!'

'Why not?' He tucked her arm in his as they walked to the car. 'Don't tell me you intend to keep up that doctor–nurse business now that we're engaged.'

'Are we?' She stopped and looked up at him with dancing eyes.

'Of course we are.' He propelled her forward again.

'Since when?'

'Since last night.'

'I don't remember being asked.'

'Actions speak louder than words.' He stopped to kiss her again. 'And last night my actions said "Will you marry me?" and yours said, "Yes, please! As soon as possible".' He raised his voice an octave in imitation of her.

'Well, that's the strangest proposal I've ever had.' Della looked up at him lovingly, but her face clouded as Jerry's youthful, romantic proposal flashed through her mind. Even then his voice had been tinged with sadness. She squeezed Jonathan's arm, comforted by his strength and self-assurance. She mustn't let unhappy memories haunt her; she was too young to live in the past.

Jonathan's deep voice broke into her reverie. 'Penny for them,' he said matter-of-factly, though his eyes searched her face.

'I just felt frightened for a moment because I'm so happy,' she said, only half truthfully.

'Della!' He stopped and faced her, taking both her hands. 'You've got to stop thinking about the past. I love you, and we've got a whole lifetime ahead of us together. This time it's forever, I promise.'

'I can see I'll have to be careful what I think in future.' She smiled up at him. 'I didn't know you were a mind reader.'

Jonathan took her arm again and continued towards the car. 'I don't need to read your mind, sweetheart; your thoughts are always written all over your face. Now get into the car.' It was an affectionate command, and Della obeyed happily as he opened the door for her.

'What treats have you got in store for me tonight – Robert Taylor, Clark Gable or Tyrone Power?'

'Sorry to disappoint you, but the star of tonight's performance is the hitherto unknown Jonathan Maddison. If you think I'm taking you to the cinema, you're out of your mind.'

'Good! I prefer live performances.' Della snuggled contentedly into her seat, savouring the thought of making love with Jonathan again.

As soon as he had closed the flat door behind them, he took her in his arms and his mouth was on hers fiercely, almost violently. Her response matched his and, even as he carried her to the bedroom, she began urgently undoing his shirt and tie. He chuckled with delight, sharing her impatience as they undressed each other quickly and almost fell on to the bed. Della heard herself moaning as they made love feverishly, their fervour heightened by the memories of the previous night. But afterwards, as they lay wrapped together, a shrill ringing pierced the air. Della jumped, startled by the unaccustomed intrusion of the telephone.

'Damn,' Jonathan muttered, pulling her back into his arms. 'Let it ring. I'm not on call tonight.'

But the jangle persisted.

'It might be urgent.' Della pushed him away from her. 'Whoever it is, they're not giving up.'

'I'll take it off the hook.' Reluctantly, Jonathan dragged himself up and strode to the hall, while Della watched his lithe naked back with pleasure.

Jonathan lifted the receiver, his fingers already on the bar to cut off the call, when an anxious female voice cried: 'Thank God! Is that Dr Maddison?'

With a sense of foreboding, he put the receiver to his

ear. 'Yes, I'm Dr Maddison.'

The distraught, disembodied voice babbled on: 'I'm Jill Carter, Charles's girlfriend. I . . . I'm afraid he's been hurt. He's in hospital. I'm calling from London.'

Jonathan sat down slowly on the chair by the telephone table. 'How badly? And what happened?'

'They're not sure how bad it is yet, but he's got severe head injuries. He's in a coma.' The girl's voice broke, and she began sobbing. 'Oh, it was awful! He had a weekend pass and he came to see me . . . and one of those rockets hit the house . . .' There was a moment's silence, followed by more sobs.

'It's all right, take your time.' Jonathan waited impatiently until she regained her voice.

'He . . . he was upstairs in the bedroom and I'd just gone down to the kitchen to make some coffee.' The voice trembled now. 'It came right through the roof and there was a tremendous bang. I ran to the shelter and the walls were falling around me, but I couldn't do anything about Charles. Oh, I feel so awful that I couldn't help him.'

'Don't worry about that. What's happened to Charles?' Jonathan urged.

'We found him later. He was pinned down by some rafters, one across his body and . . . oh, one across his head.' She started to wail and Jonathan attempted to calm her, though his voice was brusque.

'All right, pull yourself together. How bad are the head injuries?' He could hear the girl swallow hard before answering.

'Bad . . . the hospital wouldn't tell me much, only that they couldn't be certain how they would affect him until he regained consciousness.'

'Which hospital?' Jonathan almost barked now, grabbing the pen and pad he kept by the phone.

'It's the Joseph Powell in Balham, and the number's

Balham 2112. He's in ward sixteen. I'm staying with neighbours nearby. I'm going in to see him again tomorrow. Do you have a work number? I've been trying to get you all day.' Now that the girl had given voice to her burden, her tone was calmer. 'I knew he had a brother who was a doctor at Newcastle, but I couldn't remember the name of the place where his father lives.'

'That's all right. I'll see to that. I'll call the hospital now. Are you on the telephone?'

'My neighbours are. The number's Balham 3425.'

'All right! I'll keep in touch. Thank you for letting me know.' Jonathan replaced the receiver and hurriedly scribbled on the pad before dialling the operator. The jarring ringing tone seemed to resound in his ear for ever. He groaned, rapping his fingers on the table in agitation.

'Here, put this on.' Della draped his dressing gown round his shoulders.

'It's Charles,' Jonathan said dully. 'I'm trying to get the hospital.'

'I know, I heard.' She took his free hand and held it tightly.'

'The damned operator is taking forever,' he rasped.

'I'll make some coffee.' Della withdrew her hand and tied about her the oversized bath robe she had grabbed in her haste.

'Oh, thank God!' Jonathan's voice almost exploded as, at last, a female voice echoed down the line.

'Number please?'

'Operator! I want a London number – Balham 2112.' He brushed his tousled hair back from his forehead impatiently.

'Hold on, please.' It was several minutes before the voice pronounced the magic words. 'You're through now.'

'Ward sixteen, please.' Jonathan let out a long breath of relief.

But it seemed like an eternity before a male voice announced: 'Ward sixteen.'

'I'm Jonathan Maddison, and I'm enquiring about my brother, Charles Maddison.'

'He was operated on last night. He's still in a coma. I'm afraid there's nothing more I can tell you at the moment.'

'Damn you, man!' Jonathan bellowed. 'I'm a doctor! I want to know what his head injuries are and how bad. Are you his doctor?'

'No, I'm the night nurse, sir.' The voice was now respectful. 'All I can tell you is that he's got a fractured skull and there was some haemorrhaging and swelling of the brain substance.'

'Oh, God,' Jonathan moaned.

'The operation went smoothly, but we can't be sure of the extent of any brain damage until he regains consciousness. If you give me your telephone number I'll make a note for one of the staff to ring you as soon as your brother comes round.'

'Thank you.' Jonathan wearily repeated his home and hospital numbers. 'What about any other injuries? I understand his body was trapped by a beam.'

'A thigh fracture and flesh wounds, mostly superficial, sir. It's only the head injuries that leave room for any real concern.'

'That's more than enough. Please ring me immediately there's any change.'

'Yes, sir,' the man replied as if to a sergeant major.

'Thank you.' Jonathan slowly put down the receiver.

Della darted from the kitchen, looking anxiously at Jonathan's drawn face as he pulled on his dressing gown. 'How bad is it?'

'Severe head injuries.' He shook his head in despair.

'It could mean permanent brain damage.'

'Oh, no!' Della put her arms round him. 'Come into the living room. I've made some coffee and Spam sandwiches. You must eat something.'

'Thanks,' he said absently, following her and sinking into the sofa. He rubbed his forehead to clear his thoughts.

Della handed him a mug of coffee and placed the sandwich plate on his knee. 'What happened?' she asked softly as she sat beside him. 'I could only hear half the conversation.'

'It's so bloody crazy, I can hardly believe it. A pilot who's got this far through the war without a scratch, and a bloody rocket hit the house where he was staying with his girlfriend.'

Della gasped in horror. 'You mean one of those V1s?'

'Yes, and no doubt there'll be plenty more to come.' Jonathan's voice, almost a whisper, held a hopeless note. 'Hitler's secret weapon is no secret any more. I can only thank God the girl found me and not my father. This could be the end of him. Charles was always his favourite, and now his only hope of carrying on the estate.'

'Are you going to tell him tonight?'

Jonathan brushed back the stubborn fall of brown hair from his forehead. 'No, there's no point in upsetting him until I know how bad it is. I'll go to London as soon as Charles comes round and, when he's well enough to move, I'll have him transferred to the General where I can keep an eye on him myself.'

Della hated to be practical but was worried about the hospital's reaction to yet another leave. 'Won't they mind at the hospital about you taking more time off?'

'I don't give a tinker's damn whether they mind or not! Dr Simpson and I stand in for each other; it's not as though we just scarper off. And I've never taken time off for anything but compassionate reasons.' He sighed. 'There've just been too bloody many of them recently.'

'You're close to your brother, aren't you?'

Jonathan looked thoughtful for a moment before replying. 'I couldn't say we're exactly close; we were too different for that. But he was my elder brother and, as a child, I revered both my brothers. But I was always on the outside, so to speak. They were closer in age and I was just the little brother who got in the way.' He smiled wryly. 'I wanted to be like them so much, but I knew I was different. I was always getting into trouble with my parents and they never did. I used to think there was something wrong with me until I started growing up. I realised then that my mother and father weren't the gods I'd thought they were, and that my brothers were their favourites because they modelled themselves after them – not that they would have admitted it, of course . . . or perhaps they weren't even aware of it,' he added, as if the idea had just occurred to him. 'But don't get me wrong. They weren't like my parents in every way; they were both good-natured at the bottom even though they had my parents' obsession with money and worldly success. Where business was concerned they were quite ruthless.'

'Sweetheart.' Della took his hand again. 'Do you realise you're talking about them both in the past tense? Charles is still alive! You mustn't give up hope.'

Jonathan closed his eyes. 'You're right! Just a slip of the tongue.' He attempted to smile. 'Of the two, I got on better with Charles, especially as we got older. I *am* fond of him.' He drew her close and kissed her tenderly on the cheek. 'My poor darling,' he murmured. 'What an evening for you! And I had such a wonderful celebration planned.'

Della snuggled into him. 'Don't worry about *me*, you

idiot. You're the one with the problems. I'm worried about you! And please finish your sandwich.'

'Later.' He placed the plate on the coffee table. 'And worrying's not going to make either of us feel any better.' He tilted her chin and kissed her tenderly. She responded, and their touch seemed to melt them together. As their embrace comforted them both, Della thought how wonderful it was to have someone to love and to be loved in return.

But the moment was lost when the telephone bell clanged again. Jonathan was in the hall and had picked up the receiver before the second ring had ended.

'Dr Maddison?'

'Yes.' Jonathan recognised the male nurse's voice.

'Your brother regained consciousness about ten minutes ago, sir. I couldn't ring any earlier because I was the only one on the ward.'

'That's all right,' Jonathan said impatiently. 'How is he?'

There was a pause before the voice answered: 'Well, he's not coherent, sir. He keeps babbling on about jelly babies and sherbet. But it's too soon to know anything for sure.'

Jonathan's knuckles turned white as he gripped the receiver. 'I'll catch the first train in the morning. In the meantime, ring me if there's any more news. I shall be out for a while but please keep trying.'

As he replaced the telephone, Della stood behind him trembling. 'How is he?' She knew the news was bad.

'He's come round.' Jonathan hurried to the bedroom and flung on his clothes. Della followed him and dressed as he continued. 'He's not coherent, which isn't surprising at first, but in any case, I want to be there. Apparently he's babbling about jelly babies and sherbet – his two favourite sweets when he was a boy.' He paused in the act of pulling on his socks and added with a catch in his voice, 'He used to dip the jelly babies into the sherbet.'

'Oh, my poor darling!'

Jonathan pulled on his jacket. 'I'll take you home first and then I'll have to go to the hospital and clear up the stuff on my desk before Dr Simpson can take over. I'll ring him from there. The poor chap's supposed to be semi-retired, but I seem to be keeping him fully employed lately.'

On their way out to the car, Della's heart cried out for Jonathan. But there was little she could do to comfort him.

Chapter Forty-One

When the postman arrived, Rose was force-feeding Rosemary her porridge, while Bill sipped his tea and read the newspaper. 'Here, *you* do it.' Rose stuffed the spoon into Rosemary's hand. 'And I want to see that dish empty,' she added firmly as she left the room.

'No porridge,' Rosemary whined. She scooped up a spoonful and threw the contents under the table. Delighted with her new game, she continued while Bill obliviously read his newspaper.

Rose picked up the single letter on the hall floor. It was Joe's handwriting. She should put it away until Bill left, but her usual excitement at hearing from Joe outweighed her caution. Ripping open the envelope, her eyes greedily devoured the short note:

My Darling Pumpkin,

Great news! I've got seven days R and R. I didn't tell you before in case you worried, but I've been in hospital having my appendix out. A goddam stupid time to get appendicitis, but at least it's given me a whole week to spend with you.

I'm longing to hold you again. Expect me on Wednesday afternoon.

All my love, baby,

Joe

Rose stuffed the letter into her apron pocket and thought frantically. She couldn't possibly keep Joe's visit a secret this time; Bill was coming back to town on Thursday. She must tell him. Whatever the consequences, she had to see Joe. Remembering Bill's reaction when she had brought Andrew home, she shivered with apprehension as she returned slowly to the kitchen. She ignored the mess under the table and on Bill's shoes.

'All gone!' Rosemary proudly lifted up the empty bowl.

Rose sat down heavily. 'So I see. Now go out and play with your pram in the garden.'

Rosemary jumped down from her chair with alacrity, delighted that her new game had worked. 'Where's dolly?'

'In the pram,' Rose snapped, impatient for the child to leave. Obediently, Rosemary skipped out to the garden.

'What's up with you?' Bill grunted over his newspaper. 'A bit tetchy this morning, aren't you?'

Rose drew in a deep breath and looked straight at him. 'I've got something to tell you, Bill . . . I'm in love with someone else.' Every muscle in her body tensed as she spoke the final words. Bill threw the newspaper to the floor, his handsome face darkening frighteningly. Rose gripped the edge of the table.

'And how long has this been going on?' he hissed, thrusting out his lower lip in a threatening gesture.

'I met him a long time ago, when you were in London buying your mother a house.' Rose met Bill's gaze levelly, but her voice faltered. 'He . . . he . . . was only on a visit for a week. I . . . I thought it better not to tell you. I didn't know if he would ever come back, and I don't want to spoil things with us. But he's coming to see me tomorrow for a week.' She lowered her eyes, afraid of what was to come.

Bill scraped back his chair and jumped up. 'You little tart!' he screamed. 'Carrying on behind my back with another man! And all the time I'm forking out to keep you and your kid.'

'Rosemary's your child as well,' Rose reminded him, trying to keep her voice from trembling.

'And how the bloody hell do I know that?' Bill advanced towards her. 'I've caught you with another fella before.'

'There was never anyone else but you. I swear, Bill.' Rose was amazed at the sudden calmness in her voice, despite the churning of her stomach.

'Am I really supposed to believe that? And what about since then? You little bitch!' He lifted his hand as if to strike her but thought better of it. He paced the room. 'So I've been forking out all these years to keep you and the kid, while you've been entertaining your men friends here. I suppose they've been paying for your services as well,' he sneered.

Rose spoke between clenched teeth. 'There's only been one man in my life since I met you, Bill, and I didn't mean it to happen.' Her voice began to rise as she felt the injustice of his accusations. 'And it wouldn't have happened if you had been here for me.' She stood up to face him. 'I've had to hide in the background all these years, lonely and bored, just waiting for your visits, while you go home to your wife and family. You've had it both ways. I'm just your toy – your pastime.'

'You knew that from the start.' He clenched and unclenched his fists.

'No, Bill, I didn't. You lied to me. If I'd known from the start you had a wife and family, I'd never have got involved with you like this. By the time I found out, I loved you so much that I decided half a loaf was better than no bread. I needed you that much!' She shook her head. 'I was young and stupid.'

'Needed *me* or the easy life I could give you?' Bill took a step towards her and she put a restraining hand on his shoulder.

'Sit down, Bill!' The force of her voice caused him to sit on the chair she had just vacated.

She sat next to him, her face white and strained. 'I admit that when I first met you I was seduced by your sophistication and your money, but then I fell in love with you . . . or maybe I thought I did,' she added wearily. 'I really don't know. But I do know that if you had been here for me as a proper husband and a proper father to your child, I'd never have been drawn to another man.'

'Yes, it's out of sight, out of mind with you.'

'Well, I'm certainly out of your sight and mind once you get home to your precious wife and all her money.'

Bill jumped up again, his eyes wild with anger. 'You never objected to accepting my "precious wife's money", as you call it.' He loomed over her threateningly, but Rose didn't flinch. For all his faults, she knew he wasn't a physically violent man. 'I always knew you were a gold-digger,' Bill raged, his finger jabbing the air in front of her accusingly, 'but I was prepared to pay for what I got because, by God, I wanted you.' His hand fell to his side and he stepped back, his face a mixture of anger and frustration.

Rose bit her lip to stem the tears. 'I know, Bill, and I wanted you. I'd have wanted you even if you hadn't been rich; my infatuation grew to a love and a need of some sort. I just blinded myself to the future.'

'Well, you'd better look to the future now, you little hussy. If you think I'm going to go on paying for your fun with another man, you've got another think coming.' Bill glared at her venomously, angry also with himself that she still had the power to make him jealous.

'You always were an insatiable little tart,' he spat finally.

'And what about you? You used me because you couldn't get enough from your wife,' Rose reminded him hotly, now inflamed by his insults.

Bill glowered down at her, his teeth clenched in an effort to keep control. 'I've told you! I don't get *anything* from my wife.'

Rose almost laughed. 'Come on, Bill! How do you expect me to believe that when you've got three children by her?'

'Aye, well that was then,' he said more quietly now. 'I had to do my duty by her. She wanted a family, and her father wanted grandbairns to carry on the family line. But I haven't touched her since the last one was born. She was plain when I married her, and now she's plain and fat and forty. I couldn't touch her with a barge pole.' He twisted his face in disgust.

'Bill!' Rose's mouth gaped in disbelief. 'So you only married her for her family's money! You never wanted to sleep with her!' She drew her hand across her forehead, trying to take in what he had just said. 'You told me *she* was the one who didn't want sex. I suppose that means that when I get old and lose my looks, you wouldn't want me either? Is that what love means to you?' She paused, realising painfully that he had never really loved her. 'You only wanted to own me, to have my body . . . and your poor wife, you only wanted her money. That's why you wouldn't leave her – not because you felt responsible for your family at all. You've lied to me from the beginning, Bill. Oh, God! What a fool I've been!'

He almost exploded in outrage. 'And suppose I had left her for you! I'd have been penniless. Don't tell me you'd have wanted me then?'

'Yes, Bill.' Rose nodded slowly. 'By that time you'd become so much a part of me, I would have wanted you any way I could get you – money or no money.' She looked up at his handsome face, now twisted with rage. 'Oh, yes, I admit I enjoyed your money, but you could have got a job, and we could have lived like any other couple. Love is what counts in the end. It's taken me a long time, but I've finally learned that lesson.' As she finished, hot tears of hurt and disillusionment coursed down her cheeks.

'Love!' Bill spat, as if it were a dirty word. 'You can't live on love, as you call it, especially the way *you* like to live.' He stamped towards the table to pick up the newspaper from the floor. Only then did he notice the porridge on his shoes. 'And look what your bloody kid's done to my shoes!'

Rose winced. 'She's *your* daughter as well, Bill.'

'Aye, you can tell that to the marines.' He rubbed furiously at his shoes with the corner of the tablecloth. 'I was a bloody fool to give in to you and let you keep the kid, and then I even let you talk me into having her around the house when I'm here. How the hell do I know whose kid I've been forking out for?'

'Bill,' Rose entreated, 'don't you remember, she was born nine months after that night in the air raid?'

'Aye, and who else were you having it off with at the same time? That soldier for one!'

Rose ignored the insult. 'I see. I certainly don't expect anything more from you for myself, but surely – your daughter. Do you mean to say you won't take responsibility for her?'

'Let your new fancy-man do that! Let him take the pair of you, bag and baggage. And you'd better have your bags and baggage out of here before I get back on Thursday.' His face perspired with anger, and he mopped his brow with his handkerchief.

Rose was unable to believe her ears. 'But I've got nowhere to go! For God's sake, Bill, at least give me some notice. I'll pay you rent. But I'll need time to find another flat and a job. It won't be easy with Rosemary.'

Despite her pleading tone, Bill was unmoved. He picked up his briefcase and stuffed the newspaper into it. 'You must think I'm crazy if you expect me to let you stay on here and entertain your lover,' he snarled. 'Let him find a place to live! Let him keep you in the manner to which I've accustomed you . . . for as long as he hangs around, that is.' He paused and leered at her. 'And after that, you can always make a living doing what you like best.'

'Bill, how could you—' Rose began desperately, but his elegantly suited back was already half way out of the room.

Without turning, he barked, 'And that's final!'

Rose covered her face with her hands, tears tumbling till she could taste their hot saltiness.

From the hall door, Bill shouted, 'And if I see hair or hide of you here on Thursday, I'll throw you out with my own bare hands.'

The door slammed. Rose still sat at the table, her face in her hands, when Rosemary ran in, sobbing.

'Mammy! Dolly broke. She naughty. She fell.'

Rose lifted her on to her knee. 'All right! Let Mammy see,' she said wearily. The pink china face was split down the centre.

'Uncle Bill mend her?' Rosemary asked through her tears.

'No, chicken.' Rose smoothed back the wet ringlets that clung to Rosemary's face. 'Uncle Bill's gone. But Uncle Joe's coming tomorrow. He'll mend her for you. And I bet he's got something nice for you as well.'

'Uncle Joe! A present!' The tears stopped. 'What he bring?'

'We'll just have to wait and see. And we'll be going to another place to see him. Mammy has to go down the road to ring Auntie Della now.' She lifted the child from her knee and stood up slowly, feeling drained. 'Come on, let's wash your face and take you up to see Mrs James for a while. I bet she's got biscuits.'

After dispatching Rosemary to Mrs James, Rose trudged to the telephone kiosk. Della would be furious about her ringing her at work, but she had no choice.

Della was about to take her tea break when Matron intercepted her. 'A telephone call for you in my office, Nurse Davidson. It had better be important! And it had better be brief!'

'Thank you Matron.' Della's heart pumped wildly. It must be Jonathan from London.

'Hello,' she breathed into the receiver. But it was Rose's urgent tones that greeted her.

'Della, it's me! I'm sorry to ring you at work, but I'm in a terrible mess. I got a letter from Joe this morning. He's coming tomorrow for a week. I had to tell Bill – and you're not going to believe it – he's throwing me out of the flat.'

'Well, I'm not surprised.' Della tried not to show her exasperation. 'Is that what you called me about?'

'Well, that and a lot more.' Rose sniffed, on the verge of tears. 'But the point is he wants me out tomorrow, Della, and I couldn't possibly find anywhere by then. I've got enough money to pay for a hotel for a few days, but then I'd have nothing left for rent when I find somewhere . . . and Joe's coming on Wednesday. You know Mam and Dad wouldn't have me back.' Her tone turned pleading. 'Do you think your mam would let me stay at your house till I can get sorted out?' Before Della could speak, Rose went on persuasively, 'The boys' room's empty; I could pay her rent and, while Joe's here, Rosemary could sleep in your room.'

'Wait a minute, Rose! You know my mam wouldn't see you without a roof over your head, but do you really expect her to let you sleep with Joe in her house?'

'I know it's a lot to ask,' Rose admitted. 'But Joe would only be there for a week. Your mam's human; I'm sure she'd understand. You know she likes me a lot better since I decided to keep Rosemary. You're my only hope, Della. Nora and Phil would have us but they've only got one bedroom.'

Della gave in. 'All right, I'll see what I can do. I'll ask Mam tonight and I'll ring you. Be at the telephone box at seven.'

'Oh, you're an angel.' Rose sagged against the kiosk wall in relief.

That afternoon Matron again summoned Della, but this time her voice was civil, almost respectful: 'Dr Maddison's on the phone for you, Nurse Davidson. I'll get Nurse Jones to take over for you.'

'Thank you, Matron.' Della tried to appear composed, but she left the medicine trolley in the middle of the ward and almost ran to the office. 'Jonathan,' she cried as she picked up the receiver. 'How's Charles?'

'Hello, sweetheart.' His distant baritone voice sounded weary. 'He's in bad shape, still incoherent, and he doesn't know me, so there's not much point in my staying on at the moment. I'm coming home tomorrow. Would you please tell Dr Simpson I'll be back on duty on Thursday?'

'Yes, darling. Will Charles be all right?'

'Only time will tell. In the meantime I've arranged to have him transferred here as soon as he's well enough to be moved. I'm afraid it's going to be a long process.' He paused before adding, 'God, I've missed you.'

'Me, too,' Della said enigmatically. Matron's bulky figure had just passed the open doorway.

Jonathan went on. 'I'll come straight to the hospital. I haven't checked the train times yet, but if I'm late, please wait there till I pick you up. I need you.'

'Me, too.'

'Bye till then, darling.'

Della was about to make a formal reply but instead burst out: 'Bye, darling. I love you.' So what if Matron heard! Their romance would be all round the hospital soon enough anyway, and there was certainly no reason to hide it.

Della left work promptly at six, dreading the thought of approaching her mother about Rose. Mary was stirring corned beef hash on the stove when she arrived. 'Hello, Mam.' She kissed her on the cheek.

'Hello, luv. You're early,' Mary said, still stirring briskly.

Della decided to waste no time. She leaned against the scullery bench. 'I . . . I've got something to ask you, Mam.' Even though she had rehearsed her speech on the bus, she didn't know quite where to start. 'Rose has had a row with her boyfriend and he's kicked her out.'

Mary stopped stirring and looked up thoughtfully. 'Well, if it weren't for Rosemary, I'd say that was a good thing. But she'll have a tough time on her own with a child to bring up.' Her tone was sympathetic; she remembered only too well how difficult it had been bringing up David alone. 'What's she going to do?'

'Well, you know her parents refused to have any more to do with her, and she's got to be out by tomorrow.' Della was heartened by Mary's obvious compassion. 'She asked me if you would put her and Rosemary up for a while until she can find another flat and a job. She said she'll pay rent.'

'I see.' Mary put the lid on the pan and picked up the tin opener for the peas. 'Well, the boys' room's empty except when Anne and Colin come, and she and Rosemary could go in with you then. I don't see why not, till she gets settled.'

'But there's something else, Mam.' Della had to summon up the last of her courage to deliver the final message. 'She's left Bill because she's in love with Joe. And he's coming to see her for a week, starting tomorrow.'

Mary dropped the tin opener, her eyes uncomprehending. 'You mean *Joe*, Billie's friend?'

Della nodded. 'She really loves him, Mam. She's given up everything she had with Bill just to be with Joe for a week – you know that's not like Rose.'

Mary forgot about the peas and, wiping her hands on her apron, walked slowly to the kitchen. She sat at the table and stared at the white cloth. 'You mean she was having an affair with Joe while she was living with Bill?'

Della sat next to her. 'Yes, Mam,' she admitted. 'But she's crazy about him and it seems he is about her. They've been writing to each other regularly. But she didn't know if she'd ever see him again and—' She halted. It wasn't easy trying to excuse Rose's behaviour tactfully. But Mary's expression showed no disapproval. 'I know it sounds awful, Mam. But she was afraid to leave Bill because of Rosemary, so she didn't tell him about Joe.'

Mary had a faraway look in her eyes, remembering when she herself had been in a similar situation before she had married Walter. 'Yes,' she sighed, 'love isn't always as straightforward and wonderful as people like to believe.'

Della took Mary's hand. 'Does that mean Joe can stay as well?'

'Yes, Joe can stay.' Mary rose to return to her chores. 'You can sleep in the boy's room with Rose and Rosemary, and he can have your room.'

Della knew this was not what Rose had in mind, but

she also knew Rose would get around the problem. She hugged Mary. 'You're an angel, Mam! I said I'd phone her at seven, so I'd better go now.' She was also impatient to tell Rose about her new romance with Jonathan; she hadn't seen her since the eventful party. But the thought of Jonathan reminded her of his telephone call. She paused on her way out. 'With all this business about Rose, I forgot to tell you about Jonathan. He rang me today. His brother's in a bad way; he's still not coherent and he doesn't even know Jonathan.'

'Oh, that's sad, luv. Is Jonathan bringing him back with him?'

'No, he's too ill to be moved, so Jonathan's coming back tomorrow. He'll have him transferred as soon as he's well enough.'

'Please tell Jonathan how sorry I am.' Mary returned to the business of opening the tin before asking: 'And when are you going to bring Jonathan home to see his future in-laws?'

'Soon, Mam.' Della's face brightened. 'I'll bring him over while Joe's here. We can have a party.'

'Don't be long. Dinner's almost ready.' Mary lifted the lid and examined the hash. 'And your father's late as well. As if it isn't difficult enough to make a tasty meal these days.'

By nine o'clock Rosemary was tucked up in Della's room, keeping her out of the way while, in the boys' room, the two girls unpacked a couple of Rose's mountain of suitcases. The wardrobe and chest bulged by the time they had finished.

Della collapsed on to one of the bunks. 'Good Lord, Rose! Are you sure that's enough to last a week?'

Rose grinned. 'That's just a start. I'll get the rest of the stuff tomorrow while I'm waiting for Joe, *and* all the knick-knacks Bill gave me. If I had somewhere to store it, I'd take all the bloody furniture as well,' she added bitterly. 'But I can hardly believe I'll be seeing Joe tomorrow.' Her face brightened at the thought, then clouded. 'It's very good of your mam to do this for me, Della, and I feel awful about it. But you know, it would drive us both mad sleeping in separate rooms.'

Della gave her an innocent look. 'Don't worry! I'm a very sound sleeper. I wouldn't have the slightest idea whether or not you'd been in your own bed all night. And, do you know something – I don't think my mam expects you to either. I think she's just keeping up appearances.'

Rose flung her arms round her. 'Oh, I love you, and I'm so happy for both of us! It's marvellous that you and Jonathan have got together at long last. It's got to be fate,' she added wryly, 'considering all the obstacles you've had to overcome.'

'For once I agree with you, Rose. I just hope his brother gets better. He's very upset about it.'

Rose tried to console her. 'He will, luv, I'm sure. You said yourself, it's early days yet.'

'I suppose so.' Della suppressed a yawn. 'And I also suppose I should get some sleep.' She undressed and threw on her nightdress before climbing into one of the bunk beds.

'Goodnight, Della, and thanks again.' Rose made for the door. 'I'm too excited to sleep just yet. I'm going to have a long hot soak and dream about tomorrow.'

Rose arrived at the flat at nine o'clock the following morning. After finishing her packing, she sat waiting for Joe, filled with excitement. She was safe today. Bill wouldn't be back till tomorrow. Mary had been delighted to take over Rosemary for the day. Rose couldn't wait to be alone with Joe.

At three o'clock the doorbell rang. She flew down the

hall. 'Joe! Oh, Joe!' She flung herself into his arms with the velocity of a stone from a catapult.

'Oh, baby, it's good to see you,' Joe's deep voice drawled as he held her close.

'Come on in, you idiot.' Rose finally prised herself away. 'Are you trying to give the neighbours a treat?'

He picked up his bag, grinning. 'Nope, I'm saving that for you.' Inside, he took her in his arms again, his mouth devouring hers. But, after a moment, he pulled himself away. 'Where's Rosemary?' he asked hoarsely.

'Not here!' Rose smiled up at him invitingly.

'Then why the hell are we wasting time?' He took her hand and led her to the bedroom.

They made love urgently and afterwards Joe lay back on the pillows with a sigh. 'Jeez,' he breathed, exhausted. 'You've got to remember I'm still an invalid and treat me with more respect.' He placed his hand on the scar on his side and groaned in exaggerated pain.

Alarmed, Rose sat up and examined the fresh scar. 'Oh, no! Did I hurt you?'

'Yes, like hell! And will you please do it again?'

'You daft thing.' She grinned with relief. 'But really, does it still hurt?'

'Just a bit,' he admitted, 'but not enough to get in the way of my R and R.' He ruffled her hair and slipped his arm under her shoulders. 'You don't know how much I've missed you, honey. You got under my skin as fast as a Rocky Mountain tick – and now I've got Rocky Mountain fever. I never thought a woman could take me in the way you have.'

'That's not very romantic,' Rose chided him, delighted nevertheless. 'It's like me saying you grew on me like a wart.'

'Sounds good to me. And what a wonderful thought! You're not getting rid of me the entire week.' Joe pulled the coverlet over them. 'In fact, I could stay right here in bed with you for the rest of my leave, if you'd promise to get up and make me a meal now and then.'

Rose swiftly returned to reality. 'Joe,' she began slowly, summoning her courage, 'we can't stay here. I . . . I've left Rosemary's father for good. I just came round to collect the last of my things and to wait for you.'

Stunned, he sat up. 'Left him! But I thought there was nothing between you and him any more. You said he just came round to see Rosemary.'

'I lied, Joe,' Rose admitted bleakly. 'I'm so sorry I lied to you.' She sat up and faced him, her heart thumping as if she were pleading for her life. 'I never wanted anyone else from the moment I saw you. But I thought you'd forget all about me when you got away. I thought you'd have loads of wartime romances . . . and . . . and then go back to your girlfriend.' Her eyes begged forgiveness.

Joe still looked stunned. 'So the father had visitation rights to you as well as Rosemary,' he said as if to himself. He looked at her, as though still not quite comprehending. 'You told me that part of your relationship was over . . . and . . .'

He clasped his hand to his forehead with a groan, letting the news sink in, before he found his voice again. 'Dammit, woman! Now I get it! Christ, what a dumb ass I've been! This apartment isn't your parents', is it?' His dazed expression changed to one of hurt and anger.

Rose quailed at the tone of his voice. 'No, Joe, I lied to you. It's Bill's flat. Oh, please forgive me! I didn't know then that what you felt for me would last like this, and I had to think of Rosemary. You don't know how hard it is for a woman alone with an illegitimate child.' Like a child herself, she rubbed her wet eyes with the back of her hand. 'But I've done it now, Joe. Whatever the consequences, even one week with you is worth more than a lifetime with him.'

'One week! For Christ's sake! Is that all you expected from me? Is that how much you believed me when I told you I loved you? Do you think I go around saying that to every girl I meet?' Joe flung himself over the side of the bed and, grabbing his jacket from the floor, fumbled furiously in the top pocket. He pulled out a folded piece of paper and flung it at her. 'This is what I was hoping for from you.'

Her hands trembling, Rose unfolded the paper. 'A special licence!' she squeaked.

'That's right! I'm offering you a lifetime, Rose, not a week. I'm not the gay Lothario you seem to think I am.' Joe's voice was calmer now.

'But your girlfriend at home . . .?'

'I wrote to her as soon as I got back and told her I'd met someone else.'

Rose clutched her knees, the tears scalding her eyelids forming dark spots on the cover. 'Oh, Joe!' she wailed. 'And I let you down!'

Joe turned her face towards him. 'Do you really mean you gave up Rosemary's father and a life of luxury just to spend a week with me?'

Rose bit her lip and nodded.

'Oh, Rose, you dumb broad,' he murmured, gathering her in his arms. 'Then you didn't let me down in the end.' She clung to him, hardly believing her ears. He sighed heavily. 'I can't deny I hate the fact that you lied to me, and that that man's been sleeping with you, but I suppose it's hard for a guy to know what it's like to be in your position.' He rocked her gently and kissed the top of her head. 'If only you'd told me, honey, I'd have helped you out.'

'I was too ashamed to let you know that I was . . . was . . . that sort of girl. I thought you wouldn't want me any more.'

'Rose, you're *my* sort of girl.' Joe tilted her face up to his. 'And I've known enough of them to know when I've met the right one.'

Rose looked into his eyes; they were serious, yet smiling. 'Does that mean you still want to marry me?' Her voice was incredulous.

'What do *you* think?' He kissed her lips softly.

'Oh, Joe, Joe!' She clung to him. 'You'll never regret it. I'll be a good wife to you. I love you so much! I don't know how I could ever have thought I loved Bill.'

'So you didn't love him?' Joe hated himself for the question but needed to know the answer.

Rose shook her head. 'I was young and stupid and infatuated with his good looks and sophistication, but after I met you I realised that what I felt for him had never been real love. And when I told him about you yesterday . . .' She shuddered, reliving the unhappy moment. 'I learned some things about him that made me ashamed I'd ever even thought I loved him.' Tears started again at the painful memory.

'It's okay, honey,' Joe soothed. 'You don't need to go into it.' He pushed her away gently. 'I don't know about you but right now I could use a drink. And then let's get out of this damn' place.' He got up and began dressing.

Rose did the same, afterwards splashing her face in the bathroom. She smiled, not caring that she looked a mess. Joe loved her and wanted to marry her, with all her faults. As she skipped happily into the sitting room, Joe was rummaging in his bag. 'Would you like a brandy?' she asked.

'No thanks, baby – not *his* liquor! I've got a bottle of bourbon.'

Rose got two glasses and they sat on the sofa, hands entwined. Joe raised his glass. 'Maybe this'll clear my head a bit. It's been quite a lot for a guy to take in all at once.' He knocked back his bourbon and stood up.

'Now we'd better get practical. Where are you staying? Where do we go?'

'I'm staying with Billie's parents, and they said you can stay as well. Mrs Dolan's looking after Rosemary now. They're very nice people, Joe.'

'Yep, I found that out.' He poured himself another drink. 'And just how did you think you were going to earn a living after I left?'

'Don't worry.' Rose grinned. 'I've worked it all out. I'm going to get a job – munitions factories pay well – and Mrs Dolan's going to look after Rosemary during the day. She's thrilled about it. But I'm going to pay her rent and something extra for minding Rosemary.'

Joe looked at her with respect, and Rose realised that, for the first time, he wasn't simply admiring her pretty face. 'Do you mean to say you were going to do all that just to see me again?' he asked, almost humbly.

She nodded.

'Baby, you've certainly got – what do you Tommies call it? – spunk. But you won't need to work, kid. In a couple of days you'll be my wife and Rosemary will be my daughter. I can send you enough to live on until this Godforsaken war's over. Then I'll be taking care of you both in style back home. I can't wait to show you off to my folks.'

Moved to tears again, Rose bit them back. 'That sounds wonderful, Joe, but the funny thing is, I finally want to do my bit for the war effort. Even if I only do it part time. I want to work in munitions. I feel guilty. I've hardly suffered at all from the war so far. But,' she added with a grin, 'a little extra financial help from my husband wouldn't hurt. I'd still be making my war effort.'

Joe ruffled her hair and grinned back. 'You're one of a kind, honey.' He set his glass on the coffee table. 'Okay, let's get the hell out of here.'

Rose stood up. 'I'll just wash the glasses and make the bed. I don't want to rub it in that you've been here. And we'll have to take a taxi. I've still got some suitcases in Rosemary's room. Would you mind ringing for one while I clear up?'

'Sure thing!' He started for the door.

But Rose called him back, fluttering her eyelashes and simpering exaggeratedly, 'Joe, when you got the special licence, how did you know I'd say yes?'

He grinned and shrugged. 'Just a lucky guess, honey.'

In the taxi, Rose settled back in her seat, her hand in Joe's. She sighed with happiness. 'I never thought I'd rather live in Della's house than in my own flat . . . especially as we're going to have separate bedrooms.' Mischievously, she glanced sideways to enjoy his dismayed expression.

His mouth fell open. 'You've got to be kidding.'

Smiling, she patted his knee. 'Don't worry. I'll be sneaking in every night after lights out. Della said she's sure her mam's only doing it for appearances anyway.'

The wedding was set for Friday morning. It was to be a simple civil ceremony with only Della, Jonathan, Nora and Phil as guests and witnesses. Rose glowed beside Joe in a dove grey costume and matching wide-brimmed hat, while he, towering over her, looked more handsome than ever in his uniform. Even the austere, government-green painted registry office, relieved only by a vase of pink carnations on the ink-stained oak table, didn't mar the joy of the occasion.

As the registrar, a nervous, twitchy little man, began reciting his piece, Della saw Rose glance anxiously towards the door. Poor Rose! Her parents obviously hadn't responded to the invitation. And Rose had been convinced they would forgive and forget now that she had left Bill and was getting married.

Jonathan gripped Della's hand as Rose and Joe made their vows. 'Our turn next,' he whispered in her ear. Della returned the pressure of his hand.

The ceremony seemed to be over almost before it had begun and, while everyone kissed and congratulated the newlyweds, the door creaked open. Rose's parents stood awkwardly on the threshold. She ran to them, holding out her arms. 'Oh, Mam, Dad, you came!'

'Aye, I'm sorry we're late, but your letter only arrived half an hour ago.' Embarrassed, Mrs Johnson looked down at her shabby dress and shoes. 'I barely had time to take me pinny off. We got a taxi and came straight here.'

Rose flung her arms round her mother. 'Oh, it doesn't matter. It's wonderful to see you, Mam.'

Mr Johnson coughed, feeling awkward in front of his strange audience. 'Dad!' Rose cried, hugging him.

'Aye, well, we wish you all the best, luv,' he muttered. 'We're glad you came to your senses.'

'Come and meet my husband,' Rose said proudly, dragging them towards Joe. But, even in her joy, she felt sad that her parents looked older and thinner and careworn.

'Well, you look as though you could keep her in check,' Mr Johnson joked to Joe.

Joe smiled. 'I sure can, sir.' He shook his new in-laws' hands in turn. 'And I do thank you for your daughter, ma'am,' he said to Mrs Johnson.

She smiled up at him before scanning the room anxiously. 'Where's the bairn?' she asked tremulously.

Rose took her arm. 'She's staying with Della's parents. You're going to love her, Mam – she's just like me.'

'Aye,' Mrs Johnson sighed, 'we've got a lot of catching up to do.'

The registrar cleared his throat. 'Eh, I'm sorry, ladies and gentlemen, but, I, eh, have another wedding party due in two minutes. I'm afraid I must ask you to leave. But first the witnesses must sign.' He shuffled through the papers on his desk, while Jonathan and Phil stepped forward to do their appointed duty.

Outside, Rose hugged her parents once more. 'I'll bring Rosemary round as soon as I get back,' she promised.

'And why don't you bring your things an' all?' Mrs Johnson suggested matter-of-factly. 'There's no point in imposing on Mrs Dolan when you've got a home of your own to come to.'

Rose felt a lump in her throat. 'Thanks, Mam.'

Jonathan had loaned the couple his car for their long weekend in the Lake District, and he and Della climbed in the back as Joe took the wheel. 'Damned if I'll ever get used to this left-hand drive business,' he grinned as he started the engine.

'You'd better keep an eye on him, Rose,' Jonathan said. 'I'd like to have the car back in one piece, thank you – and you, too, of course. I've filled her up with petrol and there's a spare can in the boot, but just in case.' He fumbled in his pocket and threw a small envelope over Joe's shoulder. 'These are the last of my coupons.'

'Thanks, pal.' Joe was moved by Jonathan's sacrifice. 'You're a swell guy. I owe you. I promise I'll go carefully on the gas. I reckon we can see these puddles you call lakes in a couple of hours anyway,' he chuckled. 'And we'll be spending the rest of the time in the bedroom.'

Rose thumped him playfully on the shoulder. 'Joe! You're behaving like a true Yank. Our lakes are beautiful!'

'Just kidding, kid,' he grinned. 'I wanted to see if I could raise your hackles.'

As Joe dropped off Jonathan and Della outside the hospital, Rose got out and hugged them both. 'Thanks a million, both of you,' she said, near to tears. 'I've never been so happy . . . even though I'm going to miss Rosemary.'

'Rose!' Della scolded her. 'It's only for three days, and you know she loves being with my mam.'

'I know,' Rose sniffed. 'Do you think your mam would mind taking her to visit my parents while I'm away? I'd rather be there when they see her for the first time, but I want them to get to know her as soon as possible. And they could give your mam a break now and then.'

'Of course, you ninny.' Della pushed her back into the car and slammed the door. 'Now you two get off and have a wonderful time. Some of us have to work, you know.'

'Poor sods!' Rose waved as Joe started the car. 'Your turn next!' she yelled through the window.

'She's right there!' Jonathan took Della's hand as they walked towards the hospital entrance. 'I was thinking during the ceremony we should have been standing up there with them.'

'Me, too,' Della admitted. 'But I'd rather have a church wedding, darling. Would you mind? Just a very quiet, simple one.'

'I don't care if we get married in an air-raid shelter, just so long as we do it soon.'

'Well, it would take three weeks for the banns—'

'Then start them this Sunday,' Jonathan interrupted her. 'And make arrangements for the first Saturday after the time's up. I'm getting impatient.' He put his arm round her waist. 'And I'm also getting tired of taking you home in the middle of the night.'

She looked up at him with shining eyes. 'So am I.'

They made their way to the ward, Jonathan's arm still

about her waist, oblivious of the surprised glances of the staff. But Matron's strident voice brought them back to reality. 'Dr Maddison,' she shouted, bustling out of her office. 'The hospital rang about your brother.'

Jonathan's face turned grey. 'What did they say?'

'He had a violent turn this morning and attacked one of the orderlies. They had to put him in a strait-jacket. They asked you to ring as soon as you got back.'

Chapter Forty-Two

On Monday Jonathan worked late to repay some of the time he owed Dr Simpson. Della went straight to the flat from the hospital to prepare dinner. She hummed happily as she sliced carrots. The first banns had been announced the previous day.

At eight-thirty Jonathan arrived, looking tired and strained. He took her in his arms and held her close. 'God, it's wonderful to come home to you,' he whispered. 'I can't believe that soon you'll be living here.'

'Only three more weeks, darling.' She smiled up at him, but her smile faded at the sight of his grey, gaunt face. 'You look exhausted. Come and sit down,' she coaxed, leading him to the living room. 'Any more news about Charles?'

He flopped on to the sofa and ran his hand across his brow. 'I finally managed to get through at seven o'clock. Some of the lines were down. The Jerries dropped some more doodlebugs this morning, one of them on the Guards Chapel at Wellington Barracks just as the service was beginning . . . one hundred and nineteen killed and one hundred and forty-one injured,' he added wearily.

'I know, I heard it on the news.' Della sighed as she sat beside him and took his hand. 'But how's Charles?'

'He's had no more attacks since Saturday, so they've let him out of the strait-jacket, but they're keeping him in a padded cell, just in case.' Wearily, he rubbed his eyes under his glasses. 'I can't put this off any longer, Della. I've got to get him here. And I've got to tell Father. It's hopeless now to wait for a miraculous recovery. I knew I was fooling myself.' He put his arm round her shoulders and looked at her earnestly. 'And I've got to tell Father about you.'

Della's stomach turned a somersault. 'Do you have to just now? Don't you think one shock at a time's enough for him to take?'

'I'm not going to hide you in the background as if you were something to be ashamed of. Like it or not, I've got to tell him you're going to be my wife.'

'Please, Jonathan, let him get over the news about Charles first. I don't mind, honestly.'

At her pleading tone, Jonathan relented. 'All right, sweetheart, I'll hold off for the moment. But he's got to know before the wedding.'

Della breathed a sigh of relief. 'That's much more sensible, darling. When will Charles be arriving?'

'I've arranged to have him brought up on a troop train on Wednesday. He'll be sedated for the journey and there'll be medical personnel on the train. I'll ring my father this evening so he can make arrangements to get here.'

'Will . . . will he stay here?' At the thought, Della's spirits plummeted.

But Jonathan shook his head. 'No, he'll want first-class attention as usual. He wouldn't even know how to boil a kettle, and I can't be with him all the time. I'll book him in at the Station Hotel.' Struck by a sudden thought, he paused. 'Do you think it might be a good idea for you to meet him, give him a chance to get to know you before I tell him who are you – and that we're getting married?'

'Jonathan! That would be deceitful. I couldn't!' Della looked perplexed, but she was concerned more about meeting the old man than the deceit involved.

'I suppose you're right. But I'm not going to stop seeing you while he's in town, and he'll probably be here some of the time. If you do happen to meet, I'll introduce you truthfully as Della Davidson, my fiancée. He doesn't know your married name, so it won't actually be a lie, will it?' He looked at her like a small boy coaxing his mother into allowing him an illicit day off school.

Avoiding his gaze, Della examined her hands in her lap. 'Well, at school we were always told that a sin of omission is as bad as a sin of commission. But so long as we tell him before the wedding, I suppose it'll be all right.' Then she looked at him squarely and confessed: 'To tell the truth, I'm dreading meeting him. I'd like to put it off as long as possible. But I only hope it doesn't make him even more angry when he finds out we've deceived him.'

'I know he's a bastard, but he always had an eye for a pretty face.' Jonathan squeezed her hand in encouragement. 'I'm sure once he knows you, he'll realise you're not the kind of girl he thinks you are.'

Della's eyebrows arched in surprise. 'Apart from the fact that I'm my mother's daughter, what else could he possibly know about me?' she asked hotly.

'Calm down, sweetheart.' He squeezed her hand harder. 'It's just that my mother never had a good word to say about your mother or her offspring. Please don't get upset, darling,' he added quickly on seeing the hurt in her eyes. 'Don't you see how ridiculous it all is? And now you also see just what sort of woman my mother was.'

Della bit her lip. 'I'm sorry for her. She couldn't have been a happy woman.'

'She wasn't, and he's never been a happy man – even with all his money. They were well matched in a way.'

Jonathan chucked her chin and smiled encouragement. 'But he's going to realise my mother was wrong when he meets you.'

Della said nothing. The prospect of meeting her future father-in-law still daunted her.

'Don't look so scared, darling. I promise you everything will be all right.' Jonathan kissed her on the cheek. 'And now, how about dinner? I smell something interesting. And I need some inner strength before I ring my father.'

Della smiled wryly. 'Don't be fooled by the smell. It's only vegetable stew, but I cooked it with an Oxo cube.'

After dinner Jonathan lit a cigarette and inhaled heavily.

'I think I'll have one too,' Della decided. 'I feel as nervous as you look.'

Jonathan handed her one, smiling. 'Don't get the habit till after the war.' He scraped back his chair and went to the telephone.

Puffing at the cigarette, Della strained her ears. She heard Jonathan muttering in frustration as he tried to get through to the operator. After a few minutes, she stubbed out the cigarette and retreated to the kitchen to wash up. She'd rather not hear this conversation anyway.

Ten minutes later, Jonathan leaned heavily against the kitchen door post, his face white.

'How did he take it?' But Della knew the answer from his expression.

'As I predicted. He'd been at the port, though. I could tell by his voice. I'm tired of warning him off it. But maybe it was just as well tonight; it slowed down his reactions a bit. I don't think he's quite taken it all in yet, and I spared him some of it. I told him Charles has lost his memory and is incoherent. He may not need to know the rest – if a miracle happens.'

'Oh, you poor darling!' Della put down the tea towel and wound her arms round his neck. 'Why don't you lie down on the sofa and have a rest? I'll pour us both a brandy.'

'That's something like what I had in mind – except for the sofa bit.' He kissed her softly and released her arms from his neck with a smile. 'Bring the brandy to the bedroom.'

'Jonathan,' she reminded him reluctantly, 'you know we have to go home by bus tonight to pick up the car.'

He gave her a playful push into the living-room. 'We'll worry about that later.'

By the time Della carried in the drinks, Jonathan was undressed and sitting up in bed. She smiled as she handed him a glass. 'Well! That didn't take you long.'

'Stop wasting time, woman, and come here,' he said, sounding more like himself now. Sipping his brandy, he watched appreciatively while Della undressed and slipped under the sheets beside him. They made love slowly and tenderly, taking comfort in each other. 'God, Della,' he whispered as they lay entwined afterwards, 'I still can't believe it's really you in my arms.'

Fondly, she stroked back the lock of hair from his forehead. 'What more can I do to convince you?'

'I'll think of something. But not now.' He closed his eyes and, within minutes, his breathing grew heavy. Della lay still until she was sure he was asleep, then wriggled gently from his arms and slipped out of bed, taking her clothes into the bathroom. Furtively, she washed, dressed and sneaked out of the flat. She just had time for the last bus. She would pick up Jonathan in the car in the morning in time for work. She smiled at her deceit, sorry only that she couldn't see his face when he woke up.

At four o'clock on Wednesday, Jonathan received a call

from the psychiatric ward. His brother had arrived. He shot over to see him immediately. Charles was in a single room, though not padded, for which Jonathan thanked God silently. He approached the still figure in the bed, noticing the cast on the broken leg from the thigh to the knee. If only that were all, he wished in vain. 'Hello, Charles, it's Jonathan,' he said hopefully. But the rugged face, still handsome despite the shaved head, turned a blank gaze on him.

'He's still partly sedated,' the orderly said. 'He should be out of it in another hour or so.'

Jonathan nodded and picked up the chart clipped to the bottom of the bed. The records didn't look good – still incoherent when he left the hospital, and still didn't know his girlfriend. He replaced the chart with a sigh and sat on the bed, taking his brother's hand. 'How are you feeling, Charles? Is there anything I can get for you?' He expected no response, but Charles withdrew his hand abruptly and stared back at him, his mouth working as if to speak, though no sound came out. 'Father's coming to see you,' Jonathan said. 'I'm going to ring him now. He'll be here soon.'

Charles's empty gaze turned to the ceiling as Jonathan withdrew to the office to telephone the hotel. 'He's arrived, Father,' he said, as the telephonist put him through.

'How is he?' the old man asked urgently.

'He's still doped from the journey. It's difficult to say.'

'I'll get a taxi straight over.' Joseph Maddison's voice rang with the force of iron.

'He's in Ward Six . . . psychiatric,' Jonathan added hesitantly. The phone went dead.

While he waited, Jonathan spoke with the psychiatrist on duty. But the harried, white-haired doctor knew no more than he. 'It's impossible to say at this stage,' he said. 'All I know is what I've read on his chart. I'll be checking him out again when the sedation's worn off. I need to keep him under strict observation for a while before I draw any conclusions. If he shows no improvement, or if his condition worsens, there's a chance he may benefit from more surgery. But his behaviour should be strictly monitored before any decision can be reached. I'll keep you informed.' He picked up a sheaf of papers from his desk to end the interview.

Jonathan nodded his thanks and returned to sit with Charles until his father arrived. His brother looked at him momentarily before again riveting his gaze to the ceiling, the only sign of activity his fingers, which twitched against the white sheet. Jonathan sat in the visitor's chair, his head in his hands, waiting.

When Joseph Maddison arrived, Jonathan was in the same position and Charles still staring at the ceiling. 'Good God!' the old man cried when he saw his son. With the aid of his walking stick, he hobbled to the inert figure and bent over him. 'Charles!' he bawled. 'Look at me, boy!'

As his father leaned over him, Charles's blank stare turned on him for a second before reverting to the ceiling.

Jonathan stood up. 'It's no good, Father. He's still drugged. Let's have a cup of tea and something to eat until he comes round a bit more.'

'I'm not leaving him,' Joseph growled, sitting on the chair Jonathan had vacated and thumping his walking stick. 'I haven't come all this way to have tea.'

A voice in the doorway said apologetically, 'I'm afraid you'll have to leave for a while anyway. I've got to give him an enema and a bed-bath while he's still quiet.' Neither had seen the orderly enter the room.

Jonathan helped Joseph up from the chair. 'Come on, Father. I could do with a cup of tea anyway.'

557

Reluctantly, Joseph let Jonathan support his elbow as he walked to the door. Jonathan was dismayed that his father had obviously not been following his advice. Not only had his gout worsened, but he had also grown portlier, and his face was an unhealthy, blotchy red.

'We've got time to go back to the hotel and have a real drink,' Joseph said tetchily. 'I need more than a lousy cup of tea after that.'

'I can't, Father.' Jonathan strove to keep his patience. 'I'm still on duty. I have to stay where they can reach me.' He stopped outside the doctor's office. 'Excuse me for a moment while I ring the ward.'

When he emerged a few seconds later, Joseph was leaning heavily on his cane, his usually stern expression having given way to one of silent torment. Jonathan took his father's arm again, knowing Joseph was suffering but unable to voice his feelings. Funny how the old boy could let fly so easily with his negative emotions, he thought wryly. 'Come on, Father,' he said gently. 'I've got to go back to the ward for a while, but I have time for a cup of tea with you first. I'll come back for you as soon as I can.'

They made their way to the canteen in silence, Jonathan seating his father before he went for the tea. He returned with two cups, a single lump of sugar in each saucer.

'What's that filthy-looking stuff, and where's the rest of the sugar?' Joseph curled his lips in distaste.

'It's what they call tea here, Father, and we're rationed to one lump per cup.' Jonathan plopped his own lump in his father's cup. Slightly appeased, the old man grunted. He stirred the tea and, for the first time, looked Jonathan in the eye.

'All right then, let's have it! Just how bad is he?'

'I really don't know, Father, and neither does the psychiatrist yet. It's early days, and it's going to be a long job.' Suddenly Jonathan wanted to put a reassuring hand over the gnarled knuckles clenched on the table. But he restrained himself. The only emotions he'd ever felt for this man were fear and, later, anger, the latter gradually diminishing to indifference. But now he pitied him, pitied the lonely, tired old man who still knew no other way to live life except by barging his way through like a bulldozer. Jonathan watched with resignation as Joseph took out a large cigar from his pocket and lit it carefully.

'And don't tell me I'm not supposed to do this,' he said defiantly. 'I'm sick of you and that damned doctor telling me what to do.' He puffed thick clouds of smoke and was quiet for a moment before bursting out: 'Hell and damnation on those Jerries for what they've done to my family!' He thumped his fist on the table, slopping tea into his saucer.

Jonathan sought wearily for comforting words. 'I know it doesn't help much, Father, but we're not the only family to suffer from the war . . .' His voice trailed away as he remembered the futility of trying to appease his father.

'And that makes it better, does it?' Joseph bellowed.

Jonathan gritted his teeth and countered doggedly. 'No, Father, not better! But it's as well to remember that thousands of other families are suffering too. You talk as though we'd been singled out.' He looked at his watch and stood up. 'I've got to go now. I'll be back in good time. Would you like another cup of tea?'

'Not this filth!' Joseph rudely pushed his half empty cup aside.

'A magazine?' Jonathan persevered through tight lips.

'No! Nothing. All I want is to see my son.'

'All right! I'll be back soon.' Jonathan left, trying to stifle the anger he always felt when his father was in one of these moods. But, he reminded himself, this time there was good reason for him to be upset. He must try to keep his patience.

Forty minutes later, Jonathan returned. Joseph Maddison was still slumped in his chair, another cigar between his fat fingers.

'Sorry it took a bit longer than I thought,' Jonathan said lightly, 'but Charles should be ready now.'

'About time!' Joseph snapped, leaning on his stick to rise. 'I didn't come here to sit in this damned canteen.'

Charles again turned his gaze on them as they entered, his fingers still drumming on the sheet. He was sitting up in bed and seemed more alert now, though his expression was still blank.

Joseph sat down heavily on the visitor's chair by the bed, scrutinising Charles's face. 'How are you feeling, son?' he asked with a catch in his voice.

Charles looked into his father's face, though with no light of recognition. 'I want jelly babies and sherbet,' he whined like a child.

Joseph's eyes bulged, and he leaned closer to his son. 'For God's sake, man, talk sense, can't you?' He shouted, as though the force of his voice might penetrate Charles's blank mind.

'Jelly babies and sherbet!' Charles repeated.

Joseph's hands shot out and grabbed Charles by the shoulders, shaking him in an effort to get some sense out of him. 'God almighty, Charles!' he screamed again.

'Father, leave him alone!' Jonathan rushed from where he stood at the foot of the bed. But before he could pull Joseph away, Charles's eyes had narrowed and, in a flash, his hands were round the old man's neck, throttling him.

'Jelly babies and sherbet!' he screamed.

Jonathan frantically tried to loosen Charles's vice-like grip on Joseph's neck, at the same time shouting for the orderly, who appeared in seconds. It took both of them all their strength to free Charles's hands. The old man fell back in his chair gasping, his face purple, his eyes bulging.

'Get him out of the way,' the orderly shouted. Jonathan pulled Joseph's chair out of reach of the bed, while the man knelt over Charles and pinned down both his arms.

Quickly, loosening his father's collar and tie, Jonathan knelt by him, supporting his shoulders. Joseph was breathing convulsively but tried to speak. 'Don't talk!' Jonathan ordered. 'Breathe deeply.'

The orderly, also labouring for breath, cried, 'If he's all right, could you leave him for a second and press the emergency bell?'

Jonathan did so and within seconds two more orderlies rushed in, one carrying a strait-jacket. Joseph Maddison tried to scream, 'No, not my son,' but his voice came out as a cracked whisper. Seconds later, he clutched his chest and toppled sideways off the chair.

Jonathan bent over him. 'Get a stretcher!' he shouted through the door. He felt the old man's pulse; it was strong and slow. His florid colour had turned pale grey, one side of his mouth drooped, and one pupil was dilated. 'He's had a stroke,' Jonathan cried. 'For God's sake, where's the stretcher!'

It seemed an eternity before the orderlies returned and transferred the dead weight to the stretcher and on to the waiting trolley outside. Jonathan glanced back at Charles, now restrained in the jacket. His eyes moved wildly in their sockets. 'Dr Roberts in cardiology,' he ordered, running beside the trolley.

An hour later Jonathan sat with the specialist in his office. Dr Roberts shook his head. 'I'm afraid it was a bad one, Jonathan, but we'll do what we can. His age and his general health are against him.'

Jonathan lit a cigarette with trembling hands and gulped the smoke. 'I know, Malcolm. I've been telling him for years. What's the prognosis?'

The middle-aged Scotsman shook his red head. 'It depends on how much he wants to help himself. The medicine should inhibit further clotting, but he'll have to work hard to get his speech back and some movement in his right side.'

Jonathan shook his head in despair. 'You've got a hard case to deal with there. He's never done anything to help himself in his life. I can't see him starting now. The only incentive he might have would be if my brother were to recover.' He stubbed the cigarette out angrily. 'And from what I've seen today, that's a faint hope.'

'Your father must have been very upset to go for him like that,' Malcolm remarked, stroking his red moustache. 'Thank God your brother was still partly sedated. I've seen plenty like that. They can have the strength of ten men.'

'Oh, yes,' Jonathan replied bitterly, 'my father was upset all right. But whether he was upset at seeing my brother in that state, or whether his pride was damaged at seeing his favourite son reduced to a babbling idiot, is anybody's guess.' He looked straight at Malcolm. 'I'm not going to pretend my father is a saint simply because he's a sick old man now.'

'I'm sorry, Jonathan.' Malcolm looked sympathetic. 'You've certainly got your troubles. And, despite what you say, you must be fond of the old sod. You're certainly behaving like a loving son.'

'No, that's an illusion, Malcolm. I'm not a hypocrite. I'm only doing my duty by him. He brought me up – in his way. And he educated me. I have him to thank for the last part at least. I love my work.' Jonathan chewed on his lip thoughtfully. 'It's ironic, don't you think? I was always his least favourite son, and now I'm the only one he's got to look after him in his old age. Thanks for all you've done, Malcolm. You'll keep me informed immediately there's any change, won't you? I'll pop in whenever I can.'

Malcolm nodded. 'He's in good hands with me, don't worry.'

As Jonathan stood up, he glanced at his watch. 'Almost seven o'clock! My fiancée's waiting for me. I'd better tell her to go home, then I'll look in on Charles. I'll be back shortly.' Wearily, he turned to leave.

But Malcolm stood up and put a restraining hand on his shoulder, his rich Scottish voice booming, 'Och, don't be a fool, man! There's a limit to how much so-called "duty" you owe your father. You know sitting with him won't do any good. Check in on your brother if you must, then go home and get some rest. I'll ring you immediately there's any change in your father. You've got to work tomorrow. Your patients are your priority as well,' he reminded him with a pat on the shoulder.

Jonathan sighed heavily. 'I've got no argument with that. You win!'

Dreading what he might find, he trudged to his brother's ward. But Charles lay quietly, out of the strait-jacket now, his eyes blank once more.

The orderly followed Jonathan into the ward. 'He's been sedated again, doctor. He's feeling no pain. He doesn't, you know, even without the drugs; all they do is control his behaviour.'

Jonathan sighed. 'I know. Thanks.'

Chapter Forty-Three

Though still totally paralysed down the right side, within two weeks Joseph Maddison had partially recovered his speech and wholly recovered his ill temper. He never asked how Charles was and Jonathan hadn't told him that, after Charles had suffered another violent attack, injuring an orderly, the doctors had decided to try further brain surgery. They were concerned that when his leg cast was removed and he was more mobile, he might present a serious danger to himself and to the staff. Jonathan left his brother's ward, where Charles still lay unconscious from the operation, and looked in on his father.

Joseph thumped his left fist on the bed as Jonathan entered. 'Ged . . . ged . . . me oud of . . . here,' he slurred, his distorted features writhing with the effort.

Jonathan stood over him, shaking his head. 'You're too ill to go home, Father. You'd need a full-time nurse and constant attention.'

'Yesh, yesh,' Joseph said as forcefully as he could, again thumping the bed with his good hand.

Jonathan gave in. 'All right, Father. I'll ring Dr Parker and see if he can arrange to find someone. But I warn you, it won't be easy, and it'll be expensive.'

Joseph grunted, then sank his head back into the pillow, apparently satisfied.

Nervously Jonathan pushed up his spectacles. Would

565

now be a good time to bring up the subject of Charles again? The operation might give the old man renewed hope. 'They operated on Charles again today, Father,' he ventured. But his father stopped him with an angry wave of his hand.

'Nod . . . nod my shon!' His words, although pronounced with difficulty, rang with fervour.

'He *is* your son, Father,' Jonathan said tersely. He turned to leave but stopped at the door. 'I shan't be here tomorrow. It's my wedding day, remember? And the day after that is my honeymoon.'

Joseph nodded.

'Are you sure you wouldn't like to meet my fiancée?' Jonathan tried for the last time.

'No . . . no . . . nod like thish.' Joseph turned his face to the wall.

Disheartened, Jonathan left. He would ring Dr Parker, the family doctor, immediately. He hated to burden the ageing, overworked man with his father in his present condition. And it would be difficult to find a live-in nurse who'd put up with such a cantankerous patient. But if the money were good enough . . . He walked briskly to his office, determined not to let anything spoil the following day.

The sun shone feebly through the window as Anne fussed over Della in the bedroom, putting the final touches to her hair and make-up. 'Oh, sweetheart!' Anne stood back to admire her handiwork. 'You look absolutely gorgeous. And it's turning out to be a nice day!'

Della smiled at her own reflection, her deep brown eyes sparkling back at her. Her cheeks glowed without the aid of rouge. A touch of foundation and a light dusting of powder, together with an almost translucent red lipstick, was all Anne had used.

'Now for your crown,' Anne announced, ceremoniously picking up the wide-brimmed cream felt hat Della had chosen to match her costume.

Surveying herself again, Della tilted the hat brim forward and smoothed down her newly washed hair. Anne had coaxed it into its usual shining page-boy, just touching her shoulders. 'Do you think I should have plucked my eyebrows? It's more fashionable.'

'No, pet,' Anne assured her. 'You don't need to be a slave to fashion. You've got classic looks. You'd ruin them with those ridiculous pencilled arches. Now go down and show Mam.' She handed Della the little posy of violets she had chosen as a token bouquet.

'Well!' Mary said, impressed. She set the final plate of sandwiches on the table and took Della by the shoulders. 'You look perfect, sweetheart. Jonathan ought to be proud of you.'

'He is, Mam.' Della smiled. She looked at the clock on the mantelpiece. 'Only ten minutes before the car arrives. You'd better finish getting ready. I'll cover the food.'

'What there is of it,' Mary said ruefully. 'And if it hadn't been for Jonathan's and Colin's connections, there'd be nothing.'

Della surveyed the array of sandwiches and cakes. 'Don't be silly. It looks wonderful.' She put her arm round Mary's shoulders. 'Poor Mam! You must be getting fed up with catering for weddings.'

'Not this one! But thank God all the rest are boys.'

Della's face clouded. 'Oh, Mam, if only the boys could be here.'

'Well, they can't, luv, but let's just be grateful we're still hearing from them and know they're alive.'

'You're right.' Della nodded, mollified, but only for a moment. 'But I'm so disappointed Mrs M can't be here either. As soon as I've got a free day, let's go together and see her. She must be in a bad way if she can't get out of the house.'

Mary's eyes glittered with the threat of tears. 'If she could have, she'd have crawled here, you know that. I'm going to see her on Monday. I'll let you know how she is when you get back from honeymoon.'

'Give her a big kiss from me, Mam.' Della sniffed, then half smiled. 'You know, in a funny sort of way, I'm even sad that Mrs Bowman can't be here. I'll take her a piece of cake later.'

'You needn't be sad about her, luv,' Mary said wryly. 'She likes being confined to bed, since her daughter and husband moved in to look after her. I've got a funny feeling she won't want to get up again.'

'At least she's off *your* hands now.' Della grinned and, suddenly noticing the silence in the house, looked anxiously at the clock. 'Where's Dad, and what's happened to Colin and Johnny?'

'Colin took Johnny for a drive to keep him out of the way, and your dad's getting dressed.' Mary took off her apron. 'And that's what I'd better do or I'll be in my undies when the car gets here.'

Della hummed as she spread a tablecloth over the food. She smiled at her mother's latest version of a makeshift wedding cake – her famous sponge cake, layered with blackcurrant jam and covered in white icing, her favourite greeting 'to the bride and groom' written in pink icing.

Twenty minutes later, standing at the familiar altar with Jonathan by her side and hearing the words of the marriage service, Della felt almost unreal. And when the young priest, new to the parish, came to the familiar words: 'From this day forward', her heart fluttered. But Jonathan was real, standing beside her. He smiled at her and she smiled back.

The reception was quiet and simple, the sitting-room and kitchen filled only with close friends and relatives. George Greenberg was the best man, and Miriam and the others Della had met at that fateful party were present. Rose, now living with her parents and working at a munitions factory four days a week, glowed with as much happiness as the bride. She and Nora stood in a corner of the sitting room while Della circulated with her guests.

Suddenly, Rose grabbed Della's arm and pulled her excitedly toward them. 'Hey, Della, do you know what I just thought of last night?'

'Not yet.' Della smiled, fingering the unaccustomed gold ring on her finger.

'Well, just listen for a minute, Della,' Nora said. 'She's got me convinced.'

'Remember that fortune teller at South Shields?' Without waiting for an answer, Rose went on: 'You know she said I was going to go across the sea? Well, it's all coming true. And she said she saw a J and two Ds in your life. Remember, you thought she meant Jerry, but it must have been Jonathan – Maddison's got two Ds in it.'

Della looked at her thoughtfully. 'So has Davidson, if you look at it that way . . . and that woman also said you'd already met your husband, but you hadn't.'

'Aw, they can't get everything exactly right,' Rose countered. 'Remember what she said about Nora and Anne as well?'

'She's got a point,' Nora said. 'Don't forget the P and H she saw for me, and I did marry Phil. And she said Anne was going to have a lot of troubles but they'd get over, and she saw her living in a big house—'

'She also said Rose and Anne had talents they would make money from,' Della pointed out.

'But that's happened as well,' Rose insisted. 'Anne

made money with her dressmaking and she wants to do it again after the war. And I suppose you could say I made money with *my* talent.' She giggled. 'After all, Bill only kept me because I was good in bed.'

Smiling, Della cut her short. 'Mam's waiting for me to cut the cake now. And, anyway, didn't we say we'd wait twenty years before comparing our fortunes?'

'Well, there's no harm in keeping track so far, is there?' Rose persisted.

After the cake-cutting, Walter, slightly inebriated as always at weddings, muttered his rehearsed platitudes about not losing a daughter, etcetera. Della smothered a giggle and Jonathan, sitting next to her at the table, kicked her foot affectionately by way of reprimand.

By the time the bride and groom were ready to leave, Colin and Johnny, aided and abetted by Rose and Nora, had done a good job on Jonathan's car. They had festooned it with home-made newspaper streamers, tied a dozen rusty tin cans to the back, and Rose, sacrificing her best lipstick, had scrawled 'Just Married' on every window.

Jonathan grinned good-naturedly as the guests followed them to the gate, showering them with confetti. But, after Della had hugged Mary and Walter goodbye, his expression became serious. He took both Mary's hands and said, 'Thank you for your daughter, and thank you for taking me into your family.'

'You were always family, Jonathan,' she said tearfully. 'I just didn't know it. I'm sorry I was so thick-headed.'

Jonathan opened his mouth to protest, but Walter intervened. 'Stop blubbering, woman.' He quirked his brows at Jonathan. 'Women!' He shook Jonathan's hand vigorously. 'But you'll find out soon enough, lad. You've landed yourself with one just like her.'

'I'm pleased to say I have.' Jonathan beamed and took Della's hand.

'Go on then, off with the pair of you.' Walter waved them away as if shooing off flies. More confetti showered them as they climbed into the car.

'It's so strange the way life can turn full circle,' Mary said. 'In my wildest dreams I never thought our daughter would end up a Maddison.'

'Aye, fate works in funny ways sometimes,' Walter said tritely.

'The saying is "God", not "fate",' Mary chided him.

'Well, they're both the same fella to me,' he grinned, taking her hand.

Jonathan and Della drove down the road and turned the corner before stopping, where, both red-faced before the grinning passersby, they removed the cans and streamers and did the best they could to clean the windscreen with Jonathan's handkerchief. 'I'll have to go to a garage and wash off this stuff properly.' Jonathan muttered good-humouredly. 'I'll bet I know who did the lipstick job.'

'Me, too.' Della slipped back into her seat with a smile. 'If you turn left at the end, there's a garage just down the road. I hope it's open.'

It was, though the garage mechanic tried to wave them off, indicating the 'No Petrol' signs on the pumps. When Jonathan pointed to the windows, the man smiled and waved them in. He disappeared into the back and returned with a bucket of soapy water and a cloth. Jonathan was about to take the cloth from him, but the man gave him a wicked grin. 'Nah, lad! Save your energy for later on.'

Jonathan returned the grin. As he sank gratefully back into the car, Della took his hand. 'I can't quite take it in yet.' She stared at the finger with the glittering gold band. 'I'm Mrs Jonathan Maddison now.'

'And for ever,' he finished contentedly. He was about to take her in his arms when the mechanic leered through the gleaming glass.

'All right now, mate!' he yelled. Jonathan took out his wallet, but the man waved him off. 'Let's just say it's my weddin' present to you, lad. Enjoy yoursel's.'

'Thanks, mate.' Jonathan knew better than to insist.

Half an hour later they puttered up the Great North Road to Morpeth. Jonathan had booked a room at the Queen's Head, where Anne and Colin had spent their wedding night. The following evening they would return, in readiness for work the next day. Though not much of a honeymoon, Della was ecstatic at the prospect of sleeping all night in Jonathan's arms, waking up together the next morning, and spending the rest of the day in the country.

After a plain but satisfying dinner at the hotel, they returned to their room. Della blinked as they entered, her eyes unaccustomed to the busy decor. Everything was floral – the curtains, the wallpaper, the bed-spread, the two chairs – and all different designs. 'I think they've overdone the country atmosphere,' she laughed.

'Then close your eyes.' Jonathan took her in his arms. But she wriggled free.

'Oh, no!' She wagged her finger at him playfully. 'I know you've already had your way with me, but I'm going to play the bride for this one night. Be patient!' She picked up her toilet bag and nightclothes and disappeared down the hall to the bathroom, returning twenty minutes later glowing from her hot bath, and floating in a white lawn nightdress and negligee.

'Phweew!' Jonathan looked at her with approval. 'Did you walk down the corridor like that?'

Della giggled. 'No, actually, I put them on just outside the room door.'

'I've never seen you in a nightdress,' he said huskily, taking her in his arms.

She melted into him. 'That's why I wanted to do things properly tonight.'

'You look beautiful, darling,' he whispered, his face against hers. 'But I'm afraid I'm going to have to take it straight off.'

'That's exactly why I put it on.' Della chuckled as he pulled the flimsy cloth off her shoulders till it dropped in a frothy white pool on the floor.

He laid her on the bed, and she watched with pleasure and delightful anticipation as he undressed and joined her. They revelled in their first taste of married love and afterwards lay close, Jonathan stroking her silky hair.

'I can't believe I'm going to wake up beside you in the morning,' she said dreamily.

'Dead right,' Jonathan murmured. 'Thank God I don't have to get up in the middle of the night to cart you home.'

Della shook him playfully. 'You mean you didn't find that romantic?'

'Not a bit.' He grinned, then looked serious. 'Della, I've been thinking about afterwards – I mean after the war. It's got to end sometime, somehow. I hate to look too far ahead, especially the way things are, but if all goes well, I'd like to go into general practice.'

'And I'd like to have six children.'

'I thought it was four.'

'I've become more ambitious recently.' She snuggled into him. 'But let's not try to make plans at the moment. Let's just live for the present, please – at least we know we've got that.'

Chapter Forty-Four

Walter threw down his newspaper in disgust. 'They dropped more V2s on London last night. There's no knowing what that bloody maniac's got up his sleeve next – two thousand miles an hour, by God! They're bloody rockets, not aircraft. You can't even hear the buggers till they land – and just when we were beginning to get somewhere in Europe.' Angrily, he broke a cigarette in two and lit half.

Mary, sitting across the table cradling her teacup, nodded silent agreement. After a pause, she spoke. 'I've been thinking, Walter. I'd like to take some refugee children from London. Mrs Dickinson down the road's just taken her two nephews and one of their friends. But he has three brothers, so it means splitting up the family. I said we could take all four. But I told her I'd have to settle it with you first.' She examined his face to see his reaction.

Walter leaned back in his chair, blew a smoke ring, and watched it disperse. 'Aye, it seems like a mortal sin to have empty rooms up there when kids need homes. I don't see why not.'

Mary's face lit up. 'I thought I'd put them in the boys' room. Anne and Colin and Johnny can squeeze into the little room when they come home.'

'Why not take six for both rooms?' Walter suggested. 'Anne and her lot can always doss down in the sitting-room. They only stay one night anyway.'

Mary's jaw dropped in surprise. 'You mean you wouldn't mind having six children in the house? There'd be no peace and quiet.'

'Aye, well . . .' Walter stubbed out his cigarette. 'There's been a bit too much of that anyway since our lot left. If you think you can manage six, that's all right by me.'

Mary's voice rose in excitement. 'I managed six before.'

'But you're a bit older now, lass.'

'Rubbish!' She stood up, galvanised into action. 'I'll pop down to Mrs Dickinson's now, and I'll see if I can get two little girls for the small room.' On her way out, she bent to kiss the top of Walter's head. 'You're a nice man, Walter Dolan.'

Three weeks later Jonathan received a telephone call from Dr Parker: Joseph had suffered a second and fatal stroke. While going over the books with his accountant, in whose hands he had reluctantly left his financial affairs, he had discovered the receipts for the hospital and private mental home bills for Charles. The old man had ranted that that imbecile was not his son and not his responsibility, and raged that Jonathan had placed the idiot in an expensive nursing home without his knowledge. It was then the massive seizure struck.

Jonathan slowly put down the telephone receiver and returned to the living-room, where Della sat in the armchair darning socks. 'The old bastard's gone,' he announced without emotion. 'He went out with a bang, the way he lived.' He ran his fingers through his hair in agitation before sitting down heavily on the sofa.

Della forgot her darning. 'What happened?'

'He discovered Charles's bills. The shock brought on another seizure.'

576

Her face aghast, Della joined him on the sofa and took his hand. 'The old sod! Who did he think has been paying for Charles all this time – you? He knew you couldn't afford it on your income. Do you mean to say he would have let him go into an institution?'

'It seems like it,' Jonathan replied grimly. 'I could never let myself believe he would disown Charles completely, though I suppose I should have guessed when I told him the second operation had failed. No normal father would shrug on hearing news like that. But it didn't occur to me he'd refuse financial responsibility as well.' He shook his head in disbelief. 'If only he had let me talk about Charles, I'd have told him about the home. God! What else could I do? He couldn't take up a hospital bed forever, and he needs constant supervision.'

'There was nothing else you could do, sweetheart. And Charles is happy there. You did the right thing.'

Jonathan sighed heavily. 'Yes, it's ironic but comforting to think that, in his own private world, he's probably happier than most sane people – at least when he's not having an attack. God knows what he goes through then.'

'But they only last minutes, darling. For many people unhappiness lasts a lifetime.'

'Well, as long as I'm alive, Charles will be taken care of.' Jonathan spoke doggedly, as if standing his ground with his dead father, and then gave a humourless laugh. 'To think the old man slaved all his life to make money – and now it's all going to his least favourite son.' He looked at Della with a hint of grim humour in his eyes. 'And to the daughter of the niece he threw out of the house. Ironic, isn't it?'

Della returned his grim smile. 'It's just as well he didn't want to meet me. We couldn't have kept the truth from him. That would really have stuck in his craw, wouldn't it?' She breathed a deep sigh of relief. 'I have to admit, I'm glad I shan't have to go through the ordeal of facing him now.'

'I don't blame you.' Jonathan looked pensive for a moment. 'What was that saying of Joe's? "What goes around comes around." Funny, isn't it? I'll make sure your parents are all right.'

'Darling, that's nice of you, but I'm sure they would never take money from you. Dad's doing all right now; they've got everything they need.'

'But they'll have less when he retires. I'll deal with it when the time comes.' Jonathan chuckled before adding, 'Maybe your father will be less hard-headed by then.'

Della smiled. 'I doubt it. Will you sell the house?'

Jonathan stroked his chin, thinking deeply. 'Eventually, but who'd want to buy an expensive property in wartime? I'll get a temporary manager to keep the business going for the moment, but there's no point in keeping on the domestic staff. Better to close the house down for the time being. I'll sort things out when I go for the funeral.' He took off his glasses and rubbed his eyes with his thumb and forefinger. 'It's going to mean taking more time off.'

'Let me come with you this time, please.' Della's eyes begged. 'I'm your wife now, and a wife should share her husband's troubles.'

Jonathan shook his head firmly. 'No, darling! The old goat didn't want anything to do with you while he was alive; there's no need for you to go his funeral. I'll phone Dr Simpson now and see if he can take over from tomorrow. I should be back by Sunday.'

On Friday evening, while Della was ironing in the kitchen, the telephone rang. Jonathan's excited voice greeted her. 'Hello, darling, how are you?'

'Missing you,' she replied fervently.

'Me, too, but not for much longer. Listen, I've had a wonderful idea. I'm not going to close the house – I'm going to keep the staff on and take in some London refugees. God knows there's room for an army of them.'

It was a long time since Della had heard his voice so animated. 'Oh, Jonathan, that's marvellous! Do you need any help?'

'No, I've put the housekeeper in charge and told her to get any extra staff she needs. I'm just about finished here. Going through the accounts was an eye-opener. The old goat's been making a fat profit out of the war, selling part of each crop to the black market. I've put a stop to that, and I've organised everything else with the accountant. He'll pay Charles's bills with the rest of the accounts. He seems a capable chap. I'll be home on Sunday, darling. Love you!'

'I love you, too.' Della replaced the receiver and leaned against the wall, thinking how happy Mary would be to know that her childhood home was being put to such use. Tomorrow she would finish at four, Matron having given her a couple of hours off for the many hours of unpaid overtime she had put in. She would go straight home to tell Mary the good news.

As Della walked down her old street, the road was full of playing children. Childish laughter and a mixture of cockney and Geordie voices filled the air: 'Get yer flippin' 'ands off. They're mine!' A small boy of about seven jealously guarded a pile of pebbles from a curious girl a couple of years older.

She screwed up her face and shot back scornfully: 'Eey, you're as daft as a brush! It's only a pile of old stones. *I've* got shrapnel.'

'Shrapnel! Yer kiddin'! Let's see it then.'

The girl dug into her coat pocket and produced a

piece of shiny, twisted metal about two inches long and an inch wide. She waved her treasure in front of the boy and stuck out her tongue. 'There! I told you so.'

'Blimey!' He was impressed. 'Yer supposed to give that to the ARP for the war effort when they come round. My muvver says it's a crime not to 'and it over. And you can go to prison for crimes, yer know.'

The girl shrugged, aware of the value of her prize. 'I don't care. Jimmy Swithin's goin' to swap me two ounces of sweets for it the morrer. Then I'll eat the sweets and *he* can go to prison.'

Della smiled at the childish exchange. She had never seen so many children playing in the street at once. She waved to what Mary now termed 'her gang', who were using her clothes line as a skipping rope further down the street. She sighed, wishing as always for the war to be over. She was eager to have her own family, but not until life was back to normal.

She ran down the garden path and blasted into the kitchen, bursting with her news. 'Mam—' She stopped dead when she saw Mary's white face. Fearfully, she approached the seated figure in the armchair. 'What's happened, Mam?'

Mary looked up at her with pain in her eyes. 'Michael's been wounded.'

'How? What happened? How bad?' The questions bounced from Della's tongue, while her face turned as pale as her mother's.

'The Germans hit his tank and it caught fire. One of his mates dragged him out, but he's badly burned.'

'Oh, Mam, how badly?' Hot tears ran down Della's cheeks.

Mary swallowed hard before answering. 'Second and third degree burns over most of his body. He's in hospital in Lyon in France. Ellen got word today.'

Della sat slowly on the chair-arm and put her arm

round Mary. 'Is it only burns, Mam – no injuries?' Her voice was hushed.

'No, just burns. Don't you think that's enough?'

'Oh, Mam! Of course I do. Poor Michael! He'll be going through hell . . . but burns heal in time. We should be thankful he's still alive,' she added, in a vain effort to comfort her mother.

'Yes . . . *time*. He'll be in hospital for a long time, and they won't be able to move him back home for a long time either.' Mary twisted her pinafore in her lap. 'He's lying there suffering agonies in a foreign country, and we should be thankful – strange mercies we've got to thank God for these days! We've lost one, and now another's wounded.'

'I know, Mam,' Della persisted, 'but David and Billie are still alive and Michael will get better. I know it sounds like cold comfort, but Jonathan's lost both his brothers – one dead and the other a permanent imbecile.'

Mary pushed back her hair. A few strands of grey showed among the dark copper curls, and the tiny lines that used to appear only when she frowned were now etched permanently into her brow. She sighed and took Della's hand. 'I know things could be worse. It's nice to see you, luv. Is Jonathan still away?'

'Yes, he's coming home on Sunday. I came to tell you some good news . . . but it's all fallen flat now.' Della got up from the chair-arm and stared out of the window.

'Good news is good any time,' Mary said stoutly. 'What is it?'

'Jonathan's decided to keep the house on and fill it with refugees. I . . . I just thought you'd like to know that it's being put to good use.' Della turned to see her mother's reaction.

'That's generous of him. It's nice to think of the old place full of homeless children.' Mary's eyes looked

misty and far away for a moment, then she said with a
suggestion of humour in her tone, 'It's enough to make
Joseph Maddison turn in his grave.'

'I hope so,' Della said wickedly. 'They'll probably
wreck the place, but Jonathan doesn't seem to care.'

'No, it's hard to feel anything for a home where
you've been unhappy. I should know. But I had ten
happy years there, until Roseanne came on the scene.
And, now that the old tyrant's gone, I can think of it
fondly again. It's a pity Jonathan's going to sell it.'

'He didn't have *any* happy years there, Mam,' Della
reminded her. 'I can quite understand why he wants rid
of it.'

Mary nodded. 'So can I, luv.'

Chapter Forty-Five

It was a fine May day and Della hummed as she pushed the trolley down the corridor. She was four months pregnant, having decided that at twenty-five she couldn't allow Hitler to postpone her life any longer. It had been a tiring day but she felt joyful. Hitler was dead. The end of the war was close. Jonathan had been in theatre most of the day and she hadn't seen him. She checked her watch and smiled. They would be going home together soon.

As she neared the ward, Matron's burly figure blocked her way. 'Have you heard the news?' she bellowed. 'It's over! The war's over!' She grabbed Della and danced her down the ward. Out of breath and red in the face, she stopped as the patients cheered, flinging whatever they could grab from their lockers into the air – water glasses, handkerchiefs, spectacles, toiletries, all landing on the beds or on the floor.

'For we are jolly good fellows! Three cheers for the lads over there!' shouted Jimmy Davis, who was recovering from a hernia operation. He leaped out of bed and flung his pillow across the ward.

A chorus of 'Hip, hip, hoorays' followed, even the most seriously ill patients doing their best to join in.

'Mr Davis,' Matron said sternly when the cheers had died down, 'get back into bed this instant. You'll undo your stitches.'

'I don't care if I burst me bloody gut!' Mr Davis grinned, pleased at his own joke. 'Come on, Matron. Give us a kiss.'

'Aye, give the lad a kiss,' urged Mr Wilkins who, at eighty, was one of the sprightliest in the ward. 'And how about a noggin all round tonight, sweetheart? How do you expect us to celebrate on orange squash?'

'That's enough from all of you.' Matron wagged her finger, but the corners of her mouth turned up in a suggestion of a smile. 'One of the staff just rang me to say it's over, but I don't know the details yet.' She turned to Della. 'Nurse Maddison, would you go and listen to the wireless? I can't get away till eight. Jonathan – Dr Maddison,' she corrected herself quickly, 'left a message to say he's delayed in surgery. I'll send a cadet for you when he arrives.'

'Yes, Matron.' Della ran from the ward, abandoning the medicine trolley in the middle of the aisle.

The canteen was bursting with excited bodies, the loudspeakers turned up to full volume as the news announcer informed them that Admiral Donitz, Hitler's appointed successor, had accepted the Allied terms of unconditional surrender and an armistice had been signed at General Eisenhower's headquarters at Rheims. The audience listened to his voice in stunned silence. Mr Winston Churchill was expected to make the official announcement on the wireless some time within the next few hours, and it could be assumed that the King's broadcast to the nation would take place at nine o'clock.

Della fought her way back through the now cheering crowd and delivered the news to Matron, who had returned to her office and regained her composure. Her response now was to raise her eyes to heaven and boom piously, 'The Lord be praised!'

'If you ask me, it should be "the lads be praised",' Jonathan's voice cut in from the doorway. Della flung herself into his arms, knocking off his glasses in the process.

'Oh, Jonathan! You've heard? Isn't it wonderful?'

He swung her round like a child, accidentally trampling on the glasses. 'Jonathan, look what you've done.' Della gasped for breath as he put her down.

'So what!' He kicked the twisted frames and broken glass carelessly aside. 'You can drive me home, and then I'm going to get blind drunk anyway.'

The traffic was chaotic. Drivers honked their horns for victory, and passengers and pedestrians climbed on to the tops of cars. One man, extremely drunk, had climbed from a lorry to the top of a trolley bus. But while the conductor and driver, anxious to get the bus moving, frantically called him down, the passengers cheered him on.

Della inched her way through town to the quiet residential streets of Jesmond, where bonfires were already being built and fireworks set off. Jonathan, who had been unusually quiet during the hectic journey, suddenly put his hand affectionately on her knee. Della took her eyes off the road for a second and smiled at him. 'Why aren't you whooping and yelling like everyone else? Are you tired, sweetheart?'

'Nope.' He slid further down in his seat in contentment, his long legs doubled up against the dashboard. 'I'm whooping and yelling quietly because I'm thinking.'

'What are you thinking?' Della glanced again at his profile, but it divulged nothing.

'I'm not telling until we're each clutching a glass of bubbly.'

Della pressed her foot harder on the accelerator. 'And I'm going to open that tin of pâté.'

With difficulty, she parked outside the house, honking the horn at the milling crowds. All were dancing and singing and generally giving vent to their relief after five long years of war. 'I suppose we should go out and join them,' she suggested half-heartedly as Jonathan opened the flat door.

'Perhaps later.' He screwed up his eyes to see in the gloom and switched on the hall light. 'First we've got to kill that champagne and pâté.'

'Thanks to your dear old dad.' Della grinned as she ran to the living-room to turn on the wireless. Vera Lynn was giving her unmistakable rendition of *The White Cliffs of Dover* and, for the first time, the words were not simply a hopeful dream of peace. Della joined Jonathan in the kitchen, her heart thumping with excitement.

He pulled the dusty bottle from the wooden crate in the larder and grunted. 'It could be colder, but who cares!' He popped the cork with a flourish. 'Why waste time?' The foam oozed down the bottle as he carried it to the living-room. Following him, Della placed the pâté and a packet of cream crackers on the coffee table. Jonathan poured two glasses and handed one to Della. They raised them ceremoniously as he toasted: 'To the end! And to a new beginning.'

As always, Della hiccupped after her first sip of champagne. Laughing, she collapsed on to the sofa. Jonathan joined her and took her hand.

'Are you going to tell me now what you were thinking about in the car?' she asked.

'Yes . . . I was thinking about a new beginning for us.'

'But this *is* a new beginning, darling. The war's over and we're going to have a baby.'

'Precisely! That's why I was thinking that, if you like the idea, we could move into my parents' house and—'

'But Jonathan!' In her surprise, Della cut him off. 'You hate the place.'

He shook his head. 'Not any more – not since I saw it with hordes of kids in it, laughing and shouting and making a hell of a mess. It's a wonderful place to bring up a family, darling, and we have to get out of this flat before the baby comes anyway.'

'But your job, Jonathan!' Della looked stunned.

'I've got it all worked out. I've been thinking about it for a while, but I wanted to wait for the right moment to break the news.' His voice rose with excitement. 'Dr Parker's been waiting until the end of the war to retire and sell his practice in Carlisle.' Jonathan paused, searching her face for a sign of approval, but still she looked stunned. 'Well, what do you think, darling?' he probed.

Suddenly the blankness left her face and her eyes sparkled. 'Oh, Jonathan! It sounds wonderful. I . . . I just can't take it all in.'

'Then you wouldn't mind being a country doctor's wife?'

'And you wouldn't mind being a country doctor?'

'I've had my fill of the big city – and big hospitals. It's been good experience and fulfilling work, but I'd rather do general practice . . . get to know my patients over fifty years, like Dr Parker. And, most of all, I'd like to bring up my children in the country. We could give them a wonderful life there, Della, the sort of life *I* could have had with the right parents.'

She slammed her glass down on the coffee table and threw her arms round him. 'Oh, Jonathan! Why didn't you tell me you were thinking about this? It sounds wonderful!'

'Well, to tell the truth . . .' He steadied his glass, which Della had almost toppled in her enthusiasm. 'I only began toying with the idea recently. I didn't finally make up my mind until coming home in the car. The end of the war suddenly made it all seem real and possible – and immediate.'

'How immediate?' Della jumped up and down in her seat with excitement.

'We could give notice tomorrow, if you like. There'll be plenty of replacements soon.' He stood up to refill their glasses.

Closing her eyes, Della lay back in the sofa. 'I can't wait to tell Mam,' she said softly. Jonathan placed a full glass in her hand and sat by her, putting his arm round her shoulders. She snuggled into him. 'God, life's so strange! To think I'll be living in Mam's old house! She'll be thrilled to ribbons.'

'It reminds me of Joe's saying again.' Jonathan smiled wryly. ' "What goes around comes around." It *is* strange – poetic justice, eh?' He sipped his champagne thoughtfully for a moment. 'I'm working this Sunday, but do you think your folks would like to come with us the following Sunday? I'd like them to be there when I take you to see your future home.'

'Like to come? Mam would love it!' Della tipped up her glass and drained it recklessly, still bewildered by the sudden turn of events.

Jonathan smiled at her. 'I think that bubbly's going to your head. You look a bit glassy-eyed. Now that we've reached a unanimous verdict, let's have the pâté.'

Della attempted to rise. 'I'll get your other specs first so you can see what you're eating.'

'No, sit down.' He pulled her back into his arms. 'Life looks wonderful through a bleary haze.'

The following week, their happiness was tempered when victory brought to light the appalling extent of the Nazi atrocities. As the Allied armies swept through a Germany whose every major town had been levelled by the Allied Air Force, they came across the Nazi concentration and extermination camps. The nightmare scenes they uncovered shocked the world, as graphic pictures of the atrocities shouted out from the newspapers and newsreels.

'Poor Miriam,' Della whispered, appalled, as she and Jonathan read the Sunday papers over breakfast.

He put down his paper. 'I can't look at that and eat.' He pushed away his plate. 'George says Miriam's taking it badly. We should go to see them tomorrow after work.' He glanced at his watch. 'But now, we've got to pick up your parents.'

Della also pushed her plate away half finished. 'I'll just splash my face. And . . . and Jonathan, just for today, please don't let Dad draw you into discussing the war. At least we've got rid of Hitler and put an end to it. I want to think only of the positive side today . . . please.'

Jonathan looked at her quizzically. 'Any suggestions how I shut up your dad?'

Della smiled wryly. 'No, but try anyway.'

At the house, Michael, Ellen and Caroline were in the scullery. 'Hello, you two,' Michael greeted them. 'Mam's getting ready, and we're just leaving anyway. Ellen's brother came home last night and she can't wait to see him. We just stopped off because Caroline wanted to show her grandma her new doll.'

Della mentally kicked herself. In all the excitement of the week, she'd forgotten her niece's birthday. She bent to hug Caroline and took her hand. 'Come and see what I've got for you – a special birthday present,' she whispered.

'Another dolly?' Caroline asked, round-eyed.

'Something like that.' Della rummaged in the hall cupboard.

★ ★ ★

In the scullery, Jonathan shook hands with Michael. 'How are you feeling? Ready for a slap on the back yet?'

Michael grimaced. 'Not quite.' He had been home for five months and was walking normally except for a hint of stiffness in his gait. The only visible signs of his burns were a slight redness and unnatural tightness of the skin on his hands and down one side of his face.

Mary joined them and took Michael's hand. 'He looks almost like his old self.'

'Not really, Mam.' Ellen grinned. 'You should see him starkers – he looks like a map of the world.'

'I've no desire to see him starkers in any event.' Mary pulled a face. 'Those days are over.'

Della returned with Caroline, who proudly held up her new teddy bear. 'Look what I got from Auntie Della for my birthday! His name's Teddy.'

Jonathan darted a glance at Della, and she smiled. 'He's been lonely in that box all these years. He needs a new owner.'

Ellen duly admired Caroline's new treasure. 'That's lovely, sweetheart. Did you thank Auntie Della?'

Caroline nodded, her blonde ringlets bouncing.

'Then we'd better go now.' Ellen took the child's hand. 'We don't want to miss that bus. Have a nice day, you lot. We're thrilled you're going to live in the house. You can expect plenty of visitors.'

As they disappeared down the path, Jonathan took Della's hand. 'Did you really want to give your teddy away?'

'Of course not, you ninny. I wanted to keep him for our baby. But I felt bad that I'd forgotten Caroline's birthday.' She smiled and squeezed his hand. 'Anyway, Teddy was just an old toy. It's time for a new one.'

'I'd better get your dad,' Mary interrupted. She glanced in the sitting-room, where Walter's head was invisible behind the inevitable newspaper. 'Della and Jonathan are here,' she announced. 'Put that paper down. And I don't want to hear any more talk about the war today.'

Grinning at Mary's stern voice, Walter followed her meekly. He bent for Della's usual kiss on the cheek and shook Jonathan's hand, saying, 'I've been forbidden to talk war talk today, so I'll button me lip . . . It looks as if Labour will get in in July, though.'

Jonathan nodded. 'I wouldn't bet against them, but—'

'That's enough, both of you!' Mary wagged a warning finger at them. 'Politics and war are one and the same thing, if you ask me. It's the politicians who make wars.' She picked up a grey costume jacket and matching felt hat from the sofa and donned them at the mantelpiece mirror.

Della glanced at her in surprise. 'Mam, why are you all dressed up to go to the country? Look at me!' She indicated her simple tweed skirt, loose sweater and sensible flat shoes.

'Well, *I* haven't got a bump to hide. And this is one occasion I deserve to dress up for.' Mary's eyes glowed with excitement.

'You could both wear your birthday suits for all I care,' Jonathan said. 'So long as we don't stand around here all day.'

The day was cool and the air crisp, but the sun poked in and out of the clouds as they drove through the green countryside, enjoying the wild flowers in the hedgerows and the fresh green of spring. Spring! An appropriate time for a new beginning, Della thought, as she sat in the back seat holding Mary's hand. 'Have you heard when the boys are coming home?' she asked her superfluously.

Walter chortled from the front seat. 'What a daft question! You'd have heard about it before you got in the door if she had.'

'Well, I don't care how long it takes.' Mary sighed with relief. 'At least there's no more fighting. And that reminds me, Della. Rose came over on Saturday hoping you might be home. Joe's being sent back next week, so she and Rosemary are joining him down there. She said she'd ring you for a get-together before she leaves.'

Della fell silent for a moment. She would miss Rose and so would Nora but, remembering their pact that day on the beach, she smiled. She and Jonathan would certainly visit her. Would Anne and Nora still want to go, she wondered, now that their time was wholly taken up with their new daughters? Well, that was a long way off; she'd think seriously about it when the time came.

Passing the signpost to Carlisle, Jonathan took a turn-off to the left. Della felt Mary's grip tighten on her hand. She knew they must be almost there. As they curved round sharp bends in the narrow, hedge-lined roads, Della felt her throat tighten with pleasure and anticipation – it was so tranquil here after the bustle of town.

'McCauley's cottages are still there!' Mary pointed excitedly to a row of ancient stone cottages that looked as if they'd grown out of the rocky landscape.

'They're not McCauley's any more.' Jonathan turned to give Mary a wry smile. 'They're Maddison's cottages now. Father bought them ten years ago – and all the land behind. He wanted the cottages for his workers. I'll have to renovate them; they've got no indoor plumbing and they're damp, draughty and unhealthy.'

'How many workers are there now?' Mary had always preferred not to discuss her uncle and his affairs, but now she had good reason to be curious.

'Fifteen altogether, including the manager, but he lives in the lodge.'

Mary shook her head in disbelief. 'My grandfather only had six staff, including the groom. Your father must have expanded a lot.'

'Yes, and he bought the Five-Acre property and land. He rented the house but did nothing with the land.' As Jonathan spoke, he turned off the narrow road to an even narrower lane, marked 'Private – No Trespassers'. Ahead stood a huge pair of wrought iron gates, behind which a sweeping drive led to a large grey stone house with red gables.

Mary poked her head between Jonathan and Walter to get a better view. 'It's still the same!'

'How did he manage to hang on to his gates?' Walter's mouth turned down at the corners in disapproval.

'It's obvious you didn't know my father,' Jonathan replied dryly. 'He could manage anything he wanted.' He swung out of the car to open the gates and, a few minutes later, they pulled up at the ornate wooden doors. 'Home sweet home.' Jonathan turned to look at Della and smiled at her expression. Her eyes looked like two large coals, and her cheeks glowed with excitement. 'Like it, sweetheart?' he asked softly.

'Oh, Jonathan!' Della leaned forward and put her arms round his neck in a tight embrace. 'It's wonderful!' She hugged Mary in turn, noticing for the first time the tears streaming down her mother's face. 'Is it upsetting you, Mam?' she asked softly.

Mary shook her head and groped in her handbag for her handkerchief. 'No, luv. I'm just so happy to see the old place again and to know that you and Jonathan will be living in it.'

'Women!' Walter raised his eyes in his characteristic hopeless gesture. 'You never know where you are with them. They cry when they're miserable and they cry when they're happy. Why don't we get out of the damned car and go in?'

From his trouser pocket, Jonathan pulled out a large key ring festooned with keys. He fingered it, replaced it, and rang the bell. 'I don't want the staff to think we're creeping up on them,' he explained. 'I should have rung to let them know we were coming.'

After a few moments, the door swung open and a large, heavy-jowled woman stood before them. Her mouth gaped, showing a meticulous set of false teeth. 'Mr Jonathan!' She clapped her hand to her cheek. 'We weren't expecting you!'

'It's all right, Mrs Flynn. We're not staying. We've just come for the afternoon to have a look around.'

Still flustered, the woman stepped back to allow them in.

'Mrs Flynn is the best housekeeper in the North of England,' Jonathan said, before making the introductions.

Mrs Flynn looked pleased. 'Well, come on in then, all of you.' She gestured with her arm until they were all assembled in the large, stone-flagged hall. 'Would you like a bite to eat?'

'A cold lunch would do fine, Mrs Flynn, if you wouldn't mind,' Jonathan said. 'And perhaps afternoon tea later. We shan't be staying for dinner.'

'Aye, I'll see to it right away.' Though still flustered, Mrs Flynn looked delighted to have visitors to entertain. 'It's Cook's day off but she left us cold meats and salad. Minnie and Margaret are on duty today . . . not that there's much to do around here now that the bairns have gone,' she added with a note of regret.

Jonathan gave her one of his widest grins. 'You'll have plenty to do soon, Mrs Flynn. My wife and I have decided to live here, and the first of our family's already on the way.'

'Eey, Mr Jonathan, that's grand news.' Mrs Flynn looked closely at Della's small bump under the thick sweater. 'I can't wait to tell the girls.' She displayed the prize set of false teeth again before toddling down the hall.

Walter looked around at the vast, vaulted ceiling, the crystal chandeliers and the wide, curved staircase, his eyebrows raised almost to his hairline. He let out a low whistle. 'You could just about get our house into this hall.'

'Wait till you see the rest,' Mary said proudly.

Walter put her arm through his. 'Well, how about the grand tour then? Or are we going to stand here in the hall all day?'

Della stood, awestruck, until Jonathan tugged on her arm fondly. 'Where would you like to start, Mrs Maddison?'

'Let Mam decide.' Della was breathless with excitement. 'Let's see how well you remember it, Mam?'

'Well, let me see.' Mary closed her eyes and, for a moment, she was a little girl again, sitting on her grandfather's lap in the drawing-room on a Sunday afternoon, pestering him to read to her or to take her for a walk. 'Let's start with the drawing-room, shall we?' she said finally.

Jonathan was silent as Mary led them to the spacious room, French windows overlooking the magnificent lawn. She gazed in surprise at the red velvet, gilt-framed chairs and sofas. 'The furniture's all different!' Her nose turned up in an unconscious gesture.

Jonathan imitated her expression. 'No, it's the same old stuff. My mother had a taste for what she termed "French Elegance". She had everything she could covered in red velvet or painted gilt, or both – even the walls, as you can see.' He smiled down at Della, who looked around the large red room open-mouthed. 'Don't look so overwhelmed, darling,' he teased. 'We'll have it redecorated and get new furniture.'

'No, no!' Della tried out a wing chair. 'Redecorated, yes! But we'll have the furniture restored and recovered. It's beautiful! We couldn't possibly put wartime economy rubbish in a place like this.' She looked at Mary. 'Mam, would you help me to choose? I'm going to need lots of advice.'

'Don't worry. You'll get it whether you want it or not,' Walter said.

Mary sighed. 'I remember this room as it was – a soft, gentle green. But you'll have to put your own stamp on it, though I'd be happy to make suggestions,' she added quickly.

'Are we going to stay here half the day as well?' Walter asked in mild exasperation. 'It looks like a lot of house to see and I'm hungry.'

After covering the downstairs and most of the first floor, memories flooding through Mary at every turn, she opened the study door gingerly. She had deliberately left this room until last. It was still the same! Her grandfather's old mahogany, leather-topped desk, the same winged chair by the fireplace where she had sat on his lap and listened to his bed-time stories, the same oriental rug, though worn and shabby now.

Jonathan read her thoughts. 'My father refused to let my mother touch this room. He said it was the only place in the house where he didn't have to wear eye-shades.'

Della spluttered, and Walter's stomach growled simultaneously. 'Are you trying to tell us something, Dad?'

'Aye, well, you get the message, I suppose.'

Jonathan chuckled. 'I'm sure Mrs Flynn has done her thing by now.'

Four places were set at the long mahogany dining

table. In the centre stood a huge bowl of salad, a platter of cold roast beef, a large, home-baked loaf and a pitcher of water. Jonathan surveyed the table, then glanced at the pitcher and the water goblets. 'Mrs Flynn thinks she's still setting the table for the kids. Hang on till I get back.'

Five minutes later he triumphantly set two dusty bottles of champagne on the table.

Walter's eyes popped. 'For God's sake! How old are they?'

'I don't know.' Jonathan gave him an innocent grin. 'Too many years of dust on them to read the dates.' He popped the first cork solemnly and emptied the bottle into the four goblets.

'Jonathan!' Della tried to restrain him. 'This is vintage champagne. We shouldn't drink it like lemonade!'

This time his grin was wicked. 'Don't tell me what I can do in my own house.' He stood on his chair at the head of the table and held up his glass. 'To my lovely in-laws, and to my lovely wife, and to our lovely whatever-it-is in there.' He toasted Della's belly.

'Jonathan! Behave yourself!' Della sipped, then hiccuped as usual.

'Behave myself? Not a chance!' He jumped down from his chair, slopping champagne everywhere. He knocked back the remainder of his glass and opened the second bottle. 'All my life I've had to behave myself at this bloody dining table: "Jonathan, don't fidget; Jonathan, don't chew with your mouth open; Jonathan, don't speak until you're spoken to." ' He mimicked his father's voice. 'But *now* I can do whatever I like. And we're going to make pigs of ourselves.'

Needing no second bidding, Walter made a grab for the meat platter.

'You don't have to take him so literally, Walter,' Mary giggled, already a little inebriated.

★ ★ ★

After lunch they strolled through the garden and grounds. Mary gasped at the sight of the old kitchen gardens – the gardens her grandfather had extended to start the business. Joseph had expanded them to four times the size, reaching down to Larkin Meadow. 'I used to ride with my grandfather here,' she said nostalgically.

Jonathan's happy expression turned solemn. 'I used to ride here, too – with my brothers.'

Della slipped a comforting hand in his. 'Soon you can ride with your son, darling.'

'Or my daughter.' He again patted the small rise of her belly. 'I *will* say one thing for my father,' he said as he surveyed the rolling countryside. 'At least he kept the land as it was. He could have expanded and become – forgive the term – a "gentleman farmer".' He smiled sardonically. 'But he preferred to keep the produce business small and selective. "Maddison's Quality Kitchen Garden Produce". He kept up his standard – in his own way, though. Anything slightly flawed always went to the staff – in lieu of wages, of course. But, anyway!' He waved his arms expansively. 'Just about as far as you can see is Maddison land now. He bought it over the years, partly as investments and partly to control farming and building around him. It pays its way. He made sure he got his hunting and his fishing rights and, of course, his property rents.'

Mary shook her head, trying to take it all in. 'My grandfather didn't make a go of it because he made sure we and the staff got the best, and he sold the rest. And I have a suspicion you take after him, Jonathan.'

'You're right. I never cared for business. But I've got a manager to do that. Let's look at the west wing now. It's the only part you haven't seen except for the stables.'

'Aye, and then how about that cup of tea you promised?' Walter reminded him. 'I never thought my feet would get tired walking around a house.'

Jonathan smiled at Mary and Walter. 'I'd like you to see this last part because . . . when you retire, or before if you wish, I'd like you to come and live here.'

'Jonathan!' Mary shook her head adamantly. 'You're trying to make up for what your father did, aren't you?'

'Only partly,' he admitted. 'Another part is that . . . well . . . it would be nice for our kids to have their grandparents around, and I thought you would both enjoy living out here.'

'Look, lad,' Walter said firmly. 'We're not going to butt in on your lives. You're a young couple. You don't need us old fogies getting up your nose the whole time. You need your independence, and—'

'I know! And you need yours,' Jonathan interrupted. 'That's why I want you to see the west wing. I have plans to make it into a self-contained flat. So you wouldn't get "up our noses" nor we up yours. But you'd be welcome in the house any time. I was planning a connecting door.'

Mary stood speechless, Della squeaked a little cry of delight, and Walter cleared his throat. 'That's a nice offer, lad,' he finally muttered. 'But I couldn't accept without paying my way.'

'You could if you want,' Jonathan said. 'There's always work to do on the books and in the garden. You're good at both.'

'Aye!' Walter scratched his chin thoughtfully. 'I never thought I'd get to like growing vegetables.'

Mary finally found her voice. 'May I have a word about this?'

'Aye, and I know it'll be the *last* word, as usual,' Walter said.

Mary ignored his remark. 'I've been happy to live in a

cramped little council house in Newcastle with you all these years, Walter Dolan—'

'Oh, here we go!' Walter butted in, performing his eyebrow act again. 'I know what you're going to say – so I should be happy to live with you in your former luxury when I'm old and grey. I'm not saying I wouldn't be, but not till I'm forced to retire, mind you.' A smile started at the corners of his mouth.

Jonathan looked satisfied. 'Well, now that's settled, why don't you go and look at the west wing? I want to show Della the stables.' He slid his arm round her waist again.

As soon as Mary and Walter were out of earshot, Della reproached him with sparkling eyes. 'Jonathan Maddison! You've been scheming that all along, haven't you? And you didn't tell me!'

'Honestly, I haven't! May lightning strike me if I lie!' Jonathan looked down at her, as surprised as she was. 'The idea just occurred to me a few minutes ago. But I think it's a jolly good one, don't you?'

SHEILA JANSEN

MARY MADDISON

*A Newcastle saga in the bestselling tradition
of Catherine Cookson*

Mary Maddison's privileged childhood comes to an abrupt
end with the death of her beloved grandfather. Forced to
leave the family home, she and her mother face the
deprivation of one of Newcastle's poorer areas and the
harsh reality of having to earn a living. Only their cheerful
neighbour, Mrs Moynihan, makes life bearable at all.

Unable to find more congenial employment, Mary becomes
a factory worker. At first her refined air and educated voice
make her unpopular with her earthy co-workers, but in
time she wins them over, and then she meets Joe Cowley...

But Joe's charms prove superficial; war calls him away and
when Mary finds herself pregnant, he refuses to bear any
responsibility for the child. Thrown back on her own
resources once more, Mary becomes a housekeeper to a
widower and his four children.

Coping with a large family and making little money stretch
a long way is tiring and dispiriting, and Mary finds Walter
Dolan's moods difficult to cope with. But gradually they
settle into a companionable routine, and Mary even feels the
first stirrings of attraction towards her darkly handsome
employer. Then Joe comes back to town...

FICTION/SAGA   0 7472 3741 7

A selection of bestsellers
from Headline

THE GIRL FROM COTTON LANE	Harry Bowling	£5.99 □
MAYFIELD	Joy Chambers	£5.99 □
DANGEROUS LADY	Martina Cole	£4.99 □
DON'T CRY ALONE	Josephine Cox	£5.99 □
DIAMONDS IN DANBY WALK	Pamela Evans	£4.99 □
STARS	Kathryn Harvey	£5.99 □
THIS TIME NEXT YEAR	Evelyn Hood	£4.99 □
LOVE, COME NO MORE	Adam Kennedy	£5.99 □
AN IMPOSSIBLE WOMAN	James Mitchell	£5.99 □
FORBIDDEN FEELINGS	Una-Mary Parker	£5.99 □
A WOMAN POSSESSED	Malcolm Ross	£5.99 □
THE FEATHER AND THE STONE	Patricia Shaw	£4.99 □
WYCHWOOD	E V Thompson	£4.99 □
ADAM'S DAUGHTERS	Elizabeth Villars	£4.99 □

All Headline books are available at your local bookshop or newsagent, or can be ordered direct from the publisher. Just tick the titles you want and fill in the form below. Prices and availability subject to change without notice.

Headline Book Publishing PLC, Cash Sales Department, Bookpoint, 39 Milton Park, Abingdon, OXON, OX14 4TD, UK. If you have a credit card you may order by telephone — 0235 831700.

Please enclose a cheque or postal order made payable to Bookpoint Ltd to the value of the cover price and allow the following for postage and packing:
UK & BFPO: £1.00 for the first book, 50p for the second book and 30p for each additional book ordered up to a maximum charge of £3.00.
OVERSEAS & EIRE: £2.00 for the first book, £1.00 for the second book and 50p for each additional book.

Name ....

Address ....

....

....

If you would prefer to pay by credit card, please complete:
Please debit my Visa/Access/Diner's Card/American Express (delete as applicable) card no:

Signature ....Expiry Date ....